THE CONCORD COALITION

KENLEY DAVIDSON

PAGE NINE PRESS

Published by: Page Nine Press
Cover Design, Layout, & Formatting by: Page Nine Media

http://KenleyDavidson.com

For Kitty and Shari.

Literally. I only scraped together the fortitude to finish this book because of your encouragement and occasional threats. Hope it's everything you believed it could be.

PROLOGUE

THE VIEW outside the tower window had always been spectacular. A forest of soaring high-rises occupied one side, a sprawling cityscape the other, the glow of their nightlife brightening the sky as far as the eye could reach. The nearest towers sparkled with the reflected lights of air traffic, while the city below pulsed with the energy and flow of commerce.

Lindmark's headquarters loomed over it all, a wickedly sharp spire of glass and steel meant as a testament to the power wielded by its owner—the corporate giant whose holdings totaled twelve percent of Earth's land mass and fourteen percent of its economy.

At least they once did. Before Daragh.

Phillip Linden stood in the executive office on the topmost floor, gazing out over the city without really seeing the view that had once brought him such satisfaction. He didn't really smell the gently scented air wafting from the ventilation filters, feel the silk of his shirt against his skin, or hear the rasp and roar of his grandfather's voice.

Phillip had been numb since Daragh. Incandescent rage—at his own helplessness as much as the traitors' effrontery—had sustained him until the first transit, when the ship had begun to receive a series of hacked-in transmissions from a Conclave beacon.

It had all been true. Everything the Daraghn traitors had claimed. Phillip had been sent to Daragh not to apprehend a corporate spy as he'd been told, but to cover up the evidence of Lindmark's own staggering deception. Someone in his family had committed an unthinkable fraud, and they'd been willing to protect it by any means necessary.

Destruction of scientific evidence. Fabrication of data. Murder. And the slaughter of thousands of sapient creatures, their lives snuffed out to protect Lindmark's investment in the planet those innocent beings called home.

Phillip was no stranger to the darker side of business. Beginning when he was no more than fifteen, he'd been privy to the difficult decisions required by those who ruled the lives and fates of Earth's citizens. Over a billion people relied on Lindmark to protect them from threats both physical and economic—an enormous weight, and a sacred trust.

He'd believed himself to have failed that trust when he permitted an entire planet—with all its land, resources, and possibilities—to slip through his fingers. Until he learned the truth—neither the failure nor the betrayal had been his.

"Are you even listening?"

Phillip forced himself to focus on the face of the man behind the desk. Eustacius Linden was over eighty, but the most recent anti-aging treatments gave him the appearance of a man barely past fifty. His hands were still broad and strong, but they shook as though he felt every one of his eighty years as his harsh, dark gaze bored into Phillip like a pair of diamond-cored drills, aiming straight for the heart.

"Of course, sir." The words slipped out from between frozen lips, devoid of meaning. What did it matter what the old man said? Phillip knew what was coming.

"I don't know how you expect us to believe that." A third voice broke in. "You show no remorse, no respect for the gravity of this situation—a situation you created." The dark shape standing by the window turned to regard Phillip with an icy detachment that washed over him without making even a dent in his apathy.

Satrina Linden considered it her maternal duty to raise up children in her own image—ruthless, efficient, and emotionless. She'd spent the first twelve years of Phillip's life teaching him the dangers of feeling, a lesson he'd learned far more quickly than either of his siblings.

"You've destroyed us, Phillip," his mother went on, in that same cool, uninflected tone. "We may as well have sent Callista—or even Carolus—in your place. Even they have never completely bungled an investment." The derision in her voice might have made Phillip cringe, once. "And what I cannot understand is how. How could you have failed so utterly? Some people lose watches. Some people lose millions gambling. You lost an entire planet!" Her voice rose to something approaching a screech, an appalling lack of control for Satrina. "It makes no sense! You are *my* son! Mine! Not once have you ever shown the slightest hint of your father's pathetic weakness."

Of course he had not. In his mother's world, weakness always turned to pain.

"Shut up, Satrina." Eustacius stood and walked around his desk to tower in front of Phillip. "Your gutless, invertebrate son has brought down an empire, and all you can ask is how."

A brief image flashed into Phillip's mind, of the empty sack of flesh his grandfather seemed to imply. It suited him for the moment. Whatever spine or guts he might have possessed had been ripped out when he realized the extent of his naivety. He'd always assumed that Lindmark was above the criminal violence that so often characterized Earth politics in the past. He'd known his grandfather was a hard man, but he'd considered him both fair and efficient, even when his actions sometimes seemed harsh. Those who would lead had to be strong enough to make difficult decisions, to protect their interests and the people who relied on them for safety and stability.

3

But it had all been a lie.

"We will regroup. Spin the story however we choose. We are Lindmark, and we do not surrender to the sordid opinions of others," Satrina proclaimed.

"You're a bigger imbecile than your son if you believe that," her father growled. "We're finished. A wounded antelope surrounded by wolves. There's no prettying up the fact that we've lost a planet. Not only did we lose the capital already invested, we've lost centuries of profit! The most promising discovery since the fusion drive. And let's not forget that one of our most respected executives allowed a handful of traitors and thieves to trick him out of an entire damned spaceship in the process!"

Phillip felt the beginnings of a poorly timed smile. He wondered how hard his grandfather would have fought for possession of a spaceship when the alternative to capitulation was being buried alive.

"We'll cut him out," Satrina argued. "Prove that we know how to handle screw-ups."

"Damned right we cut him out!" Phillip's grandfather roared. "Cut him out, cut him down, turn him into the biggest object lesson this world has ever seen."

"It won't help our image." Satrina paced back and forth behind the desk, one hand on her pale, sculpted chin. "Even if his body is never found, no one will doubt for a moment that we were behind it."

Phillip's muscles remained locked as he listened to his mother and his grandfather debate the necessity and method of his death. He should have felt something. Shock, perhaps? Embarrassment?

He'd once prided himself on his judgment and his ability to assess people. He was good at predicting their decisions, even their impulses. Somehow he'd completely missed the fact that his family was viciously corrupt at its heart, and that they had expected him to be the same. But he'd failed them, and now he had no idea what, or who, he really was. Or whether he would be permitted to live long enough to find out.

"Exile."

The word cut through the sound of arguing and riveted the attention of his mother and grandfather firmly on himself. Had he spoken?

Oh. He had.

"My death will only further cement the prevailing sentiment that Lindmark lacks a conscience. A truth, but not one the public is willing to accept or condone at the moment. You may not require their assent, but their mistrust will not aid you in rebuilding." His voice seemed to be coming from somewhere outside himself, the words constructed by a mind he could not access. "You'd be better served by blaming the entire fiasco on me, and then condemning me to permanent exile."

Silence reigned as they stared at him. At each other.

"You may not be a complete waste of air," Eustacius mused. "The asteroid mining platforms could always use more hands. As a bonus, you wouldn't be likely to survive for long."

It was true. Asteroid miners signed up for one-year stints. They earned a fabulous wage if they survived the entire year, which only about fifty percent seemed to do.

"No." His mother's voice surprised him.

"You make no decisions here, Satrina," Eustacius said softly, his thin lips curving with contempt.

"But I do know my son better than you," she insisted, moving around the desk to stand next to him and join his perusal of Phillip's person. "Exile him. Make him live with his shame, but without money, name, or prospects. He will be nothing and no one. I can imagine no greater punishment than that."

Phillip almost smiled. His mother thought she knew him. As he thought he'd known her, but they'd both been wrong. Let them think he was Linden enough to fall on his sword for the sake of family. He was only Linden enough to believe it his duty to protect the people of Lindmark. It

5

was possible that claiming the role of scapegoat would prevent a takeover war, and for that, he would sacrifice himself.

Not for his family.

Never for them.

His grandfather regarded him and grunted in assent. "I'd rather twist his scrawny neck myself, but it just isn't done. And, this way, if we play our hand carefully, we may avoid losing everything." He turned away, clearly unwilling to continue suffering the sight of his grandson and former heir.

"Very well, Satrina. But I want him on the next boat off this planet. See to it he's legally stripped of everything. Change his name. I don't care to what as long as it's not one I share. And send for the board. We need to begin planning how to convince the Conclave that this was all Phillip's doing."

Phillip's mother nodded. "We will weather this, Father. Lindmark does not accept setbacks. We will rise again." She tilted her chin in Phillip's direction, and he knew it for a dismissal.

He opened his mouth. A thousand scathing diatribes rushed across his tongue and went unsaid. A few clever retorts, followed by bitter last words. But, in the end, he simply closed his mouth again and walked out. There was really nothing to say. The family that had borne him, trained him, and made him what he was had rejected him with the same brutal efficiency that they'd raised him to show towards others.

The family that had made him what he was... The words haunted him as he strode across the gleaming marble of the hall and entered the tube. His mother and grandfather had tried to mold him into a man after their own image, and, until very recently, he had been a full and willing participant in the process.

But they had thought to make him a monster. As the tube carried Phillip swiftly towards the ground floor and a bleak, uncertain future, one question drowned out all the others competing for his attention.

Had they succeeded?

ONE

SEPH SCRUNCHED up her nose at the battered computer terminal and scrolled through the job listings one last time, as if another perusal might produce a fabulous and hitherto unnoticed opportunity as a reward for her persistence. Her scan produced nothing more than the usual selection of underpaid menial positions—waitressing, cargo loading, and janitorial services. Not that she wouldn't accept one in the end if she had to, but that wasn't her goal. She needed more than menial wages. Somewhere on this station, there had to be a job that would pay enough for her to send money home to Earth.

Sweeping her long, curly brown hair to the side, Seph vacated her seat, leaving the public terminal to the scowling, jumpsuit-clad man who'd been waiting impatiently for her to finish.

Concord Five might be the busiest hub in space, but that didn't mean much when only five corporations were capable of space travel. She estimated there were about fifteen hundred permanent residents on the station, and a few hundred more coming or going at any one time, which severely limited her options. Ideally, one of the ships that used Concord Five as a waypoint would arrive with an open berth, but even if it did, what were her qualifications? The majority of those ships were traveling to or from one of the research stations or mining planets and had no need for extra hands.

She had nurse's training, but sadly it wasn't enough to be hired as a ship's medic. Her experience might get her a post as a medical assistant, but not many crews were large enough to need one. Corporate settlements were out too. No corporation would consider hiring an outsider for a colony job, and after the debacle on Daragh, Lindmark had no doubt washed their hands of one Seph Katsaros.

Which explained why she was on Concord Five, instead of Earth. Her family still needed the money she sent home, but once Lindmark withdrew their support from the Daragh colony, she could no longer afford to stay. Her association with the failed settlement would do her no favors with employers on Earth, so she was stuck, looking for work in the one place where the five corporations that dominated Earth politics seemed to coexist peacefully.

Seph tried to hold back a surge of discouragement as she made her way down the wide corridor of Concord Five's Third Level, dodging automated supply carts, jaded visitors, and jumpsuited station employees as she went. This part of Third was always crowded, as it was close to the docking section of the ring. To accommodate visitors, the greatest number of businesses clustered here, nearest the docks—bars, restaurants, supply depots and repair stations for everything imaginable, from ships to handhelds to armor. There were establishments that catered only to the wealthiest travelers, and others that were less discriminatory, but most of them never closed, which led to a steady stream of traffic at most hours of the day—or night. There was no telling them apart in space unless you'd managed to adjust to station time.

Seph supposed she could have found a position at one of the many enterprises offering companionship for a price—there was always a demand for attractive workers with few inhibitions—but she'd sworn long ago to value herself more highly than that. So she walked on by, savoring the smells issuing from a high-priced restaurant, wondering how long she was going to be able to afford to eat if she didn't get a job soon.

The crowds began to thin out as she walked past the entertainment sectors and into the service areas, where the unadorned outer wall curved away into the distance. Plush carpeting gave way to more utilitarian bare metal, and the continually shifting viewscreen walls became simple portholes gazing out on the empty darkness of space.

Personally, Seph preferred the simplicity and honesty of the station's bare bones, which was still a far cry from the poverty of her youth—the same poverty that still held her family in its chains, and threatened to derail her simple but heartfelt ambitions.

Just past the service sector, Seph paused a moment to wait for the tube door to open, then stepped into the pod that would take her down to Second, where her tiny rented room was tucked against the station's outer curve. She may not have much in her life to brag about at the moment, but her room let her gaze out at the stars, which served as a perpetual reminder of why she'd left Earth.

Seph wanted to have an adventure.

To some, setting foot inside a spaceship would be excitement enough, but not for Seph. She wanted to see the horizon, not just of Earth, but of human experience, so she'd left behind the mind-numbing tedium of her career in the Lindmark Security Forces to pursue a future in the wilds of Daragh—a Lindmark colony world on the outskirts of explored space.

She'd certainly found adventure, but, in the end, she'd been forced to leave it all behind in search of an opportunity that would allow her to support her family. A goal she was no longer sure was possible without giving up on her dreams.

As the tube spit her out again on Second, Seph reflected that perhaps she'd been expecting too much out of life. Few people from her poverty-stricken neighborhood ever made it out, let alone reached the stars. She was the first of her generation to complete school. First to be accepted to

9

the LSF training academy. First to earn a steady wage and actually purchase an apartment. Her parents had believed her to be destined for even greater things and constantly reminded her that she had the opportunity to carry her entire family out of privation and obscurity along with her.

Perhaps she should settle. Look for any position that would pay her way back to Earth, where she could go on supporting her family by working some safe, reliable job.

But what? She wasn't qualified for much. Her few short years as a supply officer in the LSF had required little beyond an organized mind, attention to detail, basic mechanical aptitude and the ability to do math, none of which made her uniquely suited for any shipboard jobs, even had they been available.

Or, she could simply admit to herself that she'd failed. She'd been her family's hope for the future, and the weight of it had proven to be too much for her to bear. Was she just not strong enough? Or not focused enough? Even when she'd been working hard to be accepted, to gain the next rung on the ladder of success, she'd dreamed of escaping to the stars—of waking up to new horizons and encountering sights no one had ever seen before. She still longed for the thrill of discovery, not the drudgery of a repetitive job whose only purpose was financial security.

In some ways, she was still too much a dreamer, looking for an unnamed future instead of being practical and ensuring that she could meet her immediate needs. True, she spent the better part of every day searching for a new position, but by this time next week, she'd be reduced to begging one of the eight restaurants or sixteen bars on the station to hire her, whether to wait tables or wash dishes.

To put off that inevitable moment, she'd limited herself to two meals a day, and, starting now, she'd need to begin frequenting the slightly less reputable establishments on the station's lowest level, where the majority of the not-quite-legal business transactions took place. First was known to be more dangerous than the other levels, and visitors were generally warned to stay clear, but the food was cheap, and Seph needed a change of scene. Besides, if it was all that bad, it would probably just feel like home.

Not her current home, she reminded herself, as she reached her room, keyed in her entry code, and glanced around at her meager possessions. It might not be much, but it was safe, neat, and clean, and didn't make her feel trapped despite its size. She couldn't necessarily say the same about the rest of the station.

It was always possible that going down to First would net her that feeling of adventure she'd been looking for, but more than likely it would just be dirty and dangerous. And no matter how familiar that seemed, she wasn't fool enough to ignore the warnings and go unarmed.

After tugging her hair into a low tail, Seph donned a loose canvas jacket that would cover the knife at her belt and the palm stunner in a holster on her back. Checking her reflection briefly, she stepped out into the corridor and made her way back to the tube.

Concord Five had been a miracle of modern design when it was built—constructed in a series of stacked rings, the largest in the middle, the smallest at the top and bottom, all connected by transport tubes that ran down the inside of the resulting sphere. The middle circle contained the docks, ports, and an official presence from each member of the Conclave, along with a thriving business district. The fourth and fifth levels were for maintenance, mechanical systems, and housing for influential guests, while the station workers and less reputable travelers found other forms of entertainment and hospitality on the first and second levels. In the cylindrical shape around which the circles had been formed were the guts of the station—the gravity generator and the tech that kept heat and air circulating comfortably.

It was an oddly insular world, where most residents kept to themselves or chose to associate only with their co-workers, which suited Seph for the most part. After spending her early life surrounded by innumerable family members, expected to share every detail of her life at every moment, she'd found that she rather enjoyed anonymity. Feeling alone, though, was quite a bit harder. Too much of silence and solitude and she would always find herself seeking out company, even if only for the noise.

The tube ride down to First took only a few moments, and initially, the scene outside the pod didn't look much different than the one she'd left. Like Second, there were no frills, and the mechanical bones of the station frequently showed. But an exploratory stroll soon showed unmistakable signs of neglect—broken terminals, abandoned equipment, discarded trash, and a faint layer of grime overlaying it all. The station was, if she recalled correctly, no more than forty or fifty years old. Had this level been abandoned to its fate since the beginning?

Seph took the time to walk the entire circle just to get her bearings, then selected one of the bars to provide her evening meal. A quick perusal had established it as the cleanest and quietest of the possibilities. It was spare and utilitarian, with no decor or frills, but business was good, and the clientele didn't appear to be actively involved in violence.

No door chime announced her entrance, but the man behind the bar looked up anyway, noting her arrival with a nod that seemed more assessing than welcoming. It was probably part of his job to spot potential threats before they became a problem, and, if so, she assumed he would dismiss her without much thought. She was tall, for a woman, but not exactly intimidating, and held no visible weapons.

The floor was relatively uncluttered, so Seph was able to make her way to the bar without having to dodge more than two chairs and one enthusiastic patron with a beer in his hand, who barely missed drenching the front of her shirt with his drink. He giggled an apology, having obviously consumed more than he could handle, but she had no desire to engage in drunken repartee, so she kept walking.

Picking out an empty stool at one end of the bar, she took a seat and cast a glance back out over the room. Besides the drunk man and his friends, it was relatively calm, though from the hushed conversations and items changing hands, she would guess there was a fair amount of business being done. One man in a corner booth shot her a grin and a wink that she didn't pause to acknowledge.

"Are you here to eat, drink, or make my customers nervous?"

Seph turned to find the bartender regarding her from a few feet away, his blue eyes sharp and his hands leaning on the counter with deceptive negligence. They were well-kept hands, not callused or stained, and his sandy blond hair was cut short. The week's worth of beard he wore was neatly trimmed, and what she could see of his arms appeared fit, at least for a bartender.

But it was his eyes that drew her back and made her wonder if she should have picked somewhere else for her evening meal. She could have sworn she saw assessment, judgment, and dismissal, all in the space of perhaps five seconds, and couldn't have explained her impression that he would have thrown her out but didn't care to get his hands dirty doing so.

"It's not my fault if women make your customers nervous," she answered easily, keeping her body language relaxed. "I'm here for food and drink, nothing more."

"There are safer ways of slumming it."

Seph raised an eyebrow but otherwise refused to react to the gibe. "Are you more concerned for my health or for your charming atmosphere?"

"Most of my customers come here to conduct their business in peace. Being stared at makes them uneasy. Being stared at by a beautiful woman with military training might make them downright unpredictable, and I don't like unpredictable."

Seph concealed her surprise at his accuracy by crossing her legs and leaning an elbow on the bar. "Then you've made a strange career choice," she observed. When his nostrils flared, and his fingers flexed slightly, she elaborated. "We're riding the edge of unexplored space. It's a stupid place to call home if you don't have a taste for the unexpected. Also, you should know that flattery doesn't amuse me."

Their eyes met, and Seph fought not to drop hers first. His gaze commanded, questioned, accused, and finally retreated, not because he was beaten, but because he seemed to suddenly remember he was only a bartender.

"What would you care to drink?" The question was mechanical and disinterested, and it left Seph feeling slightly deflated by the man's withdrawal.

"Whatever is cheap and won't kill me," she responded. "And whatever you're serving in the way of food."

"It's called stew," he answered, "though better than half the protein may be from insectile sources."

Now he was just trying to scare her off. Hoping to discourage the girl he assumed had descended from on high to get her kicks mingling with the riffraff.

"On purpose?"

"I've never asked the roaches about their intentions."

Seph suppressed a grin while tapping the counter with her fingers. "Well, I prefer weevil, but roach will do in a pinch if it's properly seasoned."

He cast her another assessing glance but kept his emotions well hidden. "If you're going to be a smart-ass about it, you can go up a level."

"Who says I'm being a smart-ass?" she countered. "Anybody who's ever been poor knows there's nothing wrong with eating bugs when you're hungry. Maybe I'm not the one who's slumming it."

"Look, if you're going to eat, eat. You want to complain about the food, call my boss. I was hired to keep the place clean and pour drinks. I never claimed I could cook, and it's not my fault the cook died."

"Died?" Seph hoped her dismay didn't show on her face. "How?"

"Well, he didn't die of food poisoning, so do you want to eat or not?"

"I don't know." She fought to disguise a surge of eagerness. "Does that mean you're going to need a new cook?"

The man known as Aidan leaned back, crossed his arms, and wondered whether there was a protocol for this situation, and if so, whether he wanted to follow it. The woman at the bar didn't trigger any of his instincts for danger, but she did seem familiar. Maybe not quite as beautiful as he'd implied, but definitely pretty. She was tall, with warm brown skin, curling light brown hair and hazel eyes. Even if her high cheekbones and elegant brows hadn't been arresting, her self-contained confidence would have caught his attention.

She was far outside the usual stripe of customers who frequented his establishment, and that, more than anything, was what made him want her gone. On the other hand, she wasn't just some pretty, rich girl looking for an adventure. Her gaze had gone right over Killian in the far booth, and women tended not to overlook the closest thing Concord Five had to an honest-to-goodness pirate. Also, if he wasn't mistaken, she was carrying two weapons and knew how to use them.

Whoever she was, she was different, and now she wanted to know if he was hiring a cook. Well, he ought to be, but he couldn't imagine hiring anyone who would apply for the job, especially if they made a habit of eating bugs, seasoned or not. Imagining that level of poverty almost made him uncomfortable.

He opted for a noncommittal answer. "My employer will be searching for someone qualified."

"And what are the qualifications? Do I only need to be able to cook better than you?"

Aidan listened in horror as a rusty bark of amusement issued from his own throat. He never laughed. Nothing in the last two years had seemed very amusing. When he thought back a little farther, nothing in his entire thirty-two years had been very humorous either. And now he found himself having to suppress the urge to laugh at a strange woman he'd just met in a bar, who had begun to look at him as though he might be dangerous, or even slightly insane.

"You don't get out much," she noted. "I'm not actually all that funny, and I'm pretty sure I just insulted your cooking."

Before he could answer, a crash intruded on their conversation. A trio of dock hounds—who'd been getting steadily drunker for the past hour—had finally reached their limit and begun hurtling insults and dishes at the table next to them. Unfortunately, that table was being held down by Grant Parrington, a Hastings hireling who used his legitimate shipping route as cover for a highly successful smuggling operation. Grant was short, bad-tempered, and ruthless, but he gave Aidan's boss a cut for ensuring that he could make his business deals in peace.

Being doused in cut-rate beer was probably not conducive to his peace.

As Aidan set down his towel and made his way over to the intoxicated offenders, he took stock of himself and his situation with a bitterness he'd spent two years honing to a razor edge. Could he have fallen much farther from the life he'd been born to lead? From a penthouse apartment and the power to bring down anyone who got in his way, to a broken down bar and the power to throw a few wasted fools out on their ear to protect the dealings of petty, third-rate criminals.

Perhaps his anger lent him a bit more strength. When he gripped two of the dock workers by their coveralls and literally knocked their heads together, they fell, slightly stunned, before scrambling up and looking at him with something approaching the fear and respect they would have shown had they been sober.

"Apologize." Every conversation in the bar stuttered to a halt as the icy word washed over them.

Drunk as they were, they stammered and scrambled to do as he asked. Three other patrons slipped quietly out the door, while Parrington watched through narrowed eyes. Once the appropriate words had been stumbled over, and the three offenders had staggered out, Aidan accepted an expressionless nod from Parrington and set about righting the furniture with measured deliberation. About the time he finished wiping up the mess, conversation resumed, and he returned to his station behind the bar, wondering why he had never found a compelling enough reason to quit.

When he caught the strange woman's eye, he remembered. She was looking at him with caution, maybe even a hint of respect, as if she, too, had recognized who held the most power in that space.

It was the only influence he'd managed to regain since being stripped of everything he'd been born to. Without it, he had no idea who he was, or how much farther he could fall. He would never be able to quit until he knew there was something more waiting for him than another long fall into the bleak nothing that was his life after…

"They're all afraid of you."

Aidan looked up at the woman, who he only now recalled was still waiting for her drink. "Yes."

"I'd wondered why this was the quietest place on First. It's you."

He pulled down a mug and filled it with the cheapest, nastiest beer they had. Maybe once she tasted it, she would stop talking and go away. Stop looking right through him with those bright, hazel eyes.

"You used to be someone else."

He whirled to face her, so fast that some of the beer sloshed onto his hand and down to the floor. Irritation surged, along with apprehension.

"This isn't a party," he said, his voice gone flat and hard. "Speculation and personal questions will get you thrown out."

"Good thing that was neither," she responded, not looking particularly nervous. "I was only observing that you haven't always been a bartender in the backwater of Concord Five. You come from money. Privilege. You never once considered that those men wouldn't listen, or that anyone might object to your handling of the situation. You just took care of it. Made it go away. You showed none of the hesitancy of a man who expects life to kick him in the teeth merely because it almost always does."

She wasn't afraid of him. He needed to change that.

"Look, you can eat, or you can leave. And while you're at it, consider that the situation went away for a reason. I didn't get this job because I wanted to be friends and chat with everyone who walks into my bar—I'm here because I know how to deal with problems. Don't make the mistake of being one of them."

He set the beer down with considerable force and walked to the other end of the bar. Whatever he might have expected, whatever he might have hoped for, it wasn't for her to chuckle, low in her throat, and take a sip of her beer.

"Nice try," she called after him, "but I've had worse."

Unsure whether she meant his reprimand or the beer, Aidan resisted the temptation to throw his towel. Why wouldn't the woman just leave? She didn't belong on First, and now she was making him as uneasy as she made the other customers. He could try being cruel, as he knew only too well how to be, but for some reason, the idea made him even more uncomfortable than she did.

Fortunately, she hadn't tried the stew yet. If that unbelievably toxic sludge didn't get rid of her, nothing would.

TWO

THE BARTENDER HADN'T BEEN LYING. THERE probably were bugs in the stew, but then, Seph hadn't been lying either. She'd eaten worse, bugs included. And it was cheap, which met her primary requisite.

After she finished and the bartender studiously ignored her for another half hour or so, Seph went looking for information. Why, she couldn't have said. True, she needed a job, and she'd cooked for her younger siblings often enough to be fairly competent in the kitchen. But cooking for drunks and thieves on First wasn't likely to pay any better than waiting tables for spaceship crews and businessmen on Third. Plus, she'd have to put up with a foul-tempered co-worker who would probably resent her for walking back into his bar.

But something about it had felt familiar. Comforting. Something about *him* had seemed familiar too. Maybe she had just been alone too long, which would explain this sudden fascination with human connection. She'd been on the station almost six months without making anything even close to a friend, so it was possible.

It was also possible that she was curious. The bartender was a mystery, and a good-looking one at that, with a lean, handsome face and those piercing eyes that turned his expression cold or irascible by turns.

Besides, having someone to fight with was somehow more appealing than spending her days wandering the station, looking for work. So instead of going home, Seph hunted down the name of the owner of the bar known as Dizzy's and sent her a message. A few hours later she had an answer.

———

The next afternoon—according to station-time—Seph took the tube down to First again and strolled into the mostly empty Dizzy's, where she found the blond bartender almost entirely out of sight underneath the refrigeration unit behind the bar. From the swear words that punctuated the intermittent sounds of hammering, his efforts were proving less than successful.

"Need help?" she offered.

The swearing paused, and the object of her scrutiny pulled himself out from under the counter, displaying an impressive set of biceps in the process. The moment his head came into view, his eyes locked onto hers and another muttered curse escaped his lips.

"You. I should have known when Dizzy told me she'd found a temp." He rose to his feet, wiped the worst of the sweat away with a bar towel and set his hands on his hips. "Can you even cook? And if you can, why would you want to?"

"Let's try this again." Seph held out her hand. "Hi. My name is Seph. Your boss offered me a job as cook, at least until she can find someone better."

He stared at her hand. "Contingent on my approval," he said at last.

Seph let her hand drop and sighed. "Yes. She said if we couldn't get along that I'd be gone because you're too valuable an employee to lose."

"Then I'll message her now and let her know that we don't get along." He turned away to pull a clean towel from a locker under the counter.

"You'd be lying. You don't have any way of knowing whether we would get along or not. Do you *like* having to do two jobs at once?"

A slight pause in his movements told her she'd scored a hit.

"No." He didn't turn back around. "I just dislike you more."

"That's lie number two."

He swiveled slowly to face her.

"You don't even know me enough to dislike me. I think I make you nervous, but that's not the same, and it's hardly a fair way to judge a person." She met his eyes without flinching. "Give me a chance. I need a job, you need a cook. I might even be able to fix your cooler."

It took effort to breathe evenly, as though his response didn't matter to her, even though it most decidedly did matter, for whatever ridiculous reason. It took even more effort not to sigh in relief when he nodded just once.

"Fine. You fix it, I'll give you a chance. You screw up, break anything, or annoy my customers, you're done."

"Deal." Seph put out her hand again.

The man hesitated but was at least polite enough not to ignore her twice. He took it, his lips pinched together as though the action caused him pain. His grip was firm, but he didn't try to overpower her, just shook once and then dropped her hand like it was covered in radioactive particles.

At his lengthening silence, Seph decided to prompt him. "Any help with what I'm supposed to call you?"

"I don't care as long as you get your job done."

She rolled her eyes, rolled up her sleeves, and crawled under the cooler unit. Maybe if she proved useful enough, he would deign to bestow his name upon his presumptuous employee. Otherwise, she wasn't above resorting to underhanded tactics. It would be simple enough to make him regret saying he didn't care what she called him.

Her new boss had begun to remind her of the apex predators she'd left behind on the colony world of Daragh. Chimaeras were powerful, deadly, and changeable, and if they didn't like you, no force on Earth would change their mind. They also had the ability to disappear, a talent the bartender clearly shared because he managed to stay completely out of her sight for the next hour.

It took her less than thirty seconds to diagnose the problem with the cooler, but a great deal longer to disassemble the control panel, find the faulty wiring, jury-rig it with the tools she had available, and make notes of what she would need in order to fix it more permanently. Once that was done, she rose to her feet and looked around for a wash-station to remove the grease from her hands.

She stopped when she realized one of Dizzy's customers was checking her out from the other side of the bar.

He held out a hand when he caught her eye. "Killian," he said smoothly, wearing a rakish grin that went well with his spiked hair and sparkling brown eyes.

"Seph," she answered, "and my hands are not fit to be touched at present. I would offer to get you something, but at the moment my title is temporary cooler mechanic and I wouldn't want to offend my boss by over-stepping my authority."

"Aidan?" The man on the other side of the counter chuckled, revealing dazzling white teeth. "He growls a lot, but he's only dangerous if you try to break up his bar or annoy his patrons."

So her new boss's name was Aidan. He'd probably be annoyed that she'd managed to learn what he'd gone to such pains to hide. She took another look at her new confidant, wondering what his game was.

Killian was about her height, and wiry rather than muscular, but there was an intense focus in his lean body that promised both competence and danger. His clothing was neither tailored nor expensive, merely a dark, deceptively simple jumpsuit paired with a spacer jacket and tooled black wristguards. A narrow comm-band wrapped around the back of his head, but it only complimented the deliberately rumpled hair and the single gleaming blue hoop in his ear.

"Well, if you'll excuse me," she said, holding up her hands as evidence, "I'll wash these and then see if I can find Aidan to help you."

"No rush." Killian leaned both elbows on the bar and tilted his head to one side. "I was just curious to meet you, that's all. Haven't seen anyone new in here for quite a while."

When she shrugged, he continued. "And don't let Aidan's manners get to you. He's brusque, colder than space, and occasionally downright rude, but he's like that to everyone. Plus he's fair, and trustworthy to a fault. I've been trying to convince him to move up in the world, but he seems to be attached to this dive, for reasons he doesn't see fit to share with us mortals."

"How long have you known each other?"

"Oh, around two years I think it's been. I stop by here whenever my crew and I are on station for some shore leave."

Seph felt a jolt go through her at the word "crew" but didn't let it show. She lifted a brow deliberately. "You have a ship then? What's a Conclave captain doing down here mingling with the commoners?"

Killian grinned, his eyes glittering with humor. "Who says it has to be a Conclave ship?" he asked slyly.

Seph considered that. "I didn't think there was any other kind," she admitted. "Never seemed like anyone outside of the Conclave would have access to the money or the tech required to build interstellar craft."

The dark haired man shook his head in mock censure. "Sounds like you've been taking the propaganda a little too seriously," he said.

"I suppose there is the *Harpy*," Seph noted. "It's independent, but it started as a Lindmark ship, which doesn't disprove the point."

"I've met the *Harpy* before," Killian said. "But they're only one of a growing number. There are others like me who have no allegiance to one government or another. We live on the edge. Make our living doing things the Conclave won't dirty their hands with."

"And they just *let* you?" Seph's experience with corporate governance suggested that they wouldn't look kindly on anyone who skirted their authority. The only reason Daragh was able to exist outside the Conclave's iron grip was the protective alien intelligence at its heart. "The Conclave doesn't seem inclined to turn a blind eye to rebels. They have a decided preference for controlling everything they can reach."

Something in Killian's brown eyes turned hard and dangerous, even while his smile remained undimmed and his body slouched against the bar with studied casualness. "You're assuming they have the ability to stop me. People want what they want, and as long as they're able to pay for it, there will be those who find a way to provide it, Conclave or no. The corporations aren't as all-powerful as they think they are, and someday they'll learn that the hard way."

"A seditionist, are you?" Seph had met a few before. They mostly gave speeches condemning the over-reach of the corporations and tried to build up support for a return to a world that wasn't ruled by commercial interests. As much as she agreed that it might be a better way to govern, the cause struck her as a foolish waste of time. There was no fixing the corporate cesspit that was Earth. "Or maybe the term 'pirate' is more to your taste?"

"I prefer to call myself a free-trader," Killian countered, unruffled by her insinuation. "I rarely involve myself in politics. So much more amusing to be a thorn in the side of the self-important from the far reaches of space."

"A free-trader? Is that what you're calling yourself these days?" The cool voice startled Seph. She turned to see Aidan only a few feet away, regarding his customer impassively, though the hands on his hips did seem a bit white at the knuckles. "What a civilized term for an uncivilized trade.

If you're finished distracting my employee, perhaps you'd care to make an order."

"Just being sociable," Killian said, not appearing notably upset by the accusations. "And since I doubt the lovely Seph will be inclined to suffer your scintillating personality for long, I'm considering offering her a job. I'm sure we could find a place for her if the terms of her employment here prove onerous."

Scintillating? Onerous? Big words for a man who spent his days thumbing his nose at the authorities. No matter how much she longed for the excitement —and higher pay—of a shipboard job, such a man was unlikely to offer stable or even legal employment. If he'd actually been serious, which she doubted.

"I was going to look for you," she interrupted, turning to Aidan, hoping to break the tension between the two men. "The cooler is running, but I'll need to order some parts if you want it to stay that way."

Aidan's gaze shifted to her, then to the refrigeration unit and back.

"Wiring went bad," she explained. "It's patched, but the patch won't hold, and if it isn't fixed, it may short out the control panel."

He gave a cautious nod. "Make a list, and I'll send it to Dizzy." His chin jerked towards the area behind the bar. "Then go on back to the kitchen and take inventory. I don't care what you cook as long as it's edible. If you can provide me a reasonable accounting of the basics that you'll need for the next week, I'll make sure they're covered."

Surprised by his newfound reasonableness, Seph did as he asked, even as she considered his attitude and decided it was highly suspicious. Was he truly going to treat her with more respect now that she'd proven she could be useful? Or was he just seizing the opportunity to remove her from the orbit of a charming but probably unscrupulous customer?

She supposed she'd find out eventually whether her new boss had a chivalrous streak. In the meantime, she had a kitchen to explore and prob-ably some roaches to exterminate. No matter what she'd told Aidan, nobody was going to accuse her of feeding them bugs, seasoned or otherwise.

———

After the kitchen door hissed closed behind his new cook, Aidan eyed Killian with a mixture of resignation and distrust. "Are you so bored you decided to harass my staff or do you have something for me?"

"Just waiting for a supplier," Killian replied with a shrug. "No news since last time, unless you count your sister losing her allowance as news. Your grandfather is still courting an alliance with Olaje, and there've been a few territorial squabbles between Korchek and Sarat, but, as I said, nothing new. "

Aidan wondered whether the pirate could tell how much he resented relying on someone else for information and deliberately downplayed everything as a result. Or maybe Killian did think of those details as insignificant. To Aidan, they were tiny, tantalizing drops of the drug that had once been his reason for living.

"So"—the veneer of charm slid off the dark-haired man, leaving a focused sense of intelligence and danger behind—"your new employee is a sharp one. Nice looking too. Where's she from?"

"Don't care, as long as she does her job," Aidan answered sharply. "But it's hands-off, or I'll tell Dizzy you need to take your business elsewhere."

Killian chuckled lazily. "You should know better than that." His voice was quiet but held an unmistakable edge. Probably didn't like having his hand slapped. "I might play games with rules, but not with women. And if I did happen to decide she was worth my time, are you sure you'd want to risk alienating your best source?"

"You're not the only gossip in the galaxy, Killian."

"No, just the best," he countered, and it wasn't a boast. It was true, and the man knew it.

Aidan had no idea how the pirate came by his information, but it was always accurate and considerably faster than any other news sources. He wasn't proud of it, but he'd been paying Killian Avalar for the past eighteen months to keep him up to date on Lindmark's internal struggles and the state of their holdings. There was nothing Aidan could do to change any of it, but after six months of silence, he'd been unable to cope with knowing nothing about the fate of the corporation he'd been raised to lead. Of course, that also meant he'd found out when he was declared officially dead.

"I was serious, you know," Killian informed him, flashing a speculative glance after Aidan's new cook. "I would definitely consider hiring Seph if things don't work out here."

"Hiring her for what?" Aidan growled, oddly unsettled by the offer. "I doubt she's interested in being your personal maid."

The pirate just grinned again, and his earring flashed as he rose from the barstool. "I could always use a contact here on station, and anyway, why should you care? Maybe I just find her attractive. You can't deny she's better looking than anyone else you get in here. And I won't be the only one who notices, not with your clientele. If you want to keep her, you might want to stop trying to run her off."

Whatever Aidan might have said in return died in his throat as Killian strolled over to his usual table and punched up an order on the wallscreen. Dinner for four and a bottle of Saffire. Whoever he was waiting for had expensive tastes, at least for Dizzy's.

Aidan shook off the temptation to claim he was out of the potent blue rum, for no better reason than to annoy Killian. Perhaps he'd best go and see what Seph was finding to cook before he succumbed to irritation and did something he'd regret.

He found his new employee throwing dishes into the tiny sanitizer while muttering what sounded like threats under her breath.

"Are you *sure* the last cook didn't die of food poisoning?" she demanded, glaring at him fiercely while tossing a filthy towel into the growing pile in one corner of the galley. "This is revolting. How you've managed to stay licensed is a miracle, though I'd lay bets it's based more on bribes than divine intervention."

"Licensed?" He let his disdain show for a brief moment before locking it away again. "First Level only exists because even the Conclave knows that business can't survive without its underbelly. They sneer and promise to crack down on illegal trade, but they leave us be, because they need the black market in order to pretend their own hands are clean."

"So, that would be your way of saying there *is* no license?"

"No one cares what you cook, or how, unless people start dying. And maybe not even then."

"I can't decide whether you're cynical or just very well educated."

Aidan got a grip on himself and offered her his patented, ice-cold stare. "And I can't decide whether you're insubordinate or completely unqualified."

"Both," she said immediately. And then, even in the face of his foul temper, she grinned. "But I'm still more qualified than you, so unless you want to end up slaving over dinner again, maybe you'd better give me a clearer idea what your customers are going to expect."

He didn't make the mistake of letting her see his confusion and hesitation. Few, if any, had the fortitude to endure one of his freezing stares, let alone the lash of his tongue. If anyone doubted his ability to banish unwanted friendliness or jocularity with a mere glance, he could produce references. Thousands of them, if he'd cared to broadcast his identity. Seph, apparently, was immune. Or possibly insane.

"What have you found that falls within your scope?" he asked, choosing to avoid the issue.

"Mostly synthetic crap," she announced, segueing easily into a brisk and businesslike efficiency. "There's some freeze-dried beef that's probably a million years old, three or four tubes of compressed dough, and"—she winced—"cabbage. Inexpressibly awful, dehydrated cabbage."

He was hard-pressed not to echo her wince. "That's it?"

"There's butter, eggs, and vegetables with the synths. And fish, but..." She didn't finish.

"Even roaches wouldn't eat that?" he suggested dryly.

"Luckily for you, there are plenty of people with less discrimination than roaches."

For the second time, she almost surprised a laugh out of him.

"Killian isn't one of them, and he's holding a business meeting." He hated to bring up the pirate's name, but Seph looked more thoughtful than interested.

"A connoisseur is he?"

"He's not picky, but his clients might be."

"When will he be expecting to be served?"

"Whenever I decide to tell him the food is ready." Aidan watched her tap her fingers on the counter, lost in ideas and plans. "In case you were worried, the equipment should be fully functional. Dizzy put in the latest flash models a few years ago to save wages, so prep time will be the worst of it."

Her forehead creased and she waved a hand to show she understood.

"I'll be out front then."

She nodded, but he wasn't sure how to interpret it.

"Any other questions?"

Still distracted, she shook her head. "I know where to find you if the kitchen burns down." She flashed him a staggering smile and turned to sort through the equipment, an effective dismissal that had him marching out of the kitchen before he even realized what she'd done.

It was more than a little infuriating how easily she'd handled him. If he wasn't careful, she'd be running the place—running him—before the day was out. Maybe he ought to consider letting the pirate make her a job offer after all... but no. Aidan might be a cold, inhuman bastard, but the idea still made him uncomfortable. It wasn't that he wanted her to stay. He didn't like anyone well enough to care whether they came or went. He just didn't trust Killian.

There were other ways to get rid of bothersome employees. Most likely, she didn't even know how to cook. If her first meal was a disaster, he could send her packing and tell Dizzy to find someone else.

———

About thirty minutes later, he leaned into the kitchen, hoping he'd get a chance to berate her for not having anything ready. He was met with a tray in the chest.

"I was just about to bring this out," Seph said breathlessly, her hair falling out of its twist and her face smudged with who knew what.

Aidan looked down at four plates, each one bearing a packet made out of dough topped with what he assumed was synth-butter. His skepticism must have shown, because Seph glared as if she'd been mortally insulted.

"Just take it out, would you?"

"This is your first day. You expect me to serve something you've cooked without tasting it?"

She scowled, balanced the tray on one hand, picked up another of the packets off a plate behind her and thrust it in his face. "Fine. Make fun of it if you want."

He sniffed cautiously. Besides the slightly stale scent of the dough, it smelled surprisingly good. "What is it?"

Her tone was defensive, yet somehow still nervous. "They're bierocks."

He must have heard her wrong. "What the devil are beer rocks?"

The tray dropped a few inches. "You don't get to sneer at my food until after you've tried it," she insisted.

Whatever Aidan might be, he was not normally petty, but something goaded him to hesitate just another moment before taking a bite. When he was convinced she might just hit him with the tray, he deigned to nibble at the corner of the... whatever she'd said it was.

His face remained impassive, but barely. Whatever her creation was called, it actually tasted like food. He took another bite. She'd used the beef. And something else, but no matter what it was, he wouldn't mind eating it. He glanced down... was that cabbage?

"Well?" she challenged.

He might be a bastard, but he wasn't a liar. At least not when it came to business. "They're decent," he conceded, and was surprised by the little sigh of relief she made no attempt to hide. "How many did you make?"

"Two dozen."

"Make it four," he ordered. "At least for now. And Seph?"

Her eyes jerked to his in surprise.

"Don't forget the list."

He took the tray and left before he had to see another of her blasted smiles.

THREE

IT TOOK ALMOST three weeks at her new job for the worst of Seph's sore muscles to work themselves out. She'd believed herself to be in decent shape, but the constant bending, twisting, lifting, kneading, and carrying proved to be more strenuous than she'd anticipated.

The hours were longer too. Her first night on the job, Seph didn't stagger home until after two in the morning, having made eight dozen bierocks and a supply list as long as her arm. Her boss had lifted an eyebrow at a few of her "essentials" but otherwise kept his opinions to himself. His only orders were to be back by four the next afternoon, to wear all black, and to keep the stunner but leave the knife at home.

She hadn't once mentioned or revealed her weapons, and the fact that her boss noticed them anyway only deepened her impression that he hadn't been a bartender forever. Most likely he had a background in security, or possibly even the military. Maybe he'd been a bodyguard for a wealthy businessman on Earth. After the partial collapse of Lindmark, a lot of folks had found themselves looking for new employment, and it wasn't beyond reason that a man with his skills could've ended up on Concord Five looking for work.

It did seem odd, however, that he would have chosen to be a bartender, given his antisocial tendencies. They worked together for at least ten hours every day, and he spent nearly every one of those hours studiously avoiding her, looking in on the kitchen only to convey orders or check on her progress. At best, Seph thought he had stopped actively trying to drive her away.

At least it wasn't just her—Aidan didn't seem to like anyone. He showed no particular familiarity with any of his customers and never engaged in personal conversation. His general air of hostility towards the world did ease a bit after Killian left the station to deliver a probably less-than-legal cargo, but Seph wasn't willing to interpret that as anything more than a case of extreme mutual dislike.

At the end of her third week on the job, Seph walked in early one afternoon to find a package waiting for her on the bar. When she poked at it curiously, Aidan looked up from his handheld long enough to dispel her confusion.

"Parts. For the cooler. A place up on Fourth had a busted unit, so I requested to scavenge the bits you needed."

"Perfect!" Seph brightened at the thought of doing something a little different with her day. Not that she minded the work, but cooking for so many was already beginning to grow monotonous. "I should be able to get it in before the dinner crowd gets here, but there's some leftover ragout if I'm running late."

"I won't serve the same thing two days in a row," her boss announced, not taking his eyes off the display in front of him. "Don't be late."

"If you don't want me to be late, how about you hand me tools while I work?" she suggested, by now completely unintimidated by his bluntness.

To her surprise, he looked up and slid off his stool. "If that's the only way."

It wasn't until she'd crawled under the cooler unit that she realized he had an ulterior motive. Once her head was out of sight and she was wrist deep in wires, he opened his mouth again.

"Dizzy wants to know how likely it is that you'll be interested in staying."

Seph jerked in surprise and narrowly missed bumping her head on the edge of the cooler. "Then why'd she ask you and not me?"

"I doubt she wants you to know how desperate she is to keep you."

"Desperate?" His answer was more honest than she'd expected, and Seph tried not to let him hear her grin. If Dizzy was truly desperate, maybe Seph could convince the woman to give her a raise.

"Business is up thirty percent in the last two weeks. I've been with Dizzy too long for her to believe the increase is due to my personal charm."

Was that humor or self-mockery she heard? "Well, I'm flattered," she admitted, "but I'm not sure I know how to answer the question. I don't really have any plans, but that's not for lack of hoping a plan will drop in my lap."

"Cooking at a dead-end dive on the backside of space isn't the pinnacle of your career goals?"

Definitely mockery. Though she wasn't entirely sure whom it was aimed at. "You can set the trap, but that doesn't mean I'm going to walk into it," she replied casually, with a slight grunt as she loosened a hex fastener. "Wire stripper please."

She heard him sort through the tools she'd laid out on the bar.

"This one?" He placed his selection in her line of sight.

"Nope, the black one, with a red grip and color-coded notches."

He handed it down and waited in silence for a few breaths before asking, "Where'd you work before?"

Seph rolled her eyes, secure in the knowledge that there was no way he could see her. "If Dizzy really wanted to know all of this, maybe she should have asked me before she hired me."

"Maybe Dizzy isn't the one who wants to know."

"Well, how about you tell me who's asking so I know how to answer." She paused while carefully detaching a few more wires from the old panel.

"Not that I'm preparing a lie, but there are details I might not care to share with the person paying my check."

"And if I'm the one asking?"

Curious now, Seph pulled herself out from under the unit to meet her boss's eyes. He looked back levelly, coolly, with no hint of actual interest, but she thought she was beginning to learn how to see past the icy mask. He genuinely wanted to know, for whatever reason.

"I've never done restaurant work before," she confessed. "I grew up in sub-level housing—one of Lindmark's developments on the north side of Old Texas."

There was a lot he'd be able to tell about her just from that. Sub-level housing was where the poorest families lived, the ones who couldn't even afford fresh air and sunlight. Seph scooted back underneath the cooler before she went on. "My family was big and poor, and my folks worked constantly. When we had food, I cooked for my younger siblings while my older brothers did odd jobs to help support the family. When I wasn't babysitting the littles, I managed to attend a charity school. Was the first of my relatives to actually make it all the way through."

"Any university?" Aidan's voice was carefully flat.

"Trade school," she confirmed. "Got a nurse's certification before I signed up with the Lindmark Security Forces, believing wholeheartedly in all that recruitment crap about them getting me a medic's license." A sigh escaped her. "My family wanted me to be a doctor. They thought if I could make it that far, the younger kids would be motivated to make something of themselves. If I became rich and successful, I'd be able to introduce them to the right people, find them better opportunities."

"What did you want?"

The question surprised her. How was it that Aidan, of all people, was the first to consider the reasons behind her choices? Most people who knew her story just saw wasted potential and lack of responsibility.

"Honestly, I'm not sure I've ever had any great or noble goals. I was happy to support my family and grateful for the opportunity to make enough money to give them a better life. But at the same time, all those expectations made me feel trapped." Seph winced, realizing how that would come across to a stranger. "That probably sounds ungrateful. I love my family, and I'll always put them first, but I also want something more. Something purely my own." She suppressed a sigh. "I'm sure that sounds a little ridiculous coming from a girl from the subs."

"Does your family know where you are?" Another strange question, though it sounded sincere.

"Yeah, I try to let them know whenever I move or change jobs." He probably didn't want all the details, but, for some reason, Seph felt like telling him. "I ended up a supply officer for my one and only term with the LSF, which left me pretty close to home, but then the colonization program opened up. Daragh seemed like a great opportunity to achieve both of my goals—better pay and the adventure of a lifetime." She grimaced, glad for the moment that he couldn't see her chagrin. "I'm pretty sure the whole galaxy knows what a disaster that was, and I still needed to make money, so I came here. Not exactly setting any records for great decisions, I know."

"Did they disown you?"

The bitterness of the question brought her out from under the cooler again, brows lowered. "My family?"

He nodded.

"No," she said, a little startled that he would even think to ask such a thing. "They were disappointed things went badly, especially my mom, but they're my family. If I ever go back, my mom and all my aunts will probably take turns pointing out how much better my life would have been if I'd listened to them and gone to medical school and married a nice boy from the neighborhood. But disown me?" She shook her head. "They love me. Besides, I have three sisters and seven brothers and something like fourteen hundred cousins. I'm not even sure I'm the biggest disappointment anymore."

She chuckled. "Anyway, once they realized I was leaving Earth, they started in on my youngest brother. He's ridiculously smart, and just after I left for Daragh, he got into some really fantastic engineering university that's working on the next generation of fusion drive. He's going to do more for the family than I ever did."

"So you could go home if you wanted to?"

Realizing she'd probably been talking a little too much, Seph tilted her chin challengingly instead of answering. "Why all the questions, boss? Are you looking for a reason to get rid of me or what? Afraid Dizzy might decide she needs me more than you?"

Aidan's expression never changed, except maybe for a slight clenching around his jaw. "If I decide to get rid of you, I won't need to ask Dizzy."

It sounded like a threat—one that he would have no difficulty carrying out, should he choose. As to whether he would... She grinned impishly. "Look, if you really want to interrogate me that badly, why not wait until we're both off the clock? Surely you don't work all the time. We can go up to Third and find a nice quiet spot to tell each other our life stories."

Judging by his quick jerk backward and the narrowing of his eyes, Aidan would have preferred to be murdered. Or to murder her. Instead, he picked up the tools off the bar, dumped them on the floor next to her, and walked away.

Seph resisted the urge to laugh. She probably shouldn't yank his chain, considering that he had the power to prolong or to terminate her employment and was undoubtedly more dangerous than the average bartender even pretended to be. But for some reason it was too hard to resist needling him, just a little, to see if she could get a response.

His queries about her family had been strange and made her wonder about his past. Where had he come from, and how had he ended up in a bar? Not that she had the nerve to ask him personal questions. Nor was he likely to answer them, even if he did seem more tolerant of her presence than he had at the beginning.

She would be a fool to speculate, or to indulge in the belief that Aidan might eventually stoop to sharing personal details. Even more foolish to hope that she could someday call him a friend. Her time would be better spent looking for a different job—one that paid better and came without an attractive but infuriating boss.

———

Aidan poured his frustration into reorganizing his inventory and rehearsing various scenarios in which he fired his cook and kicked her out of his bar forever. He hadn't realized how much it would bother him to feel watched, even judged, on a regular basis. The last cook had been uncommunicative almost to the point of dysfunction, a blessing Aidan hadn't sufficiently appreciated until now.

And wasn't it just his rotten luck—Seph had turned out to be from Lindmark. Perhaps the true blessing was that her family's poverty and obscurity prevented her from recognizing the resemblance between her boss and a former Lindmark overlord. He'd never been much in the public eye, preferring to run the family business from within and operate in relative anonymity, but that didn't mean no one knew his face. No doubt it had been splashed prominently on every newsfeed on Earth during his fall from grace.

He'd kept well away from news sources during those months. It was one thing to suggest that his family use him as a scapegoat, another to stand by and watch while they did it. Not that he'd needed to watch to predict their course of action, and his predictions had been confirmed by the intel Killian had provided months after the fact.

They'd used the media frenzy over Daragh to turn him into a red-eyed, baby-stealing mass-murderer, a man no woman in her right mind would stay in the same room with. Considering the reputation they'd created for him, his family had probably done him a favor by pretending he was dead. There were, of course, plenty of conspiracy theorists who still believed his death had been faked, but fortunately for him, they were in the minority.

After Seph finished with the cooler, Aidan banished her to the kitchen and spent the entire evening pretending she didn't exist. Wouldn't want her getting the idea that his questions meant he had a personal interest. He didn't. He would just as soon not have to look at her again.

But the bar got busier and louder. Two mining ships had docked at the station earlier that day, and a number of their crew had chosen to berth on First, which meant the tables were crowded, and the bar was at capacity by barely after eleven.

He had no choice but to enter the kitchen.

"We're full up out here. I need a hand with the tables, clearing away empties. Can you spare a minute?"

His cook straightened from where she'd been stowing clean trays and nodded, though not without flashing him an irritated glance. "Whatever you want, boss," she muttered. "Any instructions?"

"Don't break anything unless it's human and it's hitting on you."

Noticeably surprised, she brushed a tendril of hair behind her ear before untying her soiled apron. "Seems fair. Anything else?"

"Keep an eye on anyone who seems drunk and belligerent. Drunk I can handle, but I don't tolerate fights."

"Yes, sir!" She snapped off a mock salute and grinned, her seemingly endless good humor restored.

Damn that smile anyway. He needed her to take him more seriously, but he was too busy for a reprimand, so he stalked off and slammed mugs onto the bar with slightly more force than necessary. It didn't accomplish the goal, but it made him feel better and probably intimidated his patrons which never hurt.

He kept one eye on Seph for the first hour, but she was cool and professional, never engaging in prolonged conversation or encouraging any familiarity. Between the two of them, they managed to keep up a steady supply of clean mugs and shot glasses and prevent any altercations between the two rival mining crews.

The evening seemed to be proceeding better than he'd hoped, at least up until the moment an echo of his past walked in without warning—eight uniformed LSF officers, all visibly belligerent and well-past drunk.

The Conclave members paid their security forces enough that none of them should need to be looking for trouble on First, but perhaps that was the problem. They were definitely looking for trouble, which they wouldn't find on Third. It was just his lousy luck that they'd picked his bar to tear up in pursuit of entertainment and exercise.

They didn't even bother ordering drinks first, just swaggered in with raucous whoops and jeers, led by a tall, handsome dark-haired lieutenant. Two of them flipped a table in the center of the room—sending drinks and startled miners flying—while another two posted themselves by the door. The remaining four made their way towards Aidan, scattering regular patrons like poker chips as they went.

Their leader took a seat at the center of the bar and slapped it with an open palm. "Eight shots of your best whiskey." He leaned in and the corner of his mouth lifted. "On the house, unless you want us to turn this place into splinters."

Aidan already had a hand on his stunner and was planning a pattern of fire that would hopefully leave his other customers undamaged. Station security would respond to his emergency call eventually, but they were never in any hurry to make their way down to First, so he would have to handle the majority of the altercation on his own. Not to mention bear the brunt of the fallout when these idiots' commanding officer discovered what had become of eight of his finest.

The bar had fallen silent. No one could be in doubt as to what was about to happen, which made it that much more surprising when someone interrupted his staredown with the lieutenant.

"Brand Elliot, how can you still be such a freaking moron?"

Every head in the room swiveled towards the speaker. The officer in question turned slowly and deliberately to face her, wearing a dumbfounded expression that did nothing for his looks.

Seph stood only a few feet away, a loaded tray on her shoulder, and a look of disgust on her face. "You're on a space station, genius. It's made of titanium and steel-grade polymers, and the furniture in here is either plastic or 7068 aluminum. If you want splinters, you're going to have to go elsewhere, because nobody is stupid enough to use glass or wood in a place where the gravity generator has a ten percent chance of intermittent failure."

A sneer spread across the officer's face as he rose to his full height, which was considerable. Seph, to her credit, didn't flinch, shrink, or even take a step back in response.

Cursing the cook under his breath, Aidan palmed his stunner and prepared to intervene. This was what he got for not sending her packing. She had no idea what she was getting into, and the situation was going to be much uglier as a result.

Except... she'd called the officer Brand. She knew him?

"Well, hello, Percy." The tall lieutenant stalked forward until he loomed over Seph. "Been awhile. Looks like you've come up in the world." He glanced around pointedly and laughed. "This probably looks like paradise compared to the slum I left you in."

Percy?

"After dating you, darling, there was nowhere to go *but* up," she returned sweetly, shifting her tray slightly.

Hellfire and damnation. His cook was about to have a confrontation with her drunken ex right in the middle of the bar. And what had she ever seen in this piece of vacuum-sucking space scum anyway?

The drunken ex in question leaned forward, a lazy smile on his face, his hands flexing at his sides. "Sounds to me like a raging case of regret. If I'd known you wanted me back that badly, I'd have taken the trouble to hunt you down and rub your nose in it. Since I didn't"—he took another deliberate look around the bar—"I guess it's just a lucky coincidence that you get to be here while I trash this place. In fact, I think I might even break your new boyfriend's arms and let you watch."

She laughed. Seph always seemed to laugh in the face of a challenge. "Are you talking about the stone-faced guy behind the bar? I guess you're welcome to try breaking his arms, but I'll warn you for old times' sake"— she leaned in a little closer and whispered loudly—"that's probably not going to work out very well for you."

Her eyes were actually twinkling. Did she not have any idea how dangerous this situation was?

"And much as I hate to ruin your fun," Seph added, "he's not my boyfriend, he's my boss. But he's a good boss, and I don't feel like looking for a new job, so maybe I've changed my mind about letting you hit him."

"Aw, Percy." The officer moved in and lifted a hand to pat her cheek with a pitying smile. "You're so cute. You know, I just realized—you spent so much time scrabbling around the slums like a rat, you never watched the newsfeeds. You probably don't have any idea who he looks like, so you wouldn't know why I'm looking forward to hitting that face in particular."

Aidan cursed silently and took a fresh grip on his stunner. Nobody ever brought up his resemblance to Phillip Linden—at least not on First. And he liked it that way. There was too much chance someone might guess the truth, and he wasn't ready for his anonymity to end. Especially not where Seph was concerned. He didn't want to know how everything would change if she found out. He shouldn't care, but he did.

Seph just looked irritated. "I don't see what his face has to do with it."

Brand chuckled, a low, irritating sound. "You know, I used to think your innocence was an act, but you're really just that blind aren't you? I'm not sure which is funnier—that you don't recognize that face, or that you think you get a say in what I do." He leaned in, threateningly close. "Wise up, little girl. You never had a say. You were too stupid to know I was cheating on you then, and you're too stupid to know when you're in over your head now."

White hot rage shot straight to Aidan's fingertips, followed by ice-cold fear, and it wasn't for himself. Brand had wrapped one hand lovingly around Seph's delicate throat and was smiling like a madman. A high pitched laugh issued from one of the other officers, but Aidan didn't look or even care. He vaulted over the bar, swept the bastard's feet out from under him, took him to the floor, and ended with an iron grip on the tightly twisted front of the man's uniform, his other fist raised with every intention of landing a knockout punch.

A light pressure came to rest on the bulge of his upper arm, where his muscles strained with the effort of holding the lieutenant's weight off the floor. He glanced at it, and the red haze over his vision retreated enough for him to realize who had touched him.

Seph. Still holding her tray, now balanced on one hip.

Everyone else in the bar was frozen, listening to the harsh sound of his breathing, and the faint whistling noise as the lieutenant struggled for air. The other officers hadn't moved. Even drunk, Aidan thought distantly, they recognized a superior predator when they saw one. His regulars were probably just in shock. He rarely hurried, and he never, ever, let them see his temper.

Into that razor-edged silence, Seph spoke lightly, almost pleasantly. "I appreciate the effort, boss, but I'd rather you not rearrange his face."

It was like being doused in cold water. He'd thought her disdain indicated she was finished with the relationship, but for some reason, she still wanted to protect the jackass who had clearly never cared about her in the first place.

"Fine." His hand opened. The lieutenant, now red-faced and gasping, fell to the floor. "But if you insist on choosing your associates this poorly, consider your employment terminated."

"Oh, for the… You're almost as dense as he is," she snapped, shocking him into looking at her. "I'm grateful you wanted to help, Aidan, but you should know one very important thing about me." Her eyes narrowed in concentration as she looked down at her former boyfriend, who was beginning to rise from the floor. She waited until his feet were under him and his hands started to form fists before she spoke again.

"I can rearrange his face for myself."

Aidan almost didn't have time to jerk out of the way. Seph shifted, grasped her loaded tray with both hands, and put her entire body weight into the swing. The tray met the lieutenant's cheek and nose with an audible crunch, followed by a high-pitched shriek of pain.

As the entire crowd looked on in disbelief, blood fountained from the man's ruined nose and mixed with spilled beer to create a widening red puddle on the floor. Seph just stood back and watched it, the tray dangling from one hand, and a deeply satisfied look on her face. Until she seemed to remember where she was, and what she'd just done.

"I…" Her startled gaze met Aidan's. "Um…"

Any attempt she might have made at justification was drowned by a deafening cheer. The bar's regulars had just seen an interloper defeated by one of their own—if they hadn't claimed her before, they certainly did now —and they showed their approval by rising as one and moving threateningly in the direction of the remaining invaders.

Drunk though they were, the officers weren't stupid enough to stay. Even Brand lurched to his feet and staggered away, holding his face and screaming about the exact nature of his revenge. They all watched him go, at least until a slur against Seph's person emerged from his swollen lips, at which point at least six sets of helping hands joined together to ensure that he was ejected before he could utter any more.

Aidan looked at Seph. Her mouth was slightly open, and for the first time since he met her, she didn't seem to have any idea what to say.

"I have just one question." He folded his arms and tilted his head a trifle.

"Yes?" She winced.

"Percy?"

"Shut up," she muttered, and walked away. "I'm going to get a mop."

FOUR

DIZZY'S DIDN'T clear out until after four in the morning. Station security showed up a full half hour after the situation was resolved and were quickly sent on their way by Aidan's calm—if sarcastic—reassurances.

Seph kept out of her boss's way, not wanting to face his scrutiny or his disapproval. She wasn't sure whether she was more embarrassed by her display of temper, or by the fact that everyone in the bar now knew about one of her more appalling youthful indiscretions.

Brand Elliot had been in her class at the LSF Academy. He was rich, gorgeous and popular—a dream come true to a girl who had grown up poor and unnoticed. It had taken her months to realize he was toying with her—laughing about her naivety with his friends and dating at least two other girls at the same time.

She hadn't dated anyone since and had believed that part of her life buried in the past. She certainly hadn't expected to ever see him again. Or for him to use her hated nickname in front of a roomful of people who wouldn't understand why she despised it so much.

The sanitizer had just finished its final cycle when she heard someone enter the kitchen. She didn't turn around, hoping he would just give up and leave.

"Bar's closed. Put down the towel and come out here."

Seph shut her eyes and pinched her lips together tightly, breathing in and out through her nose in an effort to dispel the tension that spiked at her boss's tone. He wasn't happy, and no wonder. It would be a miracle if he didn't fire her on the spot. Well, fire her again. For all she knew, he'd been serious the first time.

Following him out into the empty front room, she took off her apron and threw it, rather forcefully, into the bin with the used towels. "I'm sorry," she said, before Aidan could even open his mouth. "Is that what you want to hear? I'm sorry I made a mess of your bar, and I'm sorry I lost my temper."

"Are you?" Aidan leaned back on the bar and surveyed her coolly, arms folded across his chest.

She assumed his question was rhetorical, but when he didn't say anything further, Seph realized he was actually waiting for her answer.

"No." She shrugged. Grimaced a little. "But it seemed like the right thing to say. I'm sorry he came in here at all, sorry he involved you in his stupidity, but I'm definitely not sorry I hit him. That was one of the most satisfying moments of my life."

To her surprise, his lips twitched in what was unmistakably an almost-smile. It vanished as quickly as it appeared, but it was enough to suggest that on some level, at least, he agreed.

"I haven't spoken to Brand in years," she continued. "He was a mistake in the beginning, but I was too young to see it. Never thought I'd run into him again, but I did, and it caused a problem for you. I'll understand if you stand by your termination of my employment."

Aidan grunted, his eyes on the floor. "Much as I'd like to, there were about eighty people in here tonight who now consider you something between a mascot and a good luck charm. That fight was the most entertainment they've had in years, and if I fire you, they're going to want to know why."

Seph couldn't decide whether to feel pleased or insulted. He wanted to fire her, but he couldn't because now she was popular with his customers? She was happy to be keeping her job, but it would be nice to feel wanted, rather than grudgingly tolerated.

"Then am I free to go?" Her irritation must have sharpened her tone more than she realized because Aidan's chin jerked up and his eyes narrowed in response.

"Not until you explain one other thing, *Percy*."

"Seriously?" She flung both hands in the air in frustration. "Is that going to haunt me forever?"

"At least until you explain why you entered into employment under a false name."

"It isn't a false name," she snapped. "My real name is..." Her face went hot, but she didn't drop her eyes. "Persephone."

One expressive eyebrow shot up in response. "Persephone? As in the daughter of Zeus who spends half the year trapped in the underworld? Married to Hades? That Persephone?"

"Yes," Seph answered between gritted teeth. "That Persephone. Do you know of any others?"

"Just checking," Aidan returned, his equilibrium seemingly restored. "Seems an unlikely choice for uneducated parents."

She mustered enough annoyance to glare at him. "My parents might have been uneducated, but my father's family has a tradition of choosing powerful, meaningful names for their children. And it could have been worse. I got off relatively easy. My sisters are Hera, Demeter, and Artemis, and my brothers' names don't bear thinking on."

"I can imagine." He almost sounded amused. "So why do you hate it so much?"

"Would you want to be named after someone who was doomed to be confined to a dark, hopeless kingdom of despair for half her life just because she committed the heinous crime of being hungry?"

Aidan's face changed. The hardness he wore like a shield seemed to crack and fall away, and his lips twisted. "I've always preferred to think that she was doomed to spend half her life away from the man who loved her, simply because her mother was unwilling to set her free."

Seph shifted back on her heels and eyed him suspiciously. She hadn't expected her seemingly heartless boss to have wasted much thought on ancient Greek myths, much less to have taken such a romantic interpretation. Granted, that perspective was only romantic if you happened to be Lord of the Dead.

"Of course a man *would* sympathize with Hades," she grumbled half-heartedly.

"Hmm." He appeared to consider that for a moment. "Anyway, it suits you."

"Don't get any ideas," she warned him, feeling off-balance and wondering whether he meant to compliment or insult her. "And if you do, keep in mind what happened to the last man who thought he could give me a cute nickname."

"I wouldn't dream of having ideas," Aidan said in his usual detached tone, shifting his weight off the bar and beginning to turn away. Then, in a deceptively casual voice, he asked, "Did he hurt you?"

"Who, Brand?" Seph's brow wrinkled in confusion. First Aidan teased her about her name, and now he was wondering if she was hurt? Now that she thought about it, he *had* leaped over the bar in her defense. But why?

"I'm... fine." She stammered over the words a little, unaccountably uncomfortable with his concern. "Exhausted and extremely embarrassed, but not hurt."

"Good." He finished turning away so that his next words were directed at the wall. "You're dismissed."

What did he mean "good"? Good that she was embarrassed or good that she wasn't hurt? Feeling bewildered but relieved to still have a job, Seph moved towards the door.

"I forgot to mention," Aidan called after her, "we're closed tomorrow. It's a repair day for the environmental systems so we won't have any water."

"Oh. I... Okay." For some reason, the idea of a day off depressed her. She hadn't had a day to herself for three weeks, but now that it was offered, she couldn't remember how she'd filled her hours before working at Dizzy's. Before meeting Aidan.

She should be happy. Should feel relieved that she could sleep whenever she wanted, do whatever she wanted, and not be forced to return to the scene of her embarrassment. Instead, all she could think of was the fact that she wouldn't see her boss, wouldn't have a chance to tease him, or have occasion to wonder what was going on under that grim facade for a whole day.

Had she really become so dependent on his company? It was a revelation and a severely unwelcome one. Seph strongly considered beating her head against the doorway as she walked out, but then she would have had to answer even more pointed questions about her sanity.

How could she have gone and developed some kind of fascination with the rudest, most peremptory, most taciturn man she'd ever met? Obviously, she had learned nothing from her misadventures with Brand. She might be older, and somewhat wiser, but her judgment was just as lousy where men were concerned.

Maybe she could blame it on the last five and a half months of near isolation. Or perhaps it was due to the general lack of intelligent, good-looking and capable men on Concord Five. Even if he wasn't exactly a dream come true, Aidan did fit comfortably into all three of those categories.

Come to think of it, maybe her taste in men *had* improved. Brand was neither intelligent nor capable. He had always been fit, but considering the ease with which her boss had held her ex's weight off the floor, Aidan was probably the stronger of the two. And it seemed he actually cared, at least a little, though he hid it well. It wasn't hard to care more than Brand.

But why was she even bothering to compare them? Brand had been an idiot and a mistake, and Aidan barely acknowledged her existence. She was a fool to even think of them in the same category, whatever that category was. Unavailable men? Idiotic blunders? Ways to get her heart stomped on?

Even if she could imagine a universe in which Aidan behaved more like a human being with feelings, would she really want him to treat her differently, or would she be intelligent enough to run screaming in the other direction?

Groaning and rubbing her gritty eyes, Seph stepped into the tube and wondered whether there was any chance of her getting smarter before she made a mistake there was no way to fix.

———

After Seph left, Aidan shoved his hands through his hair and tried to prepare himself for the worst. He hadn't expected this hiding place to last forever. Someone, sooner or later, was going to recognize him and begin to wonder whether the reports of his death had been accurate. But even if Brand Elliot didn't question Aidan's identity once he sobered up, he would definitely be looking to get his revenge on the man—and the woman—who humiliated him. And how better to get his revenge than to start a rumor that the common bartender who had assaulted him was one of the most feared and hated men in the galaxy?

Considering the type of customers Dizzy's attracted, they were likely to embrace such a revelation—true or not—as an enormous joke, or even a source of bragging rights. Aidan didn't want to be either.

There were times he wished he hadn't offered to be the family scapegoat. True, his sacrifice had served its intended purpose—once the Conclave had been convinced that the one responsible for circumventing their laws had been punished, they had settled for levying sanctions and banning Lindmark from claiming any further territory for the next twenty years.

No doubt the restrictions chafed his grandfather's hide. Considering that Eustacius Linden was the one who ordered the slaughter on Daragh in the first place, Aidan hoped it more than chafed. Alas, his hopes were fruitless, and he knew it. Public humiliation and poverty were the only fates his grandfather feared, and neither was likely to touch the Linden family anytime soon.

But at least Lindmark had not suffered the consequences of his grandfather's deception. Had the entire corporation dissolved over the issue of blame, there would have been war. The rest of the Conclave would have moved in, cannibalized their fallen rival's territory, and cared nothing for the lives and fates of the people that territory represented. If the price of Lindmark's continued existence was the life of Phillip Linden—the only family member besides Eustacius or Satrina who was powerful and influential enough to have perpetrated the crime of which he stood accused—at least he'd done what he must to protect what he'd spent his life building.

He had to repeat that to himself every so often, especially once he made the mistake of asking Killian for news and discovered the public outpouring of hatred and vitriol his supposed crimes had provoked. The people of Earth had been vicious in their repudiation, and Aidan had seen himself executed in effigy more than once. The experience left him wary and bitter—too bitter, perhaps, to ever be entirely sure that his sacrifice had been worth it.

The one thing he *was* sure of? He could never go home. His family had made sure of that. If he ever set foot on Earth again, his own people would eviscerate him without question or mercy.

After locking up the bar, Aidan made his way halfway around the circle to the tiny room he called home. On Earth, he'd had closets that were bigger, but the size of it rarely bothered him. He'd brought almost nothing with him, and acquired even less. And he spent virtually no time there when he was awake. It was easier to forget the past when all he did was work and sleep.

The sleep part, however, had been eluding him for days now. Mostly he worked and then laid awake wondering what would happen if Seph found out the truth. Tried to decide whether he should fire her first, so he would never have to see the betrayed look in her eyes when she finally recognized him.

Aidan removed his boots, slapped the light panel and stretched out on his bunk, resigned to another night of bitter, hopeless thoughts. Tomorrow he would have to find something better to occupy his time.

He'd spent a few maintenance days up on Third, but he preferred to stay away from the crowds. There was a greater chance someone up there might recognize him, despite his supposed death, so he hadn't been in months. Sometimes he puttered around cleaning and doing inventory, but all the orders for the quarter were complete, and everything in the bar was as clean as it was going to get.

What did normal people do on days off? Shop? Drink with friends? He hated shopping, rarely drank, and didn't have any friends.

What would Seph be doing? He didn't know whether she had any acquaintances on station either. Probably. She was pretty, and easy to talk to. For a brief instant, he thought about looking her up and asking her to... something. But the idea was just as quickly banished. She wouldn't want to spend her day off with the man who ordered her around on all the other days. And he didn't want to be friends. It would only make everything more complicated.

Aidan started to roll over on his bunk...

. . .

…and returned to consciousness on the floor.

He knew he hadn't fallen asleep. He recalled the tortured sound of metal grinding against metal. The sickening lurch.

And if he wasn't sure of his memory, there was proof in the ugly glow of the orange emergency light above his door, which made the stark bare walls of his quarters look even less homelike than usual.

Had the gravity generator malfunctioned? If so, the backup was online. The environmental systems, however, might not have been so lucky. The air retained its usual temperature, but there was a smell. Not smoke, but something acrid and chemical.

Pushing off the floor, Aidan winced as a sharp pain stabbed through his right temple. A quick exploration revealed that at some point he'd hit his head hard enough to split it open. Blood drenched his hair and made a wet, sticky spot on the floor.

He didn't have much hope, but a quick tap on the basin confirmed that there was no water. Fumbling around in the near dark produced a shirt that already needed washing, which he used to mop up as much of the mess as he could.

His boots had rolled across the room, but his jacket was still in his locker, along with a stunner and his wrist comm. None of them would help if the gravity went out again, but they made him feel more prepared to face whatever was happening. Even if that was ridiculous and illogical. If he was going to die, would it make him feel better not to be barefoot?

Aidan pressed the door latch. The panel jerked but opened only a few inches to reveal that the corridor outside his room was illuminated in the same sickly orange as the inside. Faint sounds filtered in, becoming clearer as he forced the door open and stepped out—panicked voices, and the clang of boots on the hard metal floor of the corridors.

Instinct demanded that he look out the porthole, even though he knew there would be nothing to see. Only the distant glow of stars.

Except that he was wrong. A chunk of debris floated past, moving slowly away from one of the upper levels, tumbling end over end into space. And the stars... they had changed.

The station had been damaged, and the stabilizers had gone offline, at least briefly.

Aidan broke into a run, heading for the tubes, though he guessed his errand was hopeless. The first thing to go down in an emergency would be the transportation. They would want to seal off the individual levels to isolate whatever damage had occurred.

Sure enough, a tense crowd was gathered in front of the tube doors, swearing at the doors and occasionally each other.

"You're looking spiffy this morning," a bafflingly cheerful voice announced from over Aidan's shoulder.

Aidan swallowed a heartfelt curse. Just who he didn't want to see. "Killian. When did you get back?"

"Just in time for the show, apparently." The dark-haired man jerked his head in the direction of a nearby porthole, looking as sharply put-together as always. "Stabilizers down. Must have been a ship-to-ship collision, or just a lousy pilot who couldn't handle the docking maneuvers."

"Your ship in one piece?"

"Of course." Killian's smile was lazy, but it had an edge. "My second is still on board. No doubt sending remotes to check out the damage."

Aidan threw him a speculative glance. Killian preferred to hide behind his charming, egotistical exterior, and often came off as irresponsible, but beneath the flash was a razor-sharp mind. More than once he had produced an unlikely piece of knowledge that proved his background was probably even less respectable than he claimed.

"I don't suppose you'd know an alternate route to Second," Aidan said casually, keeping his eyes on the tube doors.

"Why would I?" Killian's eyes gleamed and the corner of his mouth curved with amusement. "I'm just an innocent businessman, looking to turn a profit. Can't imagine how I would come by illicit information like the original plans to a space station."

"Then your imagination needs help," Aidan muttered, throwing a disgusted glance at the pirate. "I'm thinking you don't look nearly concerned enough for a man who's actually trapped down here like a rat in a cage."

Killian didn't seem surprised. He was too canny for that, but his grin did widen a little. "Could be you're right. You have somewhere you need to be, Linden?"

Aidan, too, had been trained well enough not to let his face show how much the casual use of his former identity angered him. "Could be," he echoed. "Also could be you don't want to push me too far, pirate. Use that name again where it can be heard, and you'll find out I was never just a soft, pampered, rich boy."

"And I was never just a pirate," Killian threw back, teeth flashing. "So let's come to an understanding, shall we? You show an appropriate amount of respect, and I'll offer the same in return. And I might just be willing to show you a thing or two. Back doors. Insurance policies. That sort of thing. Unless you don't really care enough about the welfare of your employee to swallow your pride."

Aidan forced back his retort. All of his retorts. He had no idea how the other man had known what he wanted, but it hardly mattered.

He was sick of needing a man like Killian, who cared for nothing but being a thorn in the side of the society Aidan had been raised to lead. To protect. But in this momentary crisis, he didn't have a choice. He did feel a strange compulsion to ensure that Seph was well, and not trapped somewhere with no idea what was happening. He had a responsibility to her as his employee, that was all. But it was enough.

"Agreed," he bit out. "Your move, *free-trader*."

"As beginnings go, it leaves something wanting," Killian remarked, "but I suppose it's progress. Follow me, *bartender*." His grin was fierce. "Hope you're not scared of heights."

FIVE

SEPH HAD FALLEN asleep in a bleak mood. In addition to her humiliating evening at work, she'd stopped by a terminal on her way home, only to find a message waiting for her. From her parents.

It cost a lot to send anything by way of the Conclave beacons, even words, and her parents would never have done so without a compelling reason—like impending doom, or at least their personal equivalent.

Her little brother was on the verge of losing his place at school. He was on scholarship, of course, but there were still fees that had to be paid, and they were coming due in less than a month. During the past two years, those fees had been paid out of her older brothers' meager salaries and supplemented by Seph's infrequent contributions.

But due to Lindmark's troubles over Daragh, the economy had taken a downturn. Her parents reported that her brothers had lost their jobs a few months back, and been unable to find work since.

Worst of all was their living situation. Her family had all been staying in Seph's place ever since she left—it was tiny, but at least it was above ground. Yet now her mother reported they were considering selling the apartment to help pay for necessities. Returning to sub-level housing.

All because Seph had been out of work for months. Unable to send money home.

Seph had felt like crying as she got ready for bed. What had she been thinking of coming to Concord instead of returning to Earth? She could have found something there, even if Lindmark hesitated to hire her. And how could she have been so selfish with her choices? She should have taken some kind of menial job months ago—considered more than just her own preferences and wild-eyed dreams.

But she hadn't, and now her family was in trouble. She was going to have to tell Aidan she was finished and look for something else. Something that paid more. If she'd known sooner, she could have headed directly for Earth, but it was too late for that now. By the time she returned home, there would be no time to solve the problem.

So it was little surprise that she slept fitfully, with recurring dreams of her entire family sobbing and proclaiming her heartless for abandoning them. Even Aidan appeared in that dream, his face in shadow but his voice entirely recognizable as he fired her and threw her out of Dizzy's.

Seph woke up achy, sweating and miserable, and only then did she realize that it wasn't all because of her dream. Her head hurt, her left shoulder ached, and half of her stuff was lying on the floor.

Looking for answers—or perhaps simply hoping she had yet to fully wake up—her eyes fastened on the familiar curve of her room's wall, but instead of its usual gray it was bathed in orange from the dim glow of the emergency light above her door.

That pulled her to full wakefulness faster than a splash of cold water to the face. Could the gravity generators have gone offline? Her sarcastic comment to Brand hadn't been an exaggeration—they did malfunction from time to time, but this would be the first instance since she'd arrived.

Fortunately, the backup generators seemed to be working, but the orange lights meant they were on backup power as well, which suggested that the problem extended well beyond gravity. Warm air still blew from the grate, indicating that environmental systems were still online, but who knew for how long?

Suddenly energized despite her lack of sleep, Seph dressed, grabbed her weapons, and slapped the door latch. Nothing happened. Suppressing a quick surge of panic, she tried again, with the same result. The glowing light that normally showed whether the lock was engaged blinked fitfully and failed to respond to her increasingly forceful prods.

Seph swallowed the sick taste of fear and set her hands on her hips to control their shaking. The door should have worked. If nothing else, the door controls should have been connected to the emergency power supply, but whether they had failed or been locked down, there was no way to know. All she knew was that she couldn't stay there. Couldn't bear the sensation of being trapped—locked in a small space with no way of getting out.

It had been that way for years. Darkness and close confines didn't bother her as long as she knew she could get out whenever she wanted. But this... Seph took a deep breath of slightly acrid-tasting air and shoved her panic back down. If this was a station-wide emergency, she wouldn't be able to count on a rescue. She had to remain calm enough to get herself out of her room. And she needed to do so quickly.

If the situation was bad enough, the station would be evacuated. The corporations would take their employees and leave everyone else to fend for themselves. Those who were unaffiliated would have to sink or swim along with the station itself, and as much as Seph wanted an adventure, being stuck on a dying space station wasn't her idea of excitement.

Her multitool! Maybe she could rewire the door controls to work with the emergency power. Seph fumbled around in her gear-pod with trembling hands until she found the pouch with her tools at the bottom. Removing the panel over the door latch was easy, but the circuits inside... If this emergency ended up being a whole lot of nothing—or the lockdown had happened on purpose—she was probably going to be in trouble for damaging her rented quarters, but she didn't care. She just needed a way out.

The orange light flickered briefly while she worked, lending a new source of urgency to her task. If the backup power went down, the environmental systems would soon follow, and the station's inhabitants would have only a short window in which to reach the emergency rafts before the air quality began to degrade. Anyone still trapped in their rooms would miss that window completely.

Seph distracted herself from the panic by wondering briefly about the hundreds of others who had to be in the same situation but without resources. At least she had tools and knew how to use them. Aidan couldn't even fix a cooler, so he probably wouldn't have the knowledge required to rewire his door locks. He might be trapped somewhere on First, where no one would think to look or take the time to attempt a rescue… Though he would no doubt favor her with an icy glare for insinuating that he needed help, then kick his door down and stalk off without a backward glance.

Seph grinned at the thought and kept working. The door circuits turned out to be relatively simple but surprisingly secure. It took what felt like an eternity to find the right wires and reconnect them in a way that—hopefully—she would be able to reverse if the situation was revealed to be a false alarm.

The door shuddered under her fingers just before she was ready to test her work. Seph jerked back and listened. She didn't think any power surge had come from the station itself, and anyway, there was no power to the door until she completed the circuit. When the disturbance failed to repeat itself, she said a brief prayer, slapped the door latch and stood back, just in case her slapdash electrical work proved faulty.

Nothing exploded. The latch lit up, and the door jerked open… by about an inch.

It wasn't much, but it helped her breathe a little easier. Made her feel a little less trapped. Seph was about to grab the door and try to force it open a bit farther when a large, male hand appeared in the gap.

"What the…" she took a step back and reached for her palm stunner as the hand grasped the door and pulled. The door shuddered and then receded, far enough for her to see the dark forms of two men in the corridor outside.

She swung her stunner up and pointed it at the nearest one's chest.

"Seph?"

"Aidan?" Her hands dropped along with her jaw. Here she'd been imagining her boss waiting helplessly in his quarters, while he'd not only gotten himself out but come looking for her? "You're okay!" She couldn't quite keep the relief out of her voice, on his behalf as well as her own. "What are you doing up here? And how did you find me?"

"If you want out, move fast," he said, his tone as cool as ever. "I can't hold this door forever."

She wanted to inform him that she been taking care of the door just fine without his help, but she was so relieved to be free that she swallowed the words, stowed her tool and her weapon and stepped out into the corridor. As soon as she was through, Aidan released the door, which oozed slowly back into place.

The second man stepped up next to him and offered her a congratulatory nod. "Very resourceful, Miss Seph. May I say that I never doubted your abilities for a moment."

"If you never doubted, then why are you even here?" Aidan's tone was very nearly peeved.

"Altruism, of course," Killian said with a grin. But the grin faded before he spoke again. "Truthfully, I wasn't sure whether Miss Seph had the right kind of connections to ensure she wouldn't be forgotten in the event of an evacuation. I thought to offer her a place aboard my ship, should it be necessary."

"Is it that bad?" Seph had hoped that she was only imagining the worst and that the crisis, whatever it was, would turn out to be small and quickly resolved.

"No way of knowing, I'm afraid," Killian said smoothly, tapping his comm-band. "Concord Five has locked down all unofficial communications."

"Never stopped you before," Aidan said, throwing a hard look at Killian.

The pirate appeared unrepentant. "When I have something I care to share, you'll be the first to know."

"It might be worse than it seems," Aidan said, returning his gaze to Seph, "but there was debris floating away from the station. Could have come from either an explosion or a collision of some sort."

Seph shuddered and wrapped her arms around herself. If something had in fact collided with the station, "bad" wouldn't begin to describe it. And Killian was right. She didn't know whether she'd be able to beg a ride off, especially if available seats were going to the highest bidder.

"The debris may not have come from the station," Killian reminded them. "It could have been ship-to-ship, or botched docking maneuvers. My second is checking it out. Whatever it was happened on or near Third, though it's affected systems on all levels."

Then Aidan had been right. The pirate *did* still have access to communication.

"Well, at least the tubes are still running," Seph observed. "Can't have been that bad."

"No,"—Killian winked—"they're not. We came by a different route. Now, would either of you care to accompany me on a little trip to Third to look around? This probably isn't the best place to be if more systems go down."

"I'm in," Seph announced. "Not waiting down here to be rescued. Aidan?"

"We'll both be stuck up there until the tubes are back online," he reminded her.

"Why can't we just come back down the same way we're going up?"

He shot her an indecipherable look. "Wait and see," was all he would say, before he turned away, giving Seph a glimpse of the side of his head, where his hair was matted and sticky with...

"Is that *blood*? What happened?" She stepped towards him and reached out without thinking, jerking her hand back only when he flinched.

"Gravity failure," he said, folding his arms. "It's fine."

"It's a head injury with blood loss," she insisted stubbornly. "You don't know if it's fine or not."

"Then you can fuss later," he said harshly. "I'm walking and talking. Wait until we find out whether there's an actual emergency."

"Oh, just knock it off," she snapped, stepping closer and putting her hands on her hips. "You're worse than a four-year-old. Hold still and let me at least see whether you're going to need stitches for anything besides your busted up sense of priorities."

She heard a choking sound from Killian as she put the flat of her hand on Aidan's jaw and pushed his head around until she could get a better look at the side. Somewhat to her surprise, he didn't knock her hand away, though his jaw did clench under her hand and she could swear she heard his teeth grind together.

As gently as possible, she touched his hair where the blood had begun to dry and probed the skin beneath. He winced as her fingers encountered a split in his scalp, but it didn't seem to be long or deep, and the swelling around it was minimal. She continued to feel around it, but couldn't detect any more gashes or areas of swelling.

"Probably okay," she said, letting out a long breath. "Unless you have a concussion, which I can't tell you without a bio-scanner. You don't seem disoriented. Any dizziness?"

Aidan jerked his head back, and Seph realized she'd still been holding his jaw. She dropped her hand swiftly.

"No." He moved away from her. "As I said before, it's fine. We should go."

Seph stepped back and quelled the urge to continue arguing with him. At least she'd tried. Apparently, even a station-wide power failure and a blow to the head couldn't make a dent in her boss's sunny personality. "Sure, boss." She threw him a mock salute. "Whatever you say."

Aidan's only answer was to walk off down the corridor, leaving Seph and Killian to stare after him, though with entirely different expressions. Killian was grinning.

"Just don't whine to me when you have the mother of all headaches," Seph grumbled under her breath, "because I won't feel sorry for you."

Her companion laughed. "I believe you're far too compassionate to make good on that promise, Miss Seph."

"There are exceptions to everything," she retorted. "Did he come up here to rescue me or to tell me why it's my own fault I was stuck in my room?"

"I suspect," Killian observed, "your friend there would prefer that no one find out he has a heart."

"I'd say he's doing a stellar job of hiding it," she returned with a sigh. "So." She raised an eyebrow at Killian. "Why are you really here?"

"What?" he asked slyly. "You didn't believe me?"

"That you came up here in the middle of a crisis to offer me a ride off station? Nope. You barely know me."

"You're a beautiful woman—perhaps I was interested on a personal level."

Seph laughed a little uncomfortably. She couldn't tell whether he was being serious, but it was easier to pretend he was joking. "Not that beautiful. And I'm sure a dashing pirate captain can have his pick of ladies far better looking than me. No, I'm pretty sure you want something, you're just not ready to tell me what it is."

"You wound me." The pirate looked more amused than wounded. "Perhaps you would believe that I encountered Aidan on First. He wanted to make sure you were all right, but the tubes were down. I was on my way to my ship anyway, and couldn't leave a distraught man to his own devices under such a circumstance."

"Distraught?" Seph couldn't help a humorless chuckle. "That would be an outstandingly polite lie if we didn't both know how ridiculous it is. I don't think Aidan knows how to be distraught. He was just worried about losing his cook."

"As to that, you might be surprised," Killian remarked, a little too casually. "But, feelings aside, we really ought to be on our way. Should the situation worsen, time will be of the essence."

"Do you really think we'll be forced to leave the station?"

The pirate nodded. "One way or another. You interested?"

Seph eyed him, thinking hard. "If there's an evacuation, the answer is decidedly yes."

"Then perhaps you'll want to grab anything you can't afford to lose. As Aidan said, we won't be coming back down anytime soon."

Probably wise. With Killian's help, Seph pried her door back open and dashed in long enough to stuff a pack she could sling over her shoulders on the way out. Her gear-pod would have to be abandoned, along with most of her clothes, but she could hold out hope that the situation wasn't as bad as it looked at the moment. Perhaps she'd be able to come back for them.

Once she returned to the corridor, she gestured in the direction Aidan had gone before he disappeared.

"Lead on, Captain," she said. "I'm certainly not itching to stay."

"Perhaps this is a trifle late to be asking, but... you're not afraid of heights, are you?"

"Not really, why?"

"Because"—Killian flashed her a heart-stopping grin—"I believe our friend Aidan is."

———

It took a handful of minutes for Seph and Killian to follow him down the dimly lit corridor to the access hatch, and Aidan spent all of them pulling himself together and trying not to wonder what the pirate was telling Seph.

Whatever it was, it wouldn't be flattering, which was probably for the best. He couldn't afford for anyone to find out that he had apparently developed a soft spot where Seph was concerned.

He'd known she meant something to him, but he hadn't expected to be affected by something as simple as her businesslike grip on his jaw, or her gentle fingers in his hair. Her probing had hurt, but the damage to his head had been less painful than the damage to the emotional barriers he'd hidden behind since he was old enough to understand the need for them.

Phillip Linden had been known as a heartless bastard for a lot of reasons, not the least of which was the minimizing of vulnerabilities. For as long as he could remember, his mother had ruthlessly punished even the smallest hint of affection for anyone or anything. People like him weren't permitted to love, because anything he loved could be used to hurt him. He was allowed pride, disdain, ambition. Loyalty to family and to Lindmark.

But all other feelings were a weakness, or so Satrina had taught him. As a child, when he'd developed the beginnings of a friendship with someone his own age, the moment his mother found out he would never be allowed to see that child again. If he'd expressed interest in an employee, that person was dismissed without pay. At least, he hoped that was all that had been done to them. Even toys he had become attached to were destroyed in front of him as a lesson. He'd learned fast to bury his feelings and refuse to acknowledge them, and one day he'd awakened to the gratifying belief that he no longer suffered from anything so maudlin as emotions.

Until his family's staggering betrayal breached his barriers and revealed the rage and sorrow and hurt still hiding behind them.

Now, Aidan kept his walls in place out of both necessity and habit. He still couldn't allow the world to guess the truth about who he was or what he had done, and honestly, it was simpler to go on as he had been. For his entire adult life, it had been as instinctual as breathing to protect those around him by maintaining a perspective of absolute and unrelenting indifference, and, after this long, who really knew where the lie ended and the truth began?

He did know that Seph made indifference more difficult than it had ever been before, and therefore also more important. Any vulnerability could still be used against him, in any number of ways, especially when his luck ran out, and someone realized he wasn't as dead as he was supposed to be.

Which he believed was bound to happen, sooner or later. Would it be wisest to look for a way off station now? Or wait to find out whether Concord would need to be evacuated?

He could stay, he supposed. Weather the storm, and possibly even hope that this event would prove distracting enough that none of those Lindmark officers would remember seeing a man who looked a lot like Phillip Linden.

Or he could disappear again. Killian might be willing to allow him a place on his crew. Considering the pirate's varied destinations and contacts, Aidan could jump ship at any one of a hundred ports and forge a new life for himself, somewhere far away from Seph and the betrayal she would feel when she learned the truth about his identity.

Getting off station was probably his best option, but only after he knew for sure that Seph would be safe. It was a nonsensical compulsion, but it was real, and he couldn't seem to ignore it, though he suspected

Seph would object if she ever became aware of his intentions. He even wondered himself whether he had a right to manipulate her future. But neither of those considerations weighed very heavily in balance with her life, and he didn't intend to let scruples get in the way of saving it. Not that Phillip Linden had ever possessed something so pedestrian as scruples.

Seph and Killian eventually caught up with him, momentarily interrupting his descent into self-loathing.

"We're headed up to Third," the pirate announced blithely, his mood seemingly undimmed by the grim reality of a malfunctioning space station. "Are you staying or going?"

Aidan cast a glance at Seph, who was studiously avoiding his eyes, her expression bland and her hands on her hips. She was definitely annoyed with him.

The knowing grin on Killian's face settled it.

"Going," Aidan answered flatly. "If the station implodes, this level will be a death trap."

"Then follow me, stay close, and don't look down." Killian deftly removed the cover from one of the maintenance shafts and handed each of them a tight pair of gloves with a dark, rough surface. He only had two, so it appeared that the pirate intended to go without.

"What are these for?" Seph asked curiously, securing her pack over her shoulders before pulling them on and flexing her fingers.

"Climbing," Killian said cryptically. "They should help you keep your grip, even if your hands get sweaty."

"Why would my hands get sweaty?" Seph's forehead wrinkled, though she didn't look nearly as worried as she ought to.

"You said you weren't afraid of heights," Killian responded with a wink, "so I'm sure it won't be a problem." He ducked into the shaft and disappeared.

"Depends on what you mean by heights," Seph muttered under her breath. "Probably should have asked more questions before I agreed to follow him anywhere."

"His answers wouldn't change the situation," Aidan said, keeping his voice hard. "Unless you prefer the possibility of dying down here, trapped and alone in the dark."

Her face jerked and her eyes flared, and as he recognized her fear of that brutally painted future, Aidan felt a brief stab somewhere in the region of his heart. Conscience? Surely not. He was pretty sure he didn't have one of those. Shame? He wasn't sure he could feel that either, but he did feel something like regret, for having deliberately exposed fear in someone so essentially fearless as Seph.

He'd also discovered an irrational desire to make sure that what she feared so deeply would never happen. If it had been in his power, he would have gladly bargained away his own ticket off the station in exchange for hers.

Though he would have died rather than admit it.

Aidan's first step into the maintenance tunnel left him blind. It was even darker than the corridor, forcing him to close his eyes to help them adjust. Reaching for the far wall to give himself a guide, he was caught off guard when Seph, following too closely, ran into his arm and nearly fell.

He grabbed for her in the dark, catching her around the waist by sheer luck, then waited while she gained her balance.

"Sorry," she said quietly, pulling away as quickly as she could. He couldn't see her face, but she sounded embarrassed. "And thank you." Her tone was subdued, which was unlike his cheerful, indomitable Seph. Had he really frightened her that badly?

Even if he had, there was nothing he could say that might help. He'd always been better at fear and intimidation than soothing ruffled tempers or hurt feelings.

"This way," Killian announced from the darkness up ahead, slapping a light patch onto his palm and setting off into the faint glow it cast ahead of him. "And step lively. We don't want to be stuck in here if the gravity fails."

"I can't decide if I like him or I'd like to kill him," Seph said grimly, though she seemed to be talking more to herself than to Aidan.

"Let me know if you need help with that." Aidan hadn't even meant to answer, but he was rewarded by the sound of Seph's laugh, a soft ripple in the darkness as she followed Killian down the tunnel.

———

After about a ten minute walk, much of it through narrow spaces filled with tubes and wires and machinery, Killian stopped and looked up, turning his palm to illuminate a circular hatch overhead. An agile leap left him hanging by one hand from a slight recess in the ceiling, while the other hand tapped a swift sequence into the security pad beside the hatch.

"I'm going to hazard a guess this is an unauthorized access," Seph remarked.

"It wouldn't be nearly as fun if we had permission," Killian replied, as casually as if they were chatting over drinks at Dizzy's.

The hatch slid back, and Killian grasped the lip with his free hand, pulling himself up swiftly and easily. "Come on up," he called down.

"Oh, sure," Seph grumbled. "Does he think this is zero-G?" She jumped but fell at least half a foot shy of the lip of the hatch.

"Need a lift?" Aidan heard himself ask, wincing as he contemplated her likely response. Seph probably wouldn't care for the insinuation that she might need help.

"Do I have a choice?" she asked, sighing a little as her face tilted up to regard the opening above her. "I'm in good shape, but I'm still subject to gravity."

Surprised and irrationally pleased, Aidan closed the gap between them.

"Will you be able to pull yourself up afterward?" she asked.

"Yes." How did she think he'd gotten up to Second? Or did she think he was so fragile that a tiny bit of blood would sideline him?

"Cut it out." Her elbow drove sharply into his ribs, surprising him into a grunt. "I can hear you being offended that I doubted your abilities." Then she elbowed him again. "And that's for being an idiot about your injury. If we're really pulling off some death-defying climb and you get dizzy—"

"My head is fine," he interrupted, gritting his teeth. "Stop fussing and let's get on with this."

"I'll fuss if I want to fuss," she shot back. "If I choose to care about whether or not your head is going to swell up and fall off, that's my business, not yours, and..."

Aidan wasn't really thinking about anything but stopping her from saying whatever was going to come next. He didn't want to hear that she cared about him, didn't want to confront his own impulses to protect her, so he bent slightly, wrapped his arms around her hips and lifted, bracing her weight against his shoulder.

She gasped and grabbed at his hair, but managed to balance precariously as he straightened, leaving her within an easy distance of the hatch. "I should kick you for that," she announced, reaching for the opening above her, "but I'd like to think I'm too nice for that kind of behavior."

"You're entitled to your delusions," Aidan said, focusing on holding her steady while trying to ignore the feeling of her gloved fingers in his hair and the curve of her hip beneath his hand. "But don't forget I saw you flatten a man's face with a tray."

He was pretty sure Seph glared at the top of his head. "That *was* nice. *You* were about to break him in half." She pulled herself up with ease, though she almost fell back through when her backpack caught for a moment on the edge of the hatch. Once she gained her feet, Seph turned to crouch near the opening where she could see him in the light from Killian's palm.

"Need a lift?" she asked sweetly.

Aidan leaped straight up, caught the edge and pulled himself through the hatch without much effort. "No," he said blandly.

Killian chuckled from behind them. "This way." He pointed his light upwards while Seph was still narrowing her eyes and looking as if she'd changed her mind about kicking someone.

Aidan looked up, almost against his will, and ruthlessly quelled the chill that rolled over him at the sight. A towering vertical shaft soared above them, bathed in a pale, cold light. It was flat and featureless but for the narrow grooves cut into one wall—a ladder, of sorts, for someone insane enough to climb it. The grooves were spaced evenly up the wall, all the way to the top, where he could just make out the brilliance of stars filtering through the transparent barrier.

According to Killian, the station's designers had meant the space to be a secondary tube system, but when the station was assembled, they had never installed the necessary equipment. Each shaft had both atmosphere and gravity, along with the maintenance ladder in case the tube's pods had required repairs. But any maintenance techs would have had climbing gear, including safety harnesses and anti-grav packs, and most likely would not have suffered from a crippling fear of heights.

Aidan wasn't afraid of heights either, as long as he was inside, with his feet on a sturdy foundation. Even Lindmark Tower had never troubled him when he stood by the window and looked down, but this was entirely different. Plus, he'd already done it once, which meant he knew exactly what to expect, and the prospect of repeating the experience made his stomach roil with nausea.

"So when you asked if I was scared of heights, what you really meant is whether I'm scared of falling," Seph said, sounding shocked. "We're actually going to climb that?"

"It's easier than it looks," Killian assured her, reaching for a handhold and beginning to ascend the wall. "I've done it a few times, even come down once or twice, and never had a problem."

"I've decided," Seph announced, as she watched Killian's progress. "I'm definitely going to kill him."

"I'll help," Aidan murmured, too quietly for her to hear.

"But this is the only way out," she said softly. "We don't have a choice."

Aidan heard her breathe deeply before she strode forward and began to climb in Killian's wake. He opened his mouth to tell her to give him her pack, but she was already several paces up, and anyway, he doubted she would have relinquished it.

"Just don't you fall off and take me with you," she called up to the pirate, who was moving faster than appeared even remotely safe.

"Perish the thought, Miss Seph," he called back, dangling by one hand for a moment as if to prove his point. "You'll be fine."

Aidan gritted his teeth and forced himself to move. Whether or not he cared what became of his own life beyond this moment, he'd become suddenly reluctant to let Seph out of his sight. That idiot pirate was going to take advantage of her desperate situation and end up getting her killed.

He reached up, grasped the first handhold, and began the climb, firmly resisting the almost overwhelming desire to close his eyes. The sense of panic was even worse the second time, and Aidan resolved firmly that even if the station recovered and everything returned to normal, Dizzy was just going to have to deal with his absence until the tubes were fixed. No matter what Killian said, there was no way he was ever climbing back down.

SIX

BY THE TIME they emerged from the maintenance tunnel on Third, Seph had decided she was most emphatically terrified of at least *some* kinds of heights. She was also not nearly as physically fit as she'd assumed. Her arms felt boneless, her fingers burned, and her legs trembled so hard she had to focus on walking as they made their way from the unused tube shaft to the access point.

She had lost her footing once, about halfway up, and heard a soft, desperate curse from Aidan where he clung to the wall below her. Whether it had been for her or for himself—perhaps anticipating that she might lose her grip and fall into him—she hadn't asked. Didn't want to know. In fact, she preferred to forget the experience as quickly as possible.

Killian, of course, still appeared carefree and unruffled. The effort hadn't even flattened the spikes in his dark brown hair. Aidan was pale and sweating, but she didn't think it was from exhaustion. Twice she'd looked back to find him resting, as close to the wall as he could get, with his eyes tightly shut.

Whether Killian had been right about him being afraid of heights she had no way of knowing—it wasn't exactly something she could ask—but she was concerned that his head injury might be bothering him. She'd seen the effects of a concussion creep up over time, so she quietly resolved to ambush him with a bio-scanner at the earliest opportunity.

And the pirate had probably been wrong anyway. If Aidan really did hate heights so much, he would have taken the shortest possible route to Third. There had been no need for him to stop and check on Seph, not when he had rarely shown anything warmer than indifference towards her existence. More than likely, he had been bored, or curious, or...

All speculation cut off abruptly when she stepped out of the tunnel onto Third and discovered a far different atmosphere than she'd expected.

"Well, this is cheery," Killian remarked as they closed the maintenance hatch behind them.

They'd emerged in the Platinum District, which had always seemed to Seph to be a different world from the one she lived in. Wide, carpeted halls, sophisticated multi-hued lighting, chrome accents, and a carefully curated selection of lounges, emporiums, and restaurants catered to clients with money and influence. The bare, utilitarian bones of the space station with its tubes and hatches and docking ports were hidden behind a veneer of wealth and pretense.

But all that pretense looked just as ugly when painted by the familiar orange glow of the emergency lights. Every denizen of Third appeared to have emerged from their place of business or employment to pack the halls. Jumpsuited executives, uniformed chefs, brightly painted professional companions and costumed entertainers jostled and shouted alongside armored security forces from all five Conclave corporations, their helmets sealed and weapons gripped tightly in gauntleted hands. An occasional scream cut through the general cacophony, while sobs could be heard alongside angry shouts. Even the air was hazy with smoke, and a harsh, chemical smell burned Seph's nostrils with every breath.

"Stay close!" Killian had to shout to be heard over the din. "The docking area is sealed off, access for officers and crew only, so we should be fine if we can make it past this mess."

"Doesn't look like the locking systems malfunctioned on this level," Seph shouted back. "Shouldn't more of these people be trapped like we were?"

"Third is busy at all hours," Killian responded with a shrug. "They could have locked down quarters, but nobody was in them."

"Do these people all know something we don't?" The general level of panic seemed concerning to Seph.

"I doubt it." For once, the set of Killian's mouth lacked humor. "The powers that be won't share information until it's absolutely necessary. These poor people don't know what to do other than panic." He leaned closer. "We need to get to the ship. There I'll have access to as much or more information than the station crew does."

"Which way? In case we get separated?" Seph hadn't spent enough time on Third to know exactly where the crew access was located.

Killian pointed. "All the way past the end of the Platinum District. Take a left. There's a short jog where you cross over to the inner side of the ring, and the corridor is sealed by an airtight door. I have a stop to make, so you'll have to wait for me there."

Seph nodded and turned to look at Aidan, who raised an eyebrow as if daring her to ask him if he was okay. By the time she turned back around, Killian had vanished into the crowds and the smoke and the shadows, so she gritted her teeth and plunged into the crowd herself, reasoning that Aidan would either keep up or he wouldn't. Either way, they would meet at the designated spot.

It was a mistake. Seph felt as though she'd stepped into a river, only to find that the current was deeper and faster than the surface showed. She was not a tiny person, but the weight and momentum of a panicked crowd were considerable, and she was already tired. Knots and swirls of movement pushed her from one side of the hall to the other as she fought for progress and balance. If she were to fall, Seph wouldn't give much for her chances. No one in the crowd would care who they trampled in their haste to get to safety.

Still, she pressed on, hoping she hadn't gotten turned around. It was difficult to see over the heads of the people around her, especially the armored security officers, who didn't seem to be watching where they were going and were clearly disinclined to wait for the crowds to part.

Seph took advantage of a brief space to stand on her toes and look for the end of the corridor. It was almost as far away as it had been when she started. When she sank back down, the beginnings of fear clawed at her throat. What if she became lost in the crowd? Would Killian even look for her, or merely assume she'd changed her mind about meeting him and leave without her? If he did, how could she possibly find a way off the station in the middle of all this chaos?

A heavy weight struck her pack, knocking her forward and to her knees. Panicked, she surged up but was thrown sideways by an armored officer who tramped on past, not seeming to realize or care that there was a person in his way.

The brief gap in the crowd was quickly swallowed up by a surge of people, and the only reason Seph wasn't trampled was the crush of bodies that kept her from falling completely. As it was, she couldn't gain her balance, but was thrown from side to side, dizzy, disoriented and eventually unsure which way was up and which way was down.

Until she was thrown hard into a body that didn't move, and a pair of arms that caught her before she could fall again.

The crowd still surged around her, but she was no longer carried with it. Eyes closed, Seph gasped in a breath and tried to pull back, but the arms didn't give way.

"Just take a minute. You're safe."

Aidan. Her eyes flew open. He stood like a rock in the midst of the crowd as it broke and flowed around him. Beneath her hands, his chest was solid and warm, and his hold on her never wavered. He'd followed her. Saved her.

He was never going to let her live this down.

"I'm okay now. Really." She pulled back again, and he let her, but then he reached down and took her hand instead.

"Better if we stay together," he said, leaning in until his lips were just inches from her ear. "Just in case you get dizzy. Or disoriented."

Seph stepped away and tried to ignore him, but it was impossible. In the midst of chaos and danger, a devil gleamed in his blue eyes. It was possibly the closest she'd ever seen him come to looking happy.

And drat her treacherous heart, it gave an answering leap of happiness at the feeling of her hand in his. The crowd tried to push them apart, but Aidan's grasp was warm and steady as he pivoted and began to forge a path in the direction they needed to go.

She should probably have resented him for the magic that made the crowd part and allow them a path, but she chose instead to be grateful. They reached the relative safety of the end of the district after only a few moments, took the short jog Killian had described, and ended up in front of a heavy-looking door that barred them from going farther.

"Thank you," Seph said as they gazed at the door. "For keeping me alive back there."

Aidan dropped her hand. "Mobs are dangerous," he said, once more cool and detached. "You shouldn't have tried to cut straight through."

Whatever humor or temporary insanity had possessed him, it had already vanished. Seph suppressed a sigh, took off her pack, and leaned back against the wall of the much narrower corridor. She tried to breathe a little more deeply but immediately wished that she hadn't, as the acrid taint in the air burned down her throat and into her lungs.

A rasping cough seized her for a moment, making her chest ache until it finally eased. "Whatever is burning, I don't think we should be breathing it."

"Probably not." Aidan jerked his chin in the direction from which they'd come. "Corporate security is armored up, and most of the station crew I could see are in decon suits. They may be hiding the extent of the damage."

Seph nodded her agreement. "Hopefully Killian won't be long." She paused, unsure how to ask her next question.

"About Killian..." she began, but Aidan interrupted her.

"Look, I don't know what Killian intends. Or what he meant by his offer to take you aboard his ship. But no matter what happens, even if Killian doesn't show up, you need to be very careful about trusting anyone from Lindmark." He seemed utterly serious.

"Aidan, I'm careful about trusting anyone. But Lindmark is basically my only hope. I may have burned my bridges with them on Daragh, but if Killian doesn't show and the station has to be evacuated, nobody else is going to take me."

"I'm telling you that you need to avoid them."

"You think Killian is safer? He might be charming and charismatic, but he also gets his kicks thumbing his nose at the corporations. I can't imagine his ship being a safe place." Aidan's expression grew grim when she called Killian charming, but she couldn't help it. The man *was* charming.

"Safe?" He huffed in either irritation or dismissal. "No. Killian isn't that. He's dangerous and unpredictable, but in this case he's a better option than Lindmark. He never hesitates to put his own life in danger, and rarely has fewer than five reasons for anything, but he's only one man."

Was that a vote of approval or disapproval? Was he hoping she would leave with Killian?

"Why are you so worried about Lindmark?"

Aidan didn't say anything, just folded his arms tightly across his chest.

Suddenly she understood. "This is about Brand, isn't it?" She would have laughed at his concern, but she didn't want to hurt his feelings. "I've never been afraid of him," she assured Aidan, "and I'm not about to start now. Especially not when we're in the middle of a serious emergency. If this station is failing, I'm not going to stand here and make a list of the people who aren't allowed to save my life."

"This isn't just about your ex." Aidan's grim tone forced her to look him in the eye. They stood closely enough Seph could see something beyond his usual indifference burning beneath the surface.

"Then what is it about? Aidan, I'm listening, but you can't make cryptic statements like that and expect me to agree without any explanation. Why should I avoid Lindmark?"

"Because I don't want you hurt," he said flatly. "Have I ever lied to you? Endangered you in any way?"

"No," she conceded. "Not that I'm aware of. Well, except when you threatened to fire me because you didn't like me. You lied twice then." When he glowered in response, Seph put her hands on her hips. "You did, so don't bother trying to deny it. But mostly you ignore me and pretend that I annoy you. I don't believe you'd lie to me again unless you thought it was in my best interests."

He didn't seem to have an answer to that, so she went on.

"Aidan, you may not have ever endangered me, but we barely know each other, and you're asking me to potentially stake my life on vague hints and warnings. Just give me a reason for your concern. I'm not stupid, but if the station is evacuated and Lindmark is my only way out, I need to know what I'm up against."

He was silent, but Seph could read the tension in his jaw and the set of his shoulders.

"I'm sorry, but you're just going to have to trust me."

"Not good enough," she said firmly. "I'm not some silly girl that you can manipulate with half-truths and dire portents. I need something concrete, and if you respect me at all—"

"Seph, please."

The please stopped her. She would have said he didn't even know the word, but he appeared to be in earnest, his gaze fastened on hers with burning intensity. First he'd said sorry and now please?

"Aidan, what is really going on?"

"I can't tell you any more."

"Can't or won't?" she asked wearily. "Aidan, I feel like maybe you're genuinely trying to look out for me, but it's hard to accept when you're also treating me like a child."

He opened his mouth as if to protest, but she didn't give him a chance.

"I don't know what kind of women you're used to, but this cryptic 'do what I tell you or else' nonsense isn't going to work on me. If you're just my boss, you don't get to tell me what to do when I'm off the clock. In fact, you don't even get to have an opinion about it. If you want to be a friend, treat me like one and respect me enough to tell me the truth."

Something bright and hot flared in his blue eyes, cutting through his usual mask of indifference and fracturing the icy disdain he used to keep the world at bay. Seph couldn't name the emotion because he'd shown so few, but she knew it wasn't anger, and for the briefest of moments, she held her breath, wondering if he was about to... Grab her? Shake her? Absurd. No matter how frustrated he was, he would never hurt her, not physically at least.

And a fraction of an instant later, the look was gone.

"I'm going to say this just once," he told her coolly, his folded arms forming an impenetrable barrier between them, "and only because you're not someone I want on my conscience. Whatever wrongheaded idea you have about who and what I am, you should forget it now, while you still can. I don't want to be your friend. My friendship is a curse that would destroy you and everyone you love. But believe this—if you ignore my warning and get on a Lindmark ship, there is a good chance you will spend the rest of your life regretting it."

Seph closed her eyes, swallowed the hurt and prayed for patience.

"Do you have any idea how melodramatic you sound?" she asked, opening her eyes and tilting her head to the side. "Whoever you think you are, you don't have the power to ruin my life."

Aidan shrugged. "As your employer, I feel some sense of responsibility for you, so I've done my best to warn you. If you're going to ignore me, I can't answer for the consequences."

He turned and faced the door, leaving Seph to stare at his back, gaping with confusion and frustration.

"That wasn't a warning," she muttered under her breath. "It was an order. And you're a pompous, self-important…"

"Ah, you made it. Good." Killian's breezy tone punctured whatever she'd been about to say and reminded her that this was not the best time for a verbal confrontation. "Give me a moment, and I'll have us out of this smoke."

Seph pasted a relieved smile on her face and pretended she hadn't been about to smack her boss across the back of the head.

"Can't be too soon," she said honestly. "My lungs are burning."

"Even if the docking area is affected, we'll have air filtration running on the *Fancy*," Killian assured her.

"The what?"

"My ship," he explained, grinning as he punched a long series of numbers and symbols into the security pad. "She's named for one of the fastest, most heavily armed pirate vessels ever to sail the Earth—captured two of the richest prizes ever recorded and was never destroyed or captured."

"For a man who prefers not to be called a pirate, you seem curiously eager to embrace the trappings," Seph commented dryly.

The door slid open, and Killian threw a wink over his shoulder. "All part of my image, Miss Seph. Without his image, a man has nothing but two hands and determination, and those never kept a spaceship running."

A curious perspective. As they stepped through the door and it slammed shut behind them, Seph filed that information away for the future —and for whatever that future might hold. For the moment, she was stuck with two enigmatic men who may or may not care what happened to her.

Just as she had been since leaving home, Seph was on her own, and at the moment that was not a comforting thought. She wasn't afraid, exactly. It was probably the crisis making her maudlin, but she suddenly wished she had someone she could count on—a connection, or a friend, to make her feel less small and vulnerable. But all of her connections were back home, relying on her to help them out of their own difficulties, blissfully unaware of the dire situation she now faced.

That thought was a bleak reminder of the many consequences that could result from the events of the next few hours. If the station was evacuated, she'd soon be heading back to Earth, jobless, unable to aid her family in any way. And even if she got to stay, she would be hard pressed to find anyone hiring in the midst of a disaster.

As Seph followed Killian around the curve of the station, she wondered whether the universe was conspiring against her or she simply had the worst luck imaginable. Either way, the next move was probably out of her hands, and she couldn't decide which made her feel more helpless—that she could do nothing for her family or that there was little she could even do for herself.

———

Aidan's frustration only grew as he followed Killian and Seph through the docking quarter of Third. He didn't blame Seph for wanting the truth, or for not trusting him. He probably wouldn't trust him either, but he had to make her understand the danger she could be in, without revealing his past.

Brand Elliot posed little physical danger to Seph, and Aidan had no doubt she would be able to handle the idiot in a confrontation. That wasn't his concern. His true worry was what other forms of revenge the bastard might choose. The question wasn't *whether* he would get his revenge, it was when. And if the man was even half as devious as he was violent, he would seize the opportunity to smear Seph's name by connecting her with Aidan's face.

By the time the next Lindmark ship reached Earth, the news stations would have seized the story, and speculation would be splashed from one side of the planet to the other. Phillip Linden, alive or dead? Fugitive or look-alike? Could it be that the former heir to Lindmark was now serving second-rate swill to dock-rats in a space station slum while involving himself in a clandestine relationship under an assumed name?

No matter which conclusion the public came to, Seph's name and reputation would be dragged through the gutter right alongside Aidan's, making her a target of hatred from anyone who had ever bought the Lindmark propaganda about Phillip. Which was, essentially, everyone.

But how could he possibly convince her to avoid that fate without betraying himself?

The docking quarter was largely deserted, unlike the Platinum District. A few lone souls made their way quickly along the metal-grate floors of the passage, while the occasional loiterer lingered in a corner, feigning disinterest in those who passed. It seemed to Aidan that most of the docked ships' crews were either already on board their ships or hadn't tried to return to their berths.

As they rounded the curve, they spotted a single man waiting ahead of them, standing in the middle of the corridor wearing a breastplate that appeared to have been looted from a suit of corporate armor and carrying a modified laser rifle.

"I don't suppose you'd be hiring, then," he asked Killian, shifting heavily on his booted feet and looking up at the ceiling. "Heard rumors they're evacuating. A few of my boys and I are looking for a ride off the station, figured you could use some extra hands."

"Thanks, Baxton, but no thanks." Killian was well enough acquainted with the man to call him by name, and by the curl in his lip didn't care for the acquaintance. "My ship is small, and I'm full up at the moment."

"These part of your crew?" The man named Baxton chewed thoughtfully at a gob of something inside his cheek, then spat on the floor.

"What if they are?" Killian asked, and Aidan shivered at the velvety soft tone.

Baxton either didn't hear the threat or didn't care, because he leveled his rifle at Seph's head. "If they are, and I kill them, guess you'll be back to needing new people, won't you?"

Aidan would have preferred to strip away the rifle and turn the presumptuous Baxton into a wet, red smear on the metal floor, but the unyielding point of what he assumed was another rifle was now pressed into the small of his back, making it impossible for him to reach for his own weapon. Evidently, the "loiterers" had been loitering with a purpose.

"In fact," Baxton went on, "I have a hankering to find out what it feels like to be a captain. Make my own orders. You hand over the codes, and I might feel generous enough to let you live."

"Whereas I am not feeling generous at all, Baxton." Killian appeared relaxed, but the razor-sharp edge in his voice boded ill for the man ahead of them.

On the other hand, no fewer than five rough-looking men now surrounded them, all five holding extremely illegal weapons. If they chose to press the issue, even Killian might have difficulty worming his way out of it.

"You'll be feeling dead if you don't give me what I want, Avalar."

"Will I now?" Killian murmured, his lips curving slightly. "I've often wondered what that might feel like."

Seph turned to look at him oddly, and three of the men jerked their weapons to track her movements. When they did, Killian threw a hand up and fired... something. There was no weapon in his hand, but an energy bolt flew at Baxton and knocked him twenty feet backward. The second bolt caught one of the other men just as he fired his weapon, throwing the laser rifle's aim off just enough to miss Aidan, who hadn't been standing still.

The moment the fight began, he sidestepped and pulled—hard—on the weapon digging into his back. As soon as the scumbag holding it started to pull away, he reversed course and jammed it into the man's belly.

Meanwhile, Seph had taken advantage of the distraction. She'd ankle-swept the man standing beside her before stripping his weapon and holding it to his throat, with an expression that indicated she'd just as soon shoot him as not.

That left one assailant still standing, and he judged it safer to run the opposite direction rather than face an unknown energy weapon in the hands of a vengeful pirate.

Killian sighed. "Next time, I hope the lot of you stop to consider your life choices before you attack an apparently defenseless man." He broke off to press two fingers to his comm-band. Listening.

The whimpering puddle of cowardice at Aidan's feet took the opportunity to worm away from him and flee, half on his hands and knees. Seph's victim kept both hands carefully where she could see them, and, when she removed her foot from his chest, he rolled sideways and came up running. He didn't even bother to ask her to return his weapon.

Feeling somewhat irrationally satisfied, Aidan looked back towards Killian, who was still listening, though his posture had grown tense and his eyes had closed.

"Are you certain?" he was asking. A pause. "No. No time. I'm almost back."

His gaze lifted to Aidan's, sharp and curious. "The station is about to be under evacuation orders for all personnel. Are you coming?" It was simple, direct, and left no room for hesitation.

"Do I have a choice?" Aidan said, not bothering to disguise the bitterness in his voice.

The pirate didn't answer. "If you're in, then follow me."

Killian turned and led the way to his ship at a brisk walk, leaving Aidan and Seph to either keep up or be left behind.

SEVEN

EVACUATING. All personnel. Seph's heart sank as she followed in Killian's wake, grateful she'd brought the most important of her belongings, but unable to suppress a surge of disappointment.

She was done here. With the station in peril, it would be every man and woman for themselves—as their attackers had so forcefully demonstrated—and she would have no choice but to go wherever Killian would agree to take her. She would beg him to take her to Earth, of course, but even if he was willing, her financial outlook was bleak. After this catastrophe, every corporation would have suffered losses, and no one was likely to be hiring.

But whether she was able to find a job or not, her dreams would be over—once back within the suffocating environment of her youth, she was unlikely to ever escape again. But what other option did she have?

Killian's path led them to a docking bay where he paused with his hand hovering over the keypad of the lock.

"Miss Seph." He turned his piercing gaze to meet hers. "You should know that my offer still stands. I would be pleased to allow you a place on my ship and return you to Earth if that's what you prefer." His sly smile quirked up at that. "But as I'm sure you can guess, I'm a man with secrets. Knowledge is a large part of my business, which means there are parts of this ship that are off-limits, and many questions I will refuse to answer. If you choose to come aboard, I require that you surrender any weapons and give me your word that you will follow my orders and heed my warnings. Otherwise, I will be unable to guarantee your safety."

That sounded ominous but hardly unexpected. And Seph had never been one of those people who were unable to resist a mystery. The pirate could keep his secrets. All she needed was a ride, and she was willing to work for it, if not in any way his sly hints might imply.

"Agreed," she said easily, pulling out her stunner and handing it over. They were far too dangerous to fire on board a ship anyway. "Though I would feel better if you allowed me to pay my way as a part of your crew. I'm no good at spaceship mechanics, but I know my way around a multi-tool, I have a head for logistics, and I have medic's training."

"My crew is small," Killian said with a shrug, "and my ship's needs are minimal, but we may be able to put you to use somewhere."

Seph couldn't imagine spending the entire two month trip to Earth doing nothing, but she wasn't exactly drowning in offers, so she nodded.

"I assume I'll be allowed to leave the ship as soon as we get to Earth?" she asked, almost as an afterthought.

Killian raised an eyebrow. "I can't imagine how it would be to my benefit to keep you against your will. There are rumors going around that it's unwise to tick you off."

Seph felt a blush spread across her cheeks and grinned in spite of herself. "Then, yes," she said, feeling a sudden release of a small part of the tension she'd been carrying. "Thank you. I accept your offer." A tiny internal voice suggested that trusting Killian might actually be the stupidest thing she'd ever done, but she ignored it.

"Aidan?" Killian looked over at her boss, who'd been strangely silent ever since the attack. "Last chance. If you're going to look for another ride, now's the time. Otherwise, you're welcome aboard."

Seph turned to Aidan. His arms were crossed, his face as stern and intimidating as always, while his blue eyes narrowed with icy intensity.

"You know if I had any other options, I'd take them," Aidan said bitterly. "A pirate ship wouldn't be my first choice as a lifeboat, any more than you'd be my first choice of captain. But for some reason, I'm not quite ready to die."

"I'm crushed," Killian said, with an impish grin. "Though I suppose it's a relief to know that you consider being stuck with me a step up from being dead."

Seph would have sworn his relief was more than a joke, but couldn't have said why. Did he care that much about his favorite bartender's survival? Or was Killian concocting some dastardly plot that required Aidan's presence?

Seph couldn't believe she'd just used the word "dastardly," even in her own head, but if anyone deserved the word, it was probably Killian.

"Now that it's decided," Killian continued, "welcome aboard the *Fancy*."

He pressed the lock, the hatch swept back, and Seph suddenly remembered something.

"Wait, why am I the only one who got that whole speech about secrets and doing as I'm told?" she protested.

Killian winked. "Because if Aidan decides to be a nuisance, I can just shoot him," he replied with a straight face.

It wasn't a real answer, but as the pirate crossed through the entryway, Seph realized it was the only one she was going to get.

This was going to be a very interesting ride.

As she crossed through the hatch in Killian's wake, Seph glanced back over her shoulder at Aidan to see whether he'd resigned himself to the situation, but he seemed to be pointedly avoiding her gaze. Probably still in a snit with her after that conversation outside of crew access. Since she didn't have a tray handy with which to express her annoyance at his pettiness, Seph diverted her attention to assessing the ship, hoping the distraction might allay her murderous impulses.

She hadn't traveled on many ships but had seen a fair few during her days as an LSF supply officer stationed at Midlands Spaceport. Whatever the *Fancy* was, Seph could tell within her first few steps inside that it was not a cargo ship.

It was too well-kept, for one, and too smoothly designed. The corridor they entered was almost featureless, and tunnel-like, with a curved metallic ceiling and lights in the floor. It looked more like a courier or private transport, but it obviously wasn't of Lindmark origin, so it was difficult to tell.

It was also difficult to tell how large it was. The main corridor curved rather sharply but didn't have any doors or portholes that offered clues. At least nothing visible.

"It's not a Conclave ship," Aidan said suddenly from behind her, making her jump.

"Yes, that's what Killian claimed," she answered, throwing a cautious glance at the captain's back. "But how do you know?"

"Conclave ships aren't built with war in mind. They're built for convenience. Multiple access points to make it easier for crew and passengers. This one docks at a single port on the top level, with engineering and drives located below. Whoever designed it wanted the greatest possible distance between the access point and the most vulnerable parts of the ship. There are also no lifts near the docking area, and"—he pointed at the walls curving around them—"no maintenance hatches. All hatches are probably in completely secure areas."

Aidan had told her a lot about himself in just those few sentences. He knew spaceships, and he was professionally paranoid.

"Who could have built it then, if it's not Conclave?" she asked curiously. "Is your pirate friend some super wealthy ex-pat out to set up his own private army?"

Aidan shrugged. "Who knows why pirates do anything?"

Killian's head turned, and his glance met Seph's, as if to convey that he was listening to every word and choosing not to offer answers.

They reached the bridge a few moments later, and its design offered even further proof that Killian's ship was unlike any Seph had ever seen before. The deck surface, seats, and workstations seemed to be composed of a single solid piece of material—one that flowed and curved almost organically. The space was small and contained only one other person, despite evidence of four working terminals.

"Captain." The short, pale, dark-haired woman jerked to her feet with an almost comical expression of surprise, as though Seph and Aidan were the very last thing she'd expected to see cross the threshold. "Uh. You didn't tell me you had... guests?"

"Prisoners," Killian said, straight-faced. "Prepare the brig, Rill. And the instruments of torture. We have a reputation to maintain."

"We, uh... we do?" Her face grew even paler for some reason.

Killian leaned towards her and spoke in an exaggerated whisper. "They think we're pirates."

Seph heard a growl of annoyance from behind her. Poor Aidan had probably reached the limit of his tolerance for levity.

Rill's expression had eased somewhat, as if being thought a pirate was somehow comforting.

"I see," she said. "And how long will our prisoners be staying, Captain?"

"They're evacuating with us," he announced, crossing the narrow space to pat her on the shoulder before taking his seat at the captain's station. "Anything new to report?"

Rill shot a nervous glance at Seph and Aidan. "I'm still trying to determine the cause of the damage, sir."

Killian booted up the command console with a few brisk motions. "Visual?" he asked.

Rill tapped on the screen in front of her. "There's a lot of interference," she said. "The drone signal is weak, but I almost have it compensated for…"

A few more quick taps activated a forward view screen, where Seph thought she'd been seeing the stars through a transparent barrier. It now featured silvery static, and lines of strange, interlocked shapes. Like text, only unlike any Seph had ever seen before.

They vanished so quickly Seph wasn't sure she'd seen them at all until she caught a quick, panicked look from Rill.

One of those secrets Killian guarded so closely?

Seph glanced back at the screen, then glanced again. The static had resolved, leaving behind a view not of the stars, but of the side of the space station. Or what used to be the side of the station. Seph blinked and took a step closer.

It couldn't be what it looked like. This was a picture of something else. Some other installation composed of stacked rings, surrounded by docked ships…

But denial became impossible when the image cleared even further and zoomed in to show only a small section of Third. Suddenly everyone else on the bridge was staring too, unable to look away as Rill's efforts to dampen interference brought the details of the crash site into sharp and almost painful clarity.

Seph could easily make out the remains of what had once been an exclusive and expensive restaurant—The Concordium. The establishment's glowing sign hung at an angle and flickered fitfully through the scorched, mangled hole in the side of Third, where what should have been nearly unbreakable material appeared to have shredded on impact.

But it was not the damage to the station that provoked a single, softly whispered curse from Aidan.

It was the thing that had caused it—the thing that still filled the majority of the gaping hole in the station's side.

An object entirely outside of human knowledge or experience.

It was massive—not as large as the *Fancy*, but easily the size of a small, in-system courier craft—yet it wasn't built along the lines of any ship Seph had ever seen.

Instead, it was cylindrical, with each end tapering to a rounded point. Four rippling frills, almost like sails, ran parallel to each other down its length, while its surface seemed unmarked with either weapons or ports. There was no drive—no visible means of propulsion at all, and yet it was clearly not an asteroid.

"What is it?" Seph was so stunned she spoke in a whisper, almost too quietly for anyone else to hear, but before she could ask her question again, the thing moved. It *moved*. Not the straight forward or back of a man-made craft, but almost thrashing, like a live thing caught on a hook. The rings shuddered visibly in response, and the image winked out.

Killian appeared to have turned to stone. Rill, too, had paused, her mouth hanging open, her arms dangling limply by her sides.

"Uh, Captain?" Rill finally spoke up, though she hadn't moved. Her eyes were still fixed on the now blank forward viewscreen. "What do we do?"

"We…" Killian dropped into his chair, suddenly bereft of all confidence. Even his trademark swagger had deserted him. He ran one hand through his spiked brown hair, then dropped it to his lap.

"No one believed this would happen," Rill said quietly. "You can't blame yourself."

Blame himself? Why would Killian blame himself for the crash?

"I…" He shook his head, shock on every line of his face.

Rill went on doggedly. "We can still follow the protocol."

Killian finally roused himself long enough to throw an impatient glance at his crew member. "Yes, of course we can, but what good will it do? The protocol is older than space! We aren't prepared, and neither will anyone else be because we've forgotten why it even matters. Forgotten why it exists! That's why they send screw-ups, rejects, and rebels like us. Because we can't possibly wreck anything or get in the way out here." His voice was bitter now.

"What do you want me to do, Captain?"

"The only thing we *can* do," he responded harshly. "We proceed immediately to the Rift. Launch drones and send a message. Ask for help."

"They'll expect us to have a plan."

"Then they should have sent a diplomat," he snapped, jerking to his feet. "Maybe an engineer. But my brother knew that and he chose me."

"It's four days to the Rift. Maybe we can come up with something." Rill seemed to be going out of her way to sound hopeful.

"Do you think I haven't tried?" Killian snarled. "Do you think I've spent the last ten years learning to fit in so we can go on ferrying illegal cargo and irritating the Conclave for the rest of our lives?"

"Hold on," Seph said, feeling utterly lost and hoping to derail whatever train the pirate was on before something exploded. "Take a deep breath, sit down, and let's try this again. Why would you blame yourself? What protocol? What rift? It sounds like you know what that thing is, so why don't you back up and tell the rest of the class." She glanced at Aidan for support, but he was watching Killian, and his face gave away none of his thoughts. Only his eyes burned with intensity, while his crossed arms appeared to be holding him back from taking decisive action.

Killian ignored her questions to address Rill again. "The worst of it is, we were supposed to have more time. Our nets were supposed to warn us of spawn so we would know when to act."

"Maybe one of those before us—"

"No." Killian seemed to already know what she was about to say. "I've seen the records. No one has ever followed the protocol as far as infiltrating Earth's government or developing their defenses. Why? Because no one actually expected this to happen. There's been no sign of them for centuries. And yet you saw that thing! It was almost half-grown, and now we have no time at all."

Whoa. What?

"Can we pause for a second?" Seph asked carefully. "I think it's about time you answered a few of my questions. Let's start with the first one—what exactly crashed into the station? What are rifts and protocols and spawn? And why would you infiltrate the government? More importantly, are you going to have to kill us now that we've heard you talking about it?"

Seph tried to sound as though she was joking, but no one else even smiled.

Killian shot her a single look, and his dark eyes might as well have bored holes clear through to her spine. "I won't kill you, Miss Seph. But I may not have to. If we can't get help fast enough, everything and everyone you know is as good as dead."

Seph's pulse ratcheted up a notch. He really believed what he was saying.

But he still didn't answer her questions. Instead, he looked away from her and pressed a finger to his comm-band. "It's causing power fluctuations in the station," he said quietly. "Energy surges. If our information is correct, that means it's probably dying so we won't need to stay to dispose of it."

"What's dying? Dispose of *what?*" Seph demanded. Did Killian think that thing was *alive?* And why didn't Aidan say anything? Wasn't he even the tiniest bit curious? His immediate future depended on the *Fancy's* captain—who was currently sounding more and more like a lunatic—and yet Aidan was still behaving like a slightly angry statue.

"What are your orders, Captain?" Rill said formally, as though Seph hadn't spoken at all.

"We follow the protocol," Killian said finally. "It's the only hope we have. While we make for the Rift, I'll plan a last-resort approach to Earth and prepare a bluff for whoever receives our transmission. Once the drones are away, we'll return to base and prepare for war."

"But sir, we don't have..."

"We will just have to do what we can with what we do have," Killian said sharply, his eyes fixed on the deck, his fingers laced together as if in prayer, or contemplation. "If any of us want to go home, we don't have a choice. We either find a way to win, or we die here."

Rill swallowed and bowed her head. "Aye, sir."

"Inform the rest of the crew of our departure," Killian ordered. "And let's see how far we can push the drive."

"After you return us to Earth." Seph spoke firmly, despite an unstoppable surge of curiosity. It wasn't even a question, much as part of her wanted it to be. She couldn't afford to go traipsing around the galaxy. Not even with tantalizing clues like spawn and rifts dangling before her. Not even with Killian's hints at doom and destruction—if anything, those increased Seph's desire to leave the *Fancy* far behind her. There were too many hints that the ship's captain bordered on delusional, such as his speech about infiltrating the government and preparing to defend Earth. Defend Earth from *what*?

But whether he was delusional or not, Seph's family needed her. Plus, some kind of alien *something* had just crashed into Concord Five, and she wanted to know what it was. Where had it come from? What did it want? Who launched it, and could humans communicate with them?

Humanity had discovered sapient races on several planets during the past eighty years of space exploration, but never one capable of space travel. No matter what the object was determined to be, this was an enormous moment in human history, and Earth would be the best place to experience it.

A thrill of excitement shot through her at the thought. She would see her family again. Most likely there would be new jobs available once scientists determined the alien craft's origin. Teams would be sent to its home planet, to communicate with its builders. The corporations would fight, of course, over who would be allowed to claim credit for the discovery, but no matter how that fell out, there were bound to be opportunities, and Seph wanted to be there to take advantage of them.

But Killian didn't even look at her. "We're not going to Earth," he said flatly. "There's no time."

"Then you have to let me off," Seph insisted, feeling an unwelcome surge of panic. She couldn't be stuck on the ship. Not now. "I have to get home. My family needs me, and I don't have time to go traipsing off around the galaxy."

"And yet, the answer is still no," Killian said softly. "I'm sorry, Miss Seph, but we're already making preparations to detach from the station, and I'm afraid my conscience won't allow me to let you leave the *Fancy*. That thing you saw is not a craft. It's a creature. A living thing with more than enough destructive capacity to incinerate everything in its vicinity. I won't ask you to believe me, as I know how little prepared you are to understand what you're facing. But there is a very real chance that everyone left on this station will die, and us with them unless we launch now, go for help, and pray it arrives in time."

———

Aidan found himself prey to conflicting emotions for perhaps the tenth time in as many hours, and he didn't like it. He wasn't supposed to have emotions at all. Above all, he wasn't supposed to feel or acknowledge fear, and yet it was fear that gripped him most tightly as he considered the situation.

Fear for himself? For Seph? Or for the rest of humanity? Because whatever else Killian might be guilty of, Aidan wasn't convinced he was lying. Whatever that thing was, it was definitely alive, and it was like nothing Aidan had ever seen or heard of before. After nearly dying at the hands—claws? Roots?—of the alien intelligence at the heart of the planet Daragh, he had a great deal of respect for the potential power this creature represented.

A living being capable of space travel. Strong enough to shred a material that had been designed to survive a collision with a spaceship. And Killian believed he knew what it was and what it was capable of.

The pirate also seemed to think he was going to take Seph and Aidan along on some sort of bizarre crusade, but Aidan at least had no intention of going along with it. Except...

Wherever Killian was going, it wasn't Earth. Earth had been a better option than a dying space station, but barely, and it was by no means Aidan's destination of choice. Why not go along with whatever insanity Killian was planning? Whether the bulk of his ravings turned out to be truth or delusion, his end goal had to be better than whatever awaited Aidan on Earth.

But Seph wasn't finished arguing, and her usual unflappable calm had begun to fray. "You can't keep me here," she said, the beginnings of desperation in her voice. "I need to get back to Earth. My family is relying on me, so if you'll just let me off, I'll find my own way home."

The deck jolted underfoot.

"What was that?" Seph went pale.

"I'm sorry, Miss Seph," Killian said again, and to his credit, he did look a little sorry. "We've launched. We truly don't have a moment to lose."

"No!"

After Seph's panicked cry, everyone appeared to move at once. Seph made a sudden move in Killian's direction, whether to tackle him, shoot him, or attempt to access the ship's systems, Aidan wasn't sure. Killian ducked, Rill stood up, and a bright flash of light flew from her raised hand to hit Seph in the back.

It threw her to the deck.

"Rill, stop!" Killian cried, but Seph was down, and as Aidan dropped to his knees beside her, his hands trembled with the realization that she lay still, her body limp and unresponsive.

"What was that?" he snarled, stripping off Seph's pack as Killian dropped to the deck on her other side.

"She thought Seph was attacking me," Killian replied, his exasperation apparent. "Rill, if I thought she was a threat I could have dealt with it myself! Take the helm and just fly, would you, before we have another collision."

The dark haired woman dropped into her seat, muttering under her breath, but she complied.

Aidan's fingers itched to close around the pirate's throat as he eased Seph onto her back and checked for a pulse, trying to ignore the fresh surge of fear.

She was going to be okay. She was going to wake up any minute and punch someone in the face, and at that point, Aidan wouldn't even have argued if that someone was him. He just wanted her to wake up.

Seph's eyelids fluttered after a moment, and her hands twitched. Her pulse beat strongly beneath Aidan's fingers, so she wasn't dead, but from the look of things, she was going to have an impressive bruise on her face where it had hit the deck.

"It's an energy weapon," Killian explained. "Rill wasn't shooting to kill, just to warn."

"I don't care what she was doing," Aidan said viciously. "Either you control your trigger-happy pilot, or I'm going to rip that weapon out of her hands and break it across my knee."

Killian had the nerve to burst out laughing. "You could try," he said, "but forgive me if I can't picture that going very well."

Aidan was still considering whether to take violent action when he heard a strangled "Ow!" from Seph and returned his attention to her.

Her eyes were open but narrowed with pain. "Killian, you're a freaking bastard," she said, but didn't seem to have the energy to put much heat behind it.

"Yes," he agreed soberly. "I expect I am. And I anticipate that you'll be even more convinced of that before this is over. I don't blame you for being angry, but you'd do well to understand that I don't have the luxury of caring about your injured feelings. No matter what injustice you think I've committed, it's nothing compared to what we will all be facing in the coming days."

"Then why won't you just answer my questions?" Seph asked weakly. "You have to know you sound insane when you just keep raving without explaining yourself. If you've had this knowledge all this time, and it was this important, why would you hide it?"

"Because you're as unprepared to learn the truth as you would be to walk out the nearest airlock without a suit," Killian said, his tone suddenly harsh. "It's a truth you're going to have to confront sooner or later, but for right now, I have to get us out of here. Once we've cleared the station's halo, I'll provide all the answers you think you want. Just don't blame me if you don't like what I have to say."

"You expect us to wait tamely for answers when you've just kidnapped us both?" Aidan said coldly. "You've given us no choice but to accompany you on whatever mad quest you're on, so don't expect us to just sit here and wait politely until you choose to inform us of your goals. Whatever justification you think you have, you promised Seph would be safe, and then your own crew member shot her in the back. You lied, pirate, and I won't forgive that. Not now, not ever."

"I'm sorry, bartender, but I don't really care whether you forgive me or not," Killian said softly. "As I recall, I implied the two of you would be safe if you followed my orders and heeded my warnings. That didn't just apply to the ones that made sense to you. And as I said before, this matter is far beyond any petty injustice you imagine you've suffered. Failure is not an option."

"And if you do fail?"

"Then the human species faces the probability of a painful and potentially catastrophic future event."

"Sounds dire," Aidan said, taking refuge in sarcasm to prevent himself from attempting a more drastic action. No matter how much he would prefer to beat the man bloody, the fact remained that they were at Killian's mercy. Aidan had no idea how many crew were on board, let alone how to fly the ship should he manage to take command of it. "And I suppose you're the only thing standing between humanity and that potential future?" he asked mockingly.

Killian locked eyes with him, and Aidan suddenly caught a glimpse of a much different man than the swaggering self-assured pirate he'd known for the past two years. This man was determined, but he was also more than a little afraid.

"Yes, in fact," Killian said softly. "Which should probably scare you as much as it scares me. But I am all you have, because I'm the only one who knows exactly what that "thing" is, where it came from, and what it means."

"Then tell us," Seph said, struggling to sit up. Aidan put an arm behind her shoulders to help, but she shrugged it off and rose to her knees before glaring fiercely at Killian. "Just what *does* it mean?"

His eyes fell to the deck for a moment before they lifted back to her. "It means," he said, almost apologetically, "that our mission takes precedence over everything humanity has ever said or ever done. It outweighs every personal grievance, every petty concern, every world-shaking moment your tiny planet's history has ever recorded. And if, in this moment, I require your presence aboard this ship for a short time, I hope you'll understand that I mean no harm or disrespect to you personally."

"*My* tiny planet?" Seph echoed Aidan's own thoughts exactly.

"Yours." Killian glanced at Aidan. "His. Soon to be no one's if I fail in my mission. If we do not make all possible speed, I risk failing in the one purpose my life still has."

"Get to the point, pirate." Aidan wasn't certain how long he could maintain the stranglehold he kept on his temper. He was experiencing a growing urge to destroy something and wasn't particular about his target. Though Killian's face was the most tempting one at present. "It's bad enough that you've dragged us here, without trying to impress us with your dramatic monologuing. Either tell us the truth or shut up."

"I didn't drag anyone anywhere," Killian said heatedly. "This is a necessary change of plans, and I won't apologize for it just because you're in a snit."

"And just because we have a history doesn't mean I won't twist your head off," Aidan growled back.

"And how"—Killian's reply was mocking—"would a pampered rich boy like you manage to do that?"

"Enough!" Seph interrupted, eyes blazing, hands clenched, looking as though she'd like to rip both their heads off and eat them. *"What in all the hells is going on?"*

Killian stood up from where he crouched on the deck, turned away, and brushed his hands on his pants. "I'm trying to save your species, Miss Seph," he said quietly.

Silence fell over the bridge as his words sunk in.

"What do you mean *my* species?" Seph pushed to her feet, still wobbling, and Aidan tried to stay close enough to steady her without revealing that he cared whether she fell. From the amused look Killian shot him, his efforts weren't exactly successful.

"Killian, you realize this all sounds insane, right?"

"I'm not responsible for ensuring that the truth is palatable," Killian countered smoothly, "and the fate of your planet doesn't depend on my sanity, only the knowledge that I have and you don't."

"Then tell us." Aidan crossed his arms to keep from touching Seph, whose balance remained in doubt. "That thing we saw. Where is it from? Is it yours? Do you—"

"No," Seph interrupted, looking suddenly more thoughtful than angry. "Those aren't even the most important questions, are they?"

Killian answering look was somehow both amused and regretful.

She took two strides across the deck until she was almost nose to nose with the pirate. "Killian, why do you refer to humans as though you're not one?"

"Because," he said, cocking his head to one side and grinning, "technically speaking, I'm not."

EIGHT

"TECHNICALLY SPEAKING..." The words rolled off Seph's tongue as if she could taste them and perhaps thereby make more sense of them.

For centuries, the human imagination had toyed with the idea of first contact—of encountering another race of beings like themselves, capable of space travel, communication, and cooperation. Their imaginations had usually rendered that encounter as a violent experience, fraught with ideas of conquest and destruction.

Or, their ideas had descended into farce, intended to provoke laughter and ease fears.

Somehow, when the moment came, it was both.

Rill's face showed nothing but shock. Because she knew her captain was crazy, or because she hadn't expected him to admit the truth? Killian himself was still wearing a tiny, mocking grin, but his eyes were razor sharp. Was it the face of a madman? Or the face of an alien spy? Seph found she was tempted to laugh at that idea but wasn't willing to break the tense silence that had descended on the bridge.

Her gaze rested on Aidan next. His anger was evident, in the tendons of his neck and the hard angle of his jaw, but he didn't look frightened or even surprised, only wary—of a man he seemed to regard as a threat. If not a threat to their safety, at least to their freedom.

But how would they even know? If Killian told the truth about not being human, everything they thought they knew went up in smoke. He appeared human enough, but what might be hiding beneath that seeming? Was he hostile? And if so, just how much of a danger did he pose to her? To Aidan? To Earth itself?

As she glanced between the two men, waiting for one of them to break the silence, Seph compared them silently and wondered which one was truly the more dangerous. Killian was all keen wit and sharp corners. Shiny and charming, with a razor edge beneath. He answered to no one, was backed by a loyal crew, and had a ship full of unknown technology at his disposal.

And then there was Aidan. Embattled and alone. Bitter and isolated, yet as unyielding as granite. He'd chosen his ground, and, like a cornered animal, he would run no farther. But would he fight to protect the place of his choosing? And in an even battle, who might come out the winner? There was no knowing, but at that particular time and place, the contest wasn't even close to fair. The advantage was all with Killian. If she and Aidan were to have any hope of escaping, they would have to wait, learn more, and plan their attack.

Seph tried to always be honest with herself, and in that moment she acknowledged that she was frightened. Angry. She would like to explain to Killian just how angry she was, but for now, she would pretend to a calmness she was nowhere close to feeling. One did not just walk up and throat punch an alien pirate spy.

Until, of course, one lulled said alien pirate spy into a false sense of complacency. And, if, in the process, he chose to underestimate her, that could only be to her advantage.

It was Rill who finally broke the silence with a strangled-sounding "Captain!"

"They're going back to base with us, Rill. They need time to accept the truth."

"The truth?" Seph said pleasantly, drawing a sharp glance from Aidan. "Yes, please do tell us the truth. Now that you've kidnapped us and we're completely at your mercy, feel free to give us the standard exposition of the full range of your villainy so we can decide whether you're a miracle of discovery or just plain bonkers."

"But you can't just tell them!" Rill protested. "It's against the protocol."

"Hang the protocol!" Killian glared at her. "Do you want to go home or not?"

She blanched and was silent.

"Because if we fail, this hell will never end! You saw the worm, Rill. The Bhandecki are coming, whether we're ready or not, so revealing ourselves to humanity unnecessarily has officially become the smallest of my concerns. How can I be worried about secrecy when their time is up, and we still need allies? If we don't find a way to stop this, every settled human planet will be obliterated, and there will be no more need for secrets because there will be no more humans. Ever. Better to break our rules or consign their people to annihilation?"

"I vote for rule breaking," Seph answered, containing her runaway speculation with herculean effort. "And truth-telling. I believe I'm in favor of that too. Who wants to start?"

"Aidan?" Killian tilted his head and regarded Seph's boss with pointed intensity. "How about you?"

Aidan didn't answer, but his tension spoke volumes. Seph thought he would have dearly loved to turn Killian into a lump of battered meat and broken bones.

"No?" Killian prodded.

"Enough." Aidan's blue eyes burned hot. "It's not as if I have any secrets that compare to your claims. Let's start with you not being human. And the potential destruction of Earth."

Killian sighed, and his chin dropped to his chest. "Very well," he said. "The truth is, it wasn't supposed to happen this way. We were supposed to be more prepared, but we're not, so we need all the help we can get. I'll tell you everything I can, and in return, if either of you has any ideas, I'd love to hear them.

"Rill, are we well away from the station yet?"

"Clearing the drive halo now, Captain."

"Then proceed to the Rift at the highest speed we can maintain safely. If you detect any Bhandecki scouts, worms, spawn, or the entire damned fleet, alert me immediately."

"I'm on it." The woman was suddenly all business, her hands flying over the console in front of her so quickly they nearly blurred. "All hands prepare for maximum drive," she called out over the internal comms.

How many was *all*? Seph wondered, but it didn't seem like the right moment to ask.

"Once we're past the first transit point, start programming a drone to take our message through the Rift. As soon as we dump it, we'll be heading directly to base to pick up the others and prepare for war."

"You two"—Killian gestured to Seph and Aidan—"come with me. Oh, and Rill?"

"Sir?"

"Keep the weapons hot. All banks. Lasers, cannons, and the new missile launchers."

"You think we'll need them?" Rill sat up straighter, her eyes wide.

"I think we have no idea how much time is left."

Rill jerked a nod and returned her attention to her console.

Killian turned to Seph and Aidan and raised an eyebrow. "If you'd be so kind as to follow me, we'll adjourn to my quarters so our discussion doesn't distract my pilot. I suggest you prepare yourselves to hear even more preposterous claims and please hold your questions until after the tour."

Seph's mouth had already been open, so she snapped it shut, swallowing numerous protests with an effort. How Aidan was remaining so very nearly silent under the circumstances was more than she could fathom. Until prodded, he seemed content to say nothing. Did he not have even the slightest speck of curiosity? Or even fear? Or was he so angry at Killian that he had no room for other emotions?

Aidan's face gave nothing away as Killian turned to leave the bridge. Not fear, not concern, nor even skepticism. If anything, he was even more stoic than usual, which worried Seph almost as much as Killian's flippancy.

As Concord Five receded behind them, Seph swallowed her misgivings and faced the unnerving truth.

She was about to get that adventure she'd always wanted. Either she was sailing into unknown space with a crew full of alien pirates en route to their home base, or she was trapped in the clutches of a delusional maniac, with no allies but her grim and churlish ex-boss who didn't want to be friends.

Seph choked down the fear that always came with the thought of being trapped, and focused on the fact that they were moving. They had a destination, and even if that destination wasn't her choice, she wouldn't be on this ship forever. Her family would survive, as they always had, until she could find her way back to them. And whether Killian proved to be an alien or a madman, she wasn't dead, and she wasn't alone. From this point onward she could either choose to wallow in her fear and uncertainty or she could set herself to solving the mystery and finding a way to escape.

In the end, it wasn't even a question. She'd survived too much in her life to give in now, and if nothing else, this would make a great story to tell her kids someday. If she lived long enough to have any.

Her focus renewed, Seph began taking more detailed note of her surroundings as she snagged her pack off the floor and followed Killian off the bridge. Anything she could learn might be to her advantage. What was the ship capable of? How many other crew did he have? And if it turned out that Killian really was an alien? She suppressed a shiver at the thought.

If it was true, she would be part of making human history. Unless, of course, everything else he'd said was true too, and there wouldn't be any more human history to be a part of...

But she couldn't allow herself to think that way. Couldn't permit herself to wallow in speculation. She had to remain in the moment—deal with what was happening now, then prepare to face whatever came next.

Which meant she ought to at least attempt to convince her sole remaining ally that they would need to work together. Confide in one another. Maybe even pretend to be friends.

Seph glanced back at Aidan, who trailed behind her without looking in any way as though he'd accepted the necessity of remaining optimistic in the face of overwhelming catastrophe. His face was frozen in his usual expression of cool disdain and detachment—as though he cared for nothing and no one, least of all the people and circumstances in which he now found himself—but Seph knew him better than that by now.

He was capable of caring. On the station, he'd nearly assaulted Brand on her behalf and braved a terrifying climb to come to her aid. When she'd been caught off guard by Rill's shot in the back, he'd moved to protect her. She'd returned to consciousness before he realized it and seen his face—he'd been ready to attack Killian if he'd thought she was still in danger. He might pretend to be cold and untouchable, but there were feelings beneath the mask. Even if he would probably die before he acknowledged them.

Fool that she was, Seph admitted to herself that she would rather be here with Aidan than anyone else she could name. He made her feel safer. Less alone. Which probably said more about her tendency towards self-delusion than his capacity for caring.

When he glanced up suddenly and caught her watching him, Seph felt herself blush and jerked her eyes back to the corridor ahead. Feigning nonchalance, she pulled her hair over her shoulder, began to form it into a braid, and commenced fishing for information.

"So, how long have you been pretending to be human?" she asked

Killian in her most innocent and non-threatening tone. She half-intended it to be funny, but if he was indeed not human, who knew what he might find amusing.

Killian, who'd kept a finger pressed to his comm-band ever since they left the bridge, just shook his head. "Later," was all he would say.

"Are you this cryptic with all of your abductees?"

"No," he answered blandly, shooting her an exasperated glance. "Only the nosy ones."

"Not sure whether it's a comfort or a concern to know we're not the first," Seph mused aloud. "If you've made a habit of kidnapping humans, at least you probably have some idea of how to keep us alive. Unless, of course, you're in the habit of starving and torturing your abductees. Which would be more in keeping with your obsession with piracy." She shot a glance back over her shoulder and found Aidan looking at her with one eyebrow raised and no trace of humor. Not that she'd expected anything so normal as a smile.

Killian paused, and Seph took a step back in case he intended to take action, but he appeared to just be listening.

"No." He spoke to the empty air, and Seph realized he was having a conversation over his comm-band. "Just make sure he's found. We can't have him running around right now."

He tapped the device once more then turned back to face her.

"Can't have who running around?" Seph asked, raising an eyebrow. "Someone else you've brought along on this little journey against their will?"

Killian sighed. "I get that you don't trust me. I wouldn't trust me either, but could you at least hear me out before you start mocking us?"

"You want me to stop, then start talking," Seph retorted. "I'd prefer shooting you to questioning you, but that wouldn't help me gain information, and given whatever weapon you used on Baxton, I imagine you'd only shoot me first. Again. That being the case, the only weapon I have left is words, and I intend to use them. If I have to annoy you into telling us the truth, I'm more than happy to do so."

Killian actually chuckled. "If the circumstances were any less dire, I would welcome your efforts. Being annoyed by a beautiful woman isn't exactly a hardship. But there isn't any need. As matters stand, it's actually in my best interests to tell you everything... well, almost everything."

He came to a stop in front of an unremarkable section of wall and pressed his hand to the square of blinking blue and orange lights beside it.

Part of the wall disappeared.

Seph barely prevented herself from jumping backward and settled for staring like a child who'd just seen a magic trick. It happened so quickly, she couldn't tell where the door had gone. Had it raised? Lowered? Or—though she couldn't believe she was even thinking it—somehow vaporized?

"That was fun," she murmured, as she followed Killian through the opening, giving the doorway a hard stare as she searched for any mechanism or recess where the door might have disappeared to.

Nothing.

After such a dramatic entrance, the space inside the door was almost disappointing. It appeared to be nothing more than a utilitarian captain's quarters, the immediate area set up like a conference room, with a long table and an assortment of chairs. Another opening in the far wall led to what was appeared to be a bedroom and a washroom, but the designer had apparently not been concerned with frills. Or comfort. There was no carpet on the deck, and the chairs were the same metal as those on the bridge—seeming to flow from the material of the deck itself. The only light issued from invisible recesses in the walls, and there was no decor of any kind.

Killian strode in and took a seat, and Seph followed suit, dropping her pack on the floor beside her chair. She was forced to bite back an exclamation of surprise as the chair suddenly reformed itself around her, curving up and around her shoulders and extending to the back of her knees.

"I promise it isn't going to eat you," Killian said, gesturing to the other chairs with an amused glance at Aidan.

Aidan looked as though he'd rather chew rocks, but took a seat anyway —the seat between Seph and Killian. As if he intended to protect her. Coming from anyone else, Seph would have called it sweet, but coming from Aidan, it was just as likely to be an attempt to annoy someone.

"I'll tell you what I can," Killian announced, "but you should know that my crew and I have been keeping our nature and our mission secret from humans for a very long time. We are unused to speaking openly of ourselves, so it may be easier for you to ask what you want to know."

"What *is* your species?" Seph had more than enough questions ready if Killian found it difficult to be forthcoming.

"You can call us Wyrdane," Killian told her. "It is not the word our people use, but our languages are too different for approximation."

"Then how is it that you look human?" Seph wasn't necessarily willing to accept his word on that without a little bit of proof. The ship was odd, true. But was it odd enough to convince her that they'd genuinely encountered intelligent humanoid aliens?

"You sound human," she reminded him. "You have enough cultural knowledge to blend in, and you even use human slang. I've seen no proof that you're anything but an opportunistic narcissist suffering from delusions."

Killian leaned back in his chair and tapped his fingers on the table. A very human gesture, Seph noted. Was he preparing to lie to her? And how would she know for sure if he did?

"When we first discovered your part of the galaxy," Killian began, "we quickly realized that our first order of business was to appear unthreatening. Humans simply weren't prepared to handle the knowledge of a more advanced race. Our natural form is not so dissimilar from yours, but we have different talents, and my people have been perfecting the art of bioengineering and the use of nanotech for many lifetimes. Given a genetic sample, we can shift our nature and appearance to mimic any species, leaving our... consciousness, if you will, intact."

"Well that's not creepy or anything," Seph remarked, struggling to feel more than a cool, clinical detachment. He couldn't be telling the truth, could he? "You're basically claiming you're shapeshifters, except with science instead of magic?"

"Essentially, yes," Killian said, sounding incredibly nonchalant considering his preposterous statements.

"It might be more helpful if you were prepared to prove it." Aidan had finally decided to get involved in the conversation, but he sounded more sarcastic than curious. "Maybe you'd like to shift into something else so we can trust that you're telling the truth."

Killian's lips twisted. "Sadly, that's out of the question, at least for now. Every shift uses up nanotech, which is also used for medical purposes and repairing the ship. Until we return to base, our supplies are too low to be wasted on showing off just to satisfy your curiosity."

"Convenient," Aidan said sarcastically.

"Convenient?" Killian suddenly bristled with anger. "We've been stuck in these forms for years, trying to conserve our resources. We've been forced to exist as weak, half-blind, nearly-deaf humans with no capacity for mind-speech or matter manipulation. The best we can manage in these bodies is accelerated healing and indefinite cellular replacement, and I am not going to jeopardize those tiny advantages for your amusement."

"So... you don't get sick, you can't be hurt, and you'll never die?" Seph hazarded, a little staggered by the implications. "That sounds great, but again, why would we believe it?"

Killian let out a sigh, produced a tiny laser pistol and laid it on the table between them. "If there's no other way…" He slid the weapon past Aidan, just hard enough that it came to a stop when it bumped into her folded hands.

"What am I supposed to do with this?"

Killian held one hand in the air, away from his head, and waved his fingers as if he were seeking permission to ask a question.

"Shoot me," he said.

———

Seph froze, staring at the tiny gun, so Aidan reached out, intending to follow Killian's instructions to the letter. She beat him to it, snatching it out from under his fingers as though her life depended on it.

Or as though Killian's did.

"You'd shoot him in the head," Seph accused, tucking the pistol under her arm.

"Probably." Aidan didn't bother denying it. He wasn't sure it was untrue.

"Killian, why do you want me to shoot you?" Seph's face was a bit pale. She seemed a lot more bothered by the idea than Aidan was.

"You wanted proof," Killian said. "This is the only way you're going to get it. Shoot me in the hand, and I will show you that I'm not human."

She glanced at Aidan, almost as if asking permission. Or maybe looking for a way out, but he didn't intend to give it to her.

"Don't look at me," he growled. "I would have done it already."

She pulled the pistol out from under her arm, slowly, as though she couldn't believe she was doing it, then paused. "I can't just shoot you!" she exclaimed.

"I promise I'll be fine," Killian assured her. "Just do it. Unless your aim is bad, in which case, I'll do it myself, but it's a lot harder for me to pull the trigger. No lasting damage, but it does sting a bit."

Seph shuddered and raised the pistol, slowly, face scrunched up in what appeared to be consternation.

"Don't shut your eyes," Aidan interjected dryly, leaning back and crossing his arms, not wanting to be anywhere near the line of fire if she actually worked up the nerve to pull the trigger.

"Oh, shut up," she muttered, and fired.

Despite her reluctance, her aim was spot on, and Killian's complexion grayed perceptibly as he held out his hand. A laser burn was clearly evident, smoking gently in the center of his palm.

Seph's face went dead white.

But as they watched, the skin of Killian's palm began to change color. The smoke stopped, and the burnt edges fell away, revealing new skin beneath. The hole filled in, the pale, scarred surface smoothed out, and within less than two minutes after the injury, it was as if it had never happened.

"Well. Must be nice," Seph commented, and if Aidan hadn't known her, he wouldn't have been able to hear the tight sound of dismay in her casual words.

"I wouldn't exactly call it *nice*," Killian drawled. "The truth is, we sacrifice a lot when we take human form. And none of us have done so of our own free will. We were sent here by our people as an outpost against the possibility of an invasion none of us thought would happen. Our task was to infiltrate humanity, blend in, and eventually gain enough power to be in a position to influence Earth's defenses. But now..." It was Killian's turn to look uncomfortable. "It may be too late."

Seph was still staring at Killian's hand, as though she expected it to be an illusion, but she looked up at the "too late."

"How so?" she asked, her brows lowered ominously.

Aidan watched her rather than Killian, feeling an unnatural calm, much as he had the day his family disowned him. It was easier to be calm, now that the truth of Killian's claims was evident. The discovery that Killian wasn't human didn't bother or surprise him nearly as much as he would have thought. Or perhaps he was suffering from shock. Either way, Seph seemed more curious than freaked out, so he didn't mind waiting for her to ask her questions before determining how to respond.

Killian sat back, silent for a moment, and Seph leaned forward to glare at him. "Come on, Killian. Don't sit there trying to decide what's safe to tell us. We want to hear about rifts and protocols and spawn. Tell us what that thing was. Tell us how you know about it and why you're here. What was that about Bhandecki scouts and a fleet of some sort? Considering that you seem to think it could herald the destruction of the entire human race, I think you owe us a little more than sly sideways glances and deliberate evasions."

The pirate captain grinned wolfishly. "You're an excellent listener, Miss Seph."

"I'm also extremely persistent," she snapped. "Just ask Aidan. So you can either tell me what I want to know, or I'll annoy you until you do." It was true, and Aidan almost grinned at the thought of her persistence being aimed at someone else.

"It's not so much that I don't intend to tell you," Killian answered patiently. "It's that I really don't know where to start. I imagine our story will sound unbelievable enough, even if I manage to tell it in the right order and you hear me with an open mind. But in order to do that, you need to first accept that we are who we say we are."

"I think your little demonstration was effective on that front," Seph assured him, though not without sarcasm.

"The probe that collided with the station," Killian said, flexing his fingers gingerly, "was sent by a sapient, space-faring race called the Bhandecki. Others have studied them longer than I, but I know enough to give you an idea of what you face.

"When we arrived in your part of the galaxy some two hundred years ago, we traveled through a space rift. What your scientists might call a wormhole, except this kind isn't natural. The Rift was formed by a fire-worm, part of a non-sapient species bred and trained by the Bhandecki. They use the worms as transportation and as weapons to fuel their conquest, which is, essentially, never-ending, as far as we can tell."

Seph crossed her legs and tapped her fingers on the table, suggesting that she might be more nervous than she let on. "So the Bhandecki explored this area some time ago?"

"So we believe. We've been attempting to track their movements ever since our people first encountered them, millennia ago, when they destroyed the planets of a neighboring star system. When they moved on to my homeworld, our biotechnology proved to be an effective defense, insofar as it kept them away from our planet and our people. But we also discovered that the worms are very difficult to damage, and we weren't able to destroy many. We might have convinced them to leave us in peace, but I doubt our efforts made much difference in their overall forces."

"Does their strength lie in numbers then?"

Killian shook his head. "Not entirely. The Bhandecki are certainly numerous, and technologically primitive, but they are also absurdly powerful and have learned to use their own bodies to fuel their energy weapons."

"A trick you seem to have borrowed," Aidan couldn't help remarking, remembering the weapon Killian used against Baxton, and the way Rill had shot Seph.

"Against the Bhandecki, we will take whatever advantages we can get," Killian said flatly. "In case I wasn't clear enough, bartender, this is war."

Seph jerked to her feet, moved away from the table, and began to pace behind Aidan's chair. Any one of his former underlings would have known that was a mistake, but Seph didn't seem to think in terms of vulnerabilities. He couldn't decide whether it was adorably innocent or irritatingly obtuse.

"Any idea why they're so bent on destroying things?" Seph asked, not pausing in the midst of her pacing. "Is there reasoning or a goal behind their obsession, or is it just a cultural... uh, quirk?"

"We aren't really certain," Killian replied, "but we do know they are vulnerable to certain types of electromagnetic waves. They seem to specifically seek out other civilizations that are sufficiently advanced to produce and harness those frequencies, and whatever they find in that search, they destroy."

"So the short version is," Seph mused, tapping a finger on her lips, "there's a super-powerful race that can create wormholes at will running around destroying anyone they see as a threat. Also, you were only able to come here because the Bhandecki were here first."

"Yes," Killian affirmed. "Our people are the only ones we know of to avoid annihilation, and ever since, we have tried to trace their movements and keep track of their technological advancements. At least until the past few hundred years, when it became less of a priority. Our outposts became a dumping ground for screw-ups and malcontents, or those people who were too highly placed to get rid of, but had annoyed the wrong people."

"And which one are you?" Aidan couldn't help asking. "All of the above?"

Killian smirk had a bitter edge. "Depends on who you ask."

"So what is the point of all this?" Seph wanted to know. "You said you're here to watch for an invasion and try to do something about it, right? So what are you going to do?"

"I don't know." Killian appeared to deflate before their eyes. "As I mentioned, we have a protocol. We're meant to infiltrate the government, talk them into working together, and provide them with information that will enable them to build defenses against a Bhandecki strike. But we were also meant to have more warning."

"What kind of warning?"

"Typically the Bhandecki seed a target area with fireworm spawn and wait for them to reach a certain size before returning. When my people traveled the Rift the first time, we were looking for evidence that they had done so here, but we found no trace of them. We assumed that they had come before humanity developed the kind of technology that might trigger their destruction."

"So you did nothing." Aidan said contemptuously. "You decided it wasn't worth your time and used your more advanced technology to take advantage of humanity instead."

Killian's reply sounded almost amused. "Would that suit your need for superiority, bartender? Allow me to relieve you of your delusions. We tried, but humans are irrational, violent, and xenophobic. It didn't take long to realize that if we'd come straight out and told them we'd come to save them from an alien invasion, they'd be just as likely to put us in a zoo or laboratory as listen."

"So you just gave up?" Aidan wasn't letting him off the hook that easily. The pirate had known this was coming, and instead of facing up to his responsibilities, he'd spent the last however many years cruising the galaxy, trading in illegal goods, and flirting with human women like Seph.

"We backed off," Killian said sharply. "Looked for a way in. We spent years just listening to transmissions, watching human interaction, learning to blend in and looking for opportunities. And if we've grown less vigilant of late, can you blame us? None of us wanted to be here, and humans wouldn't be thrilled to learn of our presence. Why risk our lives and freedom for people who wouldn't believe our warnings?"

"So you have no plan?"

"I'm afraid," Killian said with a slight shrug, "that you are correct."

"So that's it?" As she spoke, Seph stopped pacing directly behind Aidan's chair, causing him to grit his teeth and turn just far enough that he could see her. He thought he might actually trust Seph at his back, but old habits were too hard to break. "You're just going to quit? If you're right that they intend to destroy humanity, we can't just do nothing!"

"The presence of the probe indicates that the Bhandecki know about humanity. They won't have missed the evidence that you've advanced to the point of being a threat to them, and it seems safe to assume that they will proceed with annihilation at their earliest opportunity."

"You're saying they may not wait for spawn to develop," Seph noted, wrapping her arms around herself and shivering a little. "So how much time do we have?"

"I'm saying the spawn may already be here," Killian corrected. "We've been watching the Rift we know about, but it seems obvious that they've created another. There may already be spawn in your Earth's star system."

"So you're running away," Seph said, standing up straighter as her voice began to rise. "You're leaving, right when the event you're hoping to stop is finally imminent."

"We're not running, we're returning to our base." Killian drummed impatient fingers on the table. "We established a presence on an uncharted moon, close enough to observe from, but distant enough from human exploration to hopefully remain undiscovered. We have more crew and another ship there, plus the ability to make repairs to our technology. Also, we'll be sending a message back to my home planet, begging them for help in preparing to meet this threat."

Seph took two steps closer and placed her hands on the table, leaning in to narrow her eyes at the pirate. "Begging? If your people have been trying to prevent this exact kind of event for centuries, why would you have to beg?"

"Let's just say that my people don't necessarily agree about whether our presence here is necessary. Because we can easily protect ourselves from the Bhandecki, most have come to believe we should be content to do so and leave our enemies to their conquests."

"Let me see if I understand you," Aidan broke in, derision sharpening his tone. "You're here on a fool's errand, you have no backup and no real plan, and yet you've dragged us with you. Why?"

"Why not?" Killian countered patiently. "You were on board, the station was imploding, and if there was to be any hope for humanity, I needed to get my message off as soon as possible. Seemed like a win-win situation to me."

Seph didn't seem to believe him any more than Aidan did. "So you'd have us believe this was all serendipity, and you happened to choose the two of us out of everyone on the station to save?"

"With the station on the brink of collapse, why wouldn't I want to ensure my friends' safety?"

"Because we're not friends, pirate," Aidan interjected coldly. "We barely tolerate each other. Our arrangement is a business one, and if I didn't pay you, I would be nothing but the man who pours your drinks."

If he hadn't been paying attention, Aidan might have missed the slightly wistful look that flashed across the pirate's face, but it was gone as quickly as it came. "As quick as you are to repudiate me, we're not that different, you know," Killian said, sounding a little weary. "Both of us were born to something more, only to be cast aside when we became inconvenient. Both of us understand that sacrifices must sometimes be made in pursuit of victory. And both of us hide from reality by pretending to be something we're not."

"We are nothing alike," Aidan said viciously. "And if you think we are, then you know nothing about me."

Killian began to laugh. "I know everything about you, bartender. Except how to convince you to stop wallowing and..."

He paused. His expression went slack, and for a moment, his attention remained focused on something outside of the confines of the room, the ship, possibly even the universe.

"No," he whispered, shaking his head. And then, "Yes... Yes... Yes!"

With the final yes, he leaped to his feet and slammed both hands on the table. "It will work," he hissed, his eyes burning with intensity. "It *has* to work."

"Um..." Seph stepped back from the table, obviously dismayed by the pirate's sudden display of enthusiasm. "What will work?"

"You," Killian said, staring at Aidan, every muscle in his body suddenly taut as a bowstring. "You're the answer! And you were right in front of me all along. I just wasn't desperate enough to think of it."

"Think of what?" Seph looked as confused as Aidan felt. "What is it you think Aidan can do?"

"He can help us save Earth," Killian said, in a tone so earnest and serious that it took Aidan a moment to understand what he meant. What he was implying.

And for the first time in what felt like years, he laughed—a deep, genuine sound of amusement. The situation wasn't funny. Laughing was probably the least appropriate reaction to the moment. But what else was there to do?

Killian remained silent, his eyes fixed on Aidan, daring him to respond. Daring him to put words to this absurdity.

So he did. "You're a damned fool, Killian. A fool for imagining that I would care enough to get involved in your crusade."

"My crusade?" Killian echoed. "You think that's what this is? You think I *want* to be here? Think again, bartender." His sneer was mocking, though it seemed largely pointed at himself. "I was given this task to get me out of the way, so my brother could seize control of everything I'd worked for. He had more influence, and he used it to condemn me to a life far from everything and everyone that I loved. So forgive me if I'm not particularly excited about risking my life for humanity, but the fact is, if I don't, your entire race could be annihilated, and I find that while I am indisputably a cold, inhuman bastard, I'm not quite that cold."

Aidan bared his teeth in a smile as icy as the depths of space. "I am," he said.

"Aidan, were you even listening? We're not talking about an invasion, or damage on a recoverable level," Killian insisted. "We're talking about the potential destruction of every human planet. Everyone on Earth is in the crosshairs of a species with no conscience and no mercy, and yet you would still leave them to burn?"

A single raised brow was all the answer Aidan bothered to give. Suddenly, Killian's pleading expression disappeared behind cold, uncompromising fury. He swore and slammed his hands onto the table again. "I don't understand you, bartender. You gave up your life to save them once. Now, everyone you've ever known or cared about could be under threat of extinction, and you would rather run away and hide your head in a hole than seize a chance to save them again. I knew you for a bitter, angry, recluse, but I never thought you would turn your back on the opportunity to protect some tiny part of what you left behind."

"Then the joke's on you," Aidan said, hiding his own fury behind the smooth facade he'd perfected in the harsh school of his mother's scorn. He'd spent years learning to conceal all feeling, all vulnerability, and by now it wasn't even difficult. "I gave up that life because I wanted to, and I have no reason to care about what I've left behind. If I learned that my family was destroyed in the wreckage of Earth, I would look on it as a service to humanity and walk away without a backward glance." He heard a quick indrawn breath from Seph but ignored it.

Killian ran one hand through his hair and dropped back into his seat. "I knew you hated your family, but I had no idea you'd let that hatred spread to all of humanity."

"Well, now you know." Aidan kept his eyes on the pirate, not wanting to see Seph's face. He could only imagine what she must think of him, but it was better this way. "Must be disappointing to know that you wasted time rescuing someone who isn't what you want him to be, but it isn't like I misled you. You claimed to know exactly who I am, so if this comes as a shock, that's on you."

"Wait." Seph stepped in between them and looked from one face to the other. "Will someone please explain all this?"

"Explain what?" Killian sneered. "Why he won't lift a finger for the sake of humanity? Or why I asked him to try in the first place?"

"Why him?"

"Because he has the potential to influence Earth's government to mount a defense against the Bhandecki."

"*Aidan?*" She sounded skeptical. Shocked. Maybe even slightly amused, and rightfully so. Who, looking at him now, would believe the power he'd once wielded?

"Yes." Killian shrugged. "Whether by luck or destiny, he ended up on this ship, and now he's our best hope of succeeding."

"As I said, you're a fool," Aidan repeated grimly. "I thought I was the biggest fool alive, but even I can't compete with this."

"All I'm asking is that you talk to them," Killian argued fiercely. "Try. And if you fail, no one will be around to resent you for it—they'll be dead."

Aidan clenched his teeth until his jaw ached and his head pounded. Killian had no idea what he was asking. "I could try until I died of old age, and it would change nothing. A thousand years of effort wouldn't be enough because *I* am nothing."

"Please help me understand," Seph demanded again. "Why do you think Aidan can do this?"

"It doesn't matter," Aidan said harshly. "The answer is no. And if you have any sense, you'll stop asking questions." He stood up and fixed Killian with his iciest gaze. "Whatever hopes you may have of influencing my better nature or convincing me to be a better man, know this: I have no better nature. Even if I thought this ridiculous idea had a chance, the answer would still be no."

He turned on his heel and walked out before anyone could ask more questions that would require him to explain his reasons for refusing. Better that they believe him a heartless monster who cared nothing for humanity.

No matter what they thought of him, he only knew that he couldn't do what they asked, even if Seph hated him for his refusal. Her accusing gaze would hurt, but not as much as what awaited him on Earth should anyone learn his true identity.

They would have to find some other sacrificial lamb. Phillip Linden was already dead, and the sooner they accepted that, the better.

NINE

A DEFEATED silence reigned after Aidan's departure. Seph thought it was probably fortunate that the door had dematerialized at his approach—he'd been angry enough to walk right through the wall if necessary.

She knew she ought to say something, but what? As the sole remaining representative of humanity, how could she apologize for her fellow human's apparent disregard for the fate of his own species? Especially when she knew he wasn't as cold or inhuman as he claimed to be.

"He's not even a very good liar," Killian remarked at length. "He does care about what he left behind. He could have shoved everyone aside and taken command, but he saw the potential for the least destruction and he took it. He's a better man than he thinks he is, but I doubt he can be convinced of that."

"Aidan?" Seph queried. "I agree that he's a better man than he pretends to be, but what exactly could he have taken command of? I still don't understand how he can help, but I might be able to talk him into it if someone would tell me what his deal is."

Killian's face closed off. "Not my secret to tell, unfortunately."

Seph indulged in a disgusted look at the pirate. "Fine time to decide you have principles. If you won't tell me that, at least answer me this—why are *you* doing this? It's very nice of you to want to save humanity, but it would be a lot safer for you to just run away and leave us to our fate."

"Why not?" Killian rose from the table, and his face made it evident that the matter was closed. "I'm needed on the bridge, so I've asked Dinah—my engineer and mechanic—to show you around the ship. If you need anything, you can ask her. Otherwise please comply with any instructions from my crew, and don't wander around poking into corners. This ship contains technology beyond your experience, and I wouldn't want anyone to get hurt." He smiled, but the expression didn't reach his eyes, and before she could come up with a solid retort he was gone.

"Well, that's just ducky," she muttered softly, dropping back into her chair and folding her arms. What was she supposed to do now? Sit here and wait for Dinah while she contemplated the end of the world as she knew it?

Not that there wasn't a lot to think about. Seph didn't even know where to start. She'd encountered evidence of not one but two intelligent alien species in one day. Her temporary home was broken, her boss was being... himself, and she had no way to get back to Earth. Where her family waited, with no idea what was coming.

There was always a chance Killian was lying. But why? She couldn't think of a single reason for him to lie about something like that. There was certainly no advantage in it that she could see.

And what of Aidan? She should probably be more upset with him, and no doubt would be if she didn't know him well enough to sense the pain hiding behind his refusal of Killian's request. He might have been able to fool someone else into believing he would cheerfully watch the world burn, but she'd caught enough glimpses of his wary, damaged heart to realize that his apathy was no more than a front. But for what?

As she was considering it, the door into the compartment disappeared again to admit a woman Seph assumed must be Dinah. She was short and stocky, with dark brown skin and dark hair cut close to her head. She looked tough, competent, and incredibly annoyed.

"This is not a pleasure cruise," she announced, as though this whole thing had been Seph's idea. "There will be no reason for you to be wandering all over the ship, so I have no idea why I should waste my time giving you a tour."

"Maybe I can be helpful?" Seph suggested, but the look on Dinah's face clearly conveyed her dismissal of that suggestion. "Okay, then at least I'll be able to not get lost or wander into any areas that are off limits."

Dinah rolled her eyes and gestured to indicate that Seph should move now, move quickly, and get this over with as soon as possible.

Fortunately for both Seph's sense of direction and Dinah's patience, the *Fancy* proved to have an easily navigated design. Engineering and weapons were on the lowest level, closest to the drives, cargo holds and crew quarters occupied the middle level, while the top level was reserved for bridge, medical, and the mess. The entire ship appeared to be clean and well-ordered and, despite Killian's warnings, not as alien as Seph would have expected.

"This ship doesn't look all that different from ours," Seph noted as they returned to the lift after the tour was complete. "Did you modify it to make it blend in? If so, you did an amazing job."

"We altered the exterior to look like a ship we came across after we first came through the Rift," Dinah confirmed grudgingly, "and we've been modifying it ever since to keep up with advancements in tech. We needed to be able to pass inspections in order to haul legitimate cargo. The drives are ours though. No one in this galaxy can even come close to the specs, and no purely human ship would survive rift travel."

"How did you figure out how to mimic humans? Or whatever it is that you do."

Dinah shot her an unreadable glance. "Would it upset you if I said we stole the genetic material we needed?"

Seph shrugged. "Just wondering." Maybe the other woman would be more likely to share if she didn't think her answer mattered to Seph.

"At first, we spent a number of your years ghosting around Earth and the other human colony worlds, intercepting transmissions and learning how to look and act like one of you. While we were between planets, we came across a settlement ship that had been attacked by a mining crew turned privateers. They were looting the ship and finishing off the survivors before we figured out how to board."

"Wait, was the settlement ship the *Erin's Dream?*"

"Yes," Dinah admitted.

"That was a huge mystery! About what, five years ago? She never arrived at her destination, and they never found the wreckage!"

"All of her people were dead. We took enough genetic samples to enable us to imprint our nanotech and then pushed her into an out-of-the-way star system, hoping she'd burn up. Seemed kinder than letting anyone see what was left." Despite the grim picture she described, Dinah showed little or no emotion about the event.

Seph couldn't decide whether she ought to feel more squeamish about the fact that they'd taken genetic material from dead colonists, or more upset about their destruction of the evidence. Hundreds of families had gone for years with no closure, with no way to know whether their loved ones were alive or dead.

And did this mean Killian and his crew now looked like people whose families believed them lost? Seph hoped not, though she couldn't bring herself to ask, any more than she could allow herself to wonder whether the "mining crew" was a fabrication to cover a much worse crime.

"What ended up happening to the mining crew?"

"They'd just murdered over a hundred men, women, and children," Dinah said sharply. "Why does it matter what happened to them?"

"Because it tells me something important about you and your captain,"

Seph returned evenly. "Do you understand the concept of justice? And, if so, do you apply it in a more-or-less human way?"

Dinah was silent for a moment before answering. "They're dead," she confirmed. "At first, we imprisoned them at our base. Didn't seem like a great idea to let them roam around the galaxy, and the captain didn't feel it was his place to order their deaths. Then, about a year ago, they tried to break out, and our crew there let us know that they planned to execute them rather than risk them escaping with any of our tech."

Seph shivered in spite of herself. These aliens might have decided to help humanity for some reason, but it was clear they were more than capable of calculated ruthlessness. And while Killian claimed their tech wouldn't allow them to shift forms at present, it was downright creepy to imagine a being that could learn to look and act exactly like her if it chose.

They exited the lift and were returning to the bridge when yellow lights set into the bulkheads began to flash.

A voice came over the comm. "Dinah, please escort Seph to biotech before reporting to engineering."

"What does he expect us to do there?" Dinah wore a scowl Seph was beginning to think was her habitual expression. "Hope you're prepared for this, girl, because Harvey isn't going to be happy if he finds us in his space."

"Who's Harvey?

Dinah shot her a sideways glance. "Mess and biotech," she said tersely. "Only other crew besides myself, Rill and the captain."

It was a smaller crew than Seph would have expected for a ship this size, but with their technology, perhaps they didn't need as many people to keep it running.

"Well, it won't be the first time someone was unhappy to see me." If she could survive Aidan's initial response to her hiring, she thought she could handle whatever this Harvey could dish out.

Dinah made her way back past the lift before stopping to press her palm against another flashing light-pad on the wall—this one green and white. An opening appeared, revealing a neat, brightly lit room with three beds and... Seph didn't even see the rest of what the room contained because the middle of the three beds wasn't empty.

It held a bloody, shredded, unconscious wreck of a man.

"Where's your medic?" she gasped, racing to the side of the bed and dropping her pack as she took in the scope of the man's injuries.

"We don't have one," Dinah reminded her, crossing the room more slowly and not appearing particularly disturbed. "We don't actually need medics the way you do. The captain insisted we have the necessary equipment because he wanted to be prepared in case of a human presence aboard the ship, but we don't actually use it."

Seph's eyes shot to the unconscious man's face. For that first panicked moment, she'd assumed it would be one of Killian's crew, but this time she looked past the blood and the grotesquely swollen face... "*Aidan?*"

"I tracked him down in one of the cargo bays," Killian announced, striding through the door behind them.

Seph turned to snarl at him, and let out a near involuntary curse when she spotted the thing at his heels.

It was a...

She had no idea what it was. If she'd been at all disinclined to believe Killian's story about his origins, that impulse would have been entirely squashed by the sullen looking beast that slunk into the room and flopped onto the floor with a grunt.

It was huge, for one thing. Its shoulders probably came about even with Seph's, and in general, it resembled an enormous cat. More or less. It was covered in rippling purple-blue fur, longer over its back and whip-like tail, and shorter on its legs, while its neck was ringed by a waving mane of sinuous, tentacle-like appendages.

A broad head with forked ears swiveled to look at Seph suspiciously out of golden eyes with slit pupils, and when its jaws opened slightly, she could see a forest of needle-sharp teeth that covered even the roof of its mouth.

When it saw her staring, the beast extended one seven-toed foot and waved, exposing the tips of silvery claws.

"What..." Seph swallowed, reminded herself that she'd survived chimaeras and harpies on Daragh, and tried again. "What happened to him?"

Killian sighed. "Errol found him before I did."

"Who's Errol?"

The cat-thing waved again

"And you didn't think to warn us there was a man-eating monster roaming free around your ship?" she hissed furiously.

Seph would have sworn Errol looked offended.

"I *did* warn you," Killian replied patiently. "I warned you the ship could be dangerous. I won't take responsibility for the fact that Aidan failed to heed that warning. Errol is protective and suspicious of strangers, and he takes his duty to guard the ship very seriously." He looked down at the creature with a disgusted expression. "I suppose I ought to convince him that humans aren't very good eating."

Seph held back a growl of barely leashed rage. "A lot of good that'll do now. Damn it, Killian, he was already injured!" She picked up Aidan's wrist and felt anxiously for his pulse. He was still breathing, but for how long?

A little of her tension eased when she felt his heart beating strong and steady, but there were too many unknowns. She hadn't had a chance to assess his head injury from earlier, and there was no way to tell what kind of internal damage the beast might have done.

Seph ripped at the front of Aidan's shirt, tearing off several buttons in the process. "What kind of equipment do you have? I need a bio-scanner and an IV. Where the hell is the guy in charge of your medical equipment? How much does he know about human medicine? I can handle basic trauma, but I can't tell how badly he's hurt without a scanner."

For the first time since she'd finished nursing school, fear made her hands tremble. Fear for Aidan? Or for herself?

She didn't want to be left alone here. Didn't want to face this terrifying new reality of shapeshifters, fireworms, and the potential destruction of humanity without something familiar to cling to.

Aidan was the only familiar thing she had left. But he was also a friend, whether he wanted to be or not, and Seph realized that she'd never before had to treat anyone whose survival mattered quite so much to her.

"I've requested that Harvey report as soon as possible," Killian answered coolly. "He's fairly proficient with the equipment we've acquired, but he has no experience treating real humans."

"Acquired or stolen?" Seph challenged, turning to rummage through cabinets and lockers, hoping to find something she could use.

In one of the top cabinets, she finally uncovered a scanner, which didn't appear to have ever been used. She activated the device and attached it to the dock at the foot of the bed. "Mother of all hells. It wasn't trying to eat him, it was using him like a rag doll." She ran horrified eyes across the info that scrolled down the scanner. "Left hand and wrist broken. Right elbow dislocated. Five broken ribs, broken nose and cheekbone, jaw inconclusive, and that doesn't take into account at least four places that will need adhesive. Also a concussion, possibly two."

She looked up at Killian with murder in her eyes. "One minute you want to use him, the next minute you're letting your giant blue kitty treat him like a catnip mouse?"

Killian's expression iced over and held none of his trademark mocking humor. "Don't blame me for Aidan's temper tantrum. He had no business in that cargo hold, and Errol was only protecting his family and his ship. Besides, Errol is used to playing rough with us. He has no idea that human physiology is different from ours, or that Aidan can't heal as quickly as we do."

"Hell of an excuse!" Seph was about to start tearing the place apart looking for a neuronet at the very least when the door slid open to admit a barrel-chested gray-bearded man wearing a tight, sleeveless black shirt, gray cargoes, heavy black boots, and a furious scowl.

"Get out of my biotech, all of you. Who the hell is this? Who let her touch my scanner? Killian, have you lost your freaking mind?" He stomped over to the bed, raised an eyebrow, and turned to look at Killian. "So, you finally brought me a real human to practice on, and he's already dead?"

"Ah." Killian cocked his head, some of his equanimity restored. "Harvey, this human isn't for practice, and he's not quite dead yet. I need you to fix him up. Also, this lovely lady you're being so courteous to is Seph. Another 'real human.' I suspect she's about to become your new advisor on human medical care."

Harvey shot Seph a contemptuous glance. "Never said I wanted an advisor. I studied all those antiquated medical texts so I could figure out how these bodies worked, and I don't need some soft, whiny little human acting like she knows anything. Put her somewhere else."

"Afraid not." Killian didn't raise his voice, but his tone was firm nonetheless. "I'm sorry, but you're going to have to deal with it, Harvey. She has the proper training by human standards, and she's familiar with your patient. He might be the key to our dilemma, so I need you not to kill him, which means you need her."

Harvey folded his arms and glared at Seph across Aidan's body.

She glared back. "Are you going to do something old man, or am I going to do it for you?" Her taunt was angry, but also deliberate. She would have said anything to goad him into action. "I may not be a doctor or a biotech specialist or whatever, but at least I know better than to have a hissy fit while a man bleeds all over the floor."

Killian cleared his throat as veins popped out on Harvey's suddenly purple forehead. "Just fix him, will you? And find a way to work together without killing each other. We're already outnumbered about a million to one, so let's not make our odds any worse, eh?"

He stepped out, Errol at his heels, and the door rematerialized behind him.

Much to Seph's relief, Harvey was compassionate enough not to continue the quarrel. He handed Seph a laser knife, cleanser, and sealant—watching her surreptitiously as she began cleaning surface wounds—before producing a full-sized neuronet and booting it up. As the gentle hum of the neuronet filled the room, Harvey looked over the scan results and whistled appreciatively.

"Quite a beating. I take it you two came on board together?"

"Yes." Seph kept her answer short enough that it wouldn't betray the tremor in her voice. She was having a hard time looking at Aidan without feeling angry.

"And the captain thinks this guy is important?"

She gritted her teeth. Why wouldn't the man just work in silence?

"Apparently."

"Chatty thing, aren't you?" The medic grunted. "Well, from the look of things, I'd say he's lucky. A few more blows to the head and we'd have been spacing him instead of patching him up. As it is, not much here that we can't put to rights. He'll need some nanoplasm injections, probably a full day in the sleep tank, but that should do the job."

"Nanoplasm?" Seph couldn't help feeling skeptical and more than a little apprehensive. "What's that, and what's a sleep tank?" And how did Harvey know they wouldn't hurt a human if he'd never used them on one before?

Harvey grunted. "Homeworld bio-tech I modified to work with human DNA, in case our nanotech ever stopped functioning properly. The tank enables a patient to enter stasis, while DNA-coded nanoplasm repairs cells at over a hundred times the rate you normally do. Which is insanely slow, by the way." He looked up and huffed as though the information offended him. "It's a wonder any of your primitive species survive to adulthood."

Seph carefully stomped on her irritation. At least he was giving her information. He didn't have to be impressed with humans, he just had to be able to fix them.

"I'll just finish with the sealant then." She bent over Aidan's still form and focused on making sure his wounds were clear of dirt and grease. Fortunately, there weren't as many lacerations as there could have been—had the cat-thing intended to kill him, those teeth and claws would have shredded him in an instant.

"Now don't you be thinking that I've forgotten what I said earlier," Harvey warned her, without looking up from the neuronet. "I don't need an advisor, and I have even less use for a smart-mouthed one who doesn't respect me. Just because I learned from books doesn't mean I don't know anything, and if you're not willing to listen, I can make you disappear." He grinned, gleaming white teeth appearing in the midst of his beard. "Captain didn't say they needed *you* for anything."

On any other day, Seph might have said something apologetic, smoothed things over, and let the whole thing go, but she wasn't in the mood to deal with territorial blustering. She'd put up with a lot of it over the course of her career, but this wasn't the LSF, and she had reached pretty much the limit of her shut-up-and-play-nice.

"If that's what you feel like you have to do, then go ahead and try," she told him coldly. "If you're the kind of person who can't live without approval, you should know that I offer my respect when you show me you deserve it. You may have all the book knowledge and more advanced tech than I'll ever understand, but I know more about being a human. All I want is to work together if that means Aidan will survive, but if you'd prefer to pout because you feel slighted, that's not my problem."

To her surprise, Harvey laughed, and his face relaxed. "Fair enough. Can't say I've ever been as fond of humans as the captain, but you're not as bad as some." When she shot him a glare, he waved a hand dismissively. "Look, you surprised me. I don't like anyone rummaging around in my stuff. I'm not just a dabbler—biotech is my specialty, and no one else understands it, so they don't respect how complex it is. They come in here and either make demands or don't put anything back in the right place. But if you're willing to learn and don't do anything stupid, I'm sure we can figure something out. You've had medical training?"

"Yes." Seph was still reeling from the abrupt about-face. "It's been a few years. Haven't used it much since I joined the security forces. That's…"

"I know what it is," Harvey interrupted. "They didn't train you?"

She shook her head. "Turned out that medic slots required more influence than my family had."

He grunted as he prepped a vial. "I don't pay as much attention to human politics as the captain does, but I do know those corporations are run by damned fools."

Seph grimaced. "True, but that life wasn't for me anyway."

"You wouldn't be on this ship if it was." A quick jab at a clean section of Aidan's arm produced a small blood sample that Harvey peered at before giving a nod of satisfaction. "I'll prep the nanoplasm and code it into the tank. Finish with the sealant, and then we'll transfer him." He disappeared through a narrow door in the back of the room.

Letting out a sigh, Seph tried to release some of the tension that had gripped her chest ever since she'd entered the room, but she couldn't seem to relax while Aidan was still lying unconscious. She scanned his face, wincing at the swelling and the bruises, trying not to imagine what the cat-thing must have done to batter him so severely.

Sure, Aidan wasn't the easiest person to like or to get to know. But he already had nothing, and he certainly hadn't deserved this, no matter what she might think of his cryptic utterances earlier.

There were too many secrets crammed onto this ship. First Killian's, and now Aidan's. Why had Killian thought a bartender could help save Earth? And why had Aidan refused? He seemed reluctant to believe anyone would even accept his help, but would he truly damn all of humanity for the sake of some long-held grudge against his family?

Seph couldn't quite believe it. She'd sensed that someone or something —probably his family—had hurt him, and that his off-putting disposition was more than just a personality quirk. His words might be harsh, but his actions towards her suggested that his antipathy didn't run quite as deep as he wanted her to think. He was cold and often bitter, but he wasn't a monster. There had to be some other explanation.

Of course, his past wasn't much excuse for his behavior, either during their meeting with Killian or after. What could Aidan have been thinking, walking around the ship alone, probably too angry to notice when he'd strayed somewhere he shouldn't.

She was cursing him under her breath when he began to stir unexpectedly. One of his hands twitched, then his chin jerked, and his eyes fluttered. The tightening of his lips suggested he was alert enough to feel some of his injuries, and the harsh groan that escaped him confirmed it.

"Aidan, can you hear me?" Seph watched as his eyes closed for a few moments, then opened to mere slits. "It's Seph. Are you awake? Can you see me?"

"Get out." The harsh whisper forced its way between his swollen, bloody lips. "Not safe. Find Killian."

"I'm fine," she said quietly, holding herself back from touching him. He would never have allowed it when he was conscious, and it would only cause him more pain now. "You're in medical, or the closest thing they have. Killian found you in the cargo hold and brought you here."

His eyes flew open farther, and his head jerked so that he could meet her eyes. "There's a predator," he growled, or at least that's what Seph though he said. The rasp in his throat made it difficult to decipher his words, and talking was obviously painful for him. "Ambushed me. Too fast. Couldn't run."

Seph's anger boiled up at the thought. Why would Killian even let an animal that dangerous roam around his ship? "Don't worry," she said soothingly. "I'll make sure Killian keeps it locked up."

"No. Stay safe." His blue eyes drifted shut. "Stay away from it. From me. I told you... I'm cursed."

"Oh, shut up. If you weren't almost dead, I would kick you."

Despite his injuries, Aidan's mouth tried to curve into a grin, an expression that looked painful even to Seph. "Have to be alive... to kick me... so it's okay."

"You think I won't, you arrogant son of a monkey?" She would not cry. Even though he'd just acknowledged that he actually cared. The jerk.

"Did you learn that kind of language in medical school?" Harvey came back in from the lab and shot them both a quelling look. "Finished sealing him up yet?"

"No," Seph snapped, still fiercely determined to avoid tears. They were all each other had now. How could he think that she would stay away from him just because he had the stupid idea that his friendship would hurt her? "I say we shove him in the tank just like he is."

"I've heard that human females love scars," the medic observed. "What's your preference, Phillip?"

"His name's not Phillip, it's Aidan," Seph corrected, returning to her task with renewed focus. She sprayed the abrasions on his left hand with cleanser, but none of them were deep enough to need sealing. Grasping it lightly to turn it over, she tried to avoid unnecessary jostling of his wrist and was taken aback when his hand clenched tightly around hers despite what had to be agony from the broken bones.

"What? What is it?" She glanced up at his face, feeling a stab of guilt, despite her anger. "Did I hurt you?"

But his eyes were shut. His face contorted in pain, then his fist relaxed, and his whole body went limp. He'd passed out again.

"Harvey," she asked curiously, lifting her eyes from Aidan's injured hand, "why did you call him Phillip?"

The burly, gray-haired man regarded her impassively. "Must have been a mistake."

Seph bit her lip and swallowed her retort. Harvey might not be human, but she could tell he was avoiding her question. On another day, with another person, she might not have noticed, but this wasn't the first time someone had suggested Aidan looked like someone else. Could Phillip be his real name? Or was it the name of the person he resembled? And if so, why bother to hide it?

Killian's voice came over the comm. "Can biotech be ready for a transit in ten?"

Harvey pressed the comm button and responded, his voice gravelly but calm. "Aye. Putting the patient in the tank. I'll send the all clear when he's ready."

He turned to Seph. "I think that's all you can do for now. In fact, you might try getting some sleep."

Sleep? Seph almost couldn't tell whether or not she was tired. She'd been awakened in the middle of the night on the station, terrified by the thought that she might be trapped in her room, learned of the unknown emergency, climbed a wall, then been almost trampled by a panicked crowd. To finish, she'd been attacked, abducted, and then informed that aliens walked among them. She ought to be exhausted.

"It's ship-night for another seven hours," Harvey added, bent over the input screen of the neuronet, "and you might as well get used to it. Take one of these beds, and when you wake up I'll show you the tank, train you to use it." He looked up briefly, expression bland. "I'll see to it your boy here survives the transit."

She almost protested that he wasn't hers. Aidan... Phillip... whoever he was. But there was some foolish part of her that almost wished he was, and besides, it would feel too lonely to deny it.

"Thank you," she said. "I'll try."

TEN

IT TOOK Seph some time to fall asleep. After they cleared the transit point, Harvey dimmed the lights and disappeared somewhere, and once she was alone in the darkness, Seph couldn't seem to stop reliving the day. Was there any point at which it could have gone differently? Any of her decisions she would change if she could?

She carefully avoided wondering whether she would ever see home again, whether they would find a way to save Earth, or whether Aidan would be okay...

Actually, that one was the hardest to avoid. Even after her eyes were closed, she couldn't stop seeing his battered face. Couldn't stop hearing his voice, calling himself a fool. Telling her to run. Being glad that she was alive to kick him.

He was going to be fine. And he was going to agree to help. And they were going to save Earth. Or he would be his usual difficult self, and she would have to yell at him a little. She thought that didn't sound so bad, as long as he was there to be yelled at...

At some point, she drifted off and didn't awaken for some time.

———

When she opened her eyes, she thought she was back in her bunk on Concord Five. But when she rolled over, there was no wall to stop her, and she fell to the floor with a startled yelp.

A quick scan of her surroundings revealed three beds, dim lights, strange silvery walls, and no view of the stars. And no door.

There was no way to get out.

As the familiar panic began to set in, Seph sat up and thought deliberately about how she had come to be in her present position.

She was not on the space station. She was on a ship...

The past day fell in on her with an overwhelming flood of anxiety. Aidan was hurt and probably still unconscious. She was trapped on a ship full of aliens who claimed to be shapeshifters. She was hungry and needed to pee, and there was a bloodthirsty race of conquerors somewhere out there waiting to annihilate humanity.

It would seem she'd had a busy day. But at least she knew she wasn't trapped. The door would open. For Harvey if not for her, and she'd be able to leave whenever she wanted to.

Taking a few deep, cleansing breaths, Seph wondered how long she'd been asleep. As she stretched and rose from the floor, she took a moment to lift an arm and sniff tentatively—yep, she stank. The smell was almost overwhelming, reminding her of acrid smoke, sweat, and fear.

She was going to need a shower, and the sooner the better. If shapeshifting aliens showered.

Stiff muscles made her stumble a little as she made her way across the room to the door she'd seen Harvey disappear through before she fell asleep.

Harvey didn't even glance up from whatever he was reading when she stepped in.

"Took you long enough," he grumbled.

"You're the one who told me to sleep," she reminded him, "so if you wanted me before now you could have, oh, I don't know, woke me up? Said something sooner?"

"How was I supposed to know humans are lazy and insubordinate?"

"You're ancient and all-knowing and have been studying medical texts for years," she said sweetly. "Did you miss the sections on human psychology?"

"I didn't need a medical text to tell me that humans are smart-mouthed, ungrateful little bastards."

"Oh, is Aidan awake?"

He finally lifted his head to glower at her. "Not yet. But he's healing faster than I thought, so I'll be taking him out of the tank in a few hours. Which means you have a lot less than that to stop smelling like a chemical catastrophe and get back here ready to work."

"I don't know how you expect me to do that," Seph retorted. "I have clean clothes in my pack, but I don't have any way to get clean myself."

Harvey picked up a handheld and bellowed into it. "Captain, get this human out of biotech until she's showered!" He set the device down again. "Problem solved."

Seph was tempted to laugh until Rill appeared behind her only a few moments later, still looking pale and slightly annoyed.

"Let's go," she said, turning back around and walking off without waiting to see if Seph would follow.

Left with no choice, Seph grabbed her pack off the floor and scrambled after Rill, taking note of how the door dematerialized on their approach. At least, that was how it worked from inside a room. From the outer corridor, the light panel appeared to control access and was keyed to something in a person's hand. A DNA sample? Fingerprint?

"How do I get the doors to open?" she asked. "If I put my hand on it will it work the same for me?"

"No."

"Is there another way for me to get around the ship, then?"

"No."

Rill could have given even Aidan lessons in avoiding meaningful human interaction.

"Where are we going?"

"Captain says you need to wash."

"That's a fact," Seph agreed. "Am I going to be staying with you then?"

"No." The woman looked at her as if Seph had suggested something unimaginably horrifying. "You're a human. I'm not sleeping in the same room as you. I'm just letting you use my quarters to clean up, and then you're going back to biotech."

Huh. That was interesting. "So you find humans disgusting?"

Rill glanced at her dismissively. "You're just so... primitive."

"But you look and sound just like me."

"And believe me, I can't wait to go home and get rid of this body," Rill said with a shudder. "It's taken me *years* to learn how to deal with this clunky thing. You smell terrible, your language is confusing, and your senses are so useless you might as well be dead."

"Thanks," Seph said dryly. "We try."

"Look," Rill said, "I know it's just where you are as a species, and you can't really help it, but can you blame me for not wanting to see you or smell you any more than I have to?"

Seph thought about that. "Actually, I think I probably can," she decided aloud. "But I'll try not to? I'm sure there are plenty of things *I* don't realize I'm an insufferable snob about."

Rill rolled her eyes and edged over to leave a bit more space between them as they approached the lift.

"So where am I supposed to sleep?" Seph asked as Rill pressed her hand to the panel beside the lift door. She was annoyed enough to not want to let Rill off the hook, and questions seemed to irritate her.

"I really don't care."

"Well, I can't live in biotech," Seph argued as they stepped onto the lift.

"Can you ask the captain so I'll know where to go after Harvey is through with me?"

Rill shrugged as the door rematerialized behind them. "Captain'll tell you when he's ready I guess."

"Are humans like some sort of weird pet to you?"

The other woman snorted. "I wish. If you were a pet, you might be entertaining. You humans are nothing but a responsibility I'm stuck with. At least it's going to be over soon, one way or another."

"And what are those possible ways?"

"Either the Bhandecki kill you all, or they don't." Rill acted as though she were talking about the weather, not the destruction of a species.

"And then what happens to you?"

Rill shot her a glance out of the corner of her eye. "You won't need to worry about that, human. You'll be home safe, or you'll be dead."

The door opened, and Seph followed Rill out into the corridor. It was with a distinct twinge of suspicion that she recalled Killian's refusal to answer a similar question. He hadn't wanted to talk about why they were helping humans in the first place.

He'd said it was a post for screw-ups.

Wait. Hadn't he also said something about either finding a way to win or dying here?

Killian and his crew might be trying to save humanity, but their goals were clearly not entirely altruistic. Not if their attitude towards humans in general matched Rill's.

Seph was going to have to be more cautious. Trust even less. At least until she understood more of her hosts' motivations, and learned whatever it was they were determined to keep a secret.

What was in this for them? And how much of humanity would they be willing to sacrifice to get it?

After a short but blissful shower, Seph finger-combed her hair, put on the spare set of clothes from her pack, and retraced her path to biotech, wondering how she was going to be able to get in if the doors wouldn't work for her.

She needn't have worried. Harvey must have been aware of her approach because the door dematerialized in time for her to hear him bellowing from inside.

"You're late!"

Lateness was apparently a human concept the Wyrdane had yet to fully grasp.

"I'm not late," she pointed out as she joined him in his inner sanctuary. "You didn't tell me when I was supposed to be back."

"We don't have much time left, so if you want to know how the tank works, you're going have to learn everything I've already done in a hurry. Hope you're smarter than you look because we have a lot to cover, and I won't explain it a second time."

"They say a good teacher can teach anyone," Seph replied blandly. "Shall we test that theory?"

Harvey glowered and shoved a handheld at her with a growl. "Just shut it and try not to break anything."

———

Aidan knew something was wrong when he could hear voices, but couldn't wake himself up. His limbs wouldn't move, and he couldn't remember how he got to wherever he was. He remembered Dizzy's. The fight. Seph. And then nothing.

"...Wake them up slowly," the unfamiliar voice was saying. "It's too great of a shock to the system if they return to consciousness all at once. Can cause permanent memory loss."

Permanent memory loss? Is that what had happened to him? He couldn't lose his memory. There was something he needed to do.

Seph. Her face wavered in his memory—the waterfall of her curls, the curve of her cheek, the smile in her eyes... He needed to find her. Make sure she was okay.

"But you haven't used this on a human before. How do you know how fast is too fast?"

Seph's voice. He was sure of it. Grasping the thread of sound, he pulled himself towards wakefulness.

"No more talking," the first voice said. "Every time you open your mouth, he starts struggling to wake up. He's keying to the sound of your voice."

"Just don't tell *him* that. He'd deny everything."

Reaching towards the musical sound of Seph's quiet laughter, he was immensely pleased to find that he could move his fingers. And his toes.

"Damn it, I told you to shut up. Don't blame me if your boy doesn't remember who you are when he wakes up."

With one final wrench of effort, Aidan opened his eyes. The light seared into them painfully, so he slammed them shut again. A tiny fraction at a time, he cracked the lids until he could make out the faces leaning over him. One scowling, gray-bearded old man who looked as though he could have just as happily murdered Aidan as cured him.

And Seph. Wide-eyed, apprehensive, and beautiful.

No. He didn't think she was beautiful. Well, actually, he did, but he couldn't say it. Ever.

Because of his family. Brand. Killian. The fate of humanity.

Suddenly he wished he really had lost his memory. If he didn't remember his past, then he could tell Seph... No.

"We're still on Killian's blasted ship, aren't we?" he rasped.

"Hah!" Seph crowed, grinning at the old man. "His memory is fine." She leaned in to look closely at Aidan.

"Who am I?"

"A smart-mouthed cook."

Her grin widened. "Are we friends?"

"No," he said, without hesitation. The stab of pain that followed had nothing to do with his injuries.

"See?" Seph seemed overly excited for a woman who had just been comprehensively rejected. "Nothing wrong with his mind or his mouth anyway."

"Well, stop grinning like a fool and check the scanner." The old man made Aidan look positively genial.

"All fractures set and nearly healed," she reported, a note of awe in her voice. "No swelling around the dislocation or the jaw area, no trace of scars. Brain scan appears normal." She glanced at Aidan. "I can confidently report that appearances are entirely deceiving."

He didn't favor that comment with a response.

"In that case, you can get him out of my medical ward," the old man announced. "Keep him from doing anything strenuous for a few days and keep him away from cargo holds and dark corners. His personality is just pleasant enough to get him into trouble in spite of the captain's orders."

"Aye, aye." Seph snapped a mock salute. "Any more orders, doc?"

"Don't let me see your face again unless it's broken."

Seph chuckled. "It *has* been fun, hasn't it." She turned to Aidan and squinted thoughtfully. "Hope you're going to be able to walk soon because I'm pretty sure I can't carry you."

"Just try it," he growled.

"If you say so." She approached him, arms out, and he jerked upright. Or tried to. The sudden motion threw him too far off balance, and he fell off the bed.

"Go ahead and give him another concussion, why don't you," the old man said harshly. "Just don't bother asking me to fix it."

"That wasn't me," Seph protested, trying to sound innocent, but Aidan could hear the laughter in her voice. "It isn't my fault he's allergic to human sympathy."

She walked around the end of the bed to raise an eyebrow at him. "Shall we try this again, a little more slowly? Harvey really might refuse to patch you up again if you can't even get out of medical without bruises."

"I don't need help to walk." He did. He could tell his limbs were slow to awaken, slow to respond to his commands, but the old man didn't need to know how weak he was. No vulnerability. "Get me off the floor, and I'll be fine."

She extended a careful hand. "I'll pull you up. Slowly. Use the bed for balance."

He couldn't explain his reluctance to touch her. It was as if he knew that the moment he breached that barrier, it would be that much harder to deny his feelings. And as his hand slid into hers, at the sensation of her warm, strong fingers wrapped around his, the wall around his emotions cracked ever so slightly.

He was sick of pushing her away. Of trying, at least, because Seph didn't seem willing to be pushed anywhere, by anyone. But he couldn't be the man she thought he was—a simple bartender named Aidan. Especially not now, when Killian was determined to use his past as a weapon. If the pirate was desperate enough, Aidan had no doubt he would threaten to tell Seph the truth if he thought it would convince Aidan to cooperate.

One way or another, Seph would find out who he truly was, and she would despise him. It would only hurt that much more if he let her get close before the inevitable discovery of his deception.

And yet, she was going to be hurt anyway. She had fooled herself into thinking he was worth her time, and, after all his efforts, she refused to be persuaded otherwise. Why not indulge, just this once, in a human relationship purely because he wanted to? He and Seph were the only humans on the ship. A ship that may or may not return to Earth in time to prevent its destruction. If he were to let her in, just a little, who would blame him?

He would blame himself. But it wasn't as if he could despise himself any more than he already did. Why not steal just a few moments of happiness before the sins of his past caught up with him once more? Why not take this one opportunity to feel something—anything—other than the cold chill of apathy?

Using Seph as an anchor, he pulled himself up, keeping his head down and placing one hand on the bed to help him balance. As soon as his head cleared, he stood taller and let go of Seph's hand.

"Not sure that's a good idea yet, big guy," she informed him. "You try taking a step, and you'll be right back on the floor."

"I know," he informed her calmly. "I think I need to use your shoulder instead."

For once, he'd actually managed to shock her, and it almost made him smile. Her mouth dropped open, and she turned a little pink.

"Okay." She edged closer until he could have put a hand on her shoulder.

"I don't think that's going to be enough."

She took a few more steps until he could throw his entire arm around her. When he did, her whole body went rigid.

"You all right?" he asked.

"If you faint, I'll probably go down with you," she warned him. "But I think I can handle it for now. At least until we figure out where we're going."

She turned her head a bit to look at the grumpy old man. "Where am I taking him?"

"Don't look at me," he grumbled. "You two get to the lift and Killian will meet you down a level. Show you to your quarters."

"Right." Seph's eyes went a little wide, but she wrapped the arm closest to Aidan around his waist to help them both balance.

The medic was now pretending to ignore them, but Seph offered him a cheery wave with her free hand. "Thanks, Harvey. See you again, hopefully never."

He grunted but didn't bother to turn around as they stepped out into the corridor together.

Aidan quickly discovered it was going to be difficult even with Seph's help. His legs were stiff and struggling to remember how to move. "This is going to go away, isn't it?" He tried not to let her hear how much it worried him.

"Harvey thought so, but he's never used that tech on a real human before."

"You let him *experiment* on me?" Aidan jerked in dismay and almost took them both to the ground.

"Would you stop flailing?" she hissed. "There was no choice. You were stupid enough to get yourself nearly eaten by a giant cat monster and ended up with a half dozen broken bones, plus that concussion from earlier. Without their tech, you would have been out of commission for months, and we're headed for an uncharted moon to prepare for an alien invasion. Would you rather have been stuck in bed when we get there?"

He gritted his teeth and forced himself to admit that she was right. "No," he grunted. "But if I never get the use of my legs back, this won't be much better, will it?"

"You'll be fine, you big whiner."

And instead of being offended, he laughed. It seemed the alien tech had disrupted more than his coordination.

"If you want to hear me whine, trust me, I can do much better than that," he informed her.

"I thought Harvey fixed your concussion," she muttered, "but obviously I was wrong. I'm finding your room and putting you straight to bed because there is clearly something wrong with you."

"Aside from not being able to walk, I'm not sure I've ever felt better."

Seph reached up and pressed her hand to his forehead. "You don't feel feverish. Maybe all that nanoplasm stuff infected your brain. You do recall that we're at the mercy of shapeshifting alien space pirates who want to use you to save the galaxy?"

"It's either the best or the worst dream I ever had," he assured her complacently.

He could feel Seph's worried gaze, and it amused him. For some reason, she was more flustered by his optimism than his antipathy.

"We need to walk faster," she said.

———

Killian was waiting for them just outside the lift. His eyebrows went up a trifle as he absorbed the sight of Aidan's arm around Seph's shoulders, but he was wise enough not to comment.

"This way." He walked off down the corridor, a little too fast, leaving the two of them to stagger in his wake.

Aidan cursed softly, fighting for control of his own feet.

"Stop trying so hard," Seph murmured. "You'll be fine."

"He can't see me as weak," Aidan hissed quietly, surprised by his willingness to be honest with her.

"As long as he knows you and I are allies," Seph reminded him, "is it really that important?"

He didn't answer. He'd suddenly remembered all of the ways in which they could never be allies. Eventually, she was going to recover from her worry over his injuries and begin worrying over the fate of Earth. Humanity. Her family.

Seph was close to her relatives. She cared what happened to them. And she was very much going to care whether they died in an alien invasion. Once she recalled that Killian believed Aidan was the answer to saving Earth? And that he'd refused?

She wouldn't be so anxious to make him feel better.

All the more reason to accept what she offered now, before she realized how many reasons she had to hate him.

"And, here we are." Killian paused to swipe his hand across the now familiar square of lights." Welcome to your quarters for the duration of our voyage."

They followed Killian across the threshold into what appeared to be a typical utilitarian officer's cabin, with a comfortably sized bed, a locker, a desk and a chair, and a tiny washroom. The most unusual characteristic was the same as what they'd experienced on the bridge. The room and its furnishings appeared to have been formed out of a single piece of material —each piece flowing seamlessly into the next.

"It's nice." Seph sounded non-committal as she glanced at Aidan. "But I'm sure I don't need this much space. Aidan can have this one."

Killian grinned wickedly. "No, you don't understand. This cabin is where you'll both be staying for as long as you're on my ship."

Aidan locked incredulous gazes with Seph, whose cheeks had suddenly gone pink.

From the stiffness of her shoulders beneath his arm, she didn't care for the situation any more than he did. And who would? Being forced into close proximity with a man she barely knew wasn't likely to seem appealing. Or even safe. He couldn't tell whether she was feeling panicked or awaiting Killian's explanation of the arrangement with tense anticipation, but, either way, what was he going to do about it? Pat her shoulder and say something soothing?

On the other hand, if he just came out and said he didn't want to share with her, it might hurt her feelings, and he would prefer not to injure her. Graceful verbal exchanges weren't exactly a hallmark of his style, but now that he'd decided to stop pushing her away, he had to at least make an attempt. The idea of hurting her bothered him far too much.

In fact, he was quickly discovering that he had an unusual urge to prevent her from being hurt by anyone. First Brand, then Killian and Rill—

their interactions had proven that the protective impulses he'd only ever applied to Lindmark itself had suddenly found a new focus.

Aidan knew it wasn't merely because she was a beautiful woman—he'd known plenty of those, and they'd never moved him to any particular response. And she was certainly no damsel in distress. She might have been distressed by the discovery that humanity's destruction was imminent, but she was more likely to attempt rescuing everyone else than she was to need rescuing herself.

No, there was something else, something indefinable about Seph that he couldn't put a name to and didn't even care to try. But no matter how he felt about her, if he was forced to share her quarters, it would drive him mad.

He hadn't shared a room with anyone in… ever. Not ever. On the ship home from Daragh, he'd been crammed into crew quarters for one night and had lain awake, unable to relax with the sounds of breathing going on in all corners. To let his guard down that much in the presence of another person was impossible.

Aidan removed his arm from Seph's shoulders and took a few shuffling steps until he could lower himself carefully into the room's only chair. Then he took a deep breath and glared at Killian for putting him in such an awkward position. "We can't share this room," he said bluntly.

Seph's mouth opened, and then shut. She looked more bewildered than hurt or embarrassed, and that tiny hint of a blush was back, but she didn't seem inclined to discuss whatever emotion had caused it.

"What's wrong?" she queried, raising a quizzical eyebrow. "Are you worried I'll take advantage of you? Perish the thought. You're still injured. Besides, Brand pretty well ruined my appetite for attractive men with big muscles and delusions of godlike invincibility, and you've made it entirely clear you don't care for my company. I'm sure we can work out a system that requires you to see me as little as possible."

Aidan didn't have an immediate response. His brain had short-circuited somewhere around the moment she'd confessed that she found him attractive. It shouldn't be possible. He'd never been the type to attract female attention for his face—women lusted after his power, but generally gave up when they realized he was genuinely as cold and inhuman in private as he was in public.

A conviction Seph should share, considering how he'd treated her up until the last five minutes of their acquaintance, but she still just looked puzzled rather than afraid.

"That's not what I meant." He wanted to growl at her. Maybe even shake her. How could she remain so relentlessly even-tempered and utterly unaffected by their predicament? It wasn't just sharing a room! She'd been shot in the back, and he'd nearly died. Why couldn't she have the decency to look frightened? Or even slightly concerned?

"This is the only empty space we have," Killian said, hands on his hips and eyes on the ceiling as if he was praying for patience. "The two of you are adults, and your world is about to be swallowed up by an intragalactic conflict. Can't you figure out how to share a room without making it into some sort of elaborate mating dance?"

Aidan couldn't help but feel a slight stab of satisfaction when Seph's blush deepened to a dull red. Seeing her discomfited by someone else's plain-speaking was almost enough to make him smile.

Almost. "Look," he explained, "my objections to the living arrangements aren't about Seph." He felt her inquisitive gaze but ignored it. "I simply can't sleep with anyone else in the room."

Killian slapped a palm to his forehead and shut his eyes. "Have you always been such a princess?"

"What kind of life did you have anyway?" Seph sounded almost disgusted. "Can't sleep with anyone else in the room? Do you not have siblings?"

"I had two," he told her, uncertain what moved him to be honest about such a personal detail. "A brother and a sister."

"I'm sorry," she said soberly, her face falling. "It must have been difficult to lose them. How did they die?"

"Die? They're perfectly fine as far as I know."

She shot him an odd look. "You said you 'had' two siblings. I assumed you said that because you didn't have them anymore."

"No." He shut his mouth on any further explanation. He'd already shared more than he intended and revealed things better left unsaid.

"Did you have a falling out?" Seph, of course, wouldn't leave it alone. "Is that why you asked whether my family disowned me?"

Aidan clamped his lips tightly together and took refuge in silence as Killian's arms folded and he began to tap his foot on the floor.

"Look, this is all very touching," he said sarcastically, "but how about you both come over here and imprint the lock before you both die of old age? I really don't care how you handle this situation, but we're almost to the next transit point, and I have a remote to prep."

Seph submitted almost meekly to having her hand pressed to the lighted square beside the door. She left it there until the lights turned a pale lavender, and then it was Aidan's turn. The lights changed to red after his hand touched the plate, and returned to blue and orange after he removed it.

Killian tapped the square twice and then nodded. "Done," he announced "It should recognize you now, and your profiles will be added to the ship's database. If you need me, I'll be preparing to call for aid in a doomed attempt to save humanity. Unless you've changed your mind about helping?"

Aidan let his freezing stare make his answer for him.

Killian stared back, threw up his hands, and walked out.

ELEVEN

AIDAN WAS NOT AN INCREDIBLY large man, but if his weight was any indication, most of him was muscle. After Killian left, Seph managed to help him out of the chair and support him long enough to allow him to collapse onto the bed.

"And don't get up," she admonished. "So are you feeling more like yourself now that Killian has annoyed you properly? Or are you still suffering from..." She searched for a polite word.

"My delusion of contentment?" Aidan supplied, throwing a dark look in the direction of Killian's disappearance.

"Yes, that," she said. "Except the delusional aren't supposed to be aware of their self-deception."

"Hmmm."

Obviously, he was still under the influence of whatever Harvey had done to him because he neither muttered nor scowled. It was almost unnerving.

"Have you learned anything while I was unconscious?"

"Excuse me?" Seph folded her arms. "I'm not telling you anything until you explain to me exactly how you ended up in a cargo hold, being used as a cat-monster's chew toy after stomping out of that meeting."

"I didn't stomp," Aidan insisted. "I retreated."

"You stomped," she said firmly. "And there was huffing."

He shrugged and laced his fingers behind his head. "I went for a walk."

"You knew it could be dangerous. Why did you go wandering around?"

"I was looking to see if this ship has a lifeboat."

Seph's mouth flopped open.

"I trusted you to keep Killian preoccupied long enough for me to determine whether we could escape that way."

"You *trusted* me?" she echoed, dropping into the chair he'd just vacated and crossing her ankles in front of her. "Now I know you're still not right in the head. You'd better stop with the extravagant compliments, or I might start to doubt whether you actually dislike me."

"Maybe I've decided to stop wasting my breath. You never believe me anyway."

"Oh, I believe you," she countered, "I just don't care. I'm a little bit stubborn like that. So you're claiming you didn't just stomp off because you were in a snit about Killian's plan? Was the whole thing an act?" She wasn't buying it. He'd been genuinely furious.

"Hmm."

Another noncommittal grunt, so apparently that conversation was still off limits.

"At least that explains why you didn't try to take Killian's head off just now. You didn't want him asking questions about what you were up to in that cargo bay in the first place!"

Aidan more or less ignored her.

"Back to you," he said instead. "What have you learned?"

"Not much," she admitted. "Dinah told me they took the human DNA they needed to change their shape from the *Erin's Dream*. You remember that story?" At his nod, she continued. "They'd been attacked by a renegade mining crew. Dinah claims Killian tried to help, but the colonists were already dead, so they took some genetic material before they pushed the wreck of the ship into a nearby system, planning for her to wreck or burn up."

"And the pirates? The *other* pirates?"

"Killian took them back to his base, where they were eventually executed for trying to escape.

"Convenient."

For once, they actually agreed on something.

"Also, the ship is definitely their own," Seph added. "They've altered it to look like a human ship, but drives are still original. Sounds like they've been haunting our systems, learning about our people for a long time. Long enough to mimic our ships, adopt our slang, and even understand our sense of humor. I haven't been able to find out how many years it's been, but quite a while. I think they're probably a lot older than they look."

Aidan fell silent after that, and Seph wondered whether it was safe to ask the question she'd been dying to ask since the previous day.

"Um, Aidan," she began cautiously, "I don't know who Killian thinks you are, but after you were injured, Harvey called you Phillip by mistake. Any idea why he would have done that?"

Even the sound of his breathing stopped. After a few moments, he sat up with his back to her and stared at the floor, his hands clutching the edge of the bed so hard she thought he might leave holes in it.

"Don't ask me," he said. "Just don't, Seph." His voice was not the harsh, razor-edged weapon he'd used in the past whenever she got too personal. It was quiet. Pained.

"Okay," she said, holding up her hands in surrender. He'd been injured twice and was clearly suffering from some combination of head injury and the alien technology used to heal him. It wasn't the right time to press the issue.

She pushed to her feet and tried to sound soothing. "Are you hungry? I'm going to look for the mess. I could use some food, and Harvey didn't say you weren't allowed to eat."

He kept his back to her. "As you wish."

"Aidan," she said softly, still staring at his back, "I don't think Killian is the only one who knows whatever it is you're trying to hide. Sooner or later, someone is going to let it slip. If it matters that much to you, wouldn't it be better to tell me yourself?"

When he didn't answer, she dropped her chin and walked out.

It had been hard enough to know what to do when Aidan was being his normal irascible self, but now that he was hurt? Now that he was acting as though he might not quite resent her?

Seph wanted them to be allies. She wanted to be on his side, but that was impossible when she didn't know where he stood. Or even, it seemed, who he really was.

Killian was convinced Aidan could help him influence the government of Earth. It was still possible that Killian was utterly delusional, but he'd always struck Seph as being remarkably acute, which meant that he had good reason for his conviction. Aidan had to have been someone influential, someone high enough up in the corporate structure that others would listen to what he had to say.

Phillip. She could only think of one well-known Phillip, and he was dead. Phillip Linden, the heir to Lindmark Corporation, had been the mastermind of a mass slaughter on the colony world of Daragh, intending to hide its sapient species so Lindmark could move ahead with colonization. His deception had been discovered by the colonists, resulting in the biggest scandal to rock the Conclave since its formation.

In the ensuing chaos, Daragh had become an independent planet, and Phillip had been tried for murder, treason, and several hundred other unsavory things. His family had disowned him, and shortly afterward he had completely disappeared, penniless and disgraced.

At least, that had been the official story, but everyone knew the Lindens wouldn't have allowed him to live after such an enormous scandal. Initially, there had been a lot of speculation about what had become of him.

Some thought he'd been sent to the asteroid mines and died there, others were sure the Lindens had dealt with the problem themselves. It wouldn't be the first time a corporation had handed down swift punishment for someone in their ranks who'd overstepped. But after numerous reports indicating that Phillip's body had been found, with no way to determine how he'd died, the furor had died down to make way for fresh scandals.

Seph didn't really care what had happened to him, as long as he'd paid the price for his arrogance. Not only had he come close to destroying the sentient core at Daragh's heart, he'd also nearly caused the deaths of several of Seph's fellow colonists. The ensuing political upheaval and the uncertainty of the planet's future had convinced many of those colonists to seek their futures elsewhere, Seph included.

Which had, in the end, landed her here—alone on an alien ship, speeding further and further away from everything and everyone she'd ever known.

And yet, if Killian was telling the truth, her family's only hope lay not in her returning home and getting a job, but in helping him thwart the imminent invasion. Which might mean convincing Aidan to do what Killian asked, whether he wanted to or not.

She didn't want to press him now—not when he finally seemed to be dropping his barriers and allowing himself a moment of humanity. Not when he'd begged her to leave it alone. But what options did she have? If Killian was right, and Aidan was the only one who might have a chance of convincing Earth's governments to cooperate, could she allow him the luxury of time?

They were talking about billions of human lives.

Versus the genuine pain of a man she considered a friend, whether he wanted to be or not.

In the end, it all came down to risking her dubious relationship with Aidan on the word of a man she wasn't sure she could trust, with humanity's future hanging in the balance.

Aidan seemed to believe there was nothing he could do to affect the outcome of the conflict, which meant Seph had to find out the truth—had to persuade Aidan to tell her who he was, and discover why Killian was convinced he could help. And if it turned out Killian was right?

Then it wasn't even a question. She would risk everything to convince Aidan to act. But she would also be forced to mourn the death of Aidan's trust in her and the loss of the warmth she'd finally glimpsed in his eyes. Because no matter her motivation, no matter the reason, he would see her siding with Killian as betrayal.

———

When she reached the mess, Rill was sitting at a table, a strange looking device spread out in front of her in pieces.

"Hi." Seph decided to at least try being friendly, despite the other woman's evident distaste for human company. It would be nice to have more than one friend on the ship, even if that friend saw her as a slightly perplexing pet.

But the woman only looked up briefly, nodded once, then returned her attention to the tech in front of her.

Good thing Seph wasn't easily discouraged. "Is that one of your remotes?"

"I don't have to talk to you."

"Humanity isn't contagious," Seph returned with a sigh. "And it isn't like I asked you to come here. If my existence is that annoying, why are you trying so hard to save my species?"

"Don't mind Rill." Killian entered the mess and sat down across from his pilot with a single apologetic glance for Seph. "She doesn't actually like anybody. Except for computers."

"Good to know," Seph responded dryly. "So *is* that a remote? What does it do?"

"We'll be deploying it outside the Rift to alert us to the presence of fire-worms," Killian explained.

"How will that work? Does it have FTL communication?"

"I'm not an engineer," Killian replied, sounding amused, "so I don't know a lot more about the how than you do. I *can* tell you that it doesn't take any special tech to spot fireworms. The adults are about the length of this ship, except for the alpha worms, which can be four times that size."

Seph tried to imagine a space-faring worm four times the size of the *Fancy*. The resulting picture was not encouraging. "And they look like that thing that crashed into Concord Five?"

"Eh, more or less. That one was young. A fully grown worm will be wider in the middle, narrower on the ends. They absorb a lot of light as adults, so it's easier to see their motion than their form. No limbs. If you divide them into quadrants, lengthwise, each quadrant has a... a frill, or a fin, running the length of the body, that can be extended or pulled in, depending on their needs. The fins propel, navigate, and absorb energy."

"So I get the worm resemblance, but what about the fire part?" Seph wasn't sure she wanted to know.

"We've never captured one alive, so we don't know exactly how they work. We do know they can deflect lasers and most forms of energy, and they basically go nova when they die. The fire isn't really 'fire' as humans think of it, but a chemical compound that originates from what is, essentially, a mouth, and can burn through a metal hull in two minutes or less."

Seph wished she could believe Killian was making it up to scare her. "And these are the same critters that can make wormholes... rifts?"

"The adults only make temporary rifts," Killian corrected. "Those will collapse shortly after the worm passes through. The alphas can make permanent ones."

"With that kind of power, how do the Bhandecki control them?"

"They use the alphas." Rill spoke up from where she was still bent over the scattered pieces of her work. "They grow the worms from spawn, and, with some, they incorporate spaceship parts into their growth pattern. While they're still small, the Bhandecki use their instinctive response to energy fields to train them."

"Basically," Killian interpreted, "the alpha worms are living spaceships that control fleets of smaller spaceships."

Seph couldn't help feeling a little sick. "How do you fight that?"

"You start by killing the spawn," Killian said, but he didn't exactly sound hopeful. "They show up as a weird sort of blip in dark energy fields. At that stage, they're vulnerable to extremely powerful magnetic fields, so we hit them with an EMP."

"And the adults?"

"We had no idea how to kill them until we tricked one into entering atmosphere," he said. "Micro-organisms in the atmosphere disrupt whatever keeps them stable, so once we figured it out, we were able to build a planetary shield for our homeworld with that in mind. The worms won't fly through it."

Seph thought that through. "And you think this could work for other worlds."

Killian nodded. "I'd also like to experiment with projectile weapons. My people have nothing of that kind, and with humanity's experience in that field, I believe we could find a way to take the battle to the Bhandecki. Defeat the fireworms in space. But my main goal must be to convince Earth that they need to build a shield. I believe it can be done—if the human government is willing to cooperate. If we could get Earth working on the problem, they have a chance of being ready when the Bhandecki arrive. At least ready to hold them off until we find a way to defeat them for good."

Seph tried not to show her dismay at the casual belief that "Earth" would be able to work as a unit for any reason. If history was good for anything, it proved beyond a doubt that humanity couldn't manage to cooperate for long.

"And this is what you think Aidan could help you with?" She knew she sounded skeptical, but who wouldn't? What could a curmudgeonly bartender have to do with the salvation of Earth?

"I know he could at least try." Killian leaned forward, his eyes suddenly burning with purpose. "It might not be ideal, but there's a chance they would listen to him if he would only stop hiding behind his bitterness and make an effort to accomplish something besides wallowing."

"That was harsh," Seph remarked.

"You call me harsh?" the pirate countered. "How is my determination to convince Aidan to save humanity any harsher than his determination to see them all burn?"

"I didn't say it was," she returned mildly. "But we both know he doesn't truly want them to burn. After all, you're the one who told me he would prefer no one find out he has a heart, which means most of that was bluster. If you were listening, he told you that he couldn't help, even if he wanted to. He's convinced that you're wrong about what he's capable of, and I'd like to know his reasons. I'm not stupid, Killian. I realize what's at stake, but I don't know you all that well, and I don't have many reasons to trust you over him."

"What more do you want from me?" Killian asked, frustration evident in the tense set of his shoulders and the twist of his mouth. "I've told you what's coming. Why are you reluctant to believe it?"

"Wouldn't you be?" she countered.

"Maybe." His eyes were dark and intent on hers. "But I also wouldn't take the risk of ignoring the warning."

"I'm not ignoring you, Killian," she reminded him. "I've asked for a little more information, that's all."

"It's not my information to give. And I can't believe you aren't willing to do this. For your family if nothing else."

"I never said I'm not willing," Seph countered, beginning to feel equally frustrated, "but I'm also not a magician. Or a miracle worker. Even if I was willing to move heaven and Earth just because you said so, I don't know what makes you think I could persuade Aidan to do anything he doesn't want to do, especially when he already believes it's hopeless. I can promise you he doesn't give a flip what I think."

"Perhaps not," Killian argued, "but he has been less bitter and less closed off since he met you. Maybe the difference seems negligible to you, but it's far more evident to those of us who've known him longer. He isn't indifferent to you, no matter what he claims. You may be the only one with a hope of reaching him."

Seph ignored the leap of her traitorous heart. "You're crazy," she said firmly. "You may have been observing humans for years, but I *am* one, and that man doesn't like me—he likes telling me what to do. There's no way I have enough influence to convince him to change his mind."

When Killian didn't respond, her eyes narrowed.

"You bastard. I can't believe I didn't see it before. That isn't the only available cabin, is it?"

He didn't bother confirming, just leaned back in his seat with a faintly mocking expression.

"That's low, Killian, even for a lying, sneaking, manipulative, shapeshifting alien space pirate."

"Probably," he acknowledged, "but is it really that grievous of an offense considering the inducement? I'm trying to prevent genocide. Why should I give a damn about your sensitivity or your embarrassment?"

Seph had to admit that he had a point. "Fine. You're not wrong. But what do you expect me to do when I don't even know why you want him, let alone why he won't help? I can't just follow him around all day, nagging him to be a better person."

"You *can*," he said fiercely. "Seph, we don't have forever to change his mind. Weeks at best. We'll be launching another remote in a few days, hoping it will survive its journey through the Rift to our home-world, and that someone there will care enough to send help. Then we'll be making for our base at all possible speed, to collect our remaining crew and whatever tech we can. After that, it's two weeks journey to Earth."

"Two *weeks*?" Seph echoed incredulously.

"Our drives are considerably faster than yours," Killian said, almost apologetically. "But if we don't start formulating a plan soon, it won't matter how quickly we get to Earth. We will need time to convince Earth's government to work together. Time to develop the necessary technology. And if we are late by even an hour?"

None of it would matter. There wouldn't be any Earth left to save.

———

Seph returned to her quarters a few minutes later bearing food and a growing fear that Killian's plan for them was doomed to fail. There were too many obstacles to its success.

Even if the shield he proposed would work, their hopes rested on the nearly nonexistent chance that Aidan could somehow convince the Conclave to band together to deal with the oncoming threat. Aidan, who wanted nothing to do with returning to Earth, and was the farthest thing from a unifier that Seph had ever met.

But if the Bhandecki and their fireworms were fully as terrifying as Killian and Rill suggested, they couldn't just give up. Not if it meant that Earth and all its planets would be ravaged and consumed by the fury of the Bhandecki assault.

She entered their quarters ready to take up arms on humanity's behalf— or at least to convince Aidan to do whatever he could to help—but he had evidently succumbed to the exhaustion of healing so many injuries and fallen fast asleep.

It felt odd to see him so still and vulnerable, his face relaxed in sleep, his breathing even. With the armor of his suspicion gone and the ice of his gaze hidden, Seph caught her breath as her inconvenient attraction to her infuriating boss flared up and punched her straight in the heart.

She'd never denied that he was handsome, or that she found his hard edges appealing. But this Aidan—the softer one who'd actually unbent enough to allow her to help him—was devastating, and she was too lonely for her usual defenses to be much use.

If only she didn't care quite so much what he thought, or whether he was well. She could push him as hard as necessary until he agreed to do what Killian wanted.

But Killian was basically a stranger—more than a stranger, he was utterly inhuman. He had his crew, his ship, and his mission. Like her, Aidan had nothing. No one else to stand beside him, to respect whatever past experiences drove him to hide from the rest of humanity. Did she owe it to the rest of the human race to badger him into doing something that caused him pain just to speak of—a course of action he seemed to believe was hopeless anyway—or did she owe it to Aidan to try to understand him first?

If only he would just talk to her. The decision would be so much easier if she knew what he was hiding from, and why he refused to consider Killian's request. So much could be riding on Aidan's obstinate shoulders, but if he wouldn't even talk to her about his past, how could she convince him to take a chance on his future?

Aidan awoke to a dark room and the sound of muttering.

"I can hear you," he said, rubbing his hands across his stubbled face and wondering how bad he smelled.

"Of course you can hear me," Seph grumbled, emerging from the corner of the room to sit on the other side of the bed, one leg tucked up beneath her. "You were meant to hear me. You've been asleep for hours, you haven't eaten, and I was beginning to worry that you weren't going to wake up and I'd have to haul you back to Harvey."

He rolled to a sitting position. "Where are we?" And how had he been sleeping with her in the room? He should have woken up.

"Somewhere in space?" Seph grumbled. "How should I know? It all looks the same, and they don't exactly give me progress reports. Killian's preparing to launch his remotes, and and then we'll be heading to his base. If it exists."

She sounded annoyed.

"Maybe you should sleep," Aidan observed, still feeling curiously detached from the circumstances around him. From pirates, aliens, and cat-monsters at least. He felt anything but detached from Seph. "You sound stressed."

"You think?" Seph flopped on the other side of the bed and shut her eyes. "This is bad, Aidan. This whole situation is really bad, and they think we can help them fix it."

Aidan stood, testing his balance and waiting for his head to stop spinning before he crossed the small room to the table where Seph had left whatever food she had uncovered.

It wasn't terrible, he reflected after a few bites. Tasteless, mostly, but not offensive. "What do they want?" he asked finally. "Besides me."

Seph sighed heavily. "They want a way to defeat the fireworms. Not just repel them. Killian believes that humanity can use their experience with projectile weapons to develop something that will work against a creature that's not even vulnerable to energy weapons and can burn a hole in a starship in under two minutes."

"Humanity has traditionally been better at destroying itself than anything else," Aidan observed. "Maybe they're right."

"Aidan"—she rolled over onto her elbow—"they know how to build a planetary shield to protect our worlds from the Bhandecki. Killian just needs to convince Earth's government that the threat is real. That they need to work with the Wyrdane to build a shield. Why not help him? Even if nobody will listen to you, are you really any worse off than you are now?"

He looked at her and wondered. Was this something Seph was frightened enough to pursue on her own? Or was this something more sinister?

"Seph, what happened after I left Killian's quarters?"

She wrinkled her nose. "Killian didn't say much. Dinah gave me a tour of the ship. You basically know the rest."

"Did he..." Aidan didn't even know how to ask without being insulting. He didn't want to do that to her if he could help it, which complicated this conversation beyond measure. Life had been so much easier when he'd been insulting to everyone on purpose. "Did Killian threaten you? Imply that your safety might not be guaranteed unless you agreed to help him?"

"No!" Seph sat up, puzzlement creasing her forehead. "Why would he do that?"

"To get me to cooperate," he explained patiently.

From her answering expression, he'd managed to insult her anyway.

"No," she repeated. "I'm not doing this to save my own skin, or even because Killian asked me to. We're talking about the total destruction of humanity, so I figured it was worth asking how you can be so certain you can't help. So certain that you won't even try."

"Then I suggest you do both of us a favor and give up now, because I won't tell you, and I don't do guilt," he informed her. "I spent my whole life doing what I was told was right, and it got me nowhere. I'm done being manipulated by expectations."

"Then how *can* I manipulate you?" she asked baldly. "I don't want to be angry with you, but I just don't understand why you're letting your past get in the way of trying to accomplish something so important."

"That's because you don't have a past," he said, letting his bitterness lend his words plenty of bite. "You have an enormous loving family who has your back no matter what. You've been wandering around the galaxy doing whatever seemed interesting at the time, with nothing to tie you down, no responsibilities or expectations to get in your way."

Seph opened her mouth to respond, but when no words came out, she turned her back to him, her shoulders stiff and straight.

Aidan shut his eyes and silently cursed himself. It had been a cruel thing to say, considering what he knew about her family's expectations, not to mention what she'd blurted out about their current circumstances. He'd only wanted her to stop pushing, stop digging, stop trying to understand. It was a reflex—to say whatever he knew would make someone angry enough to divert them from their purpose. Especially if their purpose was to get to know him. Or to use him. In the corporate world, those two almost always went hand in hand.

"That was pathetic," Seph informed him, in a voice that was almost but not quite steady. "It was nothing but a juvenile attempt to upset me in order to deflect my questions."

Even after he'd wounded her, Seph had seen straight through him, just as she always did. It was maddening and confusing and somehow oddly fascinating, and it almost made him want to... No. "I'm not going to answer any of your questions, so if you want me to stop deflecting, stop asking."

She flopped back on the bed again. "You're impossible," she announced tightly. "And pigheaded and ridiculous. You have a positively inhuman resistance to logic and reason, which makes you a complete waste of my time, even taking into account that I have nothing else to do with it."

Aidan almost couldn't stop himself from smiling, despite his frustration. He couldn't seem to shake her. She didn't get angry or sulk or burst into tears or try to manipulate him with emotions. Even at his most sullen and taciturn, she was never afraid of him. She just acted like he was the one who had a problem and went on being... Seph.

When she first walked into his life, it had been thoroughly irritating, but now, he had a difficult time remembering what it felt like to be angry with her. Even her stubbornness was endearing, and he was tired of fighting to keep her at arm's length.

Of course, then he'd gone and hurt her again, so it was up to him to fix this if he wanted to. Did he still want to risk an emotional connection, knowing the probable outcome? Or had that decision been nothing more than a maudlin reaction to his concussion?

If so, he was nowhere near as completely healed as the doctor had believed.

It took more courage than he expected to stand, cross the room, and sit on the bed next to her. To meet her startled hazel eyes honestly, without his usual armor of ice cold apathy.

"I'm sorry," he said. The words sounded normal, but they felt as if they were being scraped from the darkest recesses of his soul. They hurt him, in some deep place where merely physical injuries couldn't reach. Aidan wasn't sure how many times he'd ever said them before. Surely not many. "Sorry that I implied you don't know what it's like to carry the expectations of others. I'm so used to protecting my secrets that it's too easy now to just lash out whenever someone gets close."

She sat up and swung her feet back over the edge of the bed so they were sitting side by side, their shoulders nearly touching.

"I didn't ask in order to hurt you," she said quietly.

"I know." He reached out, almost sick with apprehension as he rested one hand on top of hers where it lay on the edge of the bed. He didn't deserve to touch her. Didn't dare expect her to let him.

Maybe she would chalk it up to the head injury.

"But Seph, you have no idea what you're asking. I won't refuse to help, but I cannot do what Killian expects of me, even if I wanted to. Even if I tried, it wouldn't accomplish what he needs, and it would hurt his cause far more than it helps. He's too far removed from human affairs to understand, but I'm asking you to trust me and to stop digging for information. Please."

Her eyes went wide at the "please."

"Okay," she said hoarsely, and he closed his fingers over her hand for a moment in acknowledgment before he stood up.

"I'm going for a walk," he announced, not daring to look back at her. "It's your turn to rest. I'll try to stay away so you can sleep."

"Aidan, you know we're not going to be able to keep this up," she warned, a little of her usual teasing humor back in her voice. "Eventually, we're going to need to be awake at the same time. Which means we'll need to sleep at the same time. We have to figure out how to share this room like adults who aren't totally annoyed by each other."

"Seph, you know it has nothing to do with you," he said, exasperated. "I already told you, I can't sleep with anyone else in the room. It's always been that way."

"Hah," she retorted, stabbing a finger in his direction. "Liar. You were asleep for hours while I was pacing and muttering."

"Then it was a fluke, resulting from my healing injuries." There really wasn't any other good explanation. Unless he concluded that he really did trust her, which was almost more terrifying than blaming it on his wounds. "It won't work a second time."

Her mouth curved at one corner, a tiny, hopeful, teasing expression. "I think you're scared of me," she announced.

"I'm not afraid of you, I'm desperate to escape you," he said. "There's a difference." He wondered a little too late whether she would realize that he wasn't serious, but, just as she always did, Seph laughed.

"Fine, then go away." She huffed and threw a pillow at him without warning. "Just don't get into a fight with any cat monsters, don't go into any cargo holds, and for the love of life don't let Harvey see you out of bed because he'll probably kill me."

"What am I allowed to do?" he asked sarcastically, tossing the pillow aside.

"Go stare out at the stars and contemplate the meaning of life. Better yet, go take deep breaths and meditate on the importance of brotherhood with your fellow humans. Whatever. Just try to be calm and non-confrontational. Also, don't annoy Rill. She likes humans even less than you do, and I'd hate for her to fry you just because you irritate her."

"Basically, you want me to stay here and stop breathing."

"Perfect," she said and closed her eyes.

Aidan looked down at her suddenly peaceful face and experienced an almost overwhelming impulse to stay. Just to watch her sleep. To ensure that nothing would disturb her.

He wanted…

What did he want? To know that she was safe? To be sure that even though the whole of humanity might go up in flames around them, Seph would be all right?

Yes, but it wasn't quite that simple anymore. He also wanted…

The truth hit him then, so hard that he almost couldn't breathe.

He wanted everything. Everything that Seph was willing to give him.

He wanted to find out whether she smiled even in her sleep.

Whether her hair was as soft as he imagined.

Whether she'd ever truly been in love.

And so help him, he wanted to kiss her.

He wanted her to believe that Hades had been entirely misunderstood.

But all of those things were impossible, and her breathing had already evened out into the natural rhythm of sleep, so he slipped out quietly, closed the door and found an out of the way corner to stare out at the stars.

TWELVE

SEPH AWOKE from a dream of running endlessly and alone through a maze of towering walls and hedges, looking for something that was just beyond the next corner. The loneliness and desperation clawed at her throat and left an ache in her chest, but she couldn't stop running until she heard Aidan's voice calling her.

"Seph. Wake up. Please."

That couldn't be Aidan. He never said please. Except that once.

Warmth enveloped her shoulder. A warm pressure that grew tighter and then shifted slightly.

"Seph."

She blinked and the maze receded.

Someone was touching her, so she jerked around to find out who it was. The dream faded, her eyes opened, and she found Aidan leaning over her.

His hair was disordered, as though he'd been running his fingers through it repeatedly, and the shadow of beard on his jaw had grown deeper. His blue eyes were dark with worry, and for one sleep-befuddled moment Seph almost reached up to touch his cheek in reassurance. Or maybe just because she wanted to.

"Hi," she said, smiling up at him, and for once her smile didn't cause him to close off and turn away.

He stared down at her, and the worry changed to something softer, something that made Seph's breath catch in her throat. His eyes shifted ever so briefly to her mouth, but then he caught himself. Lifted his hand from her shoulder and moved away.

"Bad dream?" His voice was studiously bland, as though he still wasn't sure he wanted to be caught caring.

"Just an annoying one," she said, taking a deep, frustrated breath and letting it out slowly. Had he been about to kiss her? Or was that her overactive imagination and the enforced closeness of their situation making her see things that weren't there? "Did I sleep too long?"

They'd both been sleeping a lot in the days since Killian sent his message through the Rift, and, because Aidan continued to insist on sleeping alone, they'd seen little of each other.

"Probably not long enough," he told her, rising from the bed and avoiding her eyes. "Ship just went on alert for our approach to the base. Thought you might want to know."

"You thought I would want to be conscious when we arrive at an uncharted moon? Perish the thought." She yawned and sat up. "And look at you—still no blood or bruises. Did you do anything fun while I was asleep?"

"Murdered the crew and cleaned up the evidence," he said, forcing her to throw a surreptitious glance his direction to ensure that he was, in fact, joking. She hoped he was joking.

It had been hard to interpret his mood the past few days. He no longer behaved as though he was allergic to her presence, and he was undeniably less of a curmudgeon than he'd been before, but that wasn't really saying much. When they did end up together for any length of time, he seemed content to remain there, but never made any attempt to start or maintain a conversation. She would ask about his recovery, among other casual questions, but his responses were always brief, and both of them had avoided more complicated topics.

Except one.

"Have you and Killian talked?"

"No."

"So you're still stuck with me?"

He shrugged.

"Are we going to the bridge?"

"Killian didn't say we couldn't."

"Well, thanks for waking me." She got out of bed and headed for the washroom. "I'll meet you there as soon as I'm presentable."

———

Given the inducement, it took Seph less than three minutes to run a brush through her hair, splash water on her face and throw on a clean shirt. When she dashed out of their quarters, still gathering up her ponytail, Aidan was leaning against the curve of the corridor wall just outside the door.

"You didn't need to wait for me."

Aidan fell into step next to her.

"It isn't like I don't know where I'm going," she informed him, "and I look after myself just fine while you're sleeping."

"Conditions may be about to change," he said patiently. "We don't know what's waiting for us on this moon, and Killian won't tell me what he's done with his alien pet. If we're going to be disembarking, he may have let it loose again, and I don't want you to find out the hard way what it's capable of."

"I met it too, and it was perfectly civil," she retorted. "Of the two of us, you're the only one who seems to inspire it to murderous rage."

"It isn't like I'm not used to it."

"To murderous rage? What, did you serve your customers poisoned beer?" she teased, only to see his face close off completely.

"Aidan, what is it? What did I say?"

He didn't answer. Just kept walking.

"You know, this would all be a lot easier if you would just *talk* to me," she called after him. "We might be stuck with each other, but I'm not your enemy! Just tell me what you're running from. Tell me what Killian wants. Tell me about Phillip. Maybe I can help, or explain things to Killian, but I can't do anything at all if you won't trust me."

"Don't," Aidan said harshly, coming to a sudden stop in the middle of the corridor. "Don't keep asking me for what I can't possibly give you. The concept of trust was beaten out of me so long ago that I don't even remember how it feels, so don't imagine that you can change me by promising you're not my enemy, or that you'll never betray me. Everyone betrays."

"That's almost mind-blowingly cynical," Seph observed, coming to a stop directly behind him, reeling a little from the force of his repudiation. Someone had hurt him badly. Many someones, more likely, and she had no desire to add to their number. "But I'm sorry I upset you. Sort of sorry."

He finally turned back, one skeptical eyebrow raised.

"No, I'm not sorry for trying to find a way to convince you to help save the world," she said with a shrug. "But I did promise to stop digging, so I'm sorry I asked again about Phillip."

"You aren't very good at apologies," he noted.

"I try to be genuine about them," she admitted, "so I only apologize for things I'm truly repentant about. I can tell something about Phillip is a problem, so I should have left it alone. Instead of bringing it up, I should have just gone behind your back and asked Killian. Or Harvey. They would tell me eventually."

"No!" The look on his face was almost horrified.

"No, why?" Seph asked stubbornly.

He shook his head and took a step closer to her, eyes on hers with burning intensity. "Just promise me you won't ask anyone about Phillip!"

"Why would I promise that?" She folded her arms, ready to prove she could be just as stubborn as he could. "I can tell he's a big part of your past, whoever he is. I think he's the reason Killian believes you can influence Earth, and the reason you're running from everyone and everything. Harvey thinks you *are* him, which is ridiculous. After you got so angry at me for using what you thought was an assumed name, I don't think you would do that."

He had nothing to say in response. Just stared past her with empty eyes.

"I have a theory," she said tentatively, "that he's someone who looks like you—someone who had power—and Killian wants you to take his place."

He still said nothing.

"Aidan, was he talking about Phillip Linden?"

His eyes shot back to hers, a fire raging in their depths. "I won't discuss this with you. Not now, not ever."

"Why are you hiding from it?" she demanded. "At least tell me what you're afraid of. Is it Phillip that scares you? Aidan, I realize he was a monster, but it's not like he can come back from the dead and get his revenge on you for impersonating him."

Aidan laughed—a harsh, cold sound. "You're wrong about that. You have no idea how wrong."

The more Seph thought about it, the more she believed her guess was correct. Phillip Linden had remained mostly out of the public eye, but there would be many who knew what he looked like. If Aidan had grown up resembling one of the most powerful men on Earth, his life would have been incredibly complicated. Not to mention dangerous. And once Phillip Linden had been disgraced, she could see why his doppelgänger would have tried to hide in a place like Concord Five. Anyone who didn't believe Phillip was dead might have decided to take their hatred out on Aidan. Which also explained Brand's comments about his face.

And why Killian thought Aidan could help him. There had been enough doubt and speculation surrounding Phillip Linden's death, it wouldn't be impossible for him to claim the reports had been faked. The name might still carry enough influence for him to get a hearing at the highest levels.

What Killian didn't understand was how difficult such an impersonation would be, or the depth of the vitriol that would be unleashed should Phillip suddenly return from the dead. It was no wonder Aidan didn't want anything to do with the plan, or that he thought it would hurt Killian's cause more than it helped. Aidan would be completely out of his depth, expected to prove his identity with knowledge he couldn't possibly have, and to become the innocent target for all of the hatred Phillip had justly earned.

It would be a death sentence, either at the hands of the corporate elite when they saw through his facade, or at the hands of the people whose safety Phillip Linden had so callously jeopardized with his hubris.

"Okay," she said suddenly, drawing a surprised look from Aidan. "I'm sorry, again. I think maybe I understand why you don't believe Killian's plan would work, and why you don't even want to try. But you should know that I'm probably going to beg you to try anyway. Because while it would be horrible for you, if Killian is telling the truth, all of humanity could be about to die and I don't see how we have any choice but to attempt whatever has a snowflake's chance in hell of saving them. Also because I'm selfish and I want the people I love to survive. But I won't be angry with you for refusing as long as you promise to help us find another way."

She'd never been able to read him, not well, and never for sure. But right then, all of his carefully layered masks and walls and veils fell, leaving only a man with intense emotion burning in his ice-blue gaze.

He stepped towards her, once, twice, closer than he'd ever come before. Slowly, ever so slowly, he lifted a hand to her face. His touch was feather-light, but it left a trail of fire where it moved down her cheek to her jaw.

"Seph, you need to understand something," he said, his voice oddly level. "I don't care what Killian wants from me—if he's right, we're already too late. The Corporate machine moves too slowly for you or I or anyone else to talk them into working together to save Earth. So I don't give a damn about his plans, but I do give a damn about you. It's my fault you came on this ship and got caught up in this, and I want you to know that I will do whatever it takes to keep you safe."

Seph felt her mouth fall open, and her eyes begin to fill with unwelcome tears. He did care. At least a little. Even if he was truly awful at showing it most of the time, Aidan did have a heart. A carefully buried, deeply damaged one he was determined to hide, but for whatever reason, he had just chosen to give her another glimpse of it.

"I never asked you to save me," she said hoarsely. "I've never expected anything from you at all."

His hand fell away from her face, and she felt the loss like part of her heart had suddenly been chipped away.

"No. You didn't," he said. "But you're afraid."

"Yes." She fought to keep her tears at bay, unwilling to let Aidan see her cry. "At least, I think I am. Or I should be. I feel like the only reason I'm not having a meltdown in a corner is that it's all too much and I can't wrap my head around the possibility of what could happen. Of what's already happened. Aliens, fireworms, the destruction of humanity... I guess maybe I don't really believe it. I feel like I'm on some sort of strange adventure, but eventually, we're going to go home, and everything will be okay."

———

He knew what that felt like. The denial. The unshakeable belief that the situation couldn't possibly be as bad as your eyes and your ears were telling you. That someday soon it would all be over, and everything would go back to the way it was before.

Because if you acknowledged it—if you allowed it all to be real—you would lie down and give up because there was nothing you could do about it.

"I don't think that's even an option anymore," he said wearily. "Killian isn't human. The probe that crashed into the station wasn't of human origin. I don't believe we have a choice other than to trust him until we see otherwise."

She winced. "Trust Killian? You do realize that's terrifying."

"It is," he agreed.

She slugged him in the arm, smiling a little despite the worry he could see in her eyes. "That was *not* what you were supposed to say, genius."

He was surprised by the urge to smile at her in return. "I thought women liked it when men agree with them."

"You're supposed to say it's really not that bad and everything's going to work out in the end. That if there's a war, we're going to win, and everyone will live happily ever after."

"If I'd said anything so delusional, you would've hit me harder."

She laughed, and some of her tension appeared to ease. "Maybe. But I could have accepted something slightly less depressing. Couldn't you have given me a few encouraging and upbeat platitudes without actually descending into lies?"

He raised an eyebrow. "When, since we met, have I ever given you reason to believe that I can be encouraging? Or upbeat?"

"Just because I haven't seen it doesn't mean it's impossible."

"Trust me," he informed her dryly, "it's impossible. And I'm not going to bother lying to you. You're not stupid, and we're in a tough spot."

"No kidding," she responded. "I'm at a bit of a loss to see how it could be worse."

"Well, brace yourself then, because I'm about to tell you."

"Wait..." She grimaced. "Let me guess. You're actually a secret alien spy? A covert Korchek operative? Or something Harvey did is slowly killing you from the inside?"

"Nothing so morbid," Aidan replied levelly. "But I'm relieved to know that you think that would be bad news."

Seph glared at him.

"Look, I thought I knew Killian reasonably well, but obviously I was wrong, and if he's desperate enough for my cooperation, I don't know where he'll draw the line."

Her brow furrowed. "You think he'll torture you to ensure your cooperation?"

She didn't know. She had no idea how far Aidan would go to protect her, and he couldn't decide whether to feel relieved or disappointed. He could hardly claim to be surprised though. It wasn't as though he'd given her much reason to believe he cared.

He reached out and gripped her arm briefly. "Not me, Seph. Killian knows me better than that. He'll know that he can use you to get to me. And I can't predict whether or not he'll try it. You need to be careful."

She tensed and drew in a quick breath, eyes wide and lips slightly parted. "You think he would..."

Aidan turned to clasp her shoulders, wanting to erase that worried look from her face. Or maybe just needing to touch her again. He'd spent half his life learning not to need anyone or anything, but somehow Seph had bypassed those defenses when he wasn't looking. He was vulnerable now, because he needed her to be okay. Even worse, he'd let her know that she could be used against him. He'd given her the power to hurt him, and he didn't even care.

"He might threaten you in order to control me," he said honestly. "He could be counting on the fact that I don't want to see you hurt. But Killian isn't stupid either. If he uses you, he'll make me an enemy, not an ally. I hope for his sake that he doesn't decide to try it anyway."

Seph's eyes met his, and they were warm with hope. Maybe even joy. And a tiny bit of amusement.

Wait. What had he just said that could have made her happy?

"It's nice that you want to protect me," she said, starting to smile. "I really appreciate the thought. But you know that if Killian decides he wants to hurt me, no matter what his reason is, he'll have to deal with me long before he gets to you."

"Should I remind you that there probably aren't any trays full of beer mugs on this ship?"

"I'll improvise." She smiled again, her fear seemingly gone, just like he'd hoped. He just wasn't sure her current mood was an improvement. She looked... thoughtful.

"I wish you'd give yourself a chance," she said wistfully. "You try so hard to convince everyone you're heartless, but you're a much better man than you give yourself credit for."

Before he could react, before he could scoff, or step back, or even draw a breath, she did the unthinkable—she reached out, wrapped her arms around him, and hugged him.

As though it had been an irresistible impulse, she pulled him close, and her hair brushed gently against his cheek.

For the next few moments, her warmth pressed against him, filling up dark spaces and pushing back the bitter loneliness of his entire existence. For those precious few seconds, Aidan felt as though he'd been granted a glimpse of something rare and beautiful that he had never even dreamed was possible. But it was over too fast. He didn't even have a chance to respond. He could barely breathe. All he managed to do was stand there, frozen, as she pulled back and smiled.

"Bridge," she said, swiping at her eyes and walking away briskly.

It was official. Persephone Katsaros was going to be the death of him. But at the moment, it was the most enjoyable way he could think of to die.

It was almost surreal, knowing that she believed in him. That she'd looked past his ironclad walls and seen someone worth defending. Even if she couldn't possibly know what kind of monster he was, he'd been monstrous enough to her that she should have realized he was no prize.

Since the moment he was born, everyone had wanted something from him. His own family had been willing to manipulate and destroy him to get it. But Seph... When she said she expected nothing, he believed her. He didn't have a choice. She was so irritatingly earnest, she couldn't lie her way out of a paper bag.

Seph was the most genuinely worthwhile person he had ever met, and he was going to destroy her. No matter what he did, no matter what he said, from this point forward it was inevitable. She would learn the truth, and everything he had ever done, everything he had ever said, would become a lie and a betrayal—another chunk of the gaping hole he was digging for himself.

But he didn't care enough to let her go. He would take what she offered and pay the price later, even if that price was his life. It seemed like such a paltry thing in comparison with the gift of her trust, however brief.

Was this why Hades had been willing to spend those interminable months alone? Because he would do anything rather than risk losing his beloved entirely?

Not quite conscious of making the decision to do so, Aidan followed Seph in the direction of the bridge, wondering why he had ever felt sorry for Hades. Even the god of the underworld got to keep his Persephone, while Aidan didn't stand a chance.

———

The bridge was tense, even with only three people. Rill hovered over her station, Harvey sulked in the weapons chair, while Killian sat in the captain's seat watching the screen and the readouts with deceptive laziness.

"Took you long enough," he called, without taking his eyes off the readings in front of him.

"What can I say, it takes forever to do my hair," Seph quipped, her near-permanent cheerfulness firmly in place.

Aidan had finally begun to wonder whether she used her unflappable good-humor to avoid letting anyone see too much, just as he used icy dismissal.

"So," Seph inquired innocently, "are we almost there?"

Killian glanced up and nodded. "Yes, in fact. Though it's not much to look at."

The forward viewscreen lit up with an incredibly detailed image of their destination... which was just as boring as it sounded. A gray-green moon orbiting a gas-giant planet.

Aidan was watching Seph's face. Despite the fear she'd just confessed, it was now alight with interest and anticipation.

The faces of the three Wyrdane were tense. What were they anticipating, here at the home they'd built for themselves far from everything that was familiar? Were they happy to be returning? Eagerly awaiting a reunion with the crew they'd left behind at the base?

Aidan considered what that might feel like—to have someone, somewhere waiting, wondering if he would come home safely, or at all. His eyes shot to Seph again. She would never be the type of person to stay behind and wait for her loved ones to return. She would be the one to go, to ask the bold questions and take the intrepid leaps into new territory, leaving someone else behind to be afraid they would never see her again.

Her family. Did they ask themselves every day whether she was safe? Or did they go on with their lives thinking of her only occasionally, having resigned themselves to her wandering? Worst of all, had they given up on her?

He couldn't always stop himself from wondering about his own family. Had there ever been a moment that his mother regretted casting him off?

And his siblings... had they asked any questions? Fought for him to stay? Or had they believed, like the rest of the world, that their grandfather's crimes had been his own?

Carolus would probably believe whatever they told him. He took after their father—a beautiful, fun-loving man without much thought beyond his wardrobe, his mistress, and his entertainment. There was no actual malice in Aidan's brother, simply a vast well of ignorant self-indulgence. His mother despised his excessive emotions and lack of perspicacity, and as a result had left him strictly alone, preferring to invest her time in Phillip.

A much younger Phillip had been proud of his ability to impress her with his keen mind and incisive judgments, but now he'd begun to wonder whether Carolus wasn't more to be envied.

Callista was a different matter. She wouldn't believe the official story of Phillip's demise, or his supposed crimes, but then, she probably wouldn't let anyone know what she really thought.

Beautiful, willful, and devastatingly intelligent, Callista had managed to hide her talents for years behind whimsy and caprice, which Phillip had eventually learned were cultivated traits to keep their mother and grandfather at bay. Daring and mercurial, Callista went her own way and always had. At one point, Satrina had hoped to use her daughter to cement a matrimonial alliance, but Phillip guessed that would come to absolutely nothing. Callie had never done anything except what she wanted to do.

In Phillip's absence, his mother had probably tried to train Callista to assume his position as heir, which had no doubt resulted in spectacular fireworks. The idea almost amused him.

Almost.

But it was impossible not to feel a tiny surge of regret as he was forced to confront the fact that, when he died, no one would know he was gone. No matter what happened, even if he ended up trapped on this alien moon forever, no one would be affected. No one would mourn. No one would really care.

"Preparing for entry," he heard Killian say.

The ship shuddered. The hum of the drive stuttered briefly, then faded.

Killian slapped a button on his console. "Dinah, what's going on? Why are we powering down?"

"Power drain, Captain," the words crackled into the silence on the bridge. "We were running perfectly up until..."

The communication suddenly cut off as a jolt shook the ship.

Aidan staggered, and just barely managed to catch Seph as she fell towards him.

"Rill?" Killian snapped the word, whether angry or nervous Aidan couldn't tell.

"Energy weapon," she called out, her fingers flying over her console. "Scanning the source..." Her words trailed off into muttering, finally culminating in a shocked sounding "Captain!" Her eyes were wide, panicked. "The weapon is one of ours! It's coming from the moon!"

Aidan wrapped an arm around Seph's waist and braced himself against the nearest bulkhead. It was incredibly distracting to have her so close and to realize that she wasn't pulling away. If anything, the opposite.

"Don't want you to fall," he murmured in her ear, and she nodded, wide-eyed and a little breathless.

"Someone get the communications back up," Killian snarled. "Let them know it's us!"

"I'm trying, Captain," Rill confirmed, "but they're ignoring us! I don't understand why they fired before scanning our drives."

Killian turned to Harvey. "Are the weapons ready?"

A careful listener could have heard a hair fall to the deck in the silence that followed.

"Yes." Harvey wore his usual grim and forbidding expression as he shot a sideways look at his captain. "All systems prepared for battle."

"Has anyone on the surface identified themselves?"

"Negative, Captain."

"Then we prepare to fire." Killian's expression was carved from solid ice.

"Captain, we can't fire on our own." Disbelief filled Rill's voice.

"And our own people wouldn't be firing on us," Killian said sternly. "If our base is compromised, we have to destroy it."

"Captain," Dinah said over the comm, "this could be no more than a precaution..." and it sounded like she meant to say more, but never had the chance.

A blinding flash struck the ship, knocking it sideways and sending it into a spin. Aidan and Seph were thrown violently to the deck, while the other three slumped in their seats. Harvey slid all the way to the floor, while Rill folded forward over her console.

Aidan struggled to his knees as the *Fancy* continued in a slow, death-spiral towards the surface of the moon. The motion was disorienting, and he had to shake off dizziness so he could focus on Seph and make sure she wasn't hurt.

She was conscious at least, and rolled to her side before sitting up. There was blood on her temple, but only a small amount, and though pain formed creases at the corners of her mouth, her eyes were hard. Determined.

Satisfied that she would be okay for the moment, Aidan looked around the bridge with a sense of shock and dismay.

The weapon, whatever it was, appeared to have incapacitated every one of the crew. Killian alone remained in his chair, his eyes dazed, blood trickling from his ears and the corners of his mouth. He was struggling to reach the controls. Fighting for command of his own body.

Aidan pushed to his feet and staggered across the deck to the pirate's side. "What happened?" he demanded. "What is this?"

"Energy attack." Killian's words were slurred. "Fried our nanotech. They knew..."

"Did your own people do this?"

Killian began to cough, and blood flew from his mouth.

"If you can't fly, then help me right the ship," Aidan commanded. "Tell me how to land it."

The pirate pulled himself up with enormous effort and slapped both hands on the console in front of him. "Most like the new Hastings cruisers," he said, gasping for air and smearing blood across the screens as he unlocked them. "Pressure based. Light touch. Landing sensors..." He grasped Aidan's hand and pressed it onto one of the monitors until a blue light flashed. "Giving you full access," he slurred, before slumping forward over the screen, his eyes closed.

Seph appeared on Killian's other side, pale and sweating, but on her feet. She grabbed the unconscious pirate under his armpits, pulled him out of the chair and eased him to the deck. "I've got him," she said tersely. "You just figure out how to fly this thing. I really don't want to crash today."

Aidan took the captain's chair, trying to ignore the blood spattered across the floor and the console, struggling to remember the last time he'd sat in a pilot's chair. It had been three or four years. Not since he'd taken his new personal cruiser out for its maiden voyage.

He'd been a fair pilot, not so very long ago, but he'd never tried to fly something the size of the *Fancy* alone.

"I don't know if I can keep us from crashing," he told Seph coolly, as his fingers flew over the command screen, trying to boot up the systems. "You might want to leave the pirate to fend for himself and find a seat. You'll stand a better chance of survival."

He thought he could feel her glaring at him.

"I'm a medic, Aidan," she said, her voice tight and angry. "I don't leave an injured man... alien... whatever. It's my job to keep him alive, and it's your job to keep *me* alive, so how about you focus on that and I'll do what I have to."

Aidan grinned fiercely at the bite in her tone. Seph wasn't about to just lay down and give up without a fight, so neither would he. Not this time.

Maybe he could do this. Maybe he couldn't. The odds were decidedly against them as they rode an out-of-control alien ship towards the surface of an unknown moon populated by apparently hostile forces. Their only allies could be dead, and no one else in the galaxy knew where they were.

It should have seemed hopeless, but for the first time in two years, Aidan felt suddenly, startlingly alive.

THIRTEEN

WHEN AIDAN WAS A BOY, one of his tutors had taken him to a mountain resort where they'd spent a few days flying old-fashioned contraptions called hang-gliders, learning to read the wind currents as a metaphor for something or other. He couldn't remember what the lesson had been about, or even how to fly a glider, but he did remember something their instructor had said right before they ran off the side of the mountain and entrusted themselves to the flimsy polymer frame of their glider—"Any landing you walk away from is a good landing."

He clung to that memory as he fought to steady the ship, slowing her speed and straightening her trajectory as the moon's atmosphere fought back—heating the hull and buffeting them continually off-course.

They were going to walk away from this, he and Seph. He wouldn't let it be otherwise. He had failed at so many things in his life, but not this.

The glowing dot on his screen beckoned, taunting him with the vision of a safe landing site—if only he could reach it. Safety was, of course, an illusion. Even if he landed the ship, whoever had taken a pot-shot at them in the first place was still down there.

And then there was the matter of the Wyrdane crew. They were still alive, but not by much. Seph had confirmed that they were unconscious, with slow, weak heartbeats, icy skin, and barely discernible breathing. More like a coma. Blood leaked slowly from their noses, mouths, and even ears, and Seph had been able to do nothing but ensure that they weren't injured further by the motion of the ship.

When the wind currents gave him a moment, Aidan activated the forward viewscreen, which immediately filled with the murky haze of the moon's atmosphere. It was thick and dark, like storm clouds, and it took another half a minute for them to break clear and catch their first glimpse of the moon's surface.

"Homey," was Seph's dry comment from where she sat on the floor next to Killian, braced between the navigator's console and the communications chair. "I can see why this place has never been explored."

A rocky plain greeted them, pitted and scored with fissures and cracks, gray-green in color, and extending as far as they could see. No structures were visible, nor was there any other sign of habitation. What light managed to filter through the thick atmosphere was dim and eerie, and Aidan was forced to swallow considerable misgivings as he did his best to aim the ship for the glowing dot that indicated the landing pad near the Wyrdane base.

"Are we sure this is the right uninhabited moon?" Seph asked. "I'd hate to crash on the wrong one."

"We aren't going to crash," Aidan answered through gritted teeth. "I have control of our descent... We just might miss the landing site by a bit."

"How much is a bit?" Seph asked.

He spared her a sarcastic glance. "If you're going to judge my piloting skills, maybe you'd like to come over here and do better?"

She grinned, but the expression was taut and filled with tension. "Tell you what—if you crash, I'll be sure to explain how I could have done it better."

"I'm sure your crashing skills are second to none."

Aidan abruptly cut the engines and adjusted the glide to level out, activating the landing sensors at the last second. The thrusters fired, then failed. The *Fancy* dropped towards the surface like a dying bird, leaving Aidan's stomach in his throat and the taste of desperation in his mouth.

He heard only a brief yelp of surprise from Seph, but he was too busy to reassure her. An engine reset failed to engage the sensors, so he shut down the entire panel and bolted across the deck to the navigator's station, vaulting over a prone body to boot up the screens with desperate haste. When the symbol for the landing systems appeared he hit it with three fingers at once and was thrown forward when the ship's freefall came to an abrupt end.

Dropping into the chair, he gradually eased off on the power as the ship moved closer and closer to the moon's surface, ending its descent with a jolt and an ominous grinding noise as it settled to the ground.

Neither of them moved for a few moments, as if they hesitated to believe that it was over and they had survived. And for the moment, at least, it seemed the ship had survived as well. Her deck was tilted slightly to one side, but the lights were still on, and all the internal systems were up.

Seph sat on the floor, staring at him with her mouth slightly open.

"I was wrong," she said finally, taking a deep breath and closing her eyes. "Your crash-landings are the best."

Almost limp with relief, Aidan crossed the deck to collapse to the floor next to her. "Damn straight," he said. "Is this a good time to tell you I've never landed a ship of this size before?"

She elbowed him in the arm. "*Never* would have been a great time to tell me that."

Aidan realized suddenly that he was laughing. He'd never been so relieved to be alive. Reaching out abruptly, he grabbed Seph's hand and pulled her towards him. She fell willingly into his arms, so he wrapped them around her and pressed a kiss into her hair. He didn't even realize what he'd done until she pulled back slightly and stared at him, wide-eyed and breathless.

"Aidan, are you okay?"

"I don't think I've ever been better," he told her honestly, locking his eyes on hers. "You're alive, I'm alive, and right now I don't care about anything else."

Her cheeks went pink, but a slight smile curved her lips as she gazed back at him. "So is this a good time to remind you that we're on a moon with someone who wants to kill us and all of our allies are in a coma?"

He chuckled but decided not to let go. Having her this close felt like heaven, and he wasn't ready to walk back into hell just yet. "I don't care what you say as long as I don't have to get up."

To his surprise, she laughed and laid her head back on his shoulder, relaxing into him with a trust that left him breathless.

"Then I'll go ahead and tell you that I have no idea what's going to happen to the crew. If Killian was right and their nanotech is fried, it could mean that they won't be able to survive it. Or it might mean that they just need time. They could essentially just be human now and have to live or die by normal human means. I just don't know, and I won't until I get to medical and hopefully find that the equipment has survived and I can figure out how to use it."

"What do you need from me?"

She sighed. "I wish I knew." Her whole body grew tense against his. "Do you think we'll be safe here? Is the ship secure?"

He shook his head. "I don't know. If the attack came from their own people, they probably have access codes to the ship. I don't even know for sure where the landing access ports are, so I should probably find them sooner rather than later."

"I don't want to split up," Seph confessed, "but I think we'll have to. And eventually, if they don't break in, we'll have no choice but to go out."

"Unless we can get the ship off the ground without repairs."

"But we may need access to whatever technology they have here if we're going to help the crew."

"We wouldn't even know how to use it," Aidan pointed out.

Seph pulled away, sat up, and wrapped her arms around her knees. "They may still have allies here who could help us. We at least have to try."

"No, we really don't," Aidan growled. "Have you forgotten that we didn't ask to be involved? They forced us into this."

"Have you forgotten that there may be an invasion fleet headed for Earth to destroy it?" she shot back. "If we can't revive Killian, Earth may be doomed, so we have to do everything possible to keep him alive."

The fate of Earth—and Aidan's part in it—wasn't really something he wanted to argue about right then. There was a lot to be done, and numerous obstacles to overcome before their return became much of an issue. And it might not be an issue at all if Killian didn't survive. Just as Aidan's true identity wouldn't be an issue.

If the entire crew was dead, Phillip could die with them. Seph would never find out because there would be no one to tell her.

Aidan had done many unsavory things in his life, but the thoughts running through his head at that moment probably put them all to shame. For a handful of seconds, he considered it—ensuring that Killian and his crew never regained consciousness, thereby dooming Earth to destruction so that Seph would never learn the truth. Never know what he was truly capable of.

But if he did? He would lose her anyway. Her family's death would destroy her. And at his core, he was still the man who had accepted revilement and exile to save Lindmark from descending into war. No matter what he'd told Killian, he couldn't abandon it now, however much he might want to.

No, he would have to help her. Have to face the inevitable moment when she would know the truth and hate him for it.

There was no way for him to keep his Persephone and no number of pomegranate seeds that would bring her back to him in the end.

So he reached out, wrapped a hand around the back of her neck, and pulled her close until their foreheads touched.

"I'll help you," he said softly. "Just tell me what you need me to do."

———

Seph couldn't remember ever feeling so utterly exhausted. Not even on Daragh, when she and her fellow colonists had gone days without sleep as they fended off attacks from hostile aliens in the middle of an untamed wilderness.

But she learned a lot in the tense hours after their near-crash landing. With the access Killian had given Aidan, they discovered that the ship had been retrofitted far enough to pass human inspection. They were able to access most of her systems, and while there was plenty of baffling alien tech, there were workarounds available for most of what they needed to do.

Most important of which was assessing the condition of the four Wyrdane crew. The bio-scanner had confirmed internal bleeding on all of them but could offer no further explanation for the persistent loss of consciousness. It had to be their nanotech, but Seph had no knowledge or ability that could aid them in that case.

She also had no idea how long they could last without oxygen or fluids. Their best bet was the sleep tank, but since she had no idea whether it would work, she was hesitant to try it on Killian. She also didn't care to try it on Rill or Dinah—if it did help, she hoped whichever of their alien allies regained consciousness first wouldn't be quite so inclined to react with distrust. Or, in Rill's case, outright revulsion.

In the end, she chose Harvey, and prayed desperately that she remembered correctly everything he'd taught her about operating the tank. Once she'd submerged him (with Aidan's help) and programmed the nanoplasm, she spent the next several hours making the others as comfortable as she could on the available beds, while Aidan disappeared on his own errands.

When she could think of literally nothing else to be done, Seph left medical, trying to clear her mind of the image of the three people she'd been unable to help. She hated to leave them, hated feeling helpless, but knew too little of their physiology to risk experimentation. Their only hope was to find a few of the Wyrdane still alive—including someone who would know how to use the technology that enabled them to heal so quickly under normal circumstances.

Seph was plodding towards the lift when a voice came across the ship-wide comm system, making her jump halfway across the corridor.

"Seph, meet me in the mess."

Pressing a hand to her chest and breathing deeply, Seph set off to meet Aidan, determined to kick him in the shin for scaring her.

———

He was already sitting at a table with two plates of food and two handhelds when she arrived.

"You look like something tried to eat you and spit you back out," he observed, passing her a plate with a wary expression.

"Maybe it did," she said wearily, slumping into a seat across from him with a groan. She was just about to take a bite when she realized what he'd said.

"Aidan." Their eyes locked. "Where is it?"

"Where is what?"

"The cat-monster...thing. Its name is Errol, by the way."

He sat back and put down the handheld he'd been fiddling with, looking anything but happy to be reminded of the beast's existence. "Must be in crew quarters somewhere. If it survived."

"We have to find him," she insisted. "He's alone, and he could be hurt."

The look he gave her probably would have sent anyone who didn't know him running from the room. "You want to rescue the thing that almost killed me?"

"It's just an animal, Aidan. It didn't know any better."

"I wouldn't be too sure," Aidan replied grimly. "It's Killian's alien pet. It probably reads minds and shoots lasers out of its eyeballs."

"All the more reason not to leave it alone and frightened," Seph argued. "You really want it shooting lasers through the ship's hull?"

"I'm not letting you anywhere near it," he said flatly, gripping the edge of the table and narrowing his eyes.

"Better than letting it anywhere near you," she retorted. "Anyway, Killian introduced us while you were unconscious. The thing actually waved at me, so it shouldn't view me as a threat. You, on the other hand?" She smirked a little, and sat back to watch him do battle with his instincts. For some reason, he felt compelled to protect her, and this circumstance had to be pushing all of his buttons.

"You at least have to let me try," she said.

He scowled. "Fine. After you eat. And after I find a laser rifle so I can kill it if it tries anything."

"Fair enough." Seph pulled a plate towards her and contemplated the food Aidan had found. It was basically some sort of protein-loaf. Edible, but not terribly attractive or tasty.

"Please tell me you've had more luck than me," she begged after she'd choked down the first bite. "Any more information? Any signs of life from the moon?"

"Plenty," he responded grimly. "Someone out there has been trying to hack the ship's systems using old access codes. The computer recognizes them as legitimate but outdated and keeps asking for permission to grant entry."

"And are you sure they're enemies?"

"I'm not sure about anything except that they're not coming out of hiding. There's no movement on the surface, and no one has made any attempt to breach the access hatches on the lower hull."

Seph poked at her food, simultaneously starving and too tired to want to go through the effort of chewing and swallowing the unappetizing mess. "So you think they're hostile, whoever they are."

"I didn't say that." Aidan picked up a handheld and offered it to her. "But I was hoping you could look at this and tell me if it is what I think it is."

A complex map looked back at her, with several glowing dots on it.

"It's a survey of the surface that goes down about fifty meters. I figured out how to get it to show life signs, but I couldn't fine-tune it enough to identify them, beyond a basic assessment of density and temperature."

Seph glanced at the specs scrolling down the side of the screen as she pressed on each glowing dot in turn. "There are two types here," she noted. "They're all about the same size, but three of them are denser, and have a higher body temperature."

"And the others?" Aidan leaned forward intently.

She felt the hairs on her arms rise as a chill of dread swept through her body. "The other seven are human," she confirmed.

"There are no other ships nearby," Aidan told her. "Not even crash sites. I did a thorough sweep, so if Killian really does have another ship, it must be underground."

"Then how did they get here?"

Aidan began to look grim. "You remember what you told me about the pirates they took from the *Erin's Dream?*"

"Yes?"

"What if they didn't actually execute them?"

Seph thought about it. "You're thinking there's a possibility that they may have taken over the base."

"It's the only thing that makes sense. I think they've left the Wyrdane crew alive because they need them, but I also think they tried to kill us.

They may not be certain whether they've succeeded, given that we landed without crashing, so if they do gain access to the ship, they'll be coming in armed and ready to kill."

Seph shuddered. "If you're right, can they get in without our help?"

"I don't know." Aidan leaned over his handheld again. "I also don't know how long they'll wait before they decide to finish the job and just blow the ship up and us with it. They tried to crash it, so they must not need it for whatever they're planning."

A jolt of terror struck Seph, leaving a sick feeling in her stomach. "We can't let that happen. We have to save Killian and get him back to Earth."

Aidan set down the handheld and met her eyes intently. "The only way to do that is to leave the ship. We would have to find and kill the pirates—if that's who's done this—before they can destroy the *Fancy*. We also can't allow them to destroy the base. Whatever tech they have here is probably the only hope for reviving the crew."

Seph jerked a nod. "Understood. We need a battle plan." She tapped her fingers on the table. "Can you tell if the air is breathable?"

Aidan's eyes widened. "You're really contemplating this?"

"You said it yourself. It's the only way."

"Seph, I need you to listen carefully." His eyes bored into hers. "Neither of us are soldiers. I'm a bartender, and you're a medic. I can handle myself in a fight, but I'm no match for a gang of professional killers."

Seph bit her lip and tried to gauge his mood. He'd proven changeable since they'd left Concord Five, one minute cold and distant, the next swearing he would kill anyone who hurt her. There had been a few moments she would have sworn he'd thought about kissing her, and a few where she thought he would prefer never to see her again. But she had to believe that whatever she decided to do, in the end, he would have her back.

"Actually," she informed him, with a bit of a grin, "have you forgotten that I used to be part of the LSF? I was a soldier, even if I wasn't exactly the commando type."

Aidan's face went blank and neutral. "I hadn't forgotten," he said.

"And we do have some advantages," she went on. "They don't know we're alive in here. They're bound to expect that if anyone is still breathing, they're Wyrdane and they're incapacitated. There are only seven of them, so if we can ambush them, we stand a chance. Have you found any weapons while you searched the ship?"

"A few," he admitted, "but I doubt they've seen much use. Killian probably just kept them around for the look of the thing. But weapons or not, you honestly expect the two of us to ambush a bunch of pirates?"

"It isn't like I want to," she said. "But we have limited options. And I think you're more dangerous than you give yourself credit for."

"We're dead the moment we leave the safety of this ship," Aidan contended. "We can't assume they don't have the same equipment we do. They could easily be scanning us right now and making plans to blow us back past the atmosphere."

"All the more reason to move quickly," Seph countered. "Look, I need to find a way to help Killian and his crew. No matter what you might think of them, I can't just leave them to die. That's not who I am. We can figure out what comes next after that, but you have to admit, we can't just stay here either. Not forever. One way or another, we have to leave the ship, and in order to do that, we have to do something about whoever shot at us."

Aidan looked at her steadily. "Or we could let these aliens deal with their own problems. We could leave Killian and his crew here, take off, and go somewhere else. Find a new planet. Even if these Bhandecki are real, they won't be able to find us."

Seph's mouth fell open slightly as she surveyed him with a distinct sense of shock. Was he serious? And if he was, what was he thinking? What did he mean when he said "us"?

"You're joking," she said finally. Firmly. And if he wasn't, she didn't want to know about it. Didn't want to hear that he was actually cold-hearted enough to abandon four living breathing *people*—no matter whether they were human or not—just to avoid a confrontation. Not even if he was saying something about his feelings for her that part of her desperately wanted to hear. No matter how much she cared for him, she wasn't the sort of person who would burn down the world for the sake of love.

Love, or confused fascination, which was probably a more accurate representation of her feelings.

"I can't do it," she said doggedly, shoving aside her doubts, "and I won't. And I refuse to believe that you would do it either. You talk like you have ice water in your veins, but your actions say otherwise, and I won't accept that you're actually cruel enough to sacrifice so many lives for a selfish reason. We're going to find a way to save the Wyrdane, and then we're going to find a way to save Earth. If you don't want to, that's fine, but I expect you to respect me enough not to try to stop me."

Aidan's gaze was fixed on hers, intent and serious.

"Because if you do," she warned, narrowing her eyes, "I can always find a tray full of beer mugs."

"I'm supposed to be so afraid of you breaking my nose that I'm willing to charge barehanded into a nest of armed and angry pirates?" The irritating man actually started to smile. It was just the tiniest curve at the corner of his mouth, but for Aidan, it was practically a grin.

"It would certainly be helpful if you were," she said, shrugging and smiling back ruefully. "Or you could do it because you don't want me to die."

He sighed and folded his hands on the table. "I did say I would try to keep you from dying, didn't I? What do you have in mind?"

Seph smile turned anything but friendly. "I thought you'd never ask."

FOURTEEN

IT WAS NOT the most inviting place to call home. Through the plate of her helmet, Seph could see for miles across the rough, rocky surface of the moon under a dismal gray sky and wondered for the tiniest instant whether Aidan had been right. Maybe they should have left. Maybe this was hopeless.

"You don't get to chicken out now," Aidan's voice said into her earpiece. "I'm carrying enough explosives to destroy this entire moon, so you'd better be prepared to do your part in this plan."

She smiled weakly, even though he couldn't see it. "You know I'll do my best," she assured him. "I'm good with directions, so I'm positive I'll be able to find the base from the positions of the life signs on that map. I just need to find a way in, and it'll be up to them to help us after that."

He reached out suddenly and grabbed her shoulder. "Just stay safe. Remember, the air is technically breathable but not great for your lungs over a long period. If you have to remove your helmet, you'll live, but don't leave it off too long. If you don't hear the explosion, go back to the ship. We can always try again later, and this isn't worth your life. And Seph..." he paused. "I don't think I need to explain why it would be a bad idea to let them capture you."

She shook her head and swallowed a surge of nausea. "Same goes for you."

The forehead of his helmet pressed to hers, and she saw his eyes behind the faceplate, cool and grim. "But if they do capture you, I'll get you out. No matter what I have to do, I won't abandon you, and I won't leave you there. Do you believe me?"

Seph nodded once, sharp and jerky. "Yes."

"Good." He paused, as if he was about to stay something else, and then pulled back. "Let's get this over with."

He strode off, stumbling occasionally on the rough terrain, and Seph almost called him back. There was something horribly lonely about watching him walk away, leaving her to her own part in this ramshackle plan of theirs.

What if it didn't work? What if she never saw him again?

But it would work. It had to. All of Earth was depending on them, whether its inhabitants knew it or not.

Setting off in the opposite direction, Seph went looking for a way into the hidden Wyrdane base.

They'd seen no visible signs of their attackers since their landing. Wyrdane or human, they remained beneath the surface, probably—in Seph's opinion—waiting for the crew of the *Fancy* to die before they approached the ship. If it was indeed the pirates who had shot them out of the sky, they would know exactly how dangerous Killian and his crew were and would not care to run the risk of confronting them again. It was this caution that she was relying on to aid her own part in this rescue plan. She was also counting on them not having the ability to scan the moon's surface for signs of life.

Thus far, she'd seen nothing to indicate that there were any native species the Wyrdane might have needed to scan for. No animal life at all, either large or small. If that was the case, Killian probably wouldn't have bothered setting up a surface scanner, but if he had, she would stand out like a beacon, and her part in this operation might end up being short and painful. And if they'd missed the signs of any local beasties? She prayed that, unlike Errol, they wouldn't have a taste for human.

They'd never found Aidan's nemesis, though they'd searched every compartment on the ship but one. Killian's quarters wouldn't allow them access, no matter how many times they tried to get around security. Seph tried not to worry about the giant blue cat-thing, but she was soft-hearted enough to wonder whether he would know what was happening or would be feeling alone and afraid. At the very least, he could easily starve to death if they couldn't revive Killian soon, a thought that gave Seph renewed energy as she made her way carefully across the rocky ground.

The surface of the moon was liberally strewn with caves, and it was within one of these cave systems that the Wyrdane had evidently established their base. What Seph had no way of knowing was how well they'd hidden it, or how thoroughly they'd sealed it off. While the air on the moon was only mostly breathable for humans, the Wyrdane wouldn't be likely to care, considering how quickly they healed. It was possible that they hadn't bothered to use airlocks to secure their base.

In fact, she was hoping that was the case. If the base was too well sealed, it might well be impossible for her to gain access.

About an hour of exploration netted her precisely what she was looking for—a natural tunnel with a large enough opening to allow her entrance. Once she was underground, the cave system proved to be as extensive as she'd noted on the shipboard scan, with tunnels upon tunnels rising and falling and crossing one another with alarming frequency.

Fortunately, she'd been telling Aidan the truth about her sense of location. Despite her discomfort with enclosed spaces, she'd always had an excellent head for directions and had no difficulty retracing her steps whenever a particular tunnel became impassable.

It was cool underground, though not cold, and the suit kept her comfortably warm, possibly even too warm as the exertion of clambering up and down the various tunnels began to grow wearying. She'd just stopped to open her faceplate and take a drink from her water bottle when she finally heard a sound that wasn't her own footsteps.

She heard voices.

They were faint and far away. Sounds probably carried quite a distance in these tunnels, but Seph took every possible precaution as she crept towards them, irrationally relieved not to be alone, even if her company was of the violently unfriendly variety.

Despite her caution, she almost stumbled into them—two rough, bearded men standing in a cavern, smoking.

Her first thought was to wonder where they'd come from. There were no signs of habitation, only an empty cavern.

Her second thought was to wonder what on Earth they'd found to smoke—there wasn't likely to be tobacco anywhere in that part of the galaxy.

Seph settled in to wait them out, and fortunately, they didn't make her wait for long. Their conversation was almost as incomprehensible as it was coarse, and she'd had enough well before both men snubbed out their makeshift smokes and made their way to a corner of the cavern. After they stood there for a moment, in front of a seemingly solid wall, the rock lit up, a doorway opened, and they both disappeared.

Ahah.

Seph waited a solid half hour before following them, certain that someone else could be about to take a smoke break at any moment. But they didn't, and the door was not locked. A yellow light pad just beside the entryway illuminated her briefly before the door opened for her just as it had for the pirates—if that was indeed who they were. Taking a deep, steadying breath, Seph stepped across the threshold into the interior of the Wyrdane base.

A dull blue metal lined the curved walls, with occasional bulges and recesses that made it look as though they'd poured an artificial surface over the original cave tunnels without smoothing them out. Light was produced by tracks in the floor and ceiling, where glowing liquid flowed and swirled. The lighting it produced was dim, but adequate, though Seph couldn't determine the energy source.

Overall, the installation seemed well-designed and solidly built, with ventilation shafts and filters integrated into the tops of the tunnels. Rooms appeared off the main passageways, most with doors but some without, some leading to artificially constructed spaces, while others opened on natural caverns within the rock.

The base wasn't terribly large—at least, not if Aidan's readouts were correct. Large enough, hopefully, for her to hide from seven pirates while she looked for the areas where the Wyrdane were being kept. Small enough, she noted, for seven pirates to have done a thorough job of trashing it. There was refuse everywhere, piles of broken equipment, and an overwhelmingly putrid odor that Seph guessed Killian would never have tolerated from his own crew.

She opened one particular door, shock rifle held ready, and backed out again, gagging and retching in horror. It appeared that not everyone had survived the hostile takeover of the base, and it had been long enough since they died that she couldn't identify the origin of the bodies stacked in the dimly lit cavern.

At one point, footsteps echoed along the corridor ahead of her, and Seph was forced to duck into a side-chamber. It had been someone's bedroom—with not only the expected furniture but a few personal items as well. There was clothing lying on the bed, some sort of device on the table beside it, and what appeared to be a sculpture hanging from the wall.

Was whoever had lived there dead? Or merely imprisoned?

When she was sure the owners of the footsteps were gone, Seph steadied her shaking fingers, took a fresh grip on her rifle, and opened the door—

A bear of a man stood in the corridor. Shock and confusion paralyzed her for a moment too long, giving him a chance to growl and swing at her head with one meaty fist. Seph was forced to dodge back into the room where she tripped over the end of the bed and fell against the wall.

"I told them there was someone here," Harvey said, advancing towards her with a squinty-eyed leer. "That ship wasn't as dead as they thought. And here you are... a purty little piece too."

She tried to stand up, tried to tell herself that she was imagining things. This wasn't Harvey. This man was filthy, stinking and unshaven. Harvey was back on the ship in the sleep tank. She'd put him there herself.

But by the time her brain caught up with her eyes, there was no time left to react, and he knocked her down with a single slap to the side of her helmet. Seph hit the floor and rolled, came up with her rifle in her hands and fired it point blank into his chest. The charge had been dialed to maximum, and he dropped without a sound, his eyes rolled back in his head, his arms and legs twitching.

Her chest heaved for a few tense moments as she waited for him to get back up, but he stayed down. Part of her wanted to check for a heartbeat, but another part of her was repulsed at the idea of touching him.

He had Harvey's height and frame, and Harvey's face, but otherwise, nothing was the same. He was even missing most of his teeth. Plus, he would have killed her if he could, or worse. Harvey might be an unpleasant curmudgeon, but she didn't think he would ever have hurt her.

Seph repeated it to herself—she had not shot Harvey. But she nearly gagged as she realized what had actually happened.

Aidan had been right about the identity of their enemies. For whatever reason, Dinah had not told Seph the whole truth—Killian's crew had not taken all their DNA samples from the dead colonists on the *Erin's Dream*. At least some of them had taken genetic material from the pirates who had murdered the colonists, and now the captive pirates had somehow gained control of the Wyrdane base.

As she left Harvey's doppelgänger on the floor and closed the door behind her, Seph decided that it might be past time to rethink her life choices. Once again, she'd found adventure, and, much like the last time, it was perplexing, uncomfortable, and downright terrifying.

But she couldn't quit now, so she swallowed her revulsion at her discovery and moved onward with a purposeful step. She was going to find the three surviving Wyrdane. They were going to defeat the remaining pirates and save Killian. And humanity was going to survive.

She'd gone two steps further down the corridor when the entire base went dark. A concussive roar battered her ears, and the ground began to shake beneath her.

Aidan.

Seph grinned in the dark. He'd really done it. He'd set off the explosives they'd removed from one of Killian's shipboard missiles.

She heard shouts as the lights came back on, but no footsteps or loud voices came in her direction. Aidan had hoped that the pirates would abandon their base to investigate the explosion, allowing her to explore unimpeded. But that would leave him exposed and vulnerable, alone on the surface of the planet with no shelter and nowhere to hide. Assuming he'd survived that explosion.

Of course he'd survived. He was careful. Calculating. Controlled. He was fine, and he would find her.

Seph repeated those words to herself as she crept deeper into the base, searching for a corridor that would take her in the right direction and hopefully lead her to the captive Wyrdane.

He'd underestimated the blast radius. As Aidan picked himself up off the ground, his ears ringing and blood trickling down his neck, he cursed himself for potentially endangering both Seph and the people they were hoping to save.

The missile they'd dismantled had been a human design, one Aidan was somewhat familiar with. Few spaceships carried any form of weaponry, so only two corporations had devoted any energy to developing space-capable armaments. One of those was Lindmark, and he'd approved the plans for Killian's missile himself nearly five years ago.

But he was in no way an explosives expert and hadn't been able to remember the exact specs of each of the thirty individual sections of the missile's payload. So he'd chosen to detonate two of them when one would have been more than enough.

He hoped he hadn't managed to damage the *Fancy*. They might still need to make a quick escape, and while Killian claimed to have another ship, there was still no sign of it. It seemed reasonable to assume that if the pirates could have left this grim and barren moon at any time in the past months, they would have done so, which meant that wherever that ship was, it was most likely either inaccessible or inoperable.

Shaking off his dizziness, Aidan jogged off as quickly as the terrain permitted, at an angle to the Wyrdane base, hoping to avoid whatever team was sent out to investigate.

"Seph?" They hadn't had an opportunity to test their helmet comms over any kind of distance, and even if they had...

A burst of static was the only reply, but that didn't mean Seph had been discovered. The blast had probably knocked out his suit's comm-tech, and possibly every other piece of comm-tech within a five-mile radius.

Later he would blame the suit, and the disorientation caused by the blast, for hampering his ability to hear approaching footsteps. But whatever the reason for his distraction, the shock of an energy weapon hit him in the back without warning, throwing him several yards through the air to smash into a small rise in the rocky terrain. It hurt—and knocked the wind out of him—but the helmet protected him from the worst of the blow, leaving him fully conscious and fighting for breath when three figures came into view, all bristling with weapons as they loomed over him. The trio wore filthy, tattered clothing and patched together helmets that hid their expressions, but Aidan didn't need to see their faces to feel their hostility.

"Human," one of them growled. "Looks like at least something survived the crash. Maybe the ship's in good enough shape, and the captain will let you live after all. Damn fool move, firing before they even hit atmosphere."

"It will work," another one promised, almost eagerly. "And now that we have a hostage, we can get the codes. Even if any of them are alive in there, they won't last long."

"We don't even know if the weapon did anything," the first one grumbled. "We've only tested it at short range."

"It worked," the third man said coldly. "The captain made sure of that. Let's get this one back to base and get to work on him. I don't intend to spend one second more than I have to in this god-forsaken hellhole."

He removed a small handheld device from the recesses of his clothing, held it to Aidan's neck and pushed a button. The device activated with a deceptively simple click, and before Aidan could register what he'd seen, every muscle in his body seized up with painful intensity.

A nerve disruptor. He couldn't move, couldn't breathe, and wasn't screaming only because he couldn't control his lungs enough to pull in the air to make a sound. Agony coursed down his spine to the tips of his fingers and toes, arching his back and tearing at his joints until he was sure they must be wrenched from their sockets.

The weapon had been banned on Earth for over fifty years, but like many other banned items, they persisted and even evolved in the shadows of the criminal underworld. At their best, they created unimaginable pain. At their worst, they left their targets drooling and unable to speak or maintain bodily functions.

As two of the pirates picked him up by the arms and began to drag him over the rocks back towards their base, only one thought remained at the forefront of Aidan's pain-ravaged mind.

He had to kill them before they could use it on Seph.

———

She finally found what she was looking for in a side tunnel, behind a door that initially refused to open. It was a human-style door with an ordinary lock plate, and under other circumstances, Seph might have turned away. But she knew she was in the right area, and she was running out of places to search. Plus, it had been nearly five minutes since the blast, and time was not on her side.

So instead of moving on, she kicked the lock plate until it broke, fried the internal circuits with her shock rifle, and then pried the door back with her bare hands.

The interior of the room was dark, so she pulled a light patch out of the pocket of her suit and slapped it to her palm.

The glow lit up the room, sending a jolt of adrenaline through her as she took in the unmistakable outline of eight makeshift cells, three of which contained a battered, human-shaped body.

With no idea where the main light controls might be, Seph played her light nervously over the apparently unconscious forms, wondering whether she'd come all this way for nothing. Were they dead? Or had they succumbed to the same energy blast that had incapacitated the *Fancy's* crew?

She took a step closer to the cells, then another, her heartbeat loud inside the confines of her helmet.

"You must be new." The harsh, grating voice nearly sent Seph racing back out the door. She whirled and pointed her palm at the last cell on the right, where the body on the floor hadn't moved except to turn its head. Eyes gleamed as they reflected the glow of the light and fixed on her with predatory intensity.

Seph took a few cautious steps closer. The person on the floor of the cell watched her until she was within three paces, then uncoiled with inhuman speed, hitting the mesh panel of the cell with bruising force and a snarl of hatred.

Jerking back with a yelp, Seph barely kept from pressing the trigger on her shock-rifle out of sheer panic.

"I'm not with the pirates," she snapped, lowering the rifle and glaring at the apparition now leaning against the front of his cell, watching her hungrily. "I'm human, and I came here on the *Fancy*, in company with a Wyrdane captain and crew."

"Are they dead?" the rusty voice asked. "Did the weapon kill them, or did it just destroy their nanotech?"

"Last I saw, they aren't quite dead, but I don't think they have long. I left them on board the ship to look for help."

"Did you kill the pirates?"

"Not yet." She swallowed and reached up to unseal her helmet. "There are only two of us left. Both of us are human, and we needed allies."

As she carefully lifted off her helmet, hoping the air filters were still functional, the man in the cell began to laugh.

"As you can see," he said with a wave at the other cells, "we're not going to be much help."

They'd all been alive when Aidan scanned the base, so hopefully, they would stay that way. "I take it the pirates fried your nanotech too," Seph said wearily, shaking out her curls and hoping Aidan was faring better than she was at that moment. "Killian said you had more. Is it still secure? Or have the pirates destroyed it?"

The man shrugged, leaning on the mesh front of his cell for balance. "If the pirates found it, I'm sure they destroyed it, but I've been in here too long to know for sure. Let me out of here, and I'll see what I can find."

Seph looked at him carefully and throttled her unease. "I'd love to let you out," she said, "but I need to know that you've accepted me as an ally."

The battered man laughed, and it didn't sound particularly sane. "Well, it's not as if I've had a host of offers. We've been in these cells for months, and once they perfected their weapon, I'd given up hope we'd ever get out. You open the door, and I think you'll find we can be the very best of friends."

It wasn't as if she had a choice. Seph found the control panel and activated the door latch for the last cell on the right, watching cautiously as it rolled itself up starting at the floor.

The man watched it, making no move until it had not only cleared his height but furled itself fully into the ceiling, then took a single step across the threshold, his eyes fixed on her.

Seph raised her rifle reflexively, but the man grinned, a shocking expression on his bruised face.

"No need for that, then. Who might you be?"

"My name is Seph," she said simply. "I'm glad I finally—"

He hit her so fast, she didn't even have time to fire. The rifle flew out of her hands as he knocked her to the ground, where she barely kept her head from cracking against the floor. His hands went to her throat, and he bared his teeth as he crouched over her.

"My captain would never bring humans here," he snarled, beast-like in his fury. "This base was hidden for a reason. Now tell me what you did to my people before I crack your head open and pull the information straight from your scrambled brains."

Fighting for breath, Seph glared back at him fiercely, then bucked hard, trapped his leg and rolled.

If he hadn't been starved and beaten, it might not have worked, but he wasn't expecting her to fight back and lost his grip on her throat as she pinned him to the ground with a knee to his stomach.

"You stupid, lying bastard," she hissed. "I should just shoot you, but I need you, and so does Killian. Your precious captain took me from a space station that had just been hit by a Bhandecki probe. He was coming back here to prepare for war, so I don't think he really cared whether humans saw this place or not. Either you can agree to help me save your captain's life, or I will throw you back in that cell to rot and go looking for the nanotech myself. Am I clear?"

The man began to cough, and blood flew from his mouth, but she didn't let him up. She couldn't afford mercy, not when he'd proven that he didn't trust her word.

"Clear," he choked out, and Seph rose from the ground, this time keeping eye contact and maintaining a ready stance as he followed suit, wobbling dangerously until he gained his feet. She backed up until she could crouch down to reach her rifle, then held it trained on him until she likewise retrieved her helmet.

"How about we start again, this time with your name," she demanded.

"My human name is Patrick," the man said, staggering to a chair and dropping into it. He had brown skin and dark hair, and was a little shorter than Seph, though whatever his build had once been, it was now reduced to little more than bones and skin and the smoldering fire of rage.

"All right then, Patrick. Where do we go to look for the nanotech?"

"Not so fast," he said, fixing her once more with the intensity of his gaze. "You said there was a probe."

"Yes," she acknowledged. "At least that's what Killian called it. He said the Bhandecki would be following shortly to destroy humanity if we didn't find a way to counter them."

"Lousy timing," Patrick muttered, running filthy hands through his matted, shoulder-length hair. "Alrighty then. If we're going to get the nanotech, we'll need a plan. And a diversion."

"What about your friends?" Seph asked, swallowing her misgivings as she contemplated the risks of yet another diversion.

"Too far gone," Patrick said in a cold, clipped voice. "They tested that weapon on us first, and it's been days since either Forrest or Vivian were conscious. I don't know for sure whether either of them is still alive, but

I'm the only one with any nanotech left. Just enough to heal me up in between sessions."

"Okay." Seph tried not to feel discouraged. "It's just us then. I have a friend outside, but I don't know whether he'll make it back here in time to help."

"He responsible for that explosion?"

Seph nodded. She didn't even know for sure whether Aidan had made it clear of the blast before it went off. They'd estimated its strength and its radius, but neither of them knew much about explosives, and she hadn't heard from him since the power fluctuations.

Patrick booted up the screen next to him and entered commands until he pulled up what looked like a map of the base. "The nanotech is hidden in this locker near the main command center. I doubt the pirates even know what it is, so even if they found it, they may not have thought to destroy it. I'll need them drawn away so I can get to the locker and get back here without them knowing I've escaped. Once I get it back to this room, I can hopefully revive the others. Then we retake the base and get back to the ship. I assume it's close?"

Seph nodded. "And you're sure you can do all that? Do you have current access codes?"

Patrick grinned, to ghastly effect. "They kept me alive for a reason," he said, his voice heavy with self-loathing. "I'm the one who programmed the codes in the first place. The one who knew how the tech worked. The one who could operate the equipment and fix things when they went wrong."

"So they tortured you until you did what they wanted?" Seph guessed.

"They tortured the others," he snarled, "until I would have given them my own arms to make it stop."

A swell of rage caught her by surprise. "Then we make them pay," she said softly. "Here." She held out her shock rifle.

Patrick's eyes widened, but he didn't take it. "You'll need that," he said, sounding a bit more subdued. "I have a weapon, of sorts."

"But you barely have enough energy to walk," Seph insisted. "Using that energy to shoot people isn't going to help us get your crew back. All I have to do is draw attention to myself, but if you fail, we all lose. Take it."

He did, and Seph thought there was a tiny glimmer of respect in his eyes as his fingers closed around it.

"Thank you, Seph." His tone was formal. "I hope you'll forgive me for my earlier behavior."

"Done," she said briskly. "Now. Where would you like this diversion of yours?"

"Back entrance," Patrick said, pointing to a place on the map that looked like it was probably Seph's entry point. He rose carefully to his feet. "If you can get them to chase you out into the caves, so much the better. But please..." He came close enough to place a shaking hand on her arm. "Don't let them catch you. They are animals in the most violent and depraved sense of the word, and I would shoot you myself before I let them get their hands on you."

Seph tried to look unaffected. "I'll be careful," she promised, knowing it would do neither of them any good to admit what was likely to happen.

Aidan would also line up to shoot her if he knew what she was about to do, but there were no other options. Patrick was the only one who could help them. The only one who stood a chance of reviving the crew and getting them out of this situation alive.

Which meant he was the only thing standing between Earth and annihilation.

This had better be one hell of a diversion.

FIFTEEN

WHEN SEPH TRIED to open her eyes, it quickly became apparent that she was better off keeping them closed. Even her eyelids hurt.

But it had been one hell of a diversion.

She'd done what she'd set out to do, but it had come at a price, one she'd known she'd have to pay when she left Patrick to his own task. There had never been much chance she could gain the attention of the remaining pirates and somehow evade capture. That had never been her goal. Instead, she'd set out to draw them as far as possible from the area where her new ally needed to go, with the realization that his part in this adventure was far more crucial than hers. Aidan, too, was necessary, if any of the sacrifices already made were to mean something.

She, on the other hand, was expendable—an unpleasant but unavoidable fact—and if she could save the lives of the men who had the ability to save Earth, perhaps it would mean that her own life had not been wasted.

Sadly, her sabotage of the fire suppression system, the ventilation system, and the plumbing, followed by a noisy flight into the caves, hadn't been enough to convince the irritated pirates to kill her on sight. Instead, they'd bounced her off a few rock walls, pawed and leered at her for a short while, and then re-decorated her face with their boots. She'd lost consciousness somewhere, but it felt like they'd done due diligence on the rest of her as well.

"Patrick?" Her lips were so swollen and painful, the word came out as an unintelligible mumble.

No one answered, which she supposed could be good or bad. Either they hadn't caught him yet, or they'd put her someplace separate.

Attempts to move her arms and legs resulted in knifelike pains that suggested more than one bone had been broken. It hurt to breathe, and an effort to sit up left her dizzy and nauseated.

Seph tried cracking one eye and was able to get a brief glimpse of her surroundings, which looked depressingly familiar. From the mesh walls and the control panel outside, she began to suspect that she'd been placed in Patrick's cell. Which could mean that he was dead, or it might just mean that he hadn't been caught yet.

She took stock of her gear and noted that her helmet was nowhere to be seen. She'd been carrying it at the end, hoping that they'd be more likely to chase her if they knew she was a woman. It had worked, but it also left her far more vulnerable now that she'd been captured.

Her suit was intact, but a tentative probing of the various compartments suggested that her pockets had been emptied—no surprise there.

There was nothing to do but face reality—she was alone. Without food, water, tools, or weapons. The light patch had been ripped off her hand. Aidan and Patrick could both be dead. No one else knew where she was, and it was only a matter of time before Killian and his crew succumbed to dehydration.

Seph tried to take a deep breath, but that hurt too much. She tried to steady herself by thinking of something encouraging, but couldn't come up with a single hopeful thought.

And then there was the door. The locked door. She was in a cell, with a locked door, and no way to get out.

Pressure began to build in her chest. She could feel the bubble of panic trying to work its way out, the pain of it joining with the chorus of agony already coursing through her body, and she wondered whether it was possible to pass out from sheer terror.

The outer door began to open. It moved slowly, and she could hear swearing as it slid back an inch at a time. Her brief career in destruction had accomplished that much at least.

Voices filled the small room. Ugly ones.

"Throw him in with the other one. They're both too screwed up to cause any problems. Captain says catch the thief, and then we can have some fun getting these two to talk."

The door to her cell rolled upwards, but she was too broken to do anything about it. She could only lie there, watching through cracked eyelids as two men threw another body into her cell.

The mesh rolled down again, and the men retreated, leaving the room in silence once more, but the moment they muscled the main door shut behind them that changed. The limp "body" they'd thrown into her cell came to life, springing up and crossing the filthy floor to kneel by her side.

Aidan yanked off his helmet and slipped a hand carefully behind her head, his eyes filled with pain and something akin to panic.

"Damn it, Seph. You weren't supposed to get hurt."

"No choice," she tried to say. It didn't quite come out right, but she didn't even care. Aidan was alive. She wasn't alone.

"Don't try to talk," he admonished, his voice shaking, and his free hand rising to stroke her hair back from her face. "I'll figure out a way to get us out of here."

"Is no way," she managed to say, a bit more intelligibly this time. If Patrick hadn't been able to figure it out in all the time he'd been imprisoned there, what chance did they have? There was just one tiny sliver of hope— the pirates had mentioned they were going to catch a "thief." That could only mean that Patrick had done his part and was now loose somewhere with the nanotech that could save them all—if he changed his plans and rescued the crew on board ship first.

Coming back for her would be nothing but a death trap, but that decision was out of her hands.

She could feel Aidan trying to assess her injuries with gentle fingers, and swallowed whatever sounds of pain his actions provoked. He didn't need to know how badly hurt she was.

Eventually, though, he was going to find out about her fear of being trapped. She could already feel the panic digging in its claws, the pressure building in her chest again.

She would just have to hold on. Now that she knew Patrick was out there somewhere, she had something to cling to. She wouldn't look at the door. Wouldn't acknowledge that there was no way out.

"Seph can you look at me?"

She tried. Shifted her head slightly and cracked both eyes. Even the dim light hurt, so she closed them again.

"I think your head is okay," Aidan said quietly. "The rest of you not so much, but nothing we can't fix as soon as we get you out of here. Did you have something to do with that thief they mentioned?"

She nodded, and he squeezed her hand gently. "Good work. All we have to do is wait until he can access the ship."

Assuming Patrick had the right codes. Assuming he could do anything for the dying Wyrdane. Assuming he returned for them before it was too late.

But Aidan knew those things—he was just trying not to scare her. Being encouraging and upbeat, as he'd once said he didn't know how to be. And she would let him because she needed all the encouragement she could get.

"I need to lift you onto the bed," he told her, and she steeled herself against the pain as he slid one arm beneath her knees and another beneath her shoulders. The move was quick, and she had to admit that, bare and uncomfortable as it was, the bunk was better than the floor.

"I'm going to work on the door," Aidan said quietly. "Just relax if you can."

She would have laughed at the idea, but that would have hurt, so she kept her eyes closed and tried to block everything out—the sights, the sounds, the smells, the memories—but it all pressed in on her with brutal clarity.

At some point, Aidan's experiments with the door must have interrupted the power source, because the lights flickered out without warning, and Seph's panic finally overflowed.

She was trapped. There was no way out of the cell, no way out of the room, no way out of the base, no way off the moon... Her heart raced, and her entire body broke out in a cold, clammy sweat. Every breath grew labored—as if something heavy was sitting on her chest—and her body began to shake.

"Seph?"

A hand touched her cheek, while another clasped her cold, trembling fingers.

"Seph, what's going on? You sound like you can't breathe."

She clutched at his hand despite the pain. She had to get control. Had to fight it. She wasn't alone, and they would find a way out.

"You're freezing." Aidan's tone was so deliberately casual, she knew she'd scared him.

"I'm fine," she said, her voice shaking so badly she wasn't sure Aidan would understand her. "It startled me when the light went out. That's all."

"I'm a little insulted," he replied, keeping his tone steady. "That's the worst lie I think I've ever heard, and I've heard quite a few."

"If you're going to call me a liar," she slurred, "you can just go away."

He chuckled. She felt him sit down next to the bunk, her hand still in his, his head leaning back against her hip.

"Close your eyes, Seph."

It was probably a measure of just how bad the situation was that she listened, and closed her eyes without thinking too much about why.

"Breathe with me."

His breaths were deep and even. Seph hesitated, but only for a moment before trying to match her inhale and exhale with his. Eventually, the weight on her chest began to ease, and she realized her grip on his hand was probably painfully tight.

She relaxed her fingers and tried to pull away, fighting back embarrassment that threatened to feed her panic.

Aidan didn't let her go. His hand was warm, and it enveloped her cold, clammy one gently, holding on without making her feel trapped.

"Tell me what you're most afraid of."

"I don't want to," she said shakily. "I'm trying not to think about it. And if I tell you, then you'll know how pathetic I am. I'll never be able to see you without feeling embarrassed."

"Seph, I think we're a little past being embarrassed around each other," he said softly. "You're the strongest person I know, whether or not you have panic attacks, and there's no one else I'd rather be stuck here with. Except maybe a shapeshifting alien with lockpicks."

A quick bubble of laughter escaped, but died just as quickly.

"Also, I'm not going to make fun of you for having a panic attack. Sometimes it lessens the fear if you talk about it."

"Maybe you wouldn't make fun of me for panicking, but you'll definitely think I'm a fool for choosing a life that makes that panic worse."

"You're not a fool, Seph," he said quietly.

His hand on hers was warm and reassuring, and Seph felt her arm begin to relax.

"I am," she said, with a little less rancor. "A fool to think I wanted adventure." After a deep shuddering breath, she admitted what he probably could have guessed anyway. "I'm terrified of being trapped." Her words blurred together and she had to fight her swollen lips and cheeks, but she said it. "I can't handle being locked into a situation with no exit. It doesn't really matter whether it's large or small, real or imagined, I just need to know that I can get out."

When he didn't say anything, she kept talking.

"I know it's stupid for me to get on a spaceship, or live on a space station, but I can manage it as long as I know where I'm going. As long as I have a purpose. It was easy to stay distracted on the ship, but we're so screwed right now..." The tension welled up in her chest again, and she felt Aidan's grip on her hand tighten just a fraction.

"How long have you been afraid of being trapped?"

She sorted through her memories, wondering why she'd never asked herself that before. When she was small, she and her siblings had explored their neighborhood and played many games that involved crawling into tight, dark spaces, and she couldn't remember associating them with any sense of fear.

"I think it started when I was going to school. I don't remember why. I do remember the first time I encountered a lift-tube... the door closed and it started to move, and I was convinced I was going to die. The other students made fun of me for a solid month."

"I'm not going to make fun of you," Aidan said. "Everyone has their own fears."

"Are you really afraid of heights?" she couldn't help asking.

"Only heights I can fall from," he said dryly, and she smiled in the dark, realizing only afterward that he'd been right.

Talking really had helped, and she could finally breathe again.

"Aidan?"

"Seph?"

"Thank you."

"You're welcome."

He still didn't release her hand, and even though his featherlight grip caused pain to shoot down her injured fingers, Seph wasn't about to let go. She liked the feel of his skin on hers, the weight of his head resting against her leg. And if this stolen moment in a cell on an alien world was all they were ever going to get? She would take it. Every painful, regret-filled moment.

———

Aidan had learned a lot since he met Seph. She'd taught him to laugh, reminded him of his own humanity, and demonstrated a mind-boggling combination of quiet patience, cheeky humor, and steely-resolve, three things he would not have expected to coexist gracefully.

But she'd also taught him to be afraid. For the first time in his life, Aidan had discovered the uncomfortable sensation of helpless fear for another human being.

The sight of her, lying bloody and battered on the floor of the cell, had awakened feelings that terrified him with their strength.

Protectiveness. Fear. And rage.

He'd promised to protect her, and he'd failed. It had been a foolish promise anyway when made to a woman as brave and unflinching as Seph. She would always be the one to walk into an uncertain situation, always be the one to follow her curiosity wherever it led. He would never be able to put himself fully between her and the danger she so willingly confronted.

But he could have stood beside her. Should have stood beside her, instead of allowing her to go into danger alone.

He didn't think her injuries were life-threatening, at least not on their own, but there would be worse to come if they didn't escape. And he had no idea how they might accomplish that. There was nothing inside the cell to work with. He'd found an access panel, but all he'd managed was to short out the power supply to the lights, which hadn't affected the door.

They could do nothing but wait—wait, and try to hold the darkness at bay.

Talking seemed to help, so he talked. He asked questions about her family, her childhood, her career with the LSF, and learned a lot that he never would have thought to ask about otherwise. There were truths that as one of the leaders of a multi-planet corporation, he never would have imagined were reality for the people whose lives he'd once held in his hands.

Seph really had eaten bugs. Lived without power most days out of every month. Worn her brothers' clothes and gone barefoot until she was a teenager. She'd scrapped for everything she had, and especially for her education, and after hearing her stories, he thought he finally understood her need not to feel trapped.

Her very life had been a trap that she'd finally escaped. The trap of endless cycles of poverty, the trap of her family's desperation, and the trap of feeling like so much depended on her. Up until quitting the LSF, she'd sent almost her entire salary home, living on next to nothing so her family could move into better housing, eat real food every day, and send the youngest children to school.

It wasn't until her older brothers had found decent jobs that she gained the courage to quit and strike out on her own.

He hoped she wouldn't regret telling him so much. Several times she tried to dismiss his concern, to deny her own fears, or belittle her need to hear another person breathing there in the darkness of their cell so she would know that she was still alive. She expected him to lose patience with her because she didn't understand what he meant when he'd said that she mattered to him.

Not that he understood it either. He only knew that she was as necessary to him as light and air and he would do anything to ensure that the men outside that room never touched her again.

Anything.

Even the one thing he'd sworn to Killian he would never do.

Even the thing Seph asked of him, a course of action that threatened to tear down the walls he'd built around his own pain.

It would destroy him, but he would do it if he thought it would save her and protect the ones she loved.

But it wouldn't, and he knew that as clearly as if he'd seen it played out in front of him. The Conclave wouldn't listen to anything he had to say. Out of every human on Earth, Killian could have picked no one less likely to be viewed as a voice of reason and unification.

Instead, he'd chosen a man whose strengths were crushing the opposition and building his dreams out of the broken remains of his enemies. Phillip Linden knew how to win, and he knew how to rule. Given the opportunity, he could have taken Lindmark from his grandfather and built it stronger, better than it had ever been before. He'd chosen not to because the cost would have been too high, but he could have...

Yes. He could.

In the bleak darkness of the cell, Aidan allowed himself to consider what might have been and contemplate the glimmers of what still could be, and by the time he finished he knew what he needed to do.

What... and how. And there was not the tiniest sliver of doubt in his mind that he would succeed. Earth might need a unifier, but what they had was a conqueror, and if he had to conquer Earth to save it?

So be it.

He would do it to save Seph, even knowing what it would mean for their future.

If he went down this road, it would tear them apart forever. She would never look at him again without hatred in her eyes, never say his name without horror and revulsion.

If only there was a way to ensure that she would learn the truth only after he was gone.

She would eventually find out, of course, no matter how he chose to proceed. When the news hit Earth, she would know exactly who he was and what he had done, and how badly he had deceived her. Even if he disappeared now, the day would come that she would hate him, but if it happened after he was gone, at least he wouldn't have to see her face.

He could bear almost anything if he never had to see her hate him.

But even if he had to see it, even if she called him by every cutting epithet he had endured after his disgrace, even if she hit him in the face with a tray full of beer mugs, he would walk that road, and gladly, if it meant that Seph would live.

In the meantime, he was as close to Seph as he was ever going to get, so he was determined to simply exist in that moment, listening to her breathe and trying not to think about the what-ifs. He wished he'd done more with the opportunities he'd been given—told her how he felt, held her hand just because, or found out what it would be like to kiss her... assuming she would have wanted to kiss him back, which was by no means certain. They were friends, yes, because Seph wouldn't accept anything less, but as for anything more? Perhaps he was deluding himself by dreaming that it could have been possible.

And now he had to live with the realization that all he would ever have was dreams.

SIXTEEN

AIDAN EVENTUALLY FELL into a fitful doze, his head leaning back against Seph's leg, her hand still resting in his. He thought she was sleeping, as her breathing had evened out, and her hand occasionally jerked in his grasp. It was probably for the best if they could manage even a few minutes of rest. Not that it would help against what was coming, but why endure the agony of waiting if they didn't have to?

When the door finally began to open, admitting light and the hulking shadows of two ragged, unshaven men, Seph removed her hand from his and struggled to rise. Aidan could sense the pain it cost her, but he understood her need to face this moment sitting up. He elected to remain seated on the floor, and by the time the door opened enough to permit entry, Seph had righted herself and leaned her back against the wall. Hopefully it meant she was more bruised than broken, though that condition was unlikely to last.

The two men approached the cell, all swagger and hungry anticipation until they came close enough to get a good look at their prisoners. One of the men staggered to a stop, then stepped forward, his face drained of color.

He was looking directly at Aidan.

"You," he whispered.

Icy cold crept over Aidan as he regarded the filthy, bearded man, wondering if his time was finally up. He could feel the cool, distant expression habitually worn by Phillip Linden settle over his face as he looked for a clue, any hint as to the identity of the man who accosted him.

"Me?" he said, raising an eyebrow, content to deny everything as long as he could.

The pirate's agitation was visible even beneath the dirt and the beard. "You can't possibly be here," he muttered, fingers curling and uncurling repeatedly.

"Should I know you?" Aidan drawled, deliberately relaxing the surge of tension in the muscles of his jaw and the cords of his neck. Phillip Linden was afraid of no one.

"No, your majesty, of course you wouldn't know me," the pirate snarled, slamming his fists against the mesh of the cell door with a suddenness that made Seph jump. "I was never a person to you, was I? Just another face to be forgotten when you didn't need me anymore."

Aidan's shoulders tensed, preparing to move quickly, but he gave no other hint of his dismay. "Maybe you've mistaken me for someone else," he said softly.

The pirate only laughed. "Up until you destroyed me, I was a professional bodyguard," he announced, his voice cold with hatred. "So I don't make those kinds of mistakes—my reputation depended on it. You were my last job, the one I spent my entire career waiting for, the boy I protected with my life until the day I was dismissed, disgraced, and all but disappeared with no explanation, no recompense, and no way to clear my name."

Aidan locked eyes with the pirate, his wrists draped across his knees, his heart pounding with the realization that this was real. It was happening, and there was no hiding any longer.

One of his bodyguards. One of the many who had disappeared... And then he thought he remembered a pair of earnest blue eyes that always remained behind his chair, looking at him from under a carefully tamed shock of brown hair. "Buckley?" he said, the word wrenched out of him despite his reluctance.

"Then you do remember me."

He did. He remembered all of them. He knew the names and faces of every one of the people his mother had dismissed from his life, he just hadn't been able to see beneath the beard and the dirt until he knew there was a connection.

"I remember that you disappeared one day without explanation," Aidan said, his voice sounding hollow, like an echo of something nearly forgotten. "I remember that I asked about you until my mother threatened to have you killed if I didn't stop asking. So I stopped. But I looked, by every method at my disposal until it became clear that you didn't exist anymore and I was only endangering people by continuing to search."

"You're a liar!" The other man had gone hoarse with rage. "You never looked. You're the one who destroyed me in the first place. Do you think I didn't know that I was dismissed because you accused me of stealing corporate secrets?"

Suddenly Aidan felt the weariness of years drop in on him and he let his hands fall to the floor, empty and aching. "I was fourteen, Buckley. I had no knowledge of corporate secrets. And you were my favorite bodyguard—I was upset when you disappeared."

"I'm not fool enough to believe you've ever felt anything for anyone," the pirate sneered, "let alone one of those worthless invisible people who exist only to do your bidding. And even if I did believe you, I don't care anymore. I've paid for your lies with my name, my family, my dignity, and my self-respect. I don't owe any Linden anything but what they've already given me—the hell of a living death with no hope of redemption."

Aidan heard those words like the sound of a knife being driven into his own chest. The impact. The pain. And then nothing but the wet slide of blood-slicked metal as it pulled free again, leaving a gaping hole where he'd only recently realized his heart still beat.

He heard a horrified gasp from Seph. Saw bright-eyed interest on the face of the other pirate. And knew that the life he'd built for himself since his family's betrayal was over.

He rose to his feet, never once turning to look at Seph. He wouldn't explain, wouldn't ask her forgiveness, wouldn't beg her to understand. There was only one way forward now, and she couldn't be a part of it. Not if she was going to live, and that was the only reason for anything.

He opened his mouth, only to be stopped by a grip on his arm.

"No." Seph's voice was still a little slurred by her swollen lips, but he knew, suddenly, what she was about to say. "You're wrong," she said doggedly. "He might look like Phillip, but he's just pretending. He didn't do any of those things. He couldn't."

Aidan closed his eyes and wondered how it was possible that there wasn't truly a hole in his chest, because it already hurt, and now he was going to have to tear out a little more of whatever kind of heart he still had. It was going to be agony, worse than the rejection of his mother and grandfather, worse than hearing himself reviled by every news source in the Conclave.

"No, *you're* wrong," he said harshly, opening his eyes and looking directly into Seph's trusting gaze. "Every bit of it is true. Why do you think Killian asked me to help him? Because I know how he likes his gin and tonic?"

She could only stare at him helplessly, confusion and pain mingled on her face.

"But you're not," she insisted. "I know you, and you're nothing like Phillip Linden."

Buckley laughed derisively. "You *know* him? He's been lying, swindling, cheating and running the world exactly as he wants it since he first tasted solid food. He eats silly girls like you for breakfast. Whatever it is you think

235

you know, forget it. He can be anything he chooses as long as it gets him what he wants. Why wouldn't he pretend to be whatever brand of unjustly persecuted would get you into his bed?"

"Aidan?" Seph was still looking at him like she expected him to say it was all a lie.

He turned away. "What are you looking for? Proof that he's lying?" The question was infused with vicious sarcasm. "I've never claimed to be anything I'm not. I warned you I was not a decent man. I told you I would destroy you. You're the one who made me out to be something kind and good and decent—three things Phillip Linden has never known how to be."

He glanced back and saw when it hit her—when the truth finally sank in, and all of the clues he'd given since they met came together to form one undeniable conclusion. Seph's mouth dropped open, and all the fight seemed to drain out of her until there was nothing left but betrayal and defeat.

The beating she'd received at the hands of the pirates hadn't broken her, but his deception left her shattered.

"How much can we get for him?"

The gravelly voice of the second pirate startled him and shifted his attention back to where it should have remained—the true threat. He had to focus on getting himself out of here and making sure Seph would be left alone. Whatever she thought of him… It didn't matter anymore.

"Billions," he answered coolly before Buckley could say a word. "Do you know what the other Conclave members would pay to get their hands on the secrets of the Lindmark empire?"

The two men shared sharp glances, and the stranger—whose beard had been formed into a trio of crooked braids—folded his arms. "What secrets?"

"All of them." He fixed Braided Beard with the patented Linden stare until the man swore and pulled out a weapon.

"Wipe that look off your face, space-trash. You might talk big, but your life is worth less than nothing unless I say so."

Aidan laughed. "I've been threatened by far bigger men than you, and I'm still here to brag about it. Go ahead. Shoot me." He flattened his hands to the mesh and let his voice drop. "I might be the one in the cell right now, but I have the power to deny you wealth and influence beyond your wildest imagination. Or, we can work together. Sell what I know to the highest bidder and we'll all benefit."

"Or, we can beat it out of you," Buckley suggested, taking a step forward and licking his lips.

"You of all people ought to know better," Aidan said softly, "but should you feel compelled to try, know that you can take my blood but not my secrets. I'm not a dog to do any man's bidding, and I won't be forced to cooperate. Pain means nothing to me."

"Oh, but it means something to me." Buckley pulled out a weapon and leveled it at Seph. "Step back and sit down," he commanded, and to Aidan's relief, she complied, with only the tiniest whimper to betray how much pain she had to be in. "Open the door," he ordered the other pirate, and Braided Beard jumped to obey.

As the mesh rolled up, Aidan held Buckley's mad-eyed stare, only breaking contact when the pirate grabbed his arm, yanked him out of the cell and threw him to the floor. The door rolled back down, separating him from Seph, and Aidan knew he had to keep it that way.

"So, who gets to kick him first?" Braided Beard asked, a leer in his voice that suggested he would enjoy this just as much as Buckley.

"I've earned the right," Buckley snarled, and slammed his booted foot into Aidan's ribs. "I'm going to enjoy hitting you until you promise to give me everything I've ever wanted. And then I'll just laugh and hit you again."

Aidan grunted with the force of the impact and followed it with a laugh. "I hope your captain agrees that your revenge is worth sacrificing the one person who can get you off this rock."

"My captain's not here, is he?" Buckley taunted, striking a vicious blow at Aidan's kidneys.

The impact brought tears to his eyes, but he made no sound as yet another blow crashed into his hip.

A scream of rage ripped from Seph's throat, and she hurled herself off the bed to crash into the mesh door. An animal sound of pain followed the crash, but she wasn't backing down. "Stop it," she panted. "You're hitting the wrong man." She could barely stay on her feet, but she still defended him, despite the overwhelming weight of his own testimony.

Stubborn, brave, beautiful Seph.

"I think," Braided Beard said, "you have a lot to learn about who's in charge here." And he joined the assault.

Aidan tried to close himself off from everything except enduring, but he could still hear Seph's protests as they battered him again and again.

Somehow, despite his efforts to drive her away, his pain still hurt her, and with each stifled cry from the other side of the mesh, Aidan's rage began to swell. He was going to kill them before this was over. Not for hitting him—that he understood. But for causing her more pain. That he was never going to forgive.

After a particularly vicious kick snapped his head back so hard that his vision went dark, Aidan forced himself to speak up mildly, with no hint of the sorrow and fear and rage coursing through him.

"I told you pain means nothing to me. You can beat me to death and get nothing out of it but the satisfaction of seeing me dead beneath your boots."

The blows continued, and Aidan's senses began to grow hazy until he could hear nothing but the muffled sound of each kick as it landed, and quiet sobs from Seph.

She still didn't understand.

"You'd better hope your captain never finds out who I am," he said finally, between gasps for breath. He could feel blood trickling from his mouth as he spoke.

"Who's going to tell him?" Buckley sneered, drawing his foot back for another blow, but Braided Beard stopped him.

"Wait. I don't think we should kill him."

"Why not? He's a lying sack of shit, and I've been dreaming of this moment for years."

Braided Beard took hold of Buckley's arm. "But the captain won't like it. He's already pissed that Reaver shot at the ship. What if this guy can get us on board? And what if he really can sell Lindmark secrets? He could make us rich!"

"He won't betray Lindmark," Buckley said contemptuously. "If there's one thing I'm sure of, it's that. They made him what he is, and he'll never turn his back on the family, no matter what we do to him."

"That," Aidan wheezed, rolling to his back, "is where you're wrong." The answering silence told him it was time to convince them. "You've been gone too long, so I'll let you in on a little secret. I don't want my family to survive—I want them to suffer. I want them to see everything they've built, everything they've worked for, go down in flames. It's been two years since they betrayed me, destroyed me, and vilified my name, all to save themselves from their own arrogance and stupidity. I would sign a contract with the devil himself if it meant I could have a hand in their annihilation."

There was no sound but the harsh, rasping wheeze of his own breath while they considered it.

After a few moments, Buckley crouched down, grabbed a handful of Aidan's hair and lifted his head so they could look one another in the eye. "Why should I believe you?"

Aidan smiled—a wide, ghastly grin. "Why wouldn't you?" he said. "How else would I end up in a place like this with people like you?" He spat out blood before he continued. "I've been living in my own personal hell for two interminable years. I really don't give a damn about much anymore, but the one thing that would give me more joy than choking the life out of you is taking back even a fraction of what was stolen from me. And if I can't, I'd rather let you kill me than live even one more day with my disgrace."

It was a good thing the pirates had the plotting ability of a pair of toddlers.

Braided Beard began to grin. "I think maybe we understand each other, Linden. Seems you really are the cold, heartless bastard they make you out to be."

"Oh no," Aidan said softly, hoarsely, "I'm far worse. As you'll discover if you choose to accept my offer."

He managed not to hold his breath as the man considered.

"We take this to the captain," he said at last, and Buckley began to curse with frustrated rage. He would be dangerous in the future. A man who desired revenge more than money would never stop, never give up merely because revenge appeared impossible.

But fortunately, pirates were often lazy by nature. They stole and destroyed because they preferred to attain wealth without having to work for it. The lure of easy money had been too much for almost every human to encounter it, and it was bound to be far more enticing to men who'd been prisoners on a barren rock for most of the past five years.

"I'm confident your captain will see the benefits of what I propose," Aidan said, struggling to sit up and project calm confidence despite barely being able to hear and having one of his eyes nearly swollen shut.

"And if he doesn't, I can always kill you later," Buckley growled.

"Let's take him back to the command center," Braided Beard suggested. "They'll have caught the thief by now, and the captain will want to hear that we have a way to get on the ship."

"Wait." Aidan focused on ignoring the pain as he rose to his feet and surveyed his new "allies" with arrogance befitting a Linden. "There's one more thing I need to do. Open the cell door."

The two pirates shared a glance, but he'd done his work well. Whether they knew it or not, they'd already relinquished command of the situation, and Braided Beard did as he asked.

Once the door rolled up, Aidan brushed past Buckley, stepped across the threshold into the cell and went to one knee next to Seph where she slumped on the bunk, her gaze focused on nothing.

Her eyes were red, and tears made tracks through the blood and dirt left on her face from her beating at the pirates' hands.

His fault, Aidan reminded himself. He'd failed her. But he wasn't going to fail her again. No matter what he had to do, she was going to be safe.

To ensure that, he had to remove the pirates. Once they were gone, he knew she would manage. Seph was strong, and she would find a way to do what needed to be done. But he had one last chance to make her understand, one last chance to say what he should have said every day since he met her. All without betraying to the pirates how much he cared.

On his best day, he'd never been that good with words, but for Seph, he would try.

———

Seph heard the door roll up and knew the violence had finally come to an end, but when Aidan crouched beside the bunk, she didn't look at him. She didn't want to see his face, didn't want confirmation of the things he'd said about himself. She was clinging to her belief that the Aidan she knew was still in there—that she wasn't as alone as she felt. She wouldn't allow her sense of horror and betrayal to overwhelm her until he was gone.

"I'm going to lock you in," he said roughly. "You've been decently amusing, so I've decided to make them spare your life as a condition of my cooperation. Now would probably be a good time to thank me, but I doubt you're smart enough to know that. Maybe you'll find a way out, maybe you won't, but either way, it's no concern of mine after this."

His callous disregard for both her future and her feelings drove the

241

truth home at last. "You really are Phillip," she said numbly, unable to stop herself.

"Of course I'm Phillip," he snapped. "I told you not to romanticize me, but you couldn't resist, could you?"

She flinched.

"I told you to quit following me around, but you wouldn't stop. You followed me onto the *Fancy* and look where it got you."

Wait, no she hadn't! She opened her mouth to protest, but he wasn't finished.

"Maybe now you'll finally believe that I don't give a crap about anyone, least of all you." He placed a hand on her neck and shoved her sideways until she was lying on the bunk, then shifted to look down at her. "Remember everything you've ever believed about Phillip Linden and know that all of it is true. I was the man who nearly destroyed Daragh, and the one who hunted down your friends for daring to challenge me."

Each statement was a blow to her already devastated heart. She'd trusted him. Defended him. Believed in him. And he'd never shown her anything but decency. How could he be the same man who'd destroyed everything she'd dreamed of when she'd quit the LSF for the colonization program?

Apparently, he was more than willing to explain. "I went to Daragh only to protect the corporation I'd spent a lifetime building. I meant to defend her from the attack of a few upstart colonists and ended up disgraced, so believe me when I say that I am out for revenge. I am every bit the monster you fear, and I will happily ally myself with anyone who will help me regain what was stolen from me."

She shook her head. "Then everything you've said, everything you've done since I've known you was a lie? Why, Aidan? It just doesn't make sense."

"Believe it, Seph." He met her eyes and willed her to see through them to what was in his heart. "Believe that I am Phillip Linden, bogey-man of

Lindmark, destroyer of worlds. Believe that I will do whatever is necessary to take down the corporation that I built, that was stolen from me on the basis of lies and deceit." Then he bent down and whispered for her ears alone. "If you believe nothing else, Persephone, believe that the Lord of Hell would do anything to keep what he loves."

He stood up and brushed himself off.

"Goodbye," he said coldly. "It's been fun, but I have a takeover to plan. Earth is about to be hit by a corporate war so brutal it will make them dizzy, and they'll be glad to have a strong hand at the helm. Someone who knows how to handle the chaos that's coming. But you'll be locked away here, without access to anything but miles and miles of nothing. Hope you enjoy it. I wonder... is this what you had in mind when you went looking for adventure?"

Seph's jaw was clenched so hard against her tears that it shook. Even the beating she'd taken hadn't caused her this much pain.

Aidan turned away, then stopped.

"One last thing," he said, without looking at her. "No matter what happens, I'd better not find out that you've followed me. I've been amused by you to this point, but that's over. I think you'd find it wouldn't be safe for you to ever be caught in my vicinity again."

He did leave then, and stepped over to the computer console to lock her in. At a touch of the button, the door rolled down with awful finality.

The one called Buckley chuckled and ran his fingers down the mesh. "If you don't want her anymore, does this mean we can have her?"

Aidan fixed him with a glacial stare. "Leave the woman," he said coldly. "We're planning a corporate takeover, after which you can have whatever woman you choose. Why would you want one that's already broken?"

The pirate leered at her one more time and followed Aidan out into the corridor before pulling the door shut behind them.

Leaving Seph alone.

She let the tears flow then, in rivers of pain and horrified denial. She should have seen it. Should have known. He'd all but told her, and she'd been so blinded by her own infatuation that she'd ignored the signs. The first night she met him she'd seen that he was someone with an influential past, but she'd been too stupid to remember her own observations.

Anger overtook her then. At herself, at Aidan, at Killian, at the pirates...

Could it really have all come down to this? Was she going to die alone on an alien moon, knowing that humanity was doomed because she'd failed?

No.

She struggled to sit up. Pain tore through her in jagged waves, but she gritted her teeth until she was upright. Began to breathe again, first in shallow pants, then deeper, slower breaths.

The cell was not going to hold her.

She refused to die here.

Maybe Aidan was a lying bastard. Maybe he'd used her and manipulated her into thinking exactly what he wanted her to think, but she didn't have to stay here and give up. Earth still needed her. And so did Killian, if she could only...

Seph shifted her weight and felt something fall down the inside of her suit.

Her fingers protested even the weakest grip, but she managed to unseal the front of her suit far enough to reach in and retrieve a tiny piece of plastic that had fallen between her shirt and her skin. It was only about the size of a fingernail, but when she pulled it out and held it up, Seph felt the bottom drop out of the world for the second time in the last ten minutes.

It was a data chip. When Aidan pushed her down, he hadn't been trying to hurt her. He'd been giving her a data chip.

She had no idea what it held, but suddenly she began to replay everything he'd said, everything he'd done, and when she'd finished, the tiniest seed of hope had taken root in the ravaged landscape of her heart.

Phillip Linden or not, she wasn't done with him yet.

He'd been brutal in his rejection, layering cruelty upon cruelty, and perhaps he'd meant them. Or perhaps not. He might have been protecting her from being used against him. Or he might have been trying to save himself from the pain of her rejection when she discovered his true identity.

But she wouldn't know the truth until she had a chance to face him and demand some answers. And demand them she would, even if she had to hunt him down across the entire galaxy. He might have believed she would be too intimidated to follow him, or that she would be so blindsided by his revelations that she would ignore everything that had passed between them.

Idiot man. If she could get herself out of this cell, she'd show him just how badly he'd underestimated her.

And if it turned out that he was fully as terrible as history had painted him? She could always hit him with a tray.

SEVENTEEN

IF HE LIVED to be a thousand years old, Phillip knew he would never again experience an agony so piercing as the betrayal in Seph's eyes when he reviled her. Mocked her. Made her believe she'd been no more to him than an amusing diversion.

It was the only way he could think of to spare her, the only way to ensure that the pirates wouldn't attempt to use her pain against him. It was, he thought bitterly, perhaps the most unselfish thing he had ever done, which wasn't saying a great deal.

And yet, it had also been pathetically selfish—every harsh sentence seeded with desperate clues that he didn't dare hope Seph had actually heard in the midst of his excoriation.

But he had no more time, and he could not pause to dwell on the past. The future was all that mattered—the future, and his plans for whatever was left of it. When he'd looked at Seph and known he had to save her, he'd committed himself to saving more than just one woman—he was going to have the save the whole world along with her.

Which meant he had to move forward as though Aidan was dead. There would be no more hiding behind the persona of a mysterious, curmudgeonly bartender. Starting now, he would have to fully embrace his true identity once more, and do his best to re-take the empire that had once all but belonged to him. And this time, it would need to be truly his.

There was no point in lying to himself. At the end of this road lay the destruction of his family—the complete annihilation of Eustacius and Satrina, everything they'd built, and everything they stood for.

And the terrifying thing was, Phillip knew he could do it. Knew beyond a doubt that he could topple the empire of lies and deceit that his grandfather had built.

The question was, what would be left when he was finished? There had to be enough left of Lindmark to take on the other corporations if necessary. To make it clear that no takeover bid could possibly succeed. He would prefer to avoid outright war unless it was the only thing that could force the others to listen, but if they picked a fight, he would be fighting to win. Lindmark would have to be ready—to stand firm in the face of domestic threats so they could be prepared to counter galactic ones.

And that, Phillip knew, was going to be a bit harder to manage. He was going to need allies, much as the word grated against his personal preferences. Allies who weren't disgusting, murderous pirates.

He didn't spare a glance for his companions as they made their way down the underground corridor in search of the "captain." He'd taken their allegiance by little more than force of personality—with a little help from greed—and they didn't need to be reminded of how precarious his situation really was. All he had to do was remember how to act like the entitled bastard he'd been raised to be.

Which wasn't as difficult as he'd hoped it would be.

The control room was a brisk thirty-second walk from the makeshift prison, and by the time they arrived, he felt as though he'd shed Aidan like a second skin that didn't quite fit. It was Phillip Linden who entered the room filled with display screens, storage modules, and piles of trash that reeked of rot and decay—a room where four hostile strangers waited, eyeing him with a hungry sort of loathing.

It was simple to spot the captain, standing alone, farthest from the door, flanked by the others in a deferential way, whether conscious or unconscious.

But not so simple to maintain his composure when he caught sight of the face beneath the beard.

Seph had mentioned that Killian's crew had taken DNA from the *Erin's Dream*, but Killian himself must have been aiming a bit higher. Or lower, depending on your point of view.

The pirate captain wore Killian's face.

He was heavier, and beneath the layers of dirt and depravity both his stance and expression were different, but there was no mistaking his identity. Which made the whole thing more than a little creepy.

Killian was many things, but he was honorable in his own rakish way. Beneath his disregard for Conclave law, he clearly followed a code, and there were depths to which he would not sink. Perhaps Phillip shouldn't have been so quick to scoff at Killian's preference for the term "free-trader," as the realities of piracy were far uglier.

The man in front of him—if Dinah's story was to be believed—had been responsible for the violent murder of an entire colony ship. And that was only one of the crimes he had likely committed over the course of his lawless career. In addition, he was cruel and cunning enough to gain the respect of the other lawless men with whom he'd surrounded himself. He would not be so easy an opponent as Buckley or Braided Beard. But neither, Phillip reminded himself grimly, could this man have possibly matched the coldly calculating criminal career of Eustacius Linden, who had been responsible for far more murders than a mere pirate could begin to imagine.

"What's your name?" he demanded, not waiting for Killian's doppelgänger to speak first.

"That's Captain Obediah," Buckley whispered.

Captain Obediah shot his underling a look that could have peeled paint.

"I don't care what you call yourself," Phillip said shortly. "You can be Captain, Commodore, or Emperor of Earth for all I care, as long as you listen and do what you're told."

He chose his target carefully. The largest man in the room happened to be standing directly in front of a chair, so Phillip grabbed his collar and twisted, hard. Thanks to a strategically placed foot behind his ankle, the pirate fell to the floor with a surprisingly high-pitched yelp.

"Thank you for your consideration," Phillip said, with a cold glance at the other pirates as he seated himself in the chair. "In case you've been living under a rock for the past twenty years, my name is Phillip Linden. For most of my life, I was the heir apparent to Lindmark corporation, until the recent past when I was unfairly and unwisely disinherited. After conversing with these men"—he waved at Buckley and his companion—"I decided the time is right to retake what is mine. Whoever chooses to assist me will gain rewards commensurate to their assistance. Those who oppose me will discover what became of all my other enemies."

Captain Obediah chuckled, and the sound sent a chill down Phillip's spine. He might not care much for Killian, but this man made him want to take a shower simply by existing.

A compact shock pistol made an appearance from somewhere inside the pirate captain's voluminous coat. "You may find it a simple matter to subvert my flunkies," he said casually, "but I think you'll find that you've overreached just a bit, Phillip... Linden, is it?"

Then he shot Braided Beard.

No one reacted, including Phillip. He'd seen this game played out many times, even if it didn't usually involve weapons in his world. He didn't even glance at the body after it hit the floor.

"*Mr.* Linden will be fine, thank you," Phillip said coolly, leaning back in his chair and letting the fingers of one hand tap casually on his knee.

Captain Obediah chuckled. "You've got enough balls, I almost believe you."

"Believe me or don't," Phillip said with a shrug. "It won't change the fact that I plan to retake what is mine. Plus interest, if the other corporations choose not to support me. I believe there could be a place for you and your men, unless you would prefer to continue skulking behind asteroids, robbing those who were too poor to succeed on Earth."

The shock pistol twitched. "Whereas you plan to rob the rich?"

Phillip chuckled. "If it makes you happier to see it that way. When I am finished, there will be no one on Earth richer than me, so if you'd like to wait and rob me then, you're welcome to try."

"Boldly stated." The captain looked at Buckley. "I send you to interrogate prisoners, and you come back with another man holding your leash. I hope you're prepared to explain why I haven't killed you yet."

"It's really him, Captain," Buckley said hoarsely. "Phillip Linden. I knew him back on Earth, and he can really do what he says. If we go with him, we won't have to hide anymore. We can have whatever revenge we want, be rich men. Probably have our own planets." He licked his lips nervously. "Plus he can get us onto the ship."

Captain Obediah's eyes suddenly turned sharp and predatory. "The ship?" he asked softly.

"If you're speaking of the one I came here in, yes," Phillip said. "I have the access codes."

"And you didn't torture them out of him because..." The captain gave Buckley a moment to hang himself.

"We tried," Buckley protested.

"You *tried*." The captain rolled the words across his tongue as though he could taste them.

The rest of the room held its breath.

Eventually, the captain shrugged as though it didn't really matter one way or another. "I suppose we could take him with us," he said, shifting just enough to create a closed circle with his men, leaving Phillip on the outside. "And, if nothing else, perhaps someone would pay a ransom."

"If you're satisfied with a flat payout, by all means, request a ransom," Phillip said, cool condescension dripping from his tone. "I'm offering a great deal more than mere money, should you choose to ally yourself with me."

"I don't choose my allies quite so carelessly," the pirate assured him, with a near equal degree of disdain. "I might still decide to shoot you."

Phillip chuckled. "And are your men whipped enough that they would just let you? What kind of man chooses henchmen who are so easily cowed they would allow you to kill the fatted calf to save face?"

A flash of rage entered the captain's eyes, but Phillip didn't find it particularly concerning. The pirate might be canny enough amongst his own kind, but puttering about as an interstellar highwayman could hardly have prepared him to face a Linden.

"I say we wait," one of the other men insisted. "If he really is Linden, I want a part of what he's offering."

"You can't shoot us all, Obediah," said the man Phillip had thrown out of his chair. "And if he isn't Linden, and there's no money in it, I'll space him for you."

Phillip reached out, grabbed a handful of the man's greasy, disgusting hair, yanked his head back and spoke directly into his ear. "You'll wait for your captain's decision, fool, and be grateful for it."

And just that fast, he had Obediah's attention again. First, he'd taken the man's crew away and made them think for themselves. Then he'd returned them, almost as a favor, so that the men would see him as their captain's superior, and the captain would see him as an ally.

It had been almost too easy.

"If you can do as you say and get us on that ship," Captain Obediah said sharply, "then we'll listen to the rest of it."

"Couldn't ask for more," Phillip said sarcastically, rising from his seat. "Do we go now, or would you like to wait?"

"What of the crew?" The captain's attention was suddenly, fiercely focused. "What happened to the alien scum who brought us here?"

"Dead. At least the ones we came with."

"Then the weapon worked." A fierce grin crossed the man's face.

"If turning their insides to mush is what you intended to do, then yes." Phillip lied without really having to think about it. At least, he hoped it was a lie. If Killian and the others were actually dead, everything he'd done to Seph would be for nothing.

"And the thief? One of them stole our technology and escaped with it."

"Probably ran out on the surface to die once he realized the rest of his kind were gone."

"Too bad there aren't any more of them," the captain grumbled. "If the weapon actually works, we could make a fortune selling it."

"How many fortunes do you need?" Phillip remarked, thinking that the man might have more in common with his grandfather than he'd initially supposed. "Unless you've changed your mind about my offer?"

"Lead the way, Linden," the captain said with a sneer. "Let's see how much your word is worth before we start counting your money."

———

As he strode confidently up the ship's ramp, Phillip was feeling anything but confident. Had the "thief" managed to get on board? Had he revived Killian and the others, or was that a hopeless mission in the first place?

He led Obediah and his four remaining men past medical, forcing himself not to glance anxiously at the wall. The room could be a morgue by now, for all he knew, but the longer he could keep the pirates away from it and ignorant of the crew's survival, the better.

Once they reached the bridge, he accessed the systems, then deliberately allowed the captain to take the command chair, choosing the comm seat for himself. While the pirates attempted to evaluate the ship's readiness to fly, Phillip was busy, sending internal messages straight to the computer console in medical, under the guise of running functionality assessments.

Pirates aboard.

Ship preparing to launch.

Seph trapped dirtside.

How many survivors?

It wasn't until after his fourth message that a reply arrived.

Work in progress. Need exit.

Damn. He had to get the Wyrdane off the ship.

"I don't suppose any of you cook?" he inquired of his companions, leaning back lazily in his chair and propping one ankle on the opposite knee.

Five heads swiveled to look at him with something between alarm and disdain.

"Because we'll be needing to eat eventually."

"If you're so worried about it, go play kitchen boy," Obediah sneered. "We have a ship to launch."

"And I'm sure you'll do an excellent job," he said soothingly, rising from his chair. "It's a good thing I thought to recruit you all, or I might have had to do all of this by myself. Carry on, and let me know when the ship is ready."

He thought the captain might challenge the unspoken assertion that it was Phillip in charge of the situation, but Obediah was absorbed in the display in front of him and paid no attention as Phillip left the bridge and headed for medical at a pace that was not quite a run.

When pressing his hand to the light pad didn't nothing, he tapped on the wall. The door vanished, and he slipped inside, only to wish almost immediately that he hadn't. The moment the wall rematerialized behind him, his back hit it as he took two quick steps away from the thing that was occupying the center of the room.

It was tall and humanoid shaped, but only in the general sense that he could make out limbs and a head. Whatever made up its body was translucent, and flowed continually in dizzying loops and swirls that sparked with glittering lights. One of the arms began to flow towards him until the very tip of it touched Phillip's neck and a cool, tingling sensation wrapped around his throat.

As he struggled for air, an unfamiliar man appeared in the doorway on the other side of the main medical bay.

"He's the only ally we have at the moment, so I suggest you not kill him yet," the man said. "Also, I think you're ready, so it might help if you shift back."

The strange glittering creature made a sound like water flowing over stones, and then the fluid material of its body began to swirl and glow faster.

In full view of Phillip's startled gaze, the body began to change color and texture, taking on pale, pinkish skin, sprouting hair in all the usual places, plus a few unusual. By the time the graying beard had reached full length, Phillip was able to recognize the barrel-chested shape of Harvey, who did not look noticeably happier to see Phillip this time than he had the last.

"Get me my clothes, would you?" he snapped at the man behind him, who looked irritated but complied. Once Harvey was wearing pants, he shot Phillip a poisonous glare as he threw on a shirt. "You've handed this ship over to the scum we already dealt with once, and now you pretend you want to help?"

"I'm not the one who was fool enough to let them live in the first place," Phillip replied harshly, his hostility almost a reflex as he fought to contain his shock at what he'd just seen.

The Wyrdane really were shapeshifters. He'd believed it, more or less, after Killian's stunt when he asked Seph to shoot him, and even more so after meeting Captain Obediah. But seeing it happen was rather different than intellectual assent to the concept.

"There are five of them," he continued, shaking off his distraction, "and I've only barely managed to keep them from killing Seph. Right now they're more or less under my control, but only because I've promised them a part of the spoils when I return to Earth and retake what's mine."

One of Harvey's eyebrows shot up. "Revisiting your past are you?"

"Making my own future," Phillip countered icily. "And don't make me remind you of your own captain's part in this situation."

"You mean the part where we're wasting our lives on a pointless attempt to save an ungrateful species of pathetic meatbags?" Harvey growled.

"We never asked you to." Phillip wasn't in the mood to make nice. "And we're wasting time. Unless we get at least one of you off this ship, Seph isn't going to survive this mess you all have made for yourselves."

"Where is she?" Harvey's question sounded a little less hostile, even worried, which shouldn't be that surprising. Everyone seemed to like Seph.

"Back on the surface," Phillip said curtly. "She's been beaten and locked up. I gave her information that might be able to help us, but only if she can get free and head for Earth on the other ship Killian claimed is here somewhere."

"She won't find it," Harvey grunted.

"Send me," the other man said urgently. "I've done everything I can here, and I may still be able to save Forrest and Vivian."

Phillip glanced at the room's beds, two of which held the motionless bodies of Dinah and Rill. "Are any of them going to make it?"

"We've done what we can," Harvey said heavily. "The new nanotech should be enough, but we've put the captain in the sleep tank to hurry things along. Remains to be seen whether everyone will pull through. Won't know for a few days."

"They can survive that long?"

"If we were human, no," Harvey said. "But they're in a hibernation state. They'll live long enough for the nanotech to do what it can."

"And then you'll retake the ship?" Phillip asked.

"En route?" Harvey scoffed. "We can't start a firefight in the middle of nowhere. Something goes wrong, the whole ship goes up and all of us with it. We need to be docked. Should be enough of us to regain control."

"We're not going straight to Earth," Phillip informed them. "I don't want interference from the Conclave just yet."

"Then where are we headed?"

"We're returning to Concord."

"If it's still there," Harvey reminded him.

"It wasn't that badly damaged." If there was one thing Phillip understood, it was the need to be confident in order to inspire confidence in others. "Even if the Conclave abandoned it, the structure will still be mostly intact. We can dock, possibly even refuel, and deal with the pirates." No need to inform them of the rest of his plan just yet.

Phillip turned to the other man, who hadn't said much up to that point. In fact, he looked as though he barely had enough energy to stand up.

"And we're relying on you to save those left behind?" It was definitely a question.

The short, dark-haired man looked at him with something between hatred and contempt. "And we're relying on you to save your entire species?"

Touché.

"I've got the nanotech I need," the man continued, his lips pinched together either in pain or disgust. "Get me off this ship, and I'll deal with the situation below."

"You can get Seph to Earth?" Phillip didn't want her anywhere near him or the pirates.

Harvey interrupted. "That's where we'll all be in the end, Patrick. That's where the Bhandecki strike is likely to come first, and where we'll have the most chance of making a difference. Save the others, and head for Earth. We'll meet there when the pirates are dealt with."

The man named Patrick nodded wearily. "I'll do what I can."

EIGHTEEN

CONCORD FIVE FLOATED against the vast darkness of space, her five stacked rings gone dark and silent. They'd been unable to raise anyone on the station comm channel, and Phillip could see why when they came within visual range.

The station was empty. Not completely, he thought, spotting the shapes of several smaller craft docked on the third level. But none of those craft had the look of official Conclave vessels, which meant that for the moment, at least, it had been abandoned.

The probe was gone, and the hole had been patched, but apparently nothing had been sufficient to make the station fully functional again. And even if they'd sent for help via the beacons, it was a nine-week journey from Earth, plus the time it would take to examine the fireworm's corpse, assemble repair crews, and determine whose responsibility it would be to pay for the damages. By Phillip's estimation, it would be quite a while before any official presence returned.

Perhaps that should have made him feel something like gratitude towards Killian for taking him and Seph off the station—with or without their consent—but he wasn't ready to give the alien any medals just yet. The memory of Seph's battered face was still far too fresh for that.

"Looks abandoned," Buckley said. He shot a poisonous glance at Phillip. "What is this? Why'd you insist on Concord if the Conclave isn't even here anymore?"

"We need to refuel," Phillip said, as though it should have been obvious. "And I didn't know it was abandoned." He hadn't told them about the Bhandecki, or the probe. Partly because he didn't think they would believe him, and partly because they would have little interest in playing along with his takeover bid if they knew. Why risk their lives in pursuit of wealth they would never get to enjoy?

"All the better for us." Captain Obediah stood and stretched, avoiding Phillip's eyes as he did so. "Should still be plenty of fuel, and there's no one here to make us pay for it."

Phillip hadn't missed the captain's surreptitious use of the comm system over the past ten days. He'd had no way to confirm what messages had been sent or to whom, but it wasn't out of the question that the pirates would have acquaintances who were still active in the area.

Baxton, perhaps? It was theoretically possible the man was still alive, and if hygiene and morals were indicators of compatibility, he and Captain Obediah should be the very best of friends.

Phillip had stayed strictly away from medical during the voyage, other than periodically sneaking them food, leaving Harvey to do what he could for the unconscious Wyrdane. If everything had gone well, all three of the crew should be out of the sleep tank by now, and probably angry enough to chew through the bulkheads.

And even if Rill and Dinah weren't yet up to full strength, there was still a chance they could take the ship back from the pirates. They would need a better plan than a head-on assault, but there was no point preparing an ambush just yet when he had no way of knowing what Obediah was planning once they arrived. Besides, Phillip needed some time on Concord itself. He was counting on the station's comm system being repairable, assuming it hadn't merely been turned off.

Somehow, he had to leave the ship, accomplish his mission without the pirates finding out, and eventually retake the ship, without attracting the attention of the other human predators likely to be populating the abandoned station. And he would have to do it with no allies but Harvey, Killian, and, hopefully, Dinah and Rill.

As the odds against him mounted and the scale of the task he'd set himself became clearer, Phillip ought to have grown discouraged. Defeated. But what he felt was far from defeat.

For the first time since he was young, he had a goal that challenged him —that drove him to consider whether or not he could succeed.

And for the first time in potentially his entire adult life, he had a reason to succeed. Something outside himself that drove him to win the day, not just because he could, but because it *mattered*. Because he might not be able to live with himself if he failed.

As a man who had lived with his catalog of questionable deeds and decisions for thirty-two years, this was a novel experience, but not an unpleasant one. Everything he'd done, he'd done because the corporation— and by extension his mother and grandfather—required it. Because it was his duty. That duty no longer held any appeal—he had no desire to save the world they'd built.

But the world where Seph had grown up, clawing for hope, fighting to believe that her dreams were possible—that world was worth saving. Seph was worth saving. And it no longer mattered to him who he had to become in order to save her. If the world reviled him for his efforts, so be it. All he wanted was for Seph to look at him one more time with something other than confusion, anguish, and revulsion.

And if that was going to happen, he needed a better plan than "hope for the best."

"If the station is abandoned, we might want to figure out why before we dock," Phillip said casually. "The Conclave wouldn't have pulled out on a whim. Could have been an epidemic."

The captain chuckled. "Getting cold feet, are you? Well, you can stop worrying. It was a collision. Ship to ship. Disrupted the environmental systems and damaged the gravity generators. It's stable for now, and repair crews are coming from Earth."

"You're remarkably well-informed," Phillip responded dryly. "I take it you have friends on the inside?"

"My friends are none of your business, Linden," Captain Obediah responded curtly. "You'll be remaining on board while I take two men, scope out the situation and secure fuel. You're our meal ticket, and I won't risk your safety on station."

Phillip noted the attempt to regain command and rose to his feet. "I appreciate your concern for my well-being," he noted, "but there is little on station to interest me anyway. I'll be in my cabin preparing a statement for the Conclave."

"You do that." Captain Obediah smirked as the ship slowed to a crawl in preparation for docking.

———

The moment Obediah and his two most trusted men suited up and headed out, Phillip left the last two pirates on the bridge and headed for medical, barely holding himself to a brisk walk.

The remaining Wyrdane must have gained access to the ship's internal systems because the door opened on his approach as if they'd seen him coming. A hand reached out, grabbed his shirt and yanked him inside, slamming him up against the bulkhead as the door rematerialized behind him.

Killian's coldly furious brown eyes ended up inches from Phillip's nose, his fist wrapped in the front of Phillip's shirt as though he would have gladly lifted him off the deck and thrown him across the room.

Phillip was forced to swallow an unwelcome surge of relief at the sight of his slender, wiry nemesis. Even his absurdly spiked hair and the gleaming blue hoop in his ear seemed refreshing after only a short time in his doppelgänger's company.

"Bastard!" Killian hissed. "You gave my ship to *him*? If I didn't need you so badly, I would make sure you lived forever so I could invent new ways to hurt you for the next thousand years."

Phillip regarded him lazily, mostly because he knew how annoying it would be. He might have decided to give in and help Killian with his crusade, but he didn't intend for the man to get any unnecessary satisfaction from it.

"Where are we?" Killian ground out. "And where is Seph?"

"A basic *thank you* would suffice," Phillip answered coolly. "Your ship is currently docked at the abandoned shell of Concord Five. Captain Obediah and two of his attack dogs are off exploring the station, presumably to meet with any number of their piratical kin to plot how best to take advantage of me and the windfall I represent as a willing hostage. If you care to retake your ship, the time is now."

Killian relaxed his grip on Phillip's shirt. "What did you promise them?"

"The world," Phillip said flatly. "And everything in it."

"Then you've changed your mind."

"Not for you."

"I don't care who you're saving it for," Killian snapped. "But we won't have much time. Do you have a plan?"

"Yes." Phillip didn't feel even slightly inclined to make this easy for the man who'd destroyed his peaceful exile.

"And Seph. Is she safe?"

"I hope." Phillip didn't want to discuss Seph. Not with Killian. Not with anyone, really.

"You mean you don't know?"

"I left her with your friend, Patrick, back at your base. If all went well, he'll have released her, revived those of your crew that remained alive, and then headed for Earth. I gave her what she needs to take on Lindmark and blackmail the Conclave, even if we don't make it. Hopefully, it will be enough even if there's no one left but her and Patrick."

Killian slammed a hand against the bulkhead in fury. "How many did we lose?"

"No idea," Phillip said shortly. "But there were three still alive when we arrived at your base. Patrick was the only one conscious."

Killian blanched.

"We're going to be able to save Dinah and Rill," Harvey reminded him. "It's just going to take a little more time."

"We left twelve at the base," Killian whispered. "The pirates killed nine of my people because I was too foolish to kill them first."

"No, they killed nine because whoever you left behind was fool enough to lose control of them," Phillip pointed out. "But that hardly matters. Are you going to retake your ship or not?"

Killian's face might have been carved from ice. "They matter, Linden. My people will always matter."

"Then mourn them after we do what we came for," Phillip said harshly. "Or their sacrifice, as well as yours, will make you look nothing but fools when Earth is burning because we were a day too late."

Killian punched him. Or tried. Phillip dodged, and for a moment the two of them were locked together, Killian looking intent on murder, and Phillip content to hold him off.

Harvey yanked them apart and threw Killian across the room to slam against the wall.

"Enough," he snarled. "You're embarrassed, right enough. And angry, as am I. No one wants to have their ship taken with a trick like that one. But we have a chance now, and we need to take it. The human is right, and you know it."

Killian growled, a low, frustrated sound, but he stood up, brushed his hair back, and nodded.

"Fine. Where are the bastards?"

"Bridge."

Killian moved deliberately towards the door, stopping only to glare when it failed to open.

"We disabled the motion sensor, remember?" Harvey reminded him.

When Killian's glower only deepened, the older man threw up his hands and moved to the computer console.

The moment the door opened, the captain stepped out, and Phillip started to follow.

Harvey grabbed Phillip's arm. "Let him do it," he insisted. "He needs to get this out of his system."

Phillip yanked his arm from Harvey's grasp and moved to stand in the doorway. He didn't really care who dealt with the pirates. "When he's done, I'll be on station, attempting to repair the comm system. He can come find me. Or he can go hunting Obediah and his crew. Whatever makes him happy."

Harvey nodded. "Good luck."

———

Seph clenched her teeth and tried to remember to breathe as Patrick clung to the drive trail of the *Fancy*, ghosting into Concord Five behind it like a piece of space junk.

"There!" She indicated a smaller docking port a few spaces down from where Killian's ship was preparing to dock. "Lock in there. We'll wait until they've hopefully left the ship and then use your codes to break in."

Fortunately, the tiny jump-ship Killian had hidden in a cavern near his base was even faster than the *Fancy*. Despite the delay while her injuries had begun to heal, they'd managed to catch up with the others two days out from Concord and follow the larger ship in without betraying their presence.

Patrick still wasn't happy about her plan. He hadn't been happy about much of anything since he'd returned to the base and discovered that he was too late to help his friends. Eventually, he'd emerged from his rage-fueled stupor long enough to let Seph out of her cell and alter the nanotech to begin healing her injuries, but had immediately dug in his heels when she announced what she intended to do.

"We were supposed to go to Earth," he muttered, for probably the thousandth time since they left the base. "The captain won't be happy to see us here."

"The captain doesn't have the first clue where we are and didn't give us any direct orders," she reminded him. "You already told me—your instructions came from Harvey. And I'm not going back to Earth until I get an explanation for the data chip."

She'd read it, back on the Wyrdane's moon. Whatever she'd expected, it hadn't been that. The chip was several years old, and it was full, with countless files she hadn't had a chance to even glance at. But she'd seen enough.

The chip was evidence of thousands of crimes committed by Phillip's family. Primarily by his mother and grandfather, Satrina and Eustacius Linden. And those crimes included the very acts of murder and genocide that Phillip had been exiled for. It had been Eustacius, not Phillip, who had ordered the destruction on Daragh.

Seph had been forced to hold back nausea and tears as she'd read through only a handful of documents, and tried to come to terms with atrocities she'd never dreamed could occur.

Phillip wasn't innocent. She knew that. But the worst of it had happened without his knowledge or approval, and he had taken the fall for it—had sacrificed himself to save his family and their corporation from destruction, just as he'd sacrificed himself to protect her from the pirates.

She couldn't stop thinking about the words he'd whispered to her before he left her cell.

"The lord of hell would do anything to keep what he loves."

She couldn't believe it meant that he loved her. But she was definitely going to make him explain what he *had* meant. And she was sure as hell going to make certain he survived whatever damn fool thing he'd decided to do in order to accomplish it.

Maybe she was only going to save him so she could kill him herself for what he'd put her through. She felt she'd earned the right, but no one—not even her—was hurting Phillip until he'd helped her save Earth.

And if for some reason he refused, she still had the chip. She could use it to take down the bloated, corrupt behemoth that had ruled her entire life to that point, or she could blackmail her way into a position to defend the people of Earth from the coming invasion.

Much as she'd grown to despise Lindmark and everything it stood for, her decision wasn't really ever in question.

She would do whatever it took to protect humanity. Even accept the worst of allies, if it came to that. But she no longer had to sit back and wait for someone else to act. She no longer needed to be content to take life as it came to her. This time, she could beat down the doors of hell for herself.

"You ready?" Patrick activated the docking seal and turned to face her.

"Let's suit up."

———

The interior of the station was not how she remembered it.

It appeared to have been the scene of a battle. A few fitful emergency lights illuminated the scarred and pitted walls of the third level, throwing shadows from the debris littering the floor. Her helmet sensors indicated that the air in this section was breathable, but Seph didn't care to take a chance on the rest of the station being the same.

To her infinite relief, nothing moved in the corridor except for herself and Patrick, who hovered behind her with a light patch on each palm.

There was no need for him to carry a weapon, but Seph carried an arsenal worthy of an LSF commando—shock rifle, laser pistol, and palm stunner, plus two utility knives and a handful of stun grenades. She'd found them back at Killian's base—presumably taken off the captured pirates and then forgotten—and reasoned that no one was likely to miss them. Besides, under the circumstances, she needed them more than anyone else did.

The station appeared to have been essentially taken over by pirates—she hadn't seen a single Conclave insignia on any of the ships docked along its circumference. Up until recently, she'd believed what she told Killian—that non-Conclave ships didn't exist, but she'd learned differently the hard way. And whether these pirates had more in common with Killian or the men who'd shot down the *Fancy*, they weren't likely to look kindly on anyone trespassing on their territory.

No matter which kind they were, Seph couldn't wait to see the last of them—she'd had enough of pirates to last her a lifetime.

With Patrick close behind, Seph headed down the corridor in the direction of the *Fancy*'s docking bay. There was no sound but their own boots, and no other signs of life, but the corridor was creepy enough to leave her completely on edge. There were too many doors. Too many access points. And too few possibilities that anyone they encountered would be friendly.

It was none too soon that they reached the *Fancy*'s hatch, where Seph nervously guarded Patrick's back as he entered the access code.

A red light flashed as he entered the final numbers. Entry denied.

He mumbled under his breath and entered it again. The red lights flashed.

"It's been changed," he said. "But that could be good news. I don't think the humans would have known how."

"Does that mean Killian is back in command?"

"I hope so." Patrick stepped away from the hatch. "But that doesn't mean they'll let us in. They may assume we're hostile."

"Can we contact them?"

He shook his head. "I already tried, back on board ship. The internal comm system is locked down. I don't think..." He started to take a step back, and the door flashed open.

Three dark figures loomed in the entry, two of them human. One stepped in front of the others, raised a hand and fired.

Patrick threw himself in front of Seph and grunted as the energy bolt hit him in the chest.

Seph jerked the rifle to her shoulder as the man shifted his aim to her... dimly registering the spiky dark hair and blazing eyes of her opponent before she realized who she faced.

"Killian, stop!" she called out.

Miraculously, he heard her and lowered his hand.

"*Seph?*" His eyebrows lowered ominously. "You're supposed to be on Earth!"

"Sorry, Captain," she replied sarcastically. "But as it happens, you're not the boss of me, and neither is Phillip Linden."

Killian didn't look even the slightest bit mollified. "So you know."

"No thanks to you."

"It wasn't my secret to tell." Killian stepped away from the hatch, followed by Harvey and Errol, and Seph fought the urge to step back as the giant blue cat brushed past her to look both ways down the corridor. "Did the two of you have a plan or did you follow us here for lack of one?"

"My plan," Seph informed him, "is to keep Aidan from doing anything stupid. Or rather, anything more stupid than he's already done. His last words to me were full of enough cryptic clues for me to know where he planned to start, but not necessarily how he intended to proceed. Now that he's convinced it's his duty to save the universe, I'm afraid he's not going to take his own survival into account. And I've decided that nobody gets to kill him but me."

Killian raised an expressive brow. "Oh dear," he mocked. "I do believe I've inadvertently gone and played matchmaker."

Seph tried to ignore the way her heart leaped at the thought, and scowled, despite the fact that her helmet hid her expression. "There is no matching of any kind," she informed the annoying alien idiot. "He was an ass. I plan to make him pay for it."

But no matter what lies she told Killian, she was well past the point of bothering to lie to herself. Fool that she was, she'd gone and fallen for the most impossible man in the galaxy—lost her heart irrevocably to a man who claimed he didn't have one.

What Aidan might think if she told him, Seph had no idea, and she didn't plan for him to find out. At least not until he explained what he meant by those words he'd whispered in her ear.

"Well," Killian said with a shrug, "If you're planning to save him, I guess you'll have to find him first. Last I heard, he's off looking for a way to jump-start the station's comm system. Also, the halls are probably crawling with pirates and who knows what else."

"Understood." Seph turned, faced the dark uncertainty of the corridor ahead, and shrugged off the creeping tingle of fear that shot through her stomach.

"But first," Killian said softly, "I'll need you to give me whatever Phillip left with you for safekeeping."

Seph shook her head emphatically. "No. He gave it to me for a reason, and there's nothing you can do with it that I can't. It stays with me."

Killian regarded her impassively. "And if you're captured on this fool quest to save a man who doesn't really want to be saved?"

"Then the information is still in his head. I'm sure you can find him and continue on to Earth."

The alien started to turn back to his ship.

Seph had just opened her mouth to tell him she could use his help when he shot her.

He used his palm weapon, the same one Rill had used on her what seemed like forever ago, and as Seph fell heavily to the ground, she wondered whether it was possible to die from nothing more than pain.

Her muscles locked and her jaw clenched as the agony coursed along her nerves, leaving her helpless to protest as Killian knelt by her body and patted down her suit.

"Right sleeve pocket," Patrick said, and if Seph could have moved, she'd have cheerfully throttled the man who had only recently saved her life.

"I'm sorry, Seph," Killian said, as he removed the chip from her sleeve. "I have absolutely nothing against you, but I'm finished with trusting humans at my back, and there's no time to waste on Phillip's plan to retake his corporation. He says this information is enough to bring down Earth's government, and that's exactly what I plan to do. We may still be too late, but I won't make my people's deaths meaningless by continuing to hope for an alliance."

A scream of frustration and agony escaped her clenched jaw, but there was little sympathy left in Killian's brown eyes.

"You won't die," he informed her as he stood, data chip in hand. "You may wish for death, but it will wear off. Then I suppose you can go find your Phillip and the two of you can live happily ever after unless the pirates kill you, but at the moment I don't have the luxury of hanging around to find out what will happen. I'm taking my ship, and I'm completing my mission. I've lost too many friends, and I won't lose any more waiting for humans to cooperate when all we wanted was the chance to go home."

Seph darted a glance at Patrick, but he'd moved to stand with Killian. She looked at Harvey, who stood behind them both, and he at least met her eyes, but it was with sadness rather than any warmer emotion. He wasn't going to help her.

Movement caught her eye as Errol strolled back into view, sniffing her curiously before strolling up and rubbing his cheek against the top of Killian's head.

"Sorry, old friend," Killian said, stroking the animal's chin. "Back to your world for a bit. I'll let you roam again as soon as we're underway." He reached up to twist the familiar blue hoop in his ear, and Errol suddenly dissolved into a tangle of blue lights that streamed through the circle of the earring and disappeared.

Well, that explained that.

Seph watched helplessly as two pairs of boots walked back through the docking port. Killian alone remained, crouching down to where she could see his enigmatic smile.

"If you find Phillip, tell him he's going to get to save Earth after all."

While her eyes remained fixed on his face, Killian's features began to blur. He grew broader and bulkier, and when the details finally resolved themselves, Seph saw that his jaw had firmed, his eyes were blue, and his hair was now sandy blond.

Phillip Linden crouched next to her in the filthy, battle-scarred corridor of Concord Five.

"I'll do my best to ensure that his legacy is not entirely bad," Killian announced in a voice that was like Phillip's but not, "though I can't make any promises. It mostly depends on what's on that data chip, and how forgiving the people of Earth prove to be. But no matter what happens next, our friendship is finished. I hope eventually you'll realize that I never intended you any harm. All I wanted was to end my people's exile, and we will never be allowed to return home until this is resolved. One way or another."

Even if she'd been able to speak, Seph wasn't sure she could've responded to that. There was nothing to say.

Killian stood up and turned back towards his ship. "I'm leaving your weapons, and Errol said there's no one in this part of the station at the moment, so you should be safe enough until you're able to move again."

Small comfort.

"Whether you believe me or not, I hope you both survive. I wasn't lying about my reasons for wanting to save the two of you. You, Seph, are without question the kindest, most decent human I've ever met, and Phillip and I are far more alike than he will ever be willing to admit. I wish..." He seemed to catch himself, and swallowed whatever he'd been about to say.

His next words were far more flippant, as though he'd locked his emotions away. "If you do live through this, you'd make lovely caretakers for this place until the Conclave returns—if they ever get the chance—and it's possible the Bhandecki will overlook it now that it's abandoned. You never know—once you clean out the riff-raff, it might make a fairly pleasant home."

Bastard.

"Goodbye, Seph." He sounded almost wistful. "If it helps at all, I'm glad we met."

And then he left her. His footsteps receded, and the hatch closed behind him with a final, metallic clang. She listened as the docking seal retracted, and the hum of the drive made the floor beneath her head vibrate ever so slightly.

The *Fancy* was gone, and she was alone.

Alone on an abandoned space station, with an unknown number of hostile pirates and one Phillip Linden.

Seph had had about as much adventure as she could stand.

NINETEEN

SWEAT DRIPPED from Phillip's neck and trailed uncomfortably down the back of his suit as he peered around a corner, hoping to find the corridor abandoned. The maintenance hatch he needed was in the shadows on the far end.

He'd encountered three groups so far as he made his way across Third —two that appeared to be scavenging the station for parts, and one that was clearly on the hunt for live quarry.

Phillip had avoided them all so far, by a combination of luck and Killian's introduction to the maintenance tunnels, a detail that wouldn't be obvious to the casual newcomer. He also knew where to find the control center for the station's comm equipment, and it wasn't on Third.

It was only thanks to Killian that he knew how to get there, though he wasn't exactly excited about it. With the tubes powered down, his only option was one Phillip had sworn never to utilize again—a dizzying free-climb through the secondary tube system.

It was that or abandon this part of his plan, and he didn't have any other ideas. If he was really going to do this—re-establish himself as a dominant player in Earth politics and provide Killian the ally he needed to build a planetary shield—he had to begin as he meant to go on. No self-doubt. No hesitation. No holding back. He had to let them know he was coming and give them a chance to fear what he knew, fear what he was planning, fear what he might be capable of.

And that meant accessing Concord's comm array to send a message through the Conclave beacons. It would send the other members of the Conclave scrambling for information—how had he hacked the beacons? How was he even still alive? How many allies did he have? And who would he be gunning for when he set foot back on Earth?

The corridor was empty of all but shadows, and yet, Phillip had trouble making himself take that step. Seph would have already been in the maintenance tunnel, raising an eyebrow at him and wondering what was taking so long. She would say it was just another adventure.

But he didn't want any more adventures. In fact, all he'd wanted was to disappear into a quiet corner of the galaxy and be left alone. Until Seph. Before he'd met her, being alone had been enough. But now? Being alone just meant being without her.

Imagining her caustic commentary tugged him out into the corridor, set his hands to the latch and removed the cover to the maintenance tunnel. Remembering her wounds replaced the cover and dragged him down the tunnel until he found the access point to the secondary tube system—a blank round hatch set in the ceiling. Praying he could remember the code Killian entered before their first terrifying climb, he leaped up and hung by one hand as he entered the series of symbols into the recessed keypad.

The hatch opened.

Swallowing his fear, Phillip grabbed for the lip and pulled himself through the ceiling of the maintenance tunnel, into the dimly lit vertical shaft that soared all the way to the top of Fifth. From the narrow platform where he stood, he could see the handholds cut into the side—fully sufficient for a maintenance worker wearing a safety harness with an anti-grav pack. But for an ex-corporate executive with nothing but a space-suit and a deep fear of heights?

Phillip shut his eyes and began to climb.

He'd made it about halfway when his muscles began to scream at him to rest. His shoulders announced that he'd been too lax about his fitness regimen since being abducted by Killian, and his lungs insisted that they couldn't possibly provide enough oxygen.

And then he heard it—the stealthy sounds of boots and gloves climbing the wall in his wake.

He looked down.

His stomach rebelled, and his knees began to shake, and as he registered the helmeted shapes of three climbers headed his way, his toes slipped off the wall.

Phillip clung by his fingertips and sheer determination, the sick weight of fear in his belly pulling him down as he scrambled for toeholds. He gained one, and then the other, but his pursuers were not stopping to rest, so neither could he stop to indulge his desire to throw up or close his eyes again.

He climbed. Faster than he would have thought possible. Not pausing to calculate which hand or foot should be next, he simply grabbed for the next hold and propelled himself upward by will alone. He passed the access point for Fourth and kept on climbing, sensing the unknown stalkers below him increasing their speed.

Perhaps he should have done differently, but when he reached the top, he didn't stop to discourage pursuit. He threw himself off the ladder, through the hatch, and didn't even pause long enough to close it behind him. He couldn't face that climb again. He couldn't even face it long enough to push his enemies off the ladder to their own deaths. As soon as he reached the main corridor, Phillip collapsed to the deck, gasping for air inside his helmet but too afraid to remove it.

He was still sitting there, waiting, when two space-suited figures followed him out of the tunnel and approached his slumped form.

"Search him." The cold, emotionless voice came from the figure in the lead, which stood back as the second figure approached.

Their suits were old and heavily patched, but their weapons were powerful—loaded with modifications. This wasn't any kind of station security, left behind to deal with intruders. These were scavengers. Scum. After him for whatever they could steal. And the only weapon he'd been able to bring with him was a knife.

He remained limp, head lolling back, until the second figure crouched beside him, then he jerked the utility knife from his belt and stabbed, straight through the suit and into the chest behind it.

The man stumbled back with a strangled gasp, his hands going to the knife, but Phillip was already on his feet, retrieving the knife and facing the first man, who had pulled laser pistol from somewhere and leveled it at Phillip.

There was something clinical and detached about a fight where it was impossible to see an opponent's face. Phillip jerked to the side to avoid the first shot and felt the second burn the top of his shoulder. Charging forward as the pistol-wielder back-peddled, Phillip closed too fast for a third shot and slammed his enemy's wrist into the corridor wall. When the pistol dropped, he retrieved it before kicking the would-be pirate's feet out from under him and blasting his suit's environmental controls with a single shot.

"I suggest you get back to wherever you came from before you run out of air," he said, his voice little more than a harsh rasp. "Or I could have mercy on you and shoot you now, to save you from the feeling of slowly drowning in your own spit. I'll let you choose, but if I can still see you after a count of five, the choice becomes mine. And I'm not a merciful man."

His attacker ran, leaving his comrade sprawled on the deck, blood bubbling slowly from the wound in his chest.

Phillip left him there, hardening himself against the question of what Seph might think of his decisions. If she was going to live, if her family was going to survive, he couldn't afford to think like a bartender. He had to remember who he'd been before—the cold, merciless leader of one of Earth's most efficient corporations. And that man would have destroyed anyone who stood in his way.

The control center for the comm array was built into the cylindrical space at the center of Concord's rings, at the very top. Below it were the controls for the gravity generators and the environmental systems, though none of them could be accessed from the other. The security of the station demanded that each section be isolated, so that the only entrance to the comm center was from Fifth, or from emergency hatches outside the station.

And the entrance on Fifth was, as Phillip had feared, locked.

He typed in the code that had gained him access to the backup tube shaft, but the security pad flashed red, and the door remained closed.

So he lifted the laser pistol and shot the lock. It flashed and smoked, but the door remained closed. Phillip aimed a vicious kick at the lock plate, jarring it loose, then fried the wires, but the door refused to budge.

He wasn't going to come this far, only to give up. Adjusting the laser pistol to its highest possible setting, Phillip aimed it at the inner workings of the lock and pressed the trigger. Given enough time, he could burn through the door and remove the locking mechanism. He hoped.

"That door has a reinforced core," a matter-of-fact voice behind him announced. "Believe it or not, someone thought of the possibility that some crazy guy with a laser might try to burn through it, so you're not going to get in that way. I suggest you drop it before you hurt yourself."

Phillip lowered the gun slowly. He let his helmet fall forward to lean on the door and told himself that he fully deserved this torment.

He'd forgotten that there were three climbers below him on the wall, not two. And the third was a woman who sounded just like Seph.

It was probably the helmet—they tended to make everyone sound alike, and Seph was either still back on the Wyrdane base or headed for Earth. He didn't think he could bear to believe that she might be somewhere on this dark, pirate-infested hulk.

No, what he really couldn't bear was the thought of facing her after what he'd said to her last.

Not now. He had too much to do. Too much to prove.

"Are you okay?"

He lifted his head and took a step back. He had no idea what type of weapon would be pointed at him, but he knew he wouldn't be able to turn and fire fast enough. If he was careful to appear defeated, he could use the knife when she came too close...

"Look, I'm still unbelievably pissed at you, but I think I can get that door open and then make you regret your stupidity later."

Phillip swallowed painfully. It really did sound like Seph. He risked a look. She was the right height. The right size. And her suit...

It looked just like his.

"Seph?" he said hoarsely. Incredulously.

"Who else did you think would be stupid enough to chase you all the way up here?"

She wanted to see his face. To know if he was still the cold-eyed stranger who had mocked her so mercilessly, or whether he regretted those words at all. She needed to erase the last memories she had of him and replace them with better ones.

Unless there would never be any better memories. If Aidan was determined to push her away, there was nothing she could do about it. But she dared to hope that Killian had told the truth—that Aidan was up here looking for the control center because he'd changed his mind. That he truly meant to do what he'd sworn—to retake his corporation, and take a stand to defend Earth.

Even if their one-time allies had become part of what they would need to defend Earth against.

"You were supposed to go to Earth," Aidan said abruptly, turning back to stare at the door.

"I know," she told him. "But I read the chip."

She watched him tense up, saw his gloved hands clench.

"Then you should know that I gave you what you needed. You could take down Lindmark and use the instability to your advantage. Or blackmail them into allowing Killian a hearing."

She took a few steps forward until she stood next to him, staring down at the fried lock plate.

"Killian," she said dryly, "got tired of waiting."

His head jerked around, and she could feel his stare, even through the helmet. "What do you mean?"

"He stole the chip. Left for Earth." She decided Aidan didn't need to know that Killian had shot her first.

Aidan whirled and grabbed her arms, gripping them in shaking hands while pressing his helmet against hers.

"He took it and left you here? Alone?"

Seph could have cried, she was so relieved. Despite everything, he wasn't as cold or indifferent as he claimed. He cared.

"Us, Aidan," she said, in the most normal voice she could manage. "He left both of us here. Said he was tired of trusting humans at his back. Now that he has leverage, he's off to build his shield. Said we could survive here or not, but he's not willing to let his people's sacrifices go to waste."

"The deaths broke him," Aidan said, his tone flat.

"I imagine when you can heal any wound, and you never get sick, death becomes a forgotten enemy," Seph agreed. "They probably don't lose friends often. And guilt can be a powerful motivator."

As she imagined Aidan knew all too well.

Kneeling in front of the door, she began to poke at the wires, using her utility knife to strip where needed and praying the components weren't too damaged.

Aidan remained silent as she worked, and she resisted the urge to glance at him, or to wonder what he was thinking. She would help him send his message, then they would talk. They would have to. Their survival might depend on their cooperation.

The first combination of wires reactivated the security locks, and the second made the lights over the door flash purple. It wasn't until her third try that the locks disengaged and the door jerked partway open.

Seph hissed in triumph and stood up on nearly numb feet as Aidan grasped the door and shoved it open just far enough for them to fit through.

"Can you close it again?" he asked, and Seph groaned as she considered the mangled wires, but it ended up being easier than she'd feared. As soon as the door shut, Aidan stalked across the room to the computer banks and began tapping in commands. After a few moments, the lights over the door went green, indicating that the control room was back online, environmental systems running normally.

He yanked off his helmet, dropped it on the floor and turned, not to the comm equipment, but to her. Before she could react, he'd deactivated her suit seal and pulled off her helmet, abandoning it beside his own on the deck. His gloved hands cupped her jaw, and his blue eyes searched hers in pained desperation.

"I'm sorry," he said. "Seph, I'm so sorry."

And then he kissed her.

It was a desperate kiss, filled with the urgency of a moment that he'd probably believed would never come, a moment that might never come again. For that one brief moment, they were not penniless adventurer and vengeful heir—they were two lost souls who'd found a brief haven from a bleak future in one another's arms.

As the galaxy turned outside the window, as the ship that had brought them sailed farther and farther away, as the forces that could doom Earth gathered and the future should have seemed darker with every moment, Seph couldn't even seem to remember why she'd been afraid.

All she could feel was joy.

He hadn't meant any of it. He'd done it to save her, and he'd done it knowing that she might never be willing to speak to him again.

She pressed closer and kissed him back, burying her fingers in his hair and feeling the strange warmth of tears on her cheeks.

Aidan... no, Phillip. Phillip pulled back, only to rest his forehead on hers and stroke her cheek, wiping away her tears with gentle fingers. "You shouldn't forgive me," he said hoarsely. "Seph, I'm not a good man. All of those things I said about myself are true."

She closed her eyes and shook her head. "And everything you said about me?"

"I couldn't let them hit you again," he said. He sounded broken. "I couldn't watch them hurt you. So I did what I had to. I knew you'd hate me for being who I am, but it was better for you to hate me than to suffer what they would have put you through."

Seph placed a gloved hand on his cheek and felt him tremble at her touch. "Then you're not the monster you make yourself out to be. And even if you were..." She shrugged. "I suppose I already ate the pomegranate seeds. I'm doomed to keep coming back until you admit that you love me." She smiled tremulously. "But it's your actions that tell me you're not a monster, Phillip. Your words might have hurt, but they hurt you, too, and I'm not going to ignore your pain and sacrifice. I know how much it must have cost you. So no matter how hard you push me away, I'm going to stand right here, until you stop denying the truth. You're not that man anymore. You can walk away, and I won't follow, because I'm neither foolish nor desperate, but I won't be pushed. Not with all this nonsense of you being a terrible person. No more bullshit. It's time to face the fact that you've changed."

He smiled back at her then, a dizzying, jaw-droppingly gorgeous smile that almost took Seph's breath away.

She didn't think she'd ever seen him smile that way before, and she couldn't imagine that very many other women had either, because... wow.

It was hot.

"I don't know how much I've changed," he admitted. "Because I would still destroy anyone who tried to hurt you—without pause and without question. I'm willing to wade through the disgusting muck of corporate politics to save Earth, simply because you love it. And if my family doesn't take care of it first, I will hunt Killian down and hurt him for daring to endanger you for the sake of his quest."

Seph grinned. "If we're going to make this work, you're going to need to remember one very simple thing about me, Phillip."

He raised an eyebrow as he waited for her to finish.

"I've never in my life stood back and waited for someone else to deal with a problem I could deal with for myself. That means I'll be having fairly strong words with Killian over leaving us to die. It also means I'll be ready and willing to deal with anyone else who tries to hurt me, and that I'll do everything I can to save Earth. It's my home, and I want my family to live, so I'm just as responsible as anyone else."

He nodded once, lips pressed tightly together.

"But I wouldn't say no to a man who was willing to stand beside me. A man who wanted me to stand with him. Someone who wanted to take on the galaxy and its adventures together, because it would mean so much more than facing them alone."

Phillip regarded her stoically. "If you choose to stand with me," he said, "you may lose everything. You'll be reviled, dragged through the mud and just plain lied about. Your family and friends will abandon you, and your name will be synonymous with fool, for allying yourself with a criminal doomed to destruction."

Seph chuckled. "Phillip, I once quit my very stable job and tried my hand at colonizing an uncharted world. I'm not exactly queen of doing things the easy way."

"Well then," he said, and wrapped his arms around her to pull her tightly to his chest and rest his cheek against her hair. "I wouldn't say no to that either."

This. This was what joy felt like. Joy, relief, love.

"I'm a selfish man," he went on, "so I might have been willing to beg you to stay with me. But since your mind is already made up, I'll have to settle for offering you everything I have. At the moment, we are monarchs of a broken down space station infested with pirates. We have before us the task of sending a message to Earth, surviving the next few days while we eliminate the pirates, and stealing a ship to convey us back to Earth before Killian causes an interspecies incident."

"You do know how to spoil a woman, don't you?" Seph observed.

"Actually," he confessed, sounding almost thoughtful, "I have no idea. The corporate life didn't leave much time for relationships."

"You mean..." Seph stared up at him incredulously. "You've never dated? Never been serious about anyone?"

He didn't answer, but he almost appeared to be blushing.

"Then let me give you some advice," Seph announced. "The first thing you need to do is kiss me again."

So he did.

TWENTY

PHILLIP ACTIVATED THE "RECORD" function and held his breath as he waited for it to come online. The comm array seemed to be working just fine, once he'd rebooted the system, and all lights were green indicating that the beacon connections were fully functional.

Seph squeezed his hand and then stepped back, out of range of the recorder.

"Greetings to Earth," he said, into the blinking red light over the lens. "Perhaps you remember me, but perhaps you don't, so allow me to introduce myself. My name is Phillip Linden. Several years ago, I was tried and sentenced for serious crimes against the Conclave, crimes that blackened my name and doomed me to exile in the farthest reaches of space. I was stripped of my name and left to live or die according to the whims of fate."

He paused, let his eyes harden. "But the crimes for which I was exiled were not my own. I chose exile to prevent the collapse of Lindmark Corporation and the destruction that would inevitably have followed, but my period of silence has come to an end.

"I stand on the wreckage of Concord Five to tell you that war is coming. And not just a corporate war. This space station was brought to ruin by a destructive force beyond anything humanity has ever dreamed or conjured. And it is coming for Earth unless we can stop it."

He didn't expect them to believe him. Didn't imagine they would fear the Bhandecki without proof. But he could make them fear *him*, and for now, that would be enough.

"I am returning to Earth to make every attempt to save it. But that attempt will not come without a price. I intend to see justice done for the crimes of which I was accused—crimes that can be laid at the door of Eustacius and Satrina Linden.

"Believe me or don't. Ignore me or don't. That means nothing to me. I am coming, and I will be taking back what is mine. If you remember nothing else about me, remember that I will let nothing stand in the way of getting what I want. Justice *will* be served, and then we will face this threat together. Or, you can choose to oppose me and be annihilated."

As he faced the recorder, Phillip felt the same surge of adrenaline he'd experienced as he piloted Killian's ship in that death-defying dive through a hostile atmosphere. In this moment of danger and uncertainty, he felt fully and completely alive, as though he was finally doing what he was meant to do.

"Before I end this transmission, I have a special message for you, Grandfather," he said softly. "You should know that I remember every word you said at our last meeting. Know that I have finished bearing the weight of your crimes, your hubris, and your overwhelming incompetence." He leaned closer to the recorder. "Know that I am coming for you, and no matter what happens to the rest of Earth, I will ensure that you face the consequences for your actions. *All* of your actions."

He leaned back again and smiled.

"I imagine when you get this you'll make a frantic attempt to lock me out of your systems and double the guards on the doors, but it won't matter. I'll always know how to beat you because it was never you that built Lindmark, Grandfather. It was me. I made Lindmark what it is today, and I am finished letting you destroy it. And because I made it, I will always be able to find a way in.

"No matter how far you run, no matter how well you hide, I will find you. And Lindmark will be mine."

He cut the recording and dropped into a chair to finish the process of sending it by beacon across the vast distance to Earth. Seph was watching, wide-eyed, from the other side of the command center and as soon as he transmitted the message and turned to face her, she began to chuckle.

"That was..." She shook her head and grinned, apparently at a loss for words.

"Hilarious wasn't exactly the vibe I was going for."

"No," she assured him, "it was amazing, it's just that..." She smiled again and walked across the tiny room, bending down to kiss him without a hint of shyness or hesitation. "I've seen you as grumpy bartender, ice-cold heir, and tragic defender of Earth, but this is my first experience with the totally badass corporate gunslinger."

"Gunslinger?" he echoed distastefully. "I'll have you know I was *not* some kind of glorified enforcer. Other people enforced the rules that *I* made."

"I think you just need to admit that I was right about you, the first time we met."

He wanted to deny it, but couldn't. He remembered that day all too well, and every day that followed it. Days where he'd finally recognized the true cost of his agreement to his mother and grandfather's demands.

He'd been living a half-life. Buried alive in a hell of his own making, forever unable to own up to who he'd been and what he was capable of. But Seph had seen him, almost without trying. Seen who he'd once been, and who he could be. She'd seen a man he had believed was long dead, a man capable of feeling more than the icy rage and calm satisfaction that he'd confined himself to since childhood.

"You were right," he admitted. "But you were also wrong, in so many ways." He allowed himself to sink into her eyes as he bared another piece of his soul that no one else had ever seen, or bothered to look for. "You saw me as I was, and you also saw who you hoped I could be. But I was never that man, Seph. I was everything my family wanted me to be—cold, ruthless, unreachable. Every warmer feeling was trained out of me by the time I was twelve. I'd forgotten how to cry, how to laugh, how to love... they wanted a man without feelings, and they made sure of their aims by every tactic they could devise."

Seph cupped his jaw in her hand and stroked his cheek with her thumb. "You're not without feelings, Phillip. No matter what you tell yourself, they didn't succeed."

He closed his eyes, letting the warmth of her hand penetrate the icy numbness at the core of his soul. "Seph, you need to understand who I am. We're going back, and we're going to storm the fortress of one of the strongest corporations on Earth. I'm going to confront the ones who raised me, who trained me, who made me what I am. I'm going to have to become that man again if we're going to win. And that man..." He paused, the ache in his chest stealing away his breath at the thought of losing her. "You won't like him, Seph."

"How do you know?" she asked softly.

"Because I know you," he said, unable to resist grasping her waist and pulling her down to his lap where he could let her warmth hold the ice at bay. "You are fierce and stubborn and uncompromising, and you don't have the slightest idea how to quit, on life or on anyone you care about.

"I quit, Seph. When I was a child, my mother stole from me everything and everyone that mattered to me, and I just quit. I let them go and never even tried to get them back. My family needed me to be decisive and unsentimental, and that's who I became."

And because she was Seph, she glared at him and gripped his shoulder with her free hand. "You were a child, Phillip! Of course you did what you thought they wanted. Of course you tried to protect yourself from the pain they inflicted on you in whatever ways you could. You tried to make them happy because, under all those layers of indifference, you loved them."

He laughed, but it was a desperate, pain-filled sound. "Satrina would be appalled to hear you suggest that I was capable of such a thing. Or that she might be weak enough to allow it."

Seph gripped his chin and forced him to face her. "Satrina Linden is a cold-hearted, insensitive bitch, Phillip. I'm sorry, but it's the truth, and she tried to turn you into herself, but she's *failed*! You're free of her now, and she can't hurt you anymore."

"Oh, but she can," he whispered. "And she can hurt me so much more than ever before, because now there is someone I care about enough to defend. Seph, we're headed into a hurricane. And I need you to know that I won't hold it against you, I would never blame you if you decided it was more than you bargained for. I've sworn to do everything in my power to save Earth, whether you choose to stay with me or not, so you must consider yourself free. Free to leave me to do what I have to, in spite of all their efforts. They will try to hurt you. They'll use us against each other in unspeakable ways because that's what they do. And you need to know I would never blame you for choosing not to endure it."

"Well, *I* would blame me," Seph said briskly. "So, what's our next move?"

Our next move.

She didn't hate him. Wasn't going to leave him.

A part of him still struggled to believe it. A part of him insisted that he shouldn't let her sacrifice herself—shouldn't accept what she offered so freely, so innocently, with no idea what was coming.

And yet, he really hadn't changed as much as Seph believed. He was still selfish enough to know that he needed her. He simply didn't have the strength to let her go a second time.

But in exchange for his selfishness, he could give her the one thing she claimed to want from him—someone to stand beside her. Someone to take on the galaxy and its adventures by her side.

"We'll need a ship," he said.

"Killian took the *Fancy*, but the jump-ship Patrick and I used should still be here. It's fast, but they may have locked us out to make sure we stayed put."

"Then if we can't break in, we'll just have to steal a ship from one of these pirates looting the station."

Seph grinned at him. "You realize that's going to make us pirates, too."

"Arrgh," he said dryly.

"Okay, we steal a ship. What then?"

"Find and kill the men who brought me here. Head for Earth. Hunt down Killian. Punch him in the throat. Overthrow my grandfather and take control of Lindmark. Torture Killian until he tells us how to build the barrier and then threaten everyone else on Earth with annihilation unless they help us. Build the barrier and kick the Bhandecki the hell out of our galaxy."

"Excellent plan," Seph concurred cheerfully. "With only one minor hiccup that I probably should have mentioned earlier."

"I can't wait to hear the good news."

"Killian really *is* a shapeshifter, and right now he's wearing your face."

It took a moment for her words to sink in, but when they did Phillip burst out laughing. If he'd planned for months, he couldn't have come up with such a perfect form of revenge, and Killian had done it to himself.

"I hope he enjoys his moment of infamy. Earth is going to eviscerate him, and my family will make a public bonfire out of whatever is left."

"I kind of thought you'd be more upset about it," Seph observed.

Phillip chuckled again. "It might make our task a little harder, but it will be worth it. Killian deserves to suffer for what he did to you. Also, my sister will eat him alive and I wish I could be there to watch."

"So your sister deals with Killian, we defeat the enemy, then crown ourselves Emperor and Empress of Earth and live happily ever after?" Seph shrugged and grinned at her own absurdity.

"Sounds like hell," Phillip said, suddenly feeling grim as he contemplated the picture she painted of their future. "I have no desire to fight a war, or to rule anything, and neither do you."

"I'm not sure Hades had a choice." Seph sounded thoughtful. "It was a terrible job, but someone had to rule the underworld in order to prevent chaos and destruction."

"Then I imagine Persephone was the only thing that made it bearable," he told her, emotion roughening his voice as he gripped her more tightly. He'd offered to let her go, but he couldn't really imagine watching her walk away. Seeing her well and happy was the only thing that drove him to complete what he'd begun. Without her, whether he saved Earth or not, the future would be empty and bleak.

Seph didn't protest as he held her even tighter, only threaded her fingers through his hair and drew him closer. "You were right too, you know," she said quietly.

"About what?"

"Persephone must have come to hate the coming of spring and the fate that took her away from the man she loved for half of every year."

"But he always came back for her," Phillip reminded her. "Death and winter can't be stopped."

"Came back for her?" Seph echoed. "I don't think Persephone was just sitting around waiting for him to rescue her. I think she was looking for him. I think she spent every waking moment of every summer trying to find a way home."

"It wasn't home without her," Phillip whispered. "No place could ever be home when she was gone."

Seph smiled and pressed another kiss to his lips, and he closed his mind to everything except her softness and her warmth, hoping that he might become so completely lost that he would never find his way out again. She curled herself against him, a mark of trust so staggering that he almost begged her to reconsider. She shouldn't trust so easily.

It would break her someday, that trust. *He* would break her. Not intentionally, but by virtue of who he was and what he would be forced to do.

But she had taught him to hope, so until that day came, he would hope. And he would take each day with her as the gift it was, using those days to show her just how much she meant to him.

Perhaps when spring came, and she left him, as she was destined to do, it wouldn't be forever.

The sound of static interrupted his thoughts, erupting from the console beside him in loud, inconsistent bursts.

"What is it?" Seph stood next to his chair and watched as he adjusted the comm array, widening the input parameters and searching for the source of the signal.

"Incoming message," he told her, searching the database for confirmation. "From Vadim. It's a Korchek mining planet—one of the farthest from Earth."

"… Send assistance." More static. "…On fire. We've lost all but one of our satellites."

Phillip shared a look with Seph, dread overwhelming everything he'd been feeling only a moment before.

"They're everywhere! We can't stop them. I repeat, you must send assistance."

The transmission crackled again and then died.

"Time's up," Phillip said.

"No," Seph said stubbornly, taking his hand and looking into his eyes. "The clock has just started. This is a war, but we're going to win it. The Bhandecki have no idea who they're dealing with this time, and we have more to lose. We're going to make them regret ever bringing their little vendetta to this corner of the universe."

Somehow, in the face of her determination, Phillip couldn't manage to feel defeated. "Then I guess we'd better go kill some pirates and be on our way."

She grinned. "After you, Destroyer of Worlds."

He scowled at her and pulled her in for one last kiss. "You're never going to let me forget that, are you?"

"Are you kidding? It's my favorite nickname ever," she said solemnly.

"Then you won't mind if I start calling you Percy."

"I can always find another tray full of beer mugs," she threatened.

He leaned in until their noses nearly touched. "Bring it," he said darkly.

"Do my worst?" she asked with a tiny smile.

"Your best, your worst… you'll never win."

"I love you, Phillip Linden."

And just that fast, she undid him completely.

"You fight dirty," he said, wrapping an arm around her waist.

"I just fight," she corrected fiercely. "I fight for what I love, and don't you ever forget it."

"How could I?" He ran his free hand through her hair before bringing it to rest on her cheek. "How could I forget anything about you? I love you Persephone Katsaros, and I look forward to fighting beside you."

She pulled back and narrowed her eyes at him. "You'll even help me steal a ship?"

"You're going to help me steal a corporation—seems only fair."

"To piracy?" she said, holding up one fist.

"Not just to piracy," he added, tapping her knuckles with his own. "To the greatest act of piracy the world has ever seen."

"Sounds good to me." She grinned, picked up his helmet and offered it to him. "How about we go save the world?"

He took it. "Seems like a terrible first date."

"Only if we lose."

"Then I'll just have to make sure we win."

She picked up her own helmet, and they left the control center together.

———

THANK YOU

Thanks for reading! I hope you enjoyed the ride. To learn more and receive updates on new releases, be sure to visit my website and sign up for my newsletter.

http://kenleydavidson.com

If you loved The Concord Coalition and want to share it with other readers, please consider leaving an honest review on Amazon or Goodreads.

Not only do I love getting to hear how my stories are impacting readers, but reviews are one of the best ways for you to help other book lovers discover the stories you enjoy. Taking even a moment to share a few words about your favorite books makes a huge difference to indie authors like me!

ABOUT THE AUTHOR

Kenley Davidson is an incurable introvert who took up writing to make space for all the untold stories in her head. She loves rain, roller-coasters, coffee, and happy endings, and is somewhat addicted to researching random facts and reading the dictionary (which she promises is way more fun than it sounds). A majority of her time is spent being mom to two kids and two dogs while inventing reasons not to do laundry (most of which seem to involve books).

Kenley is the author of The Andari Chronicles, an interconnected series of fairy tale retellings, and Conclave Worlds, a romantic science fiction series.

She also writes sweet contemporary romance under the pseudonym Kacey Linden.

kenleydavidson.com

kenley@kenleydavidson.com

ACKNOWLEDGMENTS

As I get ready to publish this book, I'm still trying wrap my head around the realization that I've been doing the most amazing job in the world for over three years. When I started, I would have imagined that this process might get easier or shorter, but after ten novels I can say with confidence that it really doesn't—there is just as much time and care and joy and frustration in these pages as in any of my earlier books.

So thank you once again to all of those who've shared that time and care with me. My first reader, Janie, who loved the characters back when there were only four chapters and I had no idea what was going to happen next. My fellow writers—Shari, Kitty, Brittany, Melanie, and Aya—who wouldn't let me quit when the book was a half-finished disaster. My beta readers—Tiffany, Chloe, and Jeff—who read the rough draft multiple times so they could help me make it better. My amazing proofreader Theresa, who patiently pointed out my ineptitude with commas and polished the final rough edges off the manuscript. And Jeff, who I am running out of ways to thank. I might write the words, but he does everything else, which is a lot more than anyone realizes. Besides the designing, marketing, publishing, and IT work, he keeps me sane, which is not the easiest thing to do.

Readers, thank you for going on this journey with me. I've always loved science fiction, but never really dreamed I would write my own, so I'm immensely grateful to everyone who's been willing to take a chance on this new adventure in a new genre. Hope you enjoyed the ride.

Made in the USA
Columbia, SC
10 January 2021

30659604R00183